PRAISE FOR NANCY HOLDER

"Take an unfettered imagination, add an enviable skill at characterization, mix with a prose style as clear and smooth as polished crystal, and you have the fiction of Nancy Holder."
F. Paul Wilson

"Nancy Holder . . . consistently provides her readers with genuine wit, emotion, and real people in stories that always deliver what they promise."
Charles Grant, four-time winner of the World Fantasy Award, and winner of the Nebula Award

"Expect the unexpected from Nancy Holder. She makes readers hang on breathlessly to the very last word while her story moves like a thrill ride. Get ready to have fun!"
Matthew Costello, bestselling author of *The Seventh Guest*, and *Masque* (with F. Paul Wilson)

"Nancy Holder has an imagination any other writer would kill for . . . With *Gambler's Star*, she brings intrigue, suspense, humor and a sparkling characterization to a completely new kind of science-fiction universe."
Christopher Golden

"Nancy Holder's writing is fresh and fun, immensely entertaining. She packs her tales with action and fascinating characters about whom the reader must learn more. A talented writer not to be missed."
Yvonne Navarro

GAMBLER'S STAR

BOOK ONE:
THE SIX FAMILIES

NANCY HOLDER

AVON · EOS

AVON BOOKS, INC.
1350 Avenue of the Americas
New York, New York 10019

Copyright © 1998 by Nancy Holder
Published by arrangement with the author
Visit our website at **http://www.AvonBooks.com/Eos**
Library of Congress Catalog Card Number: 98-92625
ISBN: 0-380-79312-1

First Avon Eos Printing: October 1998

AVON EOS TRADEMARK REG. U.S. PAT. OFF. AND IN OTHER COUNTRIES,
MARCA REGISTRADA, HECHO EN U.S.A.

Printed in the U.S.A.

WCD   10   9   8   7   6   5   4   3   2   1

This book is for Dane Lighthart, who knows all about the Moon, and for his brother, Forrest, who knows about a lot of other things. For Tracey and Tabitha Van De Ven, who are bright stars in my firmament, and for Mr. Ken Wahl. I hope the Moon shines on brighter days for you.

A book is never written alone, although it often feels that way when you're writing one. For their help, inspiration, and support I would like to thank:

My husband, Wayne, who rose above and beyond the call of duty, many, many times. And our daughter, Belle, who makes every day a joy.

My solid rocket boosters: my wonderful agent, Howard Morhaim, who has saved me with a midcourse correction, and his assistant, Kate Hengerer, AKA the voice of Mission Control; and the founder of Moonbase Vegas, my terrific editor, Stephen S. Power. Without you all, I'd be on Apollo 13.

My ground crew: Brenda and Scott Van De Ven; Stinne Lighthart; Clara and Wayne Holder; Ruth, Gary, Bekah, Julie, and Linz Simpson; Krista Holder; Ken and Mary Holder; Tammie Bennett; Chris and Concetta Golden and their helpful Italian friends and relations; Elise Jones and Leslie Jones; Meagan Motley; the Dark Delicacies people, the Mysterious Galaxians, and the Dangerous Visions crew, including Bill Wu and Susan Ferrer.

My inspiration: Neil Armstrong, Michael Collins, and Buzz Aldrin.

From the Captain's Log of Gambler's Star :

This is what an Italian travel brochure had to say (in English) of Earthside Las Vegas in 1998:

Las Vegas, grown in the desert from Nevada like a Park Moon built to the insignia of the bad taste, she rise like a bubble of fate. Double-down, you lose your shirt. Two spins later, you marry a woman, she look like a movie star.

The mob, she say she no longer there, but you speak the language, say, *"prego, paisan,"* you get a piccolo twinkle from the eye of the cocktail waitress or croupier and wishes for good luck for you and your *mamma*. One hundred thousand people work all the twenty-four hours, some name Marco, some Tony, you do okay. More tourists than residents, still, you hear Italian. *Buon giorno! Buona sera!* Friendly place. Napoli, Venezia, Sicilia, you have a family.

Everywhere, she's gambling. You bet this, you bet that. Sixteen thousand slot machines, you find them everywhere a little bit, in the cafes, along the corridors, in the elevators and even in the baths of the hotels. Elsewhere is all forbidden, but Las Vegas, she the home of all adventures of sin. Get married or divorce in a few hours, live long nights with stupendous girls in the sparkling night-clubs and, above all, dream of open eyes.

The same could be said of Moonbase Vegas in 2142. Epperson-Roux would say it's the end of civilization as we know it (although he would certainly be fired if he did). Maybe that's a good thing. Maybe our civilization is not worth preserving. Which is why I spend most of my life aboard Gambler's Star, *above it all, as it were, above the small-mindedness and the lack of imagination and the senseless difficulties and complications they produce.*

Earth died, Earth recovered, and the carpetbaggers have arrived. My daddy would insist with every bone in his Southern body that the South (in this case, the Earth) shall rise again to its former glory. But I wonder if that's possible, or if I'm on a fool's errand. I feel the need to clean house before we make first contact. But perhaps I should spend my days rocking on the verandah of my skybound plantation with a mint julep in my hand.

Moonbase Vegas lies beneath an environmental protection dome such as we had back on Earth after the terrible Quantum Instability Wars of the 2030s. Most of my family was wiped out. Castles have suffered and died in each of the wars my family is documented to have fought in, beginning with Earth's Civil War in the 1800s. Rather than inheriting a vast fortune, as is believed of me, I took the pittance that was left and rebuilt the Castle empire. No one remembers that. No one cares. Such is the nature of class warfare—that the losers hate and envy the survivors—especially that being practiced with abandon nowadays below the surface of the Moon.

They think the universe revolves around their petty skirmishes and ugly turf wars. I know news of my arrival will strike terror in their hearts, or whatever passes for their hearts: ego, greed, insecurity. No doubt they'll take action, any action, do anything to make themselves feel that they're doing something *about me, and probably it will be the wrong action. It happens all the time Earthside. Panic never sired a smart, coherent response to a threat, especially a threat that's been magnified tenfold in someone's mind because it's coming from me, which is why I get my way so often. Most of the time, in fact.*

If only I could simply inform them of my intentions. If only they could listen. Perhaps we could progress toward the ultimate goal more efficiently and possibly, in a more orderly manner. But when in Rome . . .

On Moonbase Vegas you do as the ruling Families do.

And so I shall.

Hunter Castle
Aboard Ship, 2142.45

PART ONE

ONE

"**D**euce," the voice on the comm line said in an excited, tense whisper. It was Little Wallace, one of Deuce's most enthusiastic stoolies. Little Wallace just loved to find stuff out for him. The poor gravoid's own life was not all that exciting—he was an N.A., worked swing shift on the cargo docks—but he thought Deuce's life was the stuff of which legends are made. Anything Little Wallace could do to promote his guy, he did it.

In return, Deuce paid him well. He paid all his contacts well. But he worried for Little Wallace; the guy was so into the excitement of the informant scene—an excitement he cycled up much higher than the scene sometimes warranted—that he didn't pay sufficient attention to the danger.

Of danger, however, there was plenty.

"Yeah, *buon giorno, paisan*," Deuce said, leaning on the back legs of his chair as he swallowed his bite of pizza.

On the floor, Moona Lisa, their dachshund derivative, finished off a piece of pepperoni and waited eagerly, pencil-thin tail wagging, crooked body wiggling, as if her entire life hinged on getting the next one. They had gotten her discount because the cloning hadn't gone precisely according to Hoyle. She looked individualistic, to put it nicely, to be kind, and because he loved her: eyes a little too far apart, legs "akimbo," as Sparkle put it. Akimbo. Who talked like that, except for his baby? She had the vocabulary of a college professor. Had to have that dog, the runt of a runt litter; Deuce had never seen Sparkle so warm and fuzzy

7

over anything before or since, including him.

Sparkle would have a fit if she could see what her boyfriend and her beloved dog were eating. All that fat, all those nitrates. Divine. He'd have to hide all the evidence really, really well, or she would bust him big-time. Especially if she found out he'd been poisoning the dog.

He did not want to be busted by Sparkle. No man with a lick of sense would.

"Got something for you," Little Wallace said.

Deuce nodded, even though he wasn't on visual. These days, everybody had something for him. Ever since word got out he'd scored on the *Phoenix* crash. Little Wallace, who had no idea what was valuable and what was not, had been calling him two, three times a day for the last two weeks.

"Deuce?"

"Go ahead," Deuce said politely. "I'm all ears."

"Listen to this, man. This is juicy." Little Wallace cleared his throat. "You ready?"

Deuce grinned at Little Wallace's sense of drama. It was probably some bogus tidbit as usual. He said, "Got my notepad open, buddy."

"Well." Little Wallace's voice dropped. "The Ditwac's showing a five."

"*What*?" The front legs of Deuce's chair smacked the Mexican pavers of the kitchen floor. His eyes widened. Moona Lisa, impressed, let out a whoop and raised herself up on her hind legs, no small feat.

"Yes." Little Wallace was proud of himself. "The Ditwac. The Die That Was Cast. A five."

Deuce blinked. This had to be incorrect.

"Who messed with it?" he asked. He felt almost dizzy. You might as well announce the Moon was made of green cheese after all, you claimed that the Sacred Six of the Ditwac had been messed with.

"That's what the Scarlattis want to know. They're going darkside, Deuce. Dragging folks in and beating 'em. No one's giving anything up. I guess no one knows anything."

"Then they aren't asking the right people." It had to be the Smiths. They were in Vendetta, and the Smiths hadn't paid the Scarlattis back yet for their most recent dishonor. If the Smiths had cackled the Ditwac, they'd have more than evened the score. Way more. "How'd they get into the display cube?"

"Not a scratch on it. There wasn't anything wrong with the alarm system, either. The guard didn't even notice." Little Wallace took a breath. "Hope his loved ones don't notice, either, but he's not coming home after his shift tonight."

"Cops won't notice, you can be sure of that," Deuce said, sorry for the guard. Poor bastard. You did not mess up when you were on the Scarlattis' payroll. He was suddenly more worried than usual for Little Wallace. "Hey, man, you on a secured line?"

"Hell, who knows these days? Everybody's buying that weird spook stuff from them. We've probably got it down here." The Scarlattis had just started marketing some sophisticated new eavesdropping equipment that had everyone jumping and looking over their shoulders. People figured, *If this is the caliber of merchandise they're selling, just how good is the technology they're keeping for themselves? And how are they using this very box they just sold me for half my monthly handle to spy on my butt?*

"You shouldn't have called me from work," Deuce remonstrated.

"I had to let you know asap. I owe you. You know what I mean. I can't ever pay you back."

"Wiped clean when you told me about that Van Aadams-Smith action," Deuce assured him with a wave of his hand, which Little Wallace couldn't see. Moona Lisa could, though, and let out another yip.

"That doesn't begin to touch it, and you know it. Hey, is that Miss Sparkle?"

"I beg your pardon?" Deuce asked. "That's the dog."

"Sorry, man. But I know your lady can be frisky. Oh, gee, excuse me for being too familiar."

"It's okay. Disconnect from me, dude," Deuce said, his mind flashing warning signs that all starred Little Wallace with a shot of juice through the center of his forehead. "Right now. We'll talk more later, okay?" This was bigger than what was going down at the Chans'. Death was death, but the Six was the *Six*, man.

"You're not angry with me, are you? I didn't mean anything by that remark about Miss Sparkle."

"What? No, no. I'm just concerned for you. Don't call from work anymore. Or your aichy or your house, okay?"

"Wow, yeah, Deuce," Little Wallace said, impressed.

"And remember, it might be better if we don't use our names when we talk to each other, okay?"

"Dang, you've told me that before. I'm sorry. I get all wound up, you know. I think to myself, 'How's Deuce McNama'—I mean, 'How's *that guy* going to use *this*?' I remember the one time I told you about what that guy said about the pineapple shipment, and you made a killing at the track. How was I to know 'Pineapple Princess' was the name of a horse? But *you* knew, uh, *Tony*. I can't ever figure out how you know the things you do."

"Get off the line," Deuce urged gently. "Go now."

"Sorry, sorry. Over and out," Little Wallace said in a hushed voice, and hung up.

Deuce said to the wall speaker, "Off," and he was disconnected as well.

The Ditwac was showing a five?

Bemused, Deuce sat in the immaculate postage-stamp kitchen and shook his head while the dog bobbled up and down, still waiting for her treat. What was it, a bad moon rising? First the Chans and now this. Who would dare to mess with the Ditwac? It was the Scarlattis' most sacred object, one of the holiest things on the Moon. Almost as holy as the Beloved Blasters of Elvis, housed in the Moonbase Vegas Museum in the Caputos' House, the Lucky Star.

Deuce popped the knuckle on his left ring finger, as he did for luck when a dealer shuffled. There was going to be big-time action happening if Little Wallace was right, and once he got dealt in, opportunity was going to be knocking so loud he'd have to wear earmuffs to hear himself think.

He scratched his cheek and picked another piece of pepperoni off the pizza, glanced left, right, as if Sparkle was home to see, and flipped it like a onechip toward the pup. Moona gobbled it without a thought to tasting it. She was an unmannered, greedy little thing, but she was the best dog he'd ever had.

The first of his very own, actually. His adoptive mother, Maria della Caldera di Borgioli, had owned a one-eyed Pekingese derivative named Capone, but Capone was definitely her dog. Mean little sucker, too. Moona Lisa was the first since he'd moved out, eight years ago. Not only were pets expensive, they were big baggage. But so were ladies, and once you got one of those, you didn't mind any attendant hassles.

Sparkle said Moona Lisa was the best dog she'd ever had, too, and she had had lots of pets. Cats, birds, dogs. Men.

Deuce smoothed back his blond hair as he processed the information about the Die, turning it this way and that, fanning it out like a deck on a field of green baize. He thought about the guard who hadn't noticed the change in the Die. Maybe he had been bought off, but if so he'd been horribly stupid to stick around for the aftermath. Maybe it was a switch. If the Smiths could mess with the original Die That Was Cast, that would more than pay the Scarlattis back for stealing their shipment of Chantilly Lace. Which, rumor had it, had been stolen from some minor Chan capo who had since disappeared, but that was extraneous detail and very much beside the point.

As was the fact that he personally knew of several Moonbase Vegas artifacts that had been swiped, copied, and "returned" to their original owners. There were at least three sets of the "original" falcon feather and four-leaf clover the Apollo 17 astronauts had left, housed in various Family safes—Deuce had all three combinations—and innumerable golf balls. It was amusing, all those fat cats swaggering around believing the one they had was the real one and everybody else had a pretty good knockoff. Deuce knew where the originals were located. Just like he knew where a lot of bodies were buried.

He wondered how many people the Scarlattis had already hurt or killed trying to find out what was going down. The Lunar Security Forces wouldn't do anything about any of it. Most of them were dirty and/or scared. The others—the white knights—didn't last long. The smart ones asked for reassignment back to Earth, and the dumb ones washed out or disappeared.

Mamma had told him he was descended from a long line of crooked Irish Earthside cops, but he still didn't know if it was true or something she made up to make him feel better about being an orphan. His birth name really was Deuce McNamara, but she had registered him as Arthur (not Arturo, she said she wanted to honor his roots in a small but significant way) Borgioli and gotten him accepted into the Family on the strength of her ties to the Godfather's sister, Apogia. This effort was some kind of consolation prize for the fact that he wasn't a blood-born Family Member. As if anybody would be depressed to discover they weren't really a Borgioli.

Still, it was kind of strange that he'd never been able to make a definite genealogical connection to the dirty McNamaras of Chicago, despite the fact that he knew a couple of Mormons who worked for the Van Aadamses. Mormons were heavily into genealogy, baptizing dead people and all kind of unusual things. They used to get socked endlessly by Ponzi schemes because they were so locked into their hierarchy. The lower-echelon guys did whatever the big guns told them to. You got the leaders to buy into some idiotic pyramid thing, all the followers lined up with their credit cards in their hands.

It'd be like the Van Aadamses to have the Mormons in their back pocket. A classy, orderly organization bloodlessly co-opted into a classy, orderly Family. To a Family, trust was just another commodity, and the Van Aadamses probably bought a great deal from the Mormons by wising them up to some of the standard cons they'd long fallen for.

The Mormons were sweet people, though. The efforts of his acquaintances to convert him had failed—he figured if he was Irish, he ought to be Catholic if he was going to be anything—but those guys were still pleasant as could be.

When he was a little boy, he used to fantasize that he was the heir to one of the other Families—the Van Aadamses, the Caputos, even the Scarlattis or the Smiths—

and that he was being hidden away until some situation altered and he could be unmasked. Adulthood had erased the fantasy, but not the desire to switch Affiliations. Given his status as Maria della Caldera's adopted boy, it was an altogether unrealistic goal. But hey, he was a gambling man, wasn't he? Stranger things had happened.

After all, the Ditwac was allegedly showing a five.

"More arsenic, Moona?" he asked cheerily, giving her another pepperoni circle as he rose and stretched. He closed his eyes and checked the time on his lidclock. It was Saturday the fifteenth, 10:30 P.M., Moon Standard Time. Time to do some recon.

Lots of recon, in fact. Tonight was the night he'd set aside to find out who was stalking Sparkle and her fellow showgirls at the Down Under, the Van Aadams' casino. Sparkle was working the late show of *Venus on Ice* for an enormous private party of Shriners or whatever the heck they were, some Earthside gravoids, anyway. The backstage personnel at the Down Under had been warned to search all the girls' bouquets and gifts and what was that word they used? Sobriquets? Charcoal briquettes? Whatever. They were supposed to search everything.

Sparkle wasn't worried; she never was. But if Deuce ever caught the SOB who was harassing her and the others, the bastard was going to wish he'd never even heard of the freakin' Moon. Deuce would make the Scarlattis look like Boy Scouts. Maybe tonight would be his lucky night in more ways than one.

He went into the bedroom and sent the bed to the ceiling so he could get to the closet. He pulled out his black craterleather jacket. Checked himself in the mirror, smoothed back his yellow-blond hair, examined his clear, blue eyes—everyone insisted they were chemically enhanced, and he wasn't talking, but it had occurred to him more than once that he looked more like a Swede than an Irishman—and gave himself a smile.

The jacket smoothed itself over his arm and chest muscles, tapering to his waist. Not bad. His kickboxing sessions with Sparkle were paying off. She might not be much in the conversation department, but she was the most passionate martial artist he had ever known, and an excellent teacher. He had the bruises to prove it.

And yes, frisky. He couldn't help a smile as he glanced up at the bed. Though how Little Wallace would know about such things gave him pause.

Then he thought about whoever was stalking her, and her occasional solo off-world excursions, and made himself stop right there. She was her own person. She did what she wanted. If the man had been born who could tell her what to do, he would like to meet him.

Actually, no, he wouldn't.

With a sigh, he hissed the drawer next to the closet, got out his Borgioli colors, and pressed them onto his sleeve. The white, red, and green patch was crinkled from overuse. Most Family members permanently adhesed their colors onto their clothes, but who wanted to brag off-duty about being a Borgioli?

What major bad luck to be adopted by a Family of degenerates. It would almost have been better to have been brought up a Non-Affiliated. Hell, Sparkle didn't seem to mind being an N.A. But she didn't mind being nine feet tall, either.

Patch in place, he pinned on his comm badge, folded up his betting form, and slid it into the pocket of his black trousers. Paper betting forms were a luxury he allowed himself. He loved the feel of paper. He loved making folds neat and crisp. He loved to read about when people had paper money. Sparkle had once told him she thought his "anachronistic little habits" were cute.

He took his blaster off the charger and felt in the side pocket of the jacket for his recharge. He'd sooner forget his pants.

The dog trotted in as best she could and cocked her head. He felt guilty for giving her all that pepperoni. He wasn't even sure if she had a real stomach for it to go into. Their vet wasn't sure, either, despite all his fancy imaging equipment—cloned tissue could be tricky—but Dr. Forest got a charge out of her and assured them both she wasn't in any pain despite any appearance to the contrary.

Sometimes Deuce wondered if Sparkle was in some kind

of stray-collecting phase of her life. Sometimes he worried she'd grow out of it and go back to collecting guys with fancy aichies and penthouses. Not that he'd ever admit as much to her. More than anything—more than fat and preservatives—Sparkle hated whining.

"Watch the house for Mommy and Daddy," he ordered the dog. She yipped enthusiastically and skittered in slo-mo over the pavers to catch up with him as he went back into the kitchen. He gathered up the pizza box, wiped the table down as if for prints, and pressed the self-clean button with his elbow just for good measure. The kitchen walls hissed as the table and chairs folded inward and the walls closed up. This was sure to show up on their credit statement, but what the hell. Solar power to the people, it was fairly cheap. He gave the deodorizer button a punch, sniffed, was satisfied. It was just like living at home, when he and Joey began smoking cigarettes and charging up a fortune to hide the smell from Mamma. Of course she'd caught them.

The kitchen unfolded. With his free hand, Deuce opened the fridge and picked up the irradiated pouch with a nice mystery snack for later, which Sparkle had thoughtfully (and uncharacteristically) packed for him while her ponytail galvanized.

In the garage, he unlocked the magic locker (so named because it was armed with an extra juicer) and eased out the third of three smokin' crates of contraband toilet paper. As he carried it toward the trunk of his aichy, he grinned proudly to himself. A righteous score, that was. He wished he had thirty of these babies. He wished he held the franchise on the robot transport that brought them, no matter that something—or someone—had sent it slamming into the Sea of Tranquillity. The insurance handle alone on a craft like the *Phoenix* had to be astronomical. Deuce needed more action, some major action of his own. He was getting on. Hell, he was almost twenty-five. Of course, being a native Moonsider, and subject to less gravity than Earth folk, he didn't look a day over seventeen. Probably he would look twenty-five when he was forty or so.

"Bye, honey," he said to the dog, and sealed her into the house. She had a million ways to occupy herself, most of them benign. Sparkle had been talking about getting her a companion, which Deuce found both pleasing and a tad shocking. Only really wealthy Moonsiders owned more than one pet. Did his lady have some action she hadn't told him about? Or more properly put, just how much action did she have going she hadn't shared with him?

"Open. It's Deuce," he said to his aichy, or more properly, h.c., for "hovercraft." It didn't respond. He sighed. Typical. Theoretically, no one needed a car on—more correctly, in—the Moon, but only tourists and Non-Affiliateds used mass trans. With all the tubes and lifts and uncharted tunnels, it would take forever to get around otherwise.

Part of that was deliberate: The tourists didn't need to go anywhere but belowground to the Strip, and no one much cared how the N.A.'s got from place to place. But mostly the confusion was because Moonbase Vegas had originally been a mining operation, and later, when the Families arrived, developed privately—as in, by ambitious Godfathers who paid off anybody they needed to in order to build what they wanted.

There were all kinds of stories about people getting lost in old abandoned tunnels. Moonbase Vegas was loaded with ghosts.

As a result, most Family Members owned a private vehicle, preferably something that traveled vertically. The problem was, Deuce's something wasn't much. A two-door black bubble with worn tires and an even more worn navigational system, it drained batteries at a horrendous rate. Its bulbous chassis was completely out-of-date—the newer models were square and slanted like wicked little trapezoids—and he figured as a Casino Liaison he should have something much nicer. Something with four doors, at least.

But Sparkle made him hold that thought, patiently explaining over and over that there was this difference between income dollars and investment dollars, and that if he ever wanted to have a real handle that gave him real power, he had to save and invest as much of his filthy Family salary as he possibly could.

"Hey, buddy, open up. It's your owner," he said, rapping on the hood. The driver-side gull-wing door hissed, popped open. Deuce slid in.

"Good evening, Mr. Borgioli," the aichy said cheerily. "Where to?"

"McNamara," Deuce grumbled. Jeez, for once you'd think it could get it right. They went through this litany more often than a good Italian *mamma* said her rosary.

"But your height and weight indicate that you are Mr. Arthur Borgioli."

"Just start yourself up. And be sure to seal me in," he said tiredly.

"Sealing, Mr. Borgioli," the aichy reported, as the readouts on the black console hummed with activity. Most of Deuce's colleagues laughed at his extreme caution. Despite the fact that the enviro-dome protected Moonbase Vegas from all the hazards of the Moon environment—lack of oxygen, radiation, and the extremes of heat and cold—he always drove with his vehicle enclosed and the oxygen on, and a space suit in his trunk. He had also had the aichy—windows and chassis—coated with Kevlite. It was the same plastic they made the enviro-dome out of, derived from the old Kevlar, first used to make twentieth-century bulletproof vests. Kevlite was much stronger than Kevlar, and more lightweight.

There were a number of other domes, too, over mine shafts and transport tunnels and like that, but the big enviro-dome was the one that had gotten all the press, stretching twelve miles across the angular shaft that was the central point of Moonbase Vegas. The shaft itself came to a point over twelve miles down, where there were gold spikes in the dirt or something to commemorate the completion. In the Moonbase Museum was some old print story about how there must really be a cow that jumped over the Moon and deposited a trail of ice-cream cones, ha ha ha, because that was what a cross section of a shaft looked like. They were held up by girders made of a titanium-Kevlite composite, which were constantly checked and rechecked for stress fractures. But there had never been a significant fissure or leak or crack in any of the two dozen or so big shafts or the many tiny craterlet-sized ones, not in the 99.5 years

Moonbase Vegas had been in existence. The Feynman Field was still holding, too. Still, you never knew.

The garage door raised. Deuce waited a beat, as he always did. You were in a Family, you developed certain reflexes.

He backed out. In the white glare of the light matrix attached to the top of the tunnel, he punched on the autopilot and dithered a moment, trying to decide which route to take. He varied them at random, even though there were only so many ways to get from their complex, Moon Unit Two, to the baseline street of the Strip, Moonbase Vegas Boulevard, which was seven miles up. Finally he punched in 2-x-t-c and sat back, pulling his betting form from his pocket.

Something else came out with it. It was a thick gold chain, looked like real gold, with a holo locket. They were all the rage among people in love. He opened it. Wished he hadn't: Joey's current *amore*, Diana Lunette, appeared in her altogether and blew him a kiss. She was a sparring partner of Sparkle's down at the dojo and an occasional showgirl, although she wasn't under exclusive contract to any casino. "I love you, Mr. Borgioli," she whispered, then kind of pranced around and disappeared. Diana Lunette was very beautiful, big blue eyes, curves, that kind of thing. What was she doing in his pocket?

Absently he stuffed the locket back where he found it. He unfolded his betting form, rechecked his picks, and pressed in the code for his bookie.

"Carson."

"This is Mr. Thirteen," Deuce told him. "Check bottom figure."

Carson said, "Hold on, Thirteen. Let's see. Bottom figure is 1-29-55 in our favor."

Deuce nodded. "Okay, Carson. Run me down."

"Okay, Thirteen. Here goes the run-down. American League, Earthside: Mitchell and Buchanan 105 Pick; Clancy 15–25 over Shiflett; Grant 70–80 over Ptacek; Power 15–5 over Aponte; Alfonsi 10–20 over Santini. National League, Earthside: Van De Ven 60–70 over Sajewski; Hackett 25–35 over Wilcox; Singer and Neville 205

Pick; 50–60 Nierman over Roman. You want Moonside?"

"No, let's stick with Earthside for now." The only local things worth betting on were martial-arts tournaments and wrestling.

"Then that's it, Mr. Thirteen."

"Okay, Carson, Give me Mitchell to win, for sixteen small ones."

"Thirteen, you got Mitchell to win for sixteen small ones."

"And the Yankees and the Mets in a parlay for a big nickel, with action."

Carson repeated the bet back to him.

"And the Yankees, Mets, and Pittsburgh in a round robin for six small ones with action."

Carson repeated that bet as well. He paused. "Anything else, Mr. Thirteen?"

"That wraps it up."

"Okay, Thirteen. Lots of luck."

Deuce started to disconnect. Carson coughed, and said, "Hey, ah, got something for you."

Deuce hesitated. It had to be the Ditwac. He didn't want to pay for the same information twice if he didn't have to. On the other hand, he wanted to keep all his data links happy. And most especially his bookie.

"Yeah," Deuce said. "How about that?"

Carson chuckled. "I should've known you'd already heard. What're the Borgiolis going to do? The Caputos are for whacking him as soon as he gets here. Damn. I got an incoming. Later. Got everything punched in for you. Good luck."

"Ah, Carson?" he ventured, but the bookie had punched him off.

Now what was that all about? Mentally Deuce went through his list of informants. Everyone except the casino connections had called in within the last twenty-four hours. If any of them had had anything else, they would have called again, the way Little Wallace had. This sounded like something else he ought to know about before he hit the bricks.

After a moment's hesitation, he pressed his direct link to

his brother Joey, Mamma's biological child. Joey was the dregs, but sometimes he knew things no one else did. Dealing with him was like craps: random action, but sometimes you got lucky.

"Yeah?" Joey slurred. He was drunk. Or high. As usual.

Deuce flared with the old resentment. You think you're family. You grow up calling her Mamma and him Dirtface. You do the big brother–little brother thing, school sports, Christmases, birthdays, homework and restriction, sneaking onto Rollers and sliding down craters, all those things that make you a nuclear-family unit. Then she dies, her will is ambiguous in print but clear in intent—her two boys should share it all—but Joey, sensing that One Big Score he's always been after, requests clarification from the court. *Viola*, as Big Al likes to say, he gets awarded her entire estate. He gives Deuce a few hundred credits—about one-sixteenth of his due—and begins a career of blowing the rest.

Viola.

And no one in the Big-F Family says a word, or comes to Deuce's aid when he files a protest. If anything, they all kind of slap their collective foreheads, and say, "Oh, yeah, Arthur is *adopted*," and treat him very differently after that.

That was the Borgiolis for you.

Except for Beatrice. He winced at the thought of her, and said, "Joey, it's Deuce."

"Evenin', idiot."

"Hi, darling." Deuce waited. If Joey knew anything, he'd spill it immediately. Joey had absolutely no action except for his fat monthly check from the estate, the principal of which Maria della Caldera had at least specified be held in trust and managed by Gallagher and Talbott, a crack Earthsider investment firm with good Family ties. Deuce on the other hand, with Sparkle's help, invested his comparatively tiny monthly check and most of his salary in the stock market. He was doing pretty well, too, better than Gallagher and Talbott. Most importantly, though, he never gambled—as in gamed—with it. So for the most part, it grew.

Joey neither dealt in goods or services, nor saw any advantage to gathering, distributing, or withholding information of any sort. Deuce figured it was because Joey had never gotten what it was all about, not even when they went out for Chinese (when they'd been friendlier) and Deuce had passed him his fortune cookie fortune and looked at him hard and said, "This is true, Joey." The cookie read: *A wise man knows everything. A shrewd man knows everybody.*

Joey had read it, crumpled it up, and tossed it on the table. "I swear they put MSG in the food," he said. He was a big, dark Italian with bushy eyebrows and big, soulful eyes that said to women, *I been hurt. I need special care.* Their *mamma* had been the best friend of the sainted, virginal sister of their Godfather, Don Alberto Borgioli, but it was incredible to Deuce that Joey had actually grown up in a Family.

"Sparkle found Diana's holo locket at the dojo," Deuce improvised. "Want me to chute it over?"

"Diana? That bitch?"

Uh-oh. Another of Joey's girlfriends had left him. Deuce glanced down at his list of bets, half-listening to his brother's spew of invective—hey, a Sparkle word if there ever was one!—against this woman in particular and all women in general, especially greedy, unfaithful Non-Affiliated Moonsider showgirls.

"I'm going to Register a hit on her," Joey finished.

Deuce shook his head. Joey was always threatening to Register hits on people. "You know Big Al won't Sanction it."

"He will when I tell him she cheated on me with Wayne Van Aadams."

"The Moongoloid?" Deuce snorted. "C'mon, man. You know she wouldn't."

"*Cretino.* She did. I have proof."

This was going nowhere. Why'd he even bother? He should have known that despite his position, Joey wouldn't be in the loop of any new Family developments.

"Joey, man, got an incoming," he lied. "Gotta go."

"I'm going to hit her," Joey continued. "Uncle Al will Sanction it for *me.* I'm Maria della Caldera's boy. I—"

''Later,'' Deuce bit off, and disconnected him.

He flicked on the sender to make another call, this one to a Borgioli cousin of his, then stopped, leaning back in his chair and chewing on the inside of his cheek as he idly dangled the necklace, made it swing. Sparkle would never give him such a thing. She was not into cheap sentimentality.

He stuffed it back into his pocket. Damn Joey. Mamma had meant to include him in the will. She had never treated him differently because he was adopted. Never. And he wouldn't have pissed away her legacy. He would've taken it and built something with it. Given his family—him and Joey—a power base.

Water over, around, around, and through.

He cracked his knuckle. What the heck. He still had himself.

And himself on his recon mission slipped into a crowded corridor and zigzagged upward, dodging cars that were in no particular hurry—a foreign concept to him, to say the least. Spying the vertishaft he was after, he winked at the enormous sign advertising Sparkle and company in their revue at the Down Under—big headresses—and darted to port.

Since this was a shaft that never got much natural light, neon signs and quicktimes were plastered helter-skelter on the ends of the structures that ringed it. Who cared about a view of a bunch of traffic? Better to collect the revenue from leasing out the advertising space. In the main shaft, however, the enviro-dome was polarized to let in the sunlight whenever it was in town. It was the priciest real estate on the satellite. That was where the Families kept compounds and various high rollers lived or rented apartments.

Ninety-nine percent of the action on the Moon took place underground; despite assurances that the dome was radiation-proof, nothing much got under way Topside except for more signs the size of Sicily and a pretty lame amusement park themed around—surprise, surprise—being on the Moon. Now a few chichi condos were going in, and there was talk that the Van Aadamses were going to try out a branch casino. But the big money said everyone would always stay underground. It was a psychological thing, mostly. Like Deuce with his space suit.

Lasers had carved out the shafts and tunnels and, later, a single enormous interior canyon that contained the baseline level of the Strip. The entrances to the casinos were ranged along this level. For one brief shining moment, you might imagine yourself in old Earthside Las Vegas. Everywhere you looked there was shine and gleam and hustle. Movement and noise, a constant *ching-ching-ching* of the come-on, the shakedown, the takedown, and the score.

Only this was Las Vegas II. Huge holograms—most of holo science had been developed on, by, and for the Moon, and the holo-research brains also lived in fancy-schmancy quarters in the Big Shaft—and real neon signs reverberated off the lunaformed interior of the cavern. Then the casinos rose straight up like old-fashioned skyscrapers—who knew how far, since this was the land of the big con and the grand illusion?—their superstructures washed with revolving lights and signs, all of which were powered by the superconducting mesh that surrounded the city.

And they used to believe that magnetic fields were bad for you. Huh.

On Moonbase Vegas Boulevard, the casino entrances throbbed in a relatively straight line. First was the Lucky Star, decorated in the blue and white of the Caputo Family. FULL OF STARS! the sign read, which was basically true: The Lucky Star attracted the most and best headliners. Two of its top draws were the Blasts from the Past temporary clone celebrity lookalike contests and the annual Elvis Festival, due to start in a week. It was also home to the Moonbase Vegas Historical Museum, where all kinds of neat stuff was put on display, but not very many tourists visited it. Gravoids. *Cretinos*. If it didn't bing, boop, or promise to pay them off at less than fair odds, they weren't interested.

To the west, on Moonside Freemont Street, glittered that monument to bad taste, the Borgiolis' casino, the Palazzo di Fortuna. Deuce knew a lot about bad taste and practiced it frequently, according to Sparkle. But even he knew that holograms of the Last Supper overlaid with sparkling mosaics of gondoliers and gas movies of men and women dressed in ancient gowns drinking wine were not the way to go.

Not to mention the enormous statue of David in the lobby that activated on the hour and the half hour and made amazingly idiotic jokes about his titanic genitalia.

And at the far eastern end of the Strip (how appropriate), almost penetrating the more mundane neighborhoods of the worker bees, stood the last casino built, that of the Chans, in salmon and jade, on Bugsy Siegel Way.

Two hundred seventy-five thousand tourists a year journeyed from Mother Earth to the fabulous Moon, to get what they could no longer get on earth: vice. Clubs and casinos and hot girls and hotter boys and all the booze you could swallow. Put on your weight belt, tank up on illicit drugs, have sex at one-sixth gravity—it was all on Moonbase Vegas.

You couldn't see past the bright lights of the domes into the blackness of the sky (unless it was one of the sunlight weeks and you were in the Big Shaft), but that was okay, because there was nothing to see but stars, and they had those back on Earth. At least, so Deuce had heard. He had never been Earthside, and would do just about anything to go, even stand naked in the lobby of the Palazzo and make jokes about his own *minchia*. Unfortunately, his Family had not authorized the trip, nor had they offered to pay his way.

But someday he would get there, of that he had no doubt.

Deuce's comm badge buzzed. He tapped it, said, "Yeah."

"Deuce? It's Angelo." A Borgioli capo who provided information on occasion, in exchange for the occasional tip-off, favor, whatever. Also Deuce's cousin "What do you have on an Earthsider named Epperson-Roux?"

Ah-ha. Deuce cast back to his conversation with Carson the bookie and filled in the blanks. "The Caputos are thinking about whacking him."

Angelo laughed. "Why? He break their bank?"

Deuce cocked his head. Apparently he'd filled in the blanks wrong. "Come again?"

"All I can say, is thank God we've got a maximum bid. He's one strange guy. Swaggering around like a highroller, but he's dressed like a file clerk. Knows how to gamble but doesn't seem to get off on it. A zombie. You know the type. Everyone on the floor tastes something hinky. We're watching him, but we can't figure out what he's doing."

"Yeah," Deuce said, trying to recover without delivering bad information. "Odd guy. That's what I hear."

"Tell me what else you hear."

"That's it. I'll find out more."

"*Grazie*. Call me back asap."

"*Prego, paisan*." Deuce nodded at the disconnect. Well, well, here was something else for him to do tonight. He was going to be a busy man.

He smiled and crossed his legs on the console, and said to the aichy, "How's the weather?"

"Moonbase Vegas temperature is seventy-four degrees, sixty percent relative humidity," the hovercraft replied sincerely.

Deuce grinned. Down here it was always seventy-four degrees, sixty percent. Nights Topside could plummet to two hundred ninety degrees below zero. Sunlit days, over two hundred fifty Fahrenheit.

If you buried a recently juiced body in a crater, it would stay warm, like a cup of coffee in a Styrofoam cup.

"Perfect night for a rumble, eh?" he said to the car.

"It's a perfect night," the aichy echoed. Deuce knew it was parroting his words back to him on the default protocol. It hadn't parsed a word of what he'd said.

"Continue on course," he told it. "I've got some wheels to spin."

"It's a perfect night," the aichy said, almost hopefully.

"You got that right, babe," Deuce replied. He cracked his knuckle and put his hands behind his head.

"Finally. Some action," he said softly to himself, and smiled.

With any luck, it would be a very long, very busy, and very profitable night.

TWO

The History of the Casino Families on the Moon:

The thing about the Moon is that it's dead. There is nothing on Earth as dry and sterile as Moon seas, Moon rocks, and Moon air. There is no water, so there's no atmosphere, no weather, and no food chain.

Until the Families came, there was jack, except great views of the aforementioned stars.

Nature may abhor a vacuum, but mankind abhors boredom. By the beginning of the twenty-first century, Earth itself was getting awfully boring if you were a gangster. Vegas, Atlantic City, Reno, Washington, Monte Carlo, Johannesberg, Sydney—there were too many casino cities competing for not enough action, not enough marks. Add to that the little stuff—Native American casinos (finally erased with some clever legislation), those damn state lottos, the steamboats, and the offshore gambling—there was no room to expand.

In 2013, Don Giovanni Caputo, a Democrat and a history buff, discovered John F. Kennedy's speech about landing a man on the Moon. It became his dream to do the same for a Family man. "Earth, schmearth," he told his people. "Let's get the hell outta here."

The rest of his Family paid his grand vision lip service, but in reality, they continued to concentrate on Earth. Who could get to the Moon? And why would they want to?

26

There was no one up there, just the occasional government mission that puttered around in the dust.

Then, in 2022, the entire top half of a high-rise in Menlo Park, New Jersey, was taken out. In the building was a lab dedicated to advanced computing research. The scientists who died in the accident were posthumously labeled the Kaboomtown Rats. They were experimenting with quantum electronic devices for computers, but what they found was the Quantum Instability Effect. Once you plugged in the right formulas and pressed the right buttons, the distinction between matter and nonmatter evaporated, releasing incredible amounts of energy.

Despite the efforts of the major nations to get a corner on the research, the private sector beat them to it, and Quantum Instability bombs, about the size of a car, were soon plentiful and cheap. Every tiny country, every despot, every dictator, and every psychotic who had an axe to grind owned the means to take out whoever it was they had a beef with.

Which they did. The Instability Wars of the 2030s took out half the population of Earth and destroyed almost all the vegetation.

In secret, the major nations worked together to create countermeasures while the world was turned to radioactive dust. Never before had so many countries worked together for a common cause. As a result, a postwar world government—the Conglomerated Nations of Earth—was born. Through the heroic efforts of scientists, generals, and statesmen, many of whom died in the line of duty, the Quantum Stability Field was created. So-called Feynman Fields were raised over cities and villages, townships and rural encampments, and the fields activated. The QICs were rendered useless.

Rebuilding, reseeding, and repopulating began. The Caputos and other mob Families rubbed their hands in glee, fully expecting to put their empires back together. Moon, schmoon, there was plenty to do on Earth.

About the same time, the League of Decency sprang up. Where they came from, who they were, no one knew as they rose to power like some terrifying new clone of Mussolini's Brown Shirts. According to them, the Wars were a direct result of God's punishment on a world steeped in sin. They threatened that Armageddon would be repeated any day if Earth didn't repudiate all the fun stuff—drugs, drinking, almost all forms of sex, and all forms of gambling.

Don Giovanni, ancient now, used this new threat to renew his pressure on his Family to go to the Moon. The Earth was washed-up. There were too many obstacles to deal with, such as poisoned air and religious fanatics. The "loyal" Caputo opposition accused Don Giovanni of cooperating with the League of Decency to criminalize Earthside gambling for his own purposes, and even of creating the League himself.

Playing on the fears of the masses, the League gathered new followers every day. They held enormous rallies numbering in the hundreds of thousands all over the world. Caving to political pressure, the president of the Conglomerated Nations invited them to visit him at his official residence, Phoenix House, in Sri Lanka, and they were recognized as a legit organization.

Then, in 2042, came the match between Archangel and Gamma Lord, the two most popular wrestlers in the entire Conglomerated Nations Wrestling Federation. It was the most anticipated event of the century, exactly what the people needed after the devastation of the Wars.

It was to be held at the Gotti Memorial Coliseum, located in the heart of the Vegas strip. Every seat in the massive superarena was sold. Betting was more frenzied than the food riots had been, the amounts soaring into the ionosphere. Massive distrust arose as to the ability of all the bookmakers to keep track of the action, and a team of neuralinguists and AI experts and an elite team of crack bookmakers worked around the clock to produce a computerized system that rivaled the International Integrated Stock Exchange. All interested parties—that is to say, the big-money people—verified its integrity, and it was officially accepted as the medium through which all bets would be processed. It was known as the Betting Board.

The match was scheduled for eight o'clock in the evening on July 21, 2042. There was a prematch extravaganza that lasted two hours. A special stage had been built, crisscrossed with flashing, mechanized silver catwalks and trapdoors and trapezes and all manner of showbiz regalia. Hundreds of showgirls strutted their stuff. All the top bands and headliners performed. Jinx Adorable came out of retirement for that one memorable night and sang her signature song, "Field Around My Heart." As she climbed the highest high C on record (there was heavy action on whether she would make it or not), the arena roof slid back and fireworks went off. It was so exciting that at least three dozen people fainted.

Then, to the roar of the throng, thirty-six perfect female bodybuilders in matching blue-and-silver bikinis and glittering silver harnesses carried handsome, blond Archangel, swirling a blue-and-silver cape, on an enormous litter down the center aisle and into the ring. They proceeded to present a fifteen-minute interpretive dance called "Archangel, Messenger from Heaven," complete with fogbanks of dry ice, lasers, and chain saws.

Gamma Lord, with his misshapen features and radiation burns, his long, scraggy black hair and scars across his chest, drew hisses and boos as he dragged a dozen wrestlers he had defeated in previous matches down the same aisle in chains. They were rescued in a wild melee lasting forty-five minutes by six of Archangel's wrestling allies, who chased Gamma Lord into the ring, where he disappeared through a trapdoor. Then, as the tension built like a pressure cooker, he reappeared above their heads and soared through the air with a jet pack, spraying the crowd with thick, black smoke and shooting flames over their heads.

Then he landed on the tower where Archangel waited, and attacked. They fought; both fell off the tower to the screams of the audience. They careened through the air, saved in the nick as they grabbed on to cables and slid down into the ring.

By now, paramedics were casing the coliseum, looking for people who needed oxygen.

Archangel and Gamma Lord circled each other while the

music throbbed and the coliseum pulsed with red laser
glow. Then they got down to business, pummeling, slamming, and hurtling themselves at each other. Who would
win? The Betting Board had laid the odds on Archangel.
But who knew?

While Archangel was distracted with saving a showgirl
who had fallen off the catwalk, Gamma Lord flew at him,
slammed both feet on his chest, and hurled him into the
ropes. Though momentarily stunned, Archangel answered
with a blast of his jet pack and his famous rolling ham-
merlock.

They circled, they engaged. They bodyslammed. The
crowd was going insane. One woman had a heart attack
and died.

Archangel climbed onto the tower in the west corner of
the ring, furled his beautiful blue-and-silver cape, flexed his
muscles in time to the popular song, "Jet, Jet, Jettin' to
You, Babe" and jet-packed toward Gamma Lord. It was
going to be over. It was going to end as most people had
bet it would, with Archangel triumphing over the evil
Gamma Lord.

But just as Archangel grabbed Gamma Lord by the
shoulders, Gamma Lord's savage companion, Doom Mistress, flew up through a trapdoor and destabilized Archangel's jet pack. Archangel crashed to the floor of the ring.
Gamma Lord took advantage of the confusion and bit off
Archangel's nose. He spit it out and ground it beneath his
heel while Archangel shrieked in pain and fury.

For a split instant, there was shocked silence. Then the
fans erupted. Thousands of enraged people charged the
ring. Others ripped out chairs and hurled them at Gamma
Lord and Doom Mistress, who were jet-packing toward the
closing ceiling as lasers sliced the air around them. The
security guards drew their weapons and began firing at the
evil duo as well.

Suddenly, gunshots peppered the crowd. Some people
threw themselves to the floor. Others had no choice in falling. Everyone panicked. They fled toward the exits. Three
children were trampled to death.

In the midst of the chaos, Don Giovanni Caputo was shot

square in the forehead. He looked stunned for perhaps five seconds as blood streamed from the wound, then crumpled, stone dead. His six-year-old granddaughter soon followed him.

No one was ever fingered for the hit, because about two minutes after the don and his grandchild went down, the entire place went up.

All of the Las Vegas strip, that is. Sky-high.

The unthinkable had happened. Despite the presence of the protective Feynman Field, which should have rendered any kind of Quantum Instability device useless, a Quantum Instability Circuit had been detonated. In less than a second, every man, woman, and casino within a twenty-mile radius of the Gotti Memorial Coliseum was destroyed. Several mob Families were completely wiped out. So was most of the cabinet of the Conglomerated Nations. It would have been worse if Las Vegas had not been encased inside a protective dome to prevent the poisoned atmosphere from killing everybody. The blast was successfully contained inside.

The world quaked. A QIC shouldn't have been able to go off. This had to be some new weapon, or else the perps had been able to compromise the Feynman Field. Was this the beginning of the next round of Quantum Instability Wars?

Who had set it off? The League of Decency claimed no responsibility, but they couldn't help pointing out that they had foretold this very event. The cause was vice and sin, all of which should be eradicated.

About six months later, the Conglomerated Nations assured everyone that they had detected the nature of the QIC that had been used; that they could reveal nothing about it except that it had been much smaller than the earlier version; and retrofitted all the Feynman Fields to prevent a repeat occurrence. But rumors also spread that the Conglomerated Nations themselves had set the QIC off to hasten the criminalization of gambling and the destruction of Las Vegas, in order to please the League of Decency. Stories were circulated about hit lists of casinos. Of other crime dons slated for execution.

At Don Giovanni's funeral, Giancarlo Caputo, the new

Godfather, had begged the Family not to take up the gaunt-let flung at them by the League and by co-opted govern-ment officials. Fighting back was stupid. It was useless. The Family was like caged rats on Earth. Or fish in a barrel. Earth was death.

"Look up," he finished in a whisper, "up at the Gam-bler's Star. Then look left, just a little. See the pure white light? That's where Don Giovanni's soul waits for us. On the Moon."

By that time, transnational industrials were mining the Moon for its rich mineral deposits. They had vast resources to send and maintain their people up there, but they de-clared themselves uninterested in the working partnership the Caputos offered. That, at least, was their public posi-tion, designed to keep their rank and file happy, many of whom had joined the League.

Privately, they gave the Caputos a hand in fulfilling Don Giovanni's dream. Despite their holier-than-thou rhetoric, they knew their miners would like the booze and broads, and pay dearly to have them. The workers needed enter-tainment, and the Caputos provided the first headliner on the Moon—Cosmotica, direct from Berlin.

By this time, the helium-dust boom was on, and the min-ers began moving out of their barracks and building them-selves wacky little houses out of iron manufactured from lunar ilmenite. They started making street signs. They started marrying and having kids. Not only did the Caputos build the first casino and the first brothel, but the first su-permarket that wasn't owned by a mining company, the first library, and the first school. The miners were grateful and treated the Caputos very, very well.

However, Topside radiation was a big problem. In search of the titanium, iron, and aluminum in the soil, the miners burrowed beneath the surface, and everyone decided they liked it better down there. The Caputos went underground with them, and started building the Lucky Star casino.

As soon as it was apparent there was money to be made, the other mob groups wanted in. Twenty-one Families made their way to the Moon. With the disgruntled Caputos, who had no wish to share the spoils, they formed a loose cartel to build the enviro-dome and fit it with one of the hopefully new and improved Feynman Fields, and bring in the other amenities and utilities. But in those early days of jostling for position, more hits went down than power stations went up. It was a bloodbath, and at least two of the Families—the Mitchells and the Goldbergs—were completely wiped out. Other families disappeared through alliances, mergers, and marriages. But mostly they wasted each other.

The support types—general contractors, schoolteachers, supermarket managers, and so forth—appealed to Earthside. Now they wanted the remaining fourteen Families off the Moon. Of course the League of Decency was all for that.

But here was an interesting dilemma for the Conglomerated Nations: they had had the foresight to levy taxes on the Families' profits, and those taxes were hefty. Dressing them up in pretty clothes, they were being used for reforestation and environmental-repair projects. All of which would come to a screeching halt if the Families were put out of business.

There were studies. There were panels. There were Senate debates. What to do about the Family question?

Eventually a solution was reached: The Families would be managed. Rather than allow them to continue to run things in an atmosphere of lawlessness and chaos, their dealings would be codified and regularized. They would be overseen by a governmental watchdog organization called the Department of Fairness. Their elaborate vendettas, the various insults and dishonors and percentages of deals and house cuts and who knew what all, would be kept track of by the Betting Board. It would be reworked and called the Charter Board.

For decades, the Families fought against these measures. Finally, acknowledging defeat, they worked with the Department of Fairness, providing their own talent to assist in the retrofit of the Betting Board. As one Conglomerated Nations senator pointed out, they had cooperated in the building of the domes to assure their survival, and no one had ever tampered with them. No one had ever attempted to disable or outgun the Feynman Field. To harm one was to harm all. So it would be with the Charter Board.

In return, the League of Decency was banned from the Moon. Anyone found to be a member of the League would be instantly deported.

It was also felt that fourteen Families were too many to deal with. Romantic legend had it that the Scarlatti don, (no one could remember why it was a Scarlatti, and not, say, a Caputo) tired of the carnage, suggested the survivors get together and roll a die, see how many dots came up, and let that decide how many Families should share the Moon. That was the Scarlattis' Great Die, the Die That Was Cast—the Ditwac—the one that now showed a five. Back then, so the story went, it came up a six. So the Six were chosen as if by the gentle and loving finger of Lady Luck herself.

What actually happened, it was the first successful corruption of the new Department of Fairness, who named the Chans, the Smiths, the Van Aadamses, the Caputos, the Scarlattis, and, God help them, the poor old Borgiolis, as the only six Families allowed to own casinos on the Moon. They pointed to "studies" and "algorithms" to make sense of this seemingly arbitrary decision, and there was enough gobbledygook in their three-ring binders to glaze over any senator's eyes that wanted glazing over—and enough of them got paid to glaze. The six Families' rights were protected by Charters. If anyone else wanted in, they would have to be unanimously approved by all six Families as well as by the DOF.

Once the monumental DOF bribe was made and accepted, the six Families dissolved their brief, secret alliance created for the purpose of collecting and offering said bribe. For appearances' sake, they pretended to get along after that, and basically kept their more brutal business to themselves. But any private citizen with half a brain and two whole eyeballs knew the peace was as sincere as a crooked blackjack dealer wishing a mark the best of luck.

Then, speaking of luck, the League of Decency pushed through legislation that made Earthside gambling completely illegal. It was swift and it was total. You could not bet on anything anywhere on Earth, no matter how big a bribe you put together.

The eight other Families, having reluctantly agreed to the loss of the Moon because they assumed they would still profit from Earth gambling—dangerous though it might be—howled in protest. They killed a few people and offed the League's big honchos. But the die was most definitely cast. After a few decades, the Eight pretty much gave up and disappeared . . . or so it was said.

But you had to wonder, now and then.

Meanwhile, the legend of the Six grew. The Die That Was Cast was as precious to the Families as the Shroud of Turin, and the Scarlattis took their obligation to care for it dead—*way* dead—seriously.

So when it was messed with, it was a big deal. A very big deal. An omen, an insult, and something to be rectified. And until it was, the things that would be rolling would not be dice, but heads. Lots of them.

THREE

The Man in the Moon, according to an ancient Chinese legend (as retold for modern Moonsiders):

One night during the graveyard shift, this rich Chinese babe, Lady Heng-O, came up lucky seven and scored a cup of the Water of Life. With the first swallow, she began to whirl around, spinning like a Wheel of Fortune, and then went soaring up into space, gripping the vial with both hands while she shrieked with pleasure.

It was that good.

When Lady Heng-O landed on the Moon, the magic elixir spilled on the ground and turned into a white-jade rabbit. The rich babe turned into a frog.

Now, when you look at the full moon, you can see Lady Frog sitting at the feet of Moon Rabbit as he mixes and crushes Moon herbs with his mortar and pestle. He's trying to make a potion that will return them to Earth. But in a thousand years, he has not succeeded.

To all appearances, there was nothing unusual going on at the first of Deuce's stops, Chan's Pearl of Heaven Casino. Of all the six Chartered Establishments, the Pearl was his favorite because it was the most surreal. The designers had definitely chug-a-lugged some of that special Water of Life, or at least snorted up some Chantilly Lace (hard CH, as in Chinese wonder drug). Thirty-foot-tall rabbits of real Earthside jade perched on either side of the salmon-coral entrance. Deuce supposed most of the paying customers didn't realize that in gambler talk, a "rabbit" was an inexperienced player or a sucker, and everyone who worked in gaming, which was sixty-nine percent of the permanent population, thought the rabbits were a fantastic in-joke.

Inside, the foyer was one thermodynamic conflagration of holo ladies turning into frogs and back again in hues of jade, scarlet, blue, and all your metallic shades. Kites painted with the face of Lady Heng-O wafted in the enhanced air. Scarlet, blue, and purple "Moon herbs" as tall as apartment colonies jutted through the roof of the cavernous foyer, a holo-projection of an ancient Chinese temple.

Banners and pennants unfurled in slow motion, jeweled birds and monkeys scampering all over creation while, positioned at the ornately carved columns that towered so high there was said to be weather at their tops (which, of course, was entirely untrue; there was no weather anywhere on the Moon), seven-foot-tall temple maidens—heck, shrimps compared to Sparkle's troop—in Chinese dresses slit up to there and cut down to here bowed to each guest as fast as the tour crafts and escalators disgorged the innocent little rabbits. The Earthsiders bobbed along at one-sixth or did the sticky-walk in their Velcro shoes, or shifted their weight belts around like girdles to get to their poorly concealed credit cards, anxious as all get out to lose their life savings.

It was one of these Chinese maidens—her name badge flickered "Kwan," Deuce knew her as "Roxy," but who knew what her real name was?—Deuce met around the side of the building. It was too close to her home base to suit him, but she had insisted. He prayed none of the casino's animals had a notion about what she was doing. He'd finessed her; he felt responsible for her.

Roxy was dressed for work in her Chinese dress and platform shoes, the Chans' way of offering tall girls on the cheap: hire six-footers, artificially elevate them a couple meters. As he walked toward her, Roxy flicked her gaze at him, and he saw the edginess behind the kowtow-little-miss-peony thing she had going. You couldn't find a single person involved in Family business—Affiliated or N.A.—

whose soft glow hadn't hardened into a diamond brittleness. Everybody always looked out for number one, which was them, and always looked suspiciously at everybody else, even Sparkle. Except for lately. Deuce thought of the mystery snack with renewed uneasiness. When she had left for work, she had kissed him not only on the lips but on the forehead, too, like Mamma used to do. What, was she pregnant?

Roxy raised her brows questioningly. Deuce had always admired her body job in the past. She really did look Chinese, he thought, even though she had assured him she had originally been a beautiful shade of chocolate brown. That was still a big deal, going for a complete makeover, but sometimes it was necessary. He wondered what had happened in Roxy's life that she had to hide her old self so thoroughly.

He nodded briefly, barely registering her greeting; after all, they both might be under surveillance.

Aiming for casual, they sidled around an ornately carved column, deep into the shadows. She was sharp, this one. Not a third as smart as Sparkle, of course, but then, neither was he.

They stood in silence through the blare of a gong clanging and banging away inside. Some tourist had just hit a jackpot. As soon as it subsided, she murmured, "Have you got it?"

He held up a hand. "How's Madame Dai-tai?"

"Do you have it or not?"

"After all this time, I'd think you'd trust me," he replied in a hurt voice.

She said, "Ya gotta be kiddin'."

In response, he pulled a soft, white square from his pocket. Her eyes glowed. She reached to touch it. He drew his hand back slightly, allowing her to see but not feel. He thanked whatever equipment malfunction or Family revenge scheme or gravitational flux had sent the *Phoenix* off course, and with it the next six months' supply of sundries, including shampoo-in metallics, the classier galvanizers, educational software, and toilet paper. Deuce had some of each, but it was toilet paper everyone missed the most.

Since the crash, Deuce had never gotten so much information so fast.

How he had gotten the toilet paper was the stuff of legends. He said so himself.

"Madame is very ill." Roxy stared at the toilet paper and licked her lips. She could make a bundle off the half crate he had promised in return for good data.

"But still alive?"

Roxy moved her head almost imperceptibly.

He handed her the square of toilet paper. Goose her with the goods. It was extra nice. Fragrant. Two-ply. "Is Yuet in or out?"

"I don't know," she replied, and he almost believed her. So far, Roxy was doing pretty well in intelligence-gathering, but young babes working for minicreds weren't normally privy to the inner workings of a Family takeover. Still, you never knew. A lot of people underestimated Sparkle, too.

"Okay," he said. "I'm going back inside now."

"Wait!" she almost shouted. "What about the stuff?"

Though she hadn't produced much, he held out a Pearl onechip. No passerby would see anything unusual about giving a little generosity to a hotel staffer. Taped to it was the key to a locker at the end of the Strip, which *was* unusual.

"There'll be six rolls for you by 4 A.M.," he said.

She frowned. "It was supposed to be half a crate."

"That was for info on Madame's successor," he reminded her.

She looked disappointed. For a moment she shifted, then wiped the lipstick at the corner of her mouth with a long, lacquered finger.

"Okay. Word is that Cheung is planning a hit on Yuet."

Though Deuce was actually proud of her for holding back—after all, he had cultivated her; she'd had no prior experience divulging the secrets of her Family employers for personal gain before he'd picked her out—he was still disappointed. That Cheung would plan a hit practically went without saying. After all, he was her stepbrother. Maybe Deuce should have Registered a hit on Joey back

when the will had been read. Big Al still loved to tell him
he should have, liked to needle Deuce by reminding him
that he would have Sanctioned it. Deuce figured that for a
lie. People liked Joey. Deuce couldn't figure out why.

"When's the hit going down?" he asked Roxy.

She ruminated, shifting on her flamingo-long legs. Sparkle's were longer.

He sighed. "Okay. You get your half a crate."

"I already gave you the data for *that*."

"I'll throw in a couple of extra rolls."

"I want three-quarters of a crate." Her cheeks turned
red. She was pushing herself beyond her consciousness of
entitlement. In other words, she didn't think he'd give her
three-quarters of a crate. Passing secrets made her nervous;
she couldn't even make herself consider their value to him.
So she was thinking on the economy plan: *If I'm small
potatoes, he's small potatoes. And small potatoes don't get
in trouble.*

"No." He started to walk away, even though he was
willing. He was going to get a hell of a lot more for this
data if he could get it to Big Al first.

"Oh, all right," she said angrily. She lowered her voice,
and muttered, "If anyone finds out I told you . . ."

"How would they?" He widened his blue eyes—non-
Irish eyes are smilin'—and grinned at her, his pearly whites
shining like moonbeams. The only person they didn't work
on was Sparkle.

He thought again of the snack.

And the parting kiss on his forehead. It had been a gentle
kiss. Affectionate, even.

"They'd kill me," she said.

Probably. She was selling herself cheap. He'd never put
himself on the line for toilet paper, no matter what the
return. As he had patiently explained to her, she could sell
the rolls piecemeal to showgirls anxious for a bit of ah,
softness, or the whole score in one fell swoop to some non-
Sanctioned gambling room that had weak, if any, connections to the black market. It was to be her version of action,
and she'd been aching to get to it.

He appeared to be the only Family Liaison she had ever

sold information to, which was incredibly shortsighted of her, but which put him in the catbird seat. He thought about sweetening the deal just to be nice, but that would only frighten her at this point.

"Hurry." He glanced up at the building, where at this very minute the Eye might be staring down at them. They were talking too long. Of course he was known in the casino. He would be expected to keep up his contacts. But she worked for the Chan Family. She was expected to keep her mouth shut.

Maybe all this was occurring to her as well, because she looked very nervous and blurted, "I gotta get to work."

"When?" he insisted, smiling at her. "Where?" he added, never one to skip an angle.

"Why should I tell you? For a measly box of toilet paper?"

"No, three-quarters of a crate."

She smiled slowly. She was beginning to realize she had a good hand. "A full crate."

"You're a brat," he said, winking. He couldn't help but be proud of her. "Don't be greedy."

"As soon as Madame Dai-tai dies," she whispered. "At the funeral."

He whistled. "In the temple or at the gravesite?"

"I don't know." She pouted. "I thought I did pretty good finding this much out."

"Absolutely," he assured her. "Now go. I'll stock the locker up real nice for you."

She drifted uncertainly away. He wasn't entirely happy with the situation's outcome. She was pretty skittish. He hoped that together they could iron out the wrinkles, or he might have to cultivate another Chan informant. He had a couple others; he believed in redundant systems. His last temple maiden, code name Cheyenne, had married a guy named Jimmy-Bob or something equally polished and moved back to Earth. It had taken Deuce over two weeks to replace her with Roxy.

Big Al had not been very happy with him. In their line of work, two weeks was the same as two years.

"Just be glad my Beatrice loves you," Big Al had said,

glowering, his beefy, heavily modified bodyguards practically pounding their chests at the thought of pitching the smart-ass who didn't respect the Borgioli colors enough to sew them onto his damn clothes. Deuce sighed. Despite the threats, he doubted Big Al would ever waste him. He might be Maria's *adopted* boy, but he was her boy nonetheless. More importantly, Beatrice still carried her darn torch for him.

He walked around to the front entrance and dallied a moment, intending to cause a minor distraction with his presence—he was a rival Casino Liaison and he knew he would be picked up on surveillance—so that Roxy could sneak inside at the employee entrance.

He lit a cigarette, got a beep on his comm badge for the pollution levy, tapped back to accept it, and took a nice, deep drag. The Moonsiders Liberation Front had tried to get cigarettes banned—they were a drain on the infrastructure, and unhealthy to boot, blah de blah—but of course the MLF got outvoted. Gambling and smoking went together like any other two addictions. The MLF leaders got a lot of Family visits, some accompanied by donations to their favorite causes, some assuredly not quite so pleasant. Some of the honchos flip-flopped, most didn't. One went back to Earth.

Several went to the hospital.

The cigarette between his lips, Deuce strolled inside. The temple maidens bowed, happy-happy joy-joy, honorable sir, shall we take your money now or do you want to give it us at the tables in the more traditional, water-torture way? He swept past them, crossed the lobby, and lifted a hand in greeting at Quon, which meant "bright," but which he wasn't. Quon was the official Chan Liaison to the Borgioli Family, which was the equivalent of announcing that the Chan Family's expectations for Quon were not too great.

"*Buona sera*," Deuce said as they shook hands.

Quon replied tersely, "Let's go. I'm busy."

Yeah, yeah, yeah. Busy doing nothing else. On the other hand, maybe he was smarter than he looked. Maybe he was spending his free time trying to get reassigned to a better Family.

Quon moved on the balls of his feet, head swiveling this way and that, as if a ninja was going to leap out of whatever shadow it managed to find in the brilliantly lit casino. Deuce didn't much care for the young Chan Family member. The entire younger generation of Chans had this big Bruce Lee *tong* thing going. Not that the Chans hadn't always been tough; not for nothing was Dai-tai known as the Dragon Lady. They'd as soon break your sternum as pour you a cup of jasmine tea. But in the old days, there'd been rules of business, rules of combat. There was tradition. The Chan younger generation didn't know anything about being civilized. With no provocation they'd shake you up, shake you down. Jump you in a parking lot no matter whose colors you wore the navy and burgundy of their traditional allies, the Van Aadamses, the brown and black of the Smiths, whom they hated. It didn't matter who they had a treaty with.

Deuce figured it was the drug, Chantilly Lace. As soon as it had been patented, Earthside had banned it and the Moon had embraced it with the full fervor of a world jaded by pleasure. Naturally, the Earthside branch of the Chan Family successfully joined with the Moonside branch to smuggle Chantilly Lace onto Earth. As a result, a vigorous drug war was being waged against the Family by Earth and Lunar Security Forces, and of course individuals and groups were always trying to muscle in on the lucrative action.

Deuce did not take drugs, and he did not traffic in them. That had been his choice. He didn't swear either, and he didn't eat red meat or any facsimile thereof.

Those had been Sparkle's.

Well, okay, he fell off the wagon now and then. He hoped Moona Lisa didn't have pepperoni breath by the time Sparkle got home. He should have deodorized her, too.

Deuce pulled a sad face. "I heard about Madame Dai-tai. I'm sorry, man."

"She's fine," Quon said tersely. He narrowed his eyes at Deuce. "Anything you've heard to the contrary is a lie."

Deuce shrugged. "I'm glad to hear that."

"And anyone spreading such vicious rumors is a dead

man.'' Aiya! The guy looked like he wanted to karate-chop the nearest slot machine. Wow, he was one loyal Chan. Or maybe he was bored. As with most of the rest of the Family-based inhabitants of Moonbase Vegas, he was chafing at the lack of significant action. Nowhere to go. Promotions held up for years because with no turf wars of any significance, the capos and the godfathers were living too long.

No wonder Earthside-produced soap operas were so huge on the viso-scan ratings. Moonsiders were starved for emotional action.

Deuce held up his hands. ''Like you say, Quon, it's just a rumor. I think I heard about it over at the Smiths.''

Quon bristled. Deuce knew he wanted him to call him Mr. Chan. Like, that would be useful. You said ''Mr. Chan'' in this House, 250 heads were going to turn.

''Let's get to work,'' Quon said.

Deuce followed him through a door that read ''EMPLOYEES AND LIAISONS ONLY.'' They moved down a dingy hall. There was a second Liaison Entrance, Deuce knew, one with carpet and pictures of naked Chinese girls on the walls and those Chinese lanterns with the gold dingle balls. That was the hall the Van Aadams Liaison got led down. The Scarlattis and Caputos, too. The Smiths, as Chan Vendetta enemies, and the Borgiolis, because they were low-class, had to use the equivalent of the servants' entrance.

It made his blood boil.

They went past a nondescript, unmarked door. Deuce's interest perked. From purloined maps of the casino layout, he knew it led to the heart of the Chan casino operation, the heart of any Family's casino operation: the counting room. He knew guys who had been with the Chans for fifty, sixty years who had never been through that door. He knew Chans who had never been through that door. That was where they counted the casino's take. Dozens of people, men mostly, toted up credits night and day. Stacks of chips, stacks of chits, stacks of notepads. No one trusted the computerized tallies because when the Charter Board was created, the Families refused to put them on it on some technicality that Deuce had never understood and didn't really care about anyway. If they'd done it, he'd basically be out of a job. So everything was checked and rechecked by those dozens of people. Rumor had it the Chans used antique abacuses. Fu—that is to say, freaking—astounding.

Was Sparkle all lovey-dovey because he had been trying to clean up his mouth? She had informed him about two months before that only small-minded people swore. So he'd immediately set out to talk without using a single god-damned expletive.

But Sparkle didn't work that way. She was not into operant conditioning or any other kind of manipulation. She was straight-arrow.

"Something the matter?" Quon queried tightly. Madame Dui-tai would have this guy's head if she could see how nervous he was acting. He might as well take out an ad in the local rag, the *Moonwatcher*.

"Everything's peachy," Deuce assured Quon, and flashed him his pearly whites. They didn't work on him, either. "Just terrific."

They went into Quon's "office," which was about the size of Deuce's toilet paper locker at the end of the Strip, and pulled up two depressingly metal fold-up chairs. No fancy-schmancy stuff for these boys.

Deuce got out his minipad and punched a button, relaying his version of their various mutual transactions—Moonbase Vegas was an economy of, by, and for the Action, and the casinos placed scores, if not hundreds, of bets with each other every day. It could go up to a thousand a lunar month. Then there were various levies and tallies for infractions, debts, payoffs, takedowns, forfeitures, rewards, etc., etc. No problem. The casino accountants were up to the task. So were the security hackers who monitored the internal security of the system software twenty-five out of every twenty-four. You messed around with casino bookkeeping, you were Topside without a suit before you could say "Whoops."

It would make sense to relay everything Deuce relayed to Quon straight from one non-Charter computer to another, but it wasn't done that way. Having warm bodies move the information from one location to another gave everyone

one more fail-safe. Used to be that the casinos sent two Liaisons per visit to keep them more honest, but for some reason, they colluded more often than they spied on each other. Every Family had redundant security checks of which they did not speak. Deuce figured he knew about a fifth of what there was to know about Borgioli codeware. But he wasn't interested in messing with Family finances. He was too interested in living.

Deuce's relay was completed. Then Quon relayed his stuff. Didn't even offer Deuce a cup of tea or a bit of gossip, like the other Liaisons did. Deuce couldn't abide him.

"Okay, that about does it," Deuce said as his minipad blipped, before Quon could say it first. Deuce asserted control whenever he could. Call the meeting, close the meeting. Arrange the next one if it wasn't on a prearranged schedule that you had prearranged. If that was the case, change it.

You had to hustle constantly, especially when you wore a Borgioli patch.

He handed Quon a hard-copy printout of their business transactions. The paper levies were already taken care of. Quon flashed his signature chop over the two copies and handed one back to Deuce, who immediately scanned it into the minipad. Later on that night, Deuce would personally hand the copy over to Big Al. In some Families, a capo took care of the receipts. But the Borgiolis trusted no one.

And for good reason: no one felt any sense of loyalty to the Borgioli Family. The Family did not take good care of its own, so why take care of the Family? There was constant jostling to take over. If you had to be a Borgioli, you must as well be the number one Borgioli, *sì?*

Quon started to lead him back down the hallway. Then suddenly a door burst open with the force of an airlock and Yuet Chan stepped into the hallway.

Aiya! She was a beauty, with shiny black hair that fell in waves down her back, a startling contrast to her white-silk dress embroidered with silver moons. Her beautiful Chinese face was streaked with tears.

She started when Deuce stepped into her path, and said, "Madame Chan, good evening."

Her bodyguard raised his hand at the familiarity. Yuet shook her head and brushed past Deuce as if he didn't even exist, even though he had managed to be introduced to her on a number of social occasions. Deuce was not at all insulted. It was what he expected. Just a finger in the wind, testing; now he knew where he still stood with the upper echelons of the Chan Family. And better a brush-off than a smack from one of her animals. Someday he would find out exactly what Yuet Chan needed and get it for her.

If she was still in power.

If she was still alive.

Not that that would advance him very far in her esteem. The Chans were a true family dynasty; now and then an outsider got in by marrying one of them, but that was that exception that proved the rule. Why they weren't retarded or deformed or something no doubt had more to do with good medicine and less to do with nature.

Yuet coded a door at the opposite end of the hall. Deuce figured it must lead to the nice Liaison Entrance. He tried to peek inside at the same time that Quon was distracted by an incoming. The Chan tapped his left ear and muttered, "Earphone," into his wrist receiver. He listened, frowned. "Okay. On my way." He glared at Deuce as if Deuce had heard every word, which he had not. "I'll see you twelve sharp tomorrow. Find your way out." He jabbed a finger in the direction they had originally come.

Deuce was surprised but kept a poker face as he nodded and gave Quon a two-finger salute. In the five years Deuce had been Casino Liaison, he had always been escorted through the Liaison Entrance by at least one Chan Member or at the very least, an Affiliate. Something must be going down right now for Quon to leave him alone.

With a warning glance at Deuce over his shoulder, Quon hurried back toward his tiny office. Deuce stood in the hall, barely able to register that he was alone in the bowels of the Chan operation. He fought the urge to swear in astonishment and cracked his knuckle instead. This was an opportunity he must exploit as skillfully as possible. It would probably never come his way again.

He looked up at the surveillance cameras, verifying they

were still the old Peekissimos. Those suckers were practically obsolete. He'd pondered the Chans' ownership of them for hours, and finally decided they had to have been souped up. The Chans' deadliest enemies—the Smiths—came through here. The Family wouldn't depend upon unenhanced Peekissimos.

He waited to see what happened next. Nothing went down. No alarms, no warning voices, no shrinking walls like the Borgiolis had in their Liaison passageways for folks who got snoopy. No one seemed to even notice he was there. Or maybe they didn't care if he stood in their corridor until he rotted. Maybe everything else was armed, so they didn't bother with the corridors.

He thought hungrily of the safe he had the combination to. It was in Madame Dai-tai's office, and if he remembered the layout correctly, it was a few corridors down, and then to the left, and make another right and—

"I don't care," he heard someone announce angrily in the distance. It was Yuet, and she was somewhere to his right in another passageway. Behind the scenes, the Chan casino was like a giant Chinese puzzle box, with mazes of walls and warrens of miniature offices like Quon's. Maybe they just assumed an intruder would get lost and starve to death. "My stepmother says it's suicide to consider a hit on him."

His ears perked up. A hit? On who? Was this the same guy the Caputos were thinking of whacking? Was it that file-clerk guy, Epperson, Epperson . . . He fished for the name. In his business, detail counted. Epperson-Roux.

The door to the other corridor hissed open, the one Yuet and her beefy buddy had previously passed through. Deuce faced it expectantly. His blaster was in his aichy, naturally. No one came into a casino armed.

No one came through the door. Then it hissed shut.

After about ten seconds, it opened again.

He brightened. It couldn't be *broken*.

On impulse, he approached the door, took a breath, and hopped over the transom. He exhaled slowly as the door hissed shut. Now he was where he most definitely shouldn't be, not even by accident or the negligence of a busy Member.

Legally, they could waste him for being here.

He moved soundlessly on the plush carpet, admiring the paintings of the naked Chinese girls that were there, just like everybody claimed. They appeared to be Earth antiques, some kind of portraits. Maybe they were actually surveillance cameras. He didn't see any others anywhere around. He wasn't sure his shield would work on something as sophisticated as what the Chans were bound to have. He was starting to get nervous. This had not been the smartest of moves.

Still, the scenery was nice. The naked girls were lounging around on shimmering, embroidered fabrics, smoking long pipes. Opium dens. He smiled to himself. What was this, a little bit of bragging on their drug-trade heritage?

There was an intersection ahead of him. He debated about going left, right, or straight. His maps were a little fuzzy about the forbidden zone. Then he heard a door hiss—behind him or before him, he couldn't tell. He forced down his panic and tried to look cool, look like he belonged there, even if he did have on a Borgioli patch. It would be worse if he took it off. There weren't very many reasons an N.A. male in a black craterleather jacket would be in this hallway.

"But the Caputos—" a male voice protested.

"The Caputos are insane little dwarves," Yuet snapped. "You simply do not hit a man of his caliber. The entire Earthside government would be all over us in a flash. Those Fairness bastards are always threatening to pull the plug. All they would need is something like that."

Like what? Who was she talking about? Deuce was dying of curiosity. On a bolder night, he might have actually jumped into her path and demanded to know what was going on.

Yeah, right, if he was an insane little dwarf.

"We'll have to call a council," Yuet went on. "Of all the Families."

"*Shì de, Furén* Chan," said the man with her. "I'll get on it."

"Even the Borgiolis," she added.

Deuce's comm badge started to vibrate. He jumped. The Scarlattis' new techno-spy-stuff detected unauthorized communications in enclosed places. He slapped his hand over the badge, disconnecting the call and turning the badge off in one fell swoop, as he should have done in the first place.

There was another hiss, this one definitely behind him. Deuce turned around to see the door he had sneaked through standing open. A trap, or another piece of luck? He trotted back through it just as he heard the man announcing, "Miss Yuet. Someone's in here who shouldn't be."

He felt almost better; they should have caught him by now, or least realized they had an intruder. All he could figure was that Cheung was monkeying with the surveillance equipment in preparation for the hit. It was absolutely impossible for the Chans to be this sloppy. Not even his own Family got this careless.

The door shut behind him and he moved easily away into the public area, looking jaunty, looking untroubled, though his heart was pumping ice cubes through his body at lightspeed. Beads of sweat had broken across his forehead, and it took everything he had not to look up. Had the Eye caught it all?

He walked quickly but easily through the casino, amazed that he still hadn't been apprehended. In retrospect, he couldn't believe he'd done what he'd done. It had been a pretty stupid thing to do. Amazingly stupid. Something Little Wallace would think up.

Ching, ching, chan, chittered the slots as he made it to the main exit. Roxy was nowhere to be seen. He hoped for her sake that she was on her break, massaging her sore feet or snorting some pungent, very addictive Chan drugs. He'd had Chantilly Lace once—one toot, just to see, wasn't *doing* drugs, he'd rationalized—but once was almost too much; there were a lot of things he wouldn't normally do that he had contemplated doing to score some more of that bliss. Watching him, listening to him, Sparkle had put her lovely foot down: Never again. Chantilly Lace or her, he couldn't have both.

She was an angel, that woman.

But not a saint.

The alarm bell sounded discreetly. Just once. Casinos didn't like to upset the shills—er, paying customers—with even the hint of a problem. The sound was pleasant, unconcerned. As if to say to the heavily modified security guards who were massing on either side of each exit, "Oh, yoo-hoo, gentlemen, we have a little problem."

Through some miracle, he was out the door and in his aichy and on down the Strip. He started to tremble, then threw back his head and laughed. Man, he wished he could tell Sparkle this story. But she'd be so angry at him for the chance he'd taken that he'd wish the Chans had caught him.

Well, that wasn't quite true. But it almost was.

And the night was young. There were still lots of stupid chances to be taken.

FOUR

The Strip was kickin' that night. Some guy tried to rob Donna MaDonna's, the Biggest and Sexiest Lingerie Shoppe on the Moon (Fashions All the Way from Earthside Paris!), and came out blasting at the Moonforces wearing a lime green padded bustier, a green-and-purple garter belt, and fishnet stockings.

They juiced him good, to the applause of onlookers lured away from the staged flying-saucer landing in front of the Lucky Star and the tom-tom band advertising Comanche Nights!, the new show at the Smiths' Wild West. Of course the perp was higher than the price of toilet paper, ha ha ha. Donna MaDonna, once a fixture in a lounge act at the Caputos' Lucky Star, took advantage of the publicity by immediately announcing a donation to the governor's task force on illegal drugs. What she and the handsome viso reporter, Ram Chander, also on the take, neglected to point out was that on the Moon, there were no illegal drugs. The tourists didn't need to know that, the Families were glad of it, and the locals had no say either way.

The Elvises were beginning to arrive for their convention. Deuce took a moment to chat with Giuliano, the bouncer at the Moondo Bizarro, one of those exotic-dancer places where they did all kinds of weird, floating stuff. They both admired the fancy rhinestone capes of the Elvises, the pompadours, the tummies.

At the same time, under his breath, Giuliano let on that the Scarlattis had put out a reward of one hundred million credits for information on who had rerolled the Ditwac, although they didn't advertise it. Officially, the Ditwac was just fine. Officially, no one in the media made mention of it.

Unofficially, Deuce put finding that sucker at the top of his list of things to do. Hell, you could practically buy the Moon for one hundred million credits.

Not that the Families would let you buy even an inch of usable Moon at any price. All the decent territory, including the radiation-heavy Topside, was spoken for, them having done the speaking a long time ago. Having a lot of money and having a lot of power were not the same thing. Even though they were both a lot of fun.

Or so he'd heard.

"Heya, Deuce."

It was the girls, prostitution also being legal on the Moon. They liked Deuce because he was nice to them, treated them with respect, and gave them little presents in exchange for the tidbits of news and gossip they fed him like chocolates. Tall and skanky, tall and lovely, he made them all feel what deep down they did not, which was desirable on a higher level and worthwhile as human beings. Rumor had it that his birth mother had been a hooker, and so he had a soft spot for them. But that's all it was, a rumor, as far as he knew. Deuce had no idea what his birth mother had been.

"How's it shakin', ladies?" he drawled, sharing a cigarette with Queenie, his favorite girl. She loved to dress up. One day it was sunflowers, with golden sunflower barrettes in her hair, sunflower earrings that glittered and gleamed, and a green dress sporting sunflowers where, er, ah, the sun don't shine. The next day she was an Egyptian princess.

As with the Elvises, she had a rich imagination.

Queenie tapped her comm badge to pay for the levy; he inclined his head in a gesture of thanks. "Shakin' hard, big boy." It was okay for them to talk to him. They weren't official casino employees, and not bound by the same rules of *omertà* as someone like, say, Roxy. "Shakin' so hard I can hardly keep myself from shakin' along with it."

Queenie's girlfriends—about seven of them—all chuckled.

"Got anything for me?"

"I've got everything for you, honey. Everything you need and everything you want." Queenie undulated and put her hand on his chest. "Including this: James Atherton Van Aadams—the Moongoloid's younger brother?—was seen leaving the Van Aadams charity do—that one for illegal drugs?—with the daughter of the chief of Lunar Security."

This Deuce already knew, but Queenie was so proud of herself that he made a show of looking shocked and covering his mouth. "What did Chairman William Atherton say?"

"What would he say? He's happy. You know how snooty they are. It just makes them feel even more superior." She drew herself up. The Van Aadams hookers were snooty, too. They had often hurt the feelings of Deuce's girlfriends.

"Hey, maybe if James gets married to the chief's daughter, William Atherton will dump the Moongoloid. You know he's big on legal marriage. Says it provides stability. Says the Family's C.E.O. has to be stable."

Queenie shook her head. "Dump Wayne? That ain't gonna happen in your lifetime or mine, handsome. He's crazy about that boy. Sometimes I wonder if the kid's got something on the old man. Why else would such an image-conscious Family man allow a *thing* like that to live?"

Deuce had wondered the same thing. "No accounting for taste, I guess. Listen, I got some T.P. I'll be bringing you tomorrow night."

"You're so good to us, baby," Queen purred. "Is it scented?"

"And patterned. Has little roses on it."

They all sighed.

"Heard anything on the Ditwac?" he asked casually.

Queenie's face fell. She looked left, right. The other girls cast their gazes at their hands, their feet, the pavement. "They're being so mean," Queenie whispered. "They're killing people, Deuce. Sloooowly."

"Yeah, I know."

"We girls are terrified. All those big Family mucky-mucks, they always think we know everything." That was because they often did. The pillow talk on the Moon would make some folks' hair stand on end.

"I'll do whatever I can to protect you all," he said, and meant it. He was a good guy that way, if he did say so himself. "But meanwhile, tell everybody to watch their butts." She nodded. You did not mess with the Families, and especially you did not mess with them when they were pissed off about something, and most especially you did not mess with the Scarlattis, ever, for any reason.

"You're our big sugar daddy," Queenie simpered. She gave him a tender kiss on his cheek. "Something else is going on," she whispered in his ear. Something even bigger than the Ditwac."

"Get outta town," he said.

"No. Everyone's jittery, not just the Scarlattis. We keep almost hearing things." The other women nodded vigorously. "No one's spilled it yet, but there's something very big, very major."

"Nothing's bigger than the Ditwac," Deuce asserted, then added quickly, "but if you hear anything, comm me asap. There'll be more than toilet paper in the treasure chest."

"You should visit my treasure chest," Queenie cooed at him.

They all kissed him good-bye.

And speak of the Devil, the next stop on Deuce's route was the Inferno itself, the Scarlattis' fabulous casino where music was king: they boasted no fewer than two dozen clubs inside, each featuring a different kind of music, from the very, very latest in vibratory resonances to the Shriner Shuffle, as the younger Moonsiders termed it: music with melodies, music you could hum to. Boring music.

In the Inferno, the vibes were not only resonating but sizzling off the walls. Everyone was freaked: croupiers, cocktail waitresses, even old Fredo, the shoeshine man who was really a Scarlatti bookmaker for their offtrack betting operation. They were all hitching around like they had fleas, which was impossible, because there were no fleas on the Moon. Rats and cockroaches, of course—nothing, not even a vacuum, could stop them—but no animal with fleas made it out of quarantine until either the fleas were gone or the poor carrier had been reduced to recombinant DNA.

As nonchalantly as he could, Deuce ticked his glance toward the dais where the Great Die was kept on display. Usually, huge plaster cupids playing violins held up spotlights that beamed like halogens down on the holy relic. But tonight the cube was surrounded by a visual obstruction field, an admission that something was wrong. They couldn't just cart the sucker away; when they'd built the casino, they'd sunk shafts of concrete down into the Moon and reinforced the casing with titanium. You'd have to aim a military-strength laser just to slice off the case.

Or you could detonate a Quantum Instability Circuit. Deuce shivered. That was another rumor that made the rounds—that the Smiths had invented the next generation of QICs, and that they were virtually undetectable. It was a priority with all the other Families, as well as more legitimate Moon and Earth organizations, to conduct extreme industrial espionage in order to find out more about their Doomsday Machine—including if they really even had one.

The Smiths liked to tell people they were descended from the original developers of Smith & Wesson firearms. The amassing of power—pure power, as in boom—was their game. They were gunrunners, possessing an endless arsenal of offensive and defensive weapons. Their motto was, ''If it moves, kill it. If it doesn't move, kick it until it moves.''

The Smiths were blue-collar, union-organizing, brutal, and unpredictable. When the Twenty-one Original Families winnowed down to fourteen before the Six were selected, they merged with the Badrus, who were from Africa. Most Smiths were dark, and Deuce, like most Moonsiders, thought they were extremely attractive. No one around here got so much as a tan unless they paid for it. It had always intrigued him that Roxy had gone lighter. You'd think it would be the other way around.

The Smiths were scary, no doubt about it, and the notion that they would jeopardize themselves by developing a device that could blow the dome was even scarier. But of all the Families, it was the Scarlattis who scared Deuce the most. Sparkle said he was wise to be frightened. The Scarlattis were the nouveau riche of the lunar crime world, all trend, flash, and dash. They were brainy and weird, the next wave, as opposed to, say, the Caputos, who were real old world, real Mafia. Shriners who walked through the holo-viso-electro-whatevero doors of the Inferno were more likely to die of heart attacks than poverty, because the joint jittered and blasted with the latest in techno. Hypnotic tattoos? Piercings with lasers? They had 'em, they gave 'em. They were the black-market brokers of anything on the fringe.

Deuce took a deep breath and plunged into the Inferno. There were Scarlatti Members and Affiliates everywhere, in their signature crimson, silver, and black. During the early turf war years, they had wiped out another family, the Mitchells, in a horrendous purge the likes of which had never been seen. Not a single survivor was left. The other Families, shocked by their ruthlessness, said nothing about it. They were run by a Select of Six, who were elected to six-year terms, with a vote of confidence allowed every year.

Their number one of the Six was a humorless man named Tito Scarlatti, but their most popular member was Andreas Scarlatti, who now turned from a discussion with a pit boss and waved casually at Deuce. Deuce gave him respect with a more sincere wave and continued on his business. They were all acting cool, acting like nothing was wrong when the Ditwac had been capered.

Deuce kept an eye on the back of Andreas's shaved and tattooed head. Andreas had a lot of charm, but he was just as scary as the rest of the Family. He had more action going on than Deuce could keep up with. At the moment, rumors were flying of an alliance between him and Edward Jones, who was with the Smith Family, with plans either for forcing their Families to make peace, to merge, for creating a new Family, or for who knew what? Deuce should know; the Borgiolis needed to know. But he also knew he would live a lot longer the less he knew about the Scarlattis. A rock and a hard place for an ambitious young man.

Just like getting a wave from Andreas: With a few changes in the gesture, he could have had Deuce gunned down on the floor literally before Deuce knew what hit him.

Deuce ticked his gaze to Beniamino, one of the bartenders and one of his informants. Bennie looked away and nearly dropped a glass as he positioned it under the beer tap. Uh-oh, not a good sign. Deuce hoped they weren't coming down hard on him with questions about the Die.

He remembered that he hadn't turned on his comm badge and tapped it. He had not yet met with the House Liaison; it was rude not to have it on. Instantly it began to vibrate.

"Yeah," he said, wincing, hoping Big Al hadn't been trying to reach him.

"It's me."

He smiled. "Sparkle. Baby. Wait until you hear what's been going on."

"I wanted to make sure you did."

"I'm standing in the Inferno. The display cube is cloaked." He lowered his voice. He should be more discreet.

"Deuce," she said impatiently, "that's old news. You know about Hunter Castle, right?"

"What?"

"He's on his way to the Moon. If he's not here already."

"Hunter Castle?" he echoed, stunned, as all the evening's little hints and strange conversations lined up like X's on a bingo card. It was what Yuet Chan and Carson the bookie had both been talking about. Wow. Talk about your Moonshaking event. "Thanks, baby, gotta go."

He disconnected her and patched himself into Big Al. "Don Alberto, *buona sera*. It's Deuce. When's the meeting?" he asked without further ado, remembering that Yuet had talked about a council meeting that had to include the Borgiolis. And guessing that Big Al would call one of his own first.

"Damn it, Deuce, didn't you get my voice mail? I already started the meeting, and you're already late for it. Get your butt over here right now, or you won't have a butt," Big Al growled at him, and clicked off.

Gino, the Scarlatti Liaison to the Borgiolis, saw him and began his approach. Gino was a walking nightmare, with neuron enhancers sutured directly into his forehead and skull that pulsed inside tiny clear body shields. His nose had been split and ringed. His lips were tinted blue—a sign of drug addiction, but also currently a fashion statement as well—and large S's were branded onto his cheeks. It was said that every Scarlatti Family Member and Affiliate got branded, some in less obvious places.

"*Buona sera*," Gino said. His pupils jittered. He was biting his fingernails like they were pieces of uncooked linguine. People addicted to Chan drugs craved carbohydrates. "You heard?"

"Yeah," Deuce said, trying to guess if he meant about Castle or about the Ditwac. His heart pounded just being in the casino, almost as if he himself had messed with the Great Die. "Listen, I can't meet tonight. I came down personally because I wanted to give you respect, but my Number One has just called me in."

Gino nodded. He was sweating. He looked scared. "To talk about Castle."

"*Sì*," Deuce said, lowering his voice. Gino had no sense of discretion. Maybe it was because he was a drug addict. Or maybe—unfortunately—it was because he truly liked Deuce and figured two good *amici* like them could talk about anything.

As usual, the Borgiolis were given the dregs to work with. Still, Deuce had learned how to use Gino's loose lips—studded with hooks—to his advantage. Anything he wanted the Scarlatti higher-ups to know, he told Gino. Deuce was pretty sure they had figured out the game, and appreciated it. Especially when Deuce, pretending to get drunk one night with Gino, had made him swear never to tell Andreas that were Deuce a free man, he would love to Affiliate himself with the Scarlattis. He wasn't sure if Andreas had taken the bait or seen right through him, but either way he came off as someone trying to curry favor with the House of Scarlatti. And that was not a bad thing.

"How late are you working tonight?" Deuce asked

Gino, even though he knew the schedules of all the Borgioli Liaisons. Gino was on until 4 A.M.

"Four," Gino said, glancing over his shoulder. Sweat was rolling off him.

Deuce was deeply intrigued by his nervousness. Did the guy know something about the Ditwac? "I'll try to come back before your shift is up." To see what had developed.

Gino nodded. "Comm my badge. We'll do our business and have a nice *espresso*. I have a brand-new machine, the best." His smile was more like a facial tick. "It's in my office. Want to take a look?"

"Um, that'd be great, but my Godfather's waiting on me." Deuce kept his blue eyes wide and innocent. "Like I said, I wanted to show my respect by personally coming down." In a pig's eye. "That's why I didn't comm you in the first place."

Gino drew himself up. Deuce figured the assho—jerk— didn't get much respect from anyone. You could almost feel sorry for him if you didn't know he had beaten his wife so severely she'd gone blind.

"That's good," Gino said like a freakin' prince. He glanced covertly in Andreas's direction and caught his breath as the big man walked across the floor and headed toward the door marked "CASINO STAFF ONLY." Gino's office was the first cubicle on the left behind that door. Gino laughed and said, "Uh-oh, he'd better not touch my machine." Deuce watched with interest as Gino's right eye began to twitch. Speaking of which, it was all over the Moon that Andreas had bought Mrs. Gino her nice—and expensive—ocular implants and sent her three years ago to Earth. Why he hadn't wasted Gino in the bargain had been an endless topic of speculation for the three nights it had been the hot topic. The Family granted a divorce, no Vendetta on Mrs. Gino's behalf was Registered, and that was that.

Then something else to discuss endlessly and in mindless detail had come along. It was like that in closed-in places. Everything was briefly intense. Despite the illusions Chairman William Atherton Van Aadams clung to, the average life span of a legal marriage was 2.3 years. Which actually,

Deuce thought, was pretty good. Before Sparkle, he'd never had a full-time girlfriend. But he and Sparkle had already been together almost an entire year, even though she didn't want a single living, breathing soul to know. It had crossed his mind to negotiate for legal status, but he couldn't figure where her head was at. And he didn't want to jinx things.

He thought about the kiss on his forehead and the snack. Why did he play with fire, pull juvenile stunts like with the pizza? He'd been thrown out for less.

Of course, Beatrice, his Godfather's daughter, would never throw him out. It gave him a sense of power and a bigger sense of terror to realize she loved him that much.

Maybe Beatrice would give up if he got legal with someone else.

And then maybe Big Al really would have his butt.

He said to Gino, "I'll come back as soon as I can."

"Take your time," Gino replied magnanimously. "I'll be here." Yeah, poking through the Dumpsters for used vials of Chantilly Lace and licking out the residue. Gino didn't wash enough. He always smelled. Deuce didn't know why the Scarlattis allowed him in public. Maybe it was to grab the Borgiolis' noses and stick them in their collective armpits: *This scumbag's good enough to work with you lowlifes.*

He turned on his heel and nearly ran into one of the Scarlatti She-Devils. They were the tallest showgirls on the Moon, bounding through the Sea of Fertility at eleven feet. It was unnatural; the poor girls broke their legs on a regular basis. Some women's group had protested for a while, going on about irresponsible surgery and choking the Council with studies about bone mass, estrogen, and some other stuff. Then they got the standard Family treatment—the visits, the bribes, a couple of hospital stays.

And Scarlatti girls kept ending up in wheelchairs with misshapen hips and shins at the ripe old ages of twenty-five and twenty-six.

No one managed to get equally worked up about the boy dancers, who were so modified people called them "steroid droids." They looked less human than actual androids. In fact, Deuce didn't know why the casinos didn't replace all the human dancers with androids and be done with it, except there was a lot of cachet in having real humans dressed in sequined thongs, full-length gloves, and crowns of bird feathers.

Sparkle looked fabulous in her thongs and headdresses. Maybe she could get some data on the Chairman William–nephew Wayne–nephew James situation. It was handy that she worked in the Van Aadams casino, the Down Under, (jokingly called the Down and Out by locals, although it was raking it in just like the other Houses, even the Borgiolis) because his Liaison there never told him anything, either by accident or on purpose. Sparkle skated on real ice to a medley of Earthside oldies: "My Venus in Blue Jeans," "I'm Your Venus," "Venus Was a Woman," etc., etc., etc. *Venus on Ice* was a beautiful show, if for no other reason than that Sparkle was in it. But the icing—heh-heh—on the cake was that she also did a spectacular kick-boxing routine. In her feather crown. On ice skates.

What a woman.

Deuce commed his aichy and went outside in the seventy-four/sixty to wait for it. Speaking of ice, all that wishing they used to do Earthside about there being ice on the Moon had turned out to be a lot of hooey. Only ice there was on the Moon was gambling ice, as in protection money for the cops. It was the same the galaxy over: Even though gambling was legal here, you still had your corners you needed to cut, and someone needed to give you the scissors.

Same with their grand designs for hydroponics. Hooey. *Sciocchezza.* Oh, they grew some stuff on the Moon, but despite all the transportation costs, it was still usually a better deal to import from Earthside. Of course, that made them more dependent on the mother planet, which was part of the reason the MLF'ers had their knickers in a knot.

And why Deuce was able to rake in a fairly decent handle doling out toilet paper.

Some poor jerk N.A. shuffled by with his left hand out; the right one held a hand-lettered sign that read, WILL WORK FOR OXYGEN. Poor schmuck. Deuce gave him an Inferno onechip. Then another. What the hell.

"Bless you, sir," the guy said. Deuce figured himself for a putz—the guy probably made more panhandling than he did semihonestly—but he shrugged and continued to wait for his aichy.

"They're hiring dishwashers at the Palazzo," he said after a beat. "Tell 'em Deuce sent you." Yeah, like the guy would go. Will work for drugs and booze, more like.

"Thank you, sir." The man's rheumy eyes gleamed. "I will."

"Don't forget. Deuce." Maybe the guy would go. Maybe get some self-respect. Turn his life around.

"Hey, Deuce, hi, honey," said one of the Scarlatti hookers lounging by the entrance. They provided their girls with uniforms. She was dressed much like a She-Devil, in a brilliant red dress decorated with silver pitchforks stabbing crescent moons. "How ya doin' tonight?"

He sidled over to her. Her badge identified her as Bambi, but he was sure her name was Kimba. Maybe she was working the shift for someone else. "Hey, I heard about the Ditwac."

"Weird, huh," Kimba said, looking concerned. "But there's something even weirder going on." He looked dubious so she'd go on. "Hunter Castle's coming here."

"Get outta town."

"It's true. He's coming in a weird spaceship from another planet," she added.

Deuce raised his brows. "Say what?"

"Yes."

"Kimba, you know we're alone in the universe." So far, anyway. They'd searched and sent out signals and done large array things and all manner of other searches, and no one had replied to any of their knock-knock jokes: *Mars you glad to see me? Jupiter car in the garage?*

"Well, he's got this alien ship. Everyone's talking about it." She had the reddest mouth he'd ever seen, and now, when she smiled with it, it seemed to float in space all on its own.

"Thanks for that, sweetie. I'll bring you by a little present tomorrow."

She winked at him. "What I want is your big present, Deucie."

"You wanton creature," he said. They both smiled. "*A domani.*" See you tomorrow.

"I'll be looking forward to that, baby." She sauntered back to her post.

His aichy pulled up. Deuce swiped his card in the meter for the required tip and climbed inside.

"Where to, Mr. Borgioli?" his aichy asked politely.

"McNamara, McNamara, McNamara," Deuce grumbled.

"But you are listed as Mr. Arthur—"

Deuce sighed. "Look, doll, register my height and weight again," he commanded the aichy. "Now take my palm and retinals again." He held up his right hand and opened his pretty-blues very wide. There was a hum and a bing.

"Scan complete," said the aichy. "Again."

Sassy thing. "Register my measurements as Deuce McNamara. Again."

"Yes, sir. At once, Mr. Borgioli."

Deuce groaned. There must be some kind of Family override. His vehicle was his own—kind of; actually, it was the collateral on an uncollected loan—but he got his batteries from the Family.

"Take me to the Borgioli Building." Which was separate from the casino itself. "Fastest route possible."

"Legal speed?"

"No way. Step on it."

"Please insert your card for moving violation levics."

He swiped his card in the slot next to the voice console. "Authorization to pay double-parking fines as well."

"Yes, Mr. Borgioli."

His badge vibrated. "Why aren't you here yet?" Big Al barked.

"I'm on my way," Deuce assured him. "I had to make nice with my Scarlatti Liaison on account of we had to delay our business transactions."

"I'll make nice with that snotty little SOB. Freakin' junkie. You get over here *now.*" Big Al disconnected.

Deuce sighed and pulled out his card one more time. "Authorization for illegal passing fines," he instructed the aichy.

"Yes, Mr.—"

"McNamara," Deuce said warningly. He leaned back. "What's the weather like?"

"It's a perfect night, Mr. McNamara," the aichy declared with a note of triumph. Chalk one up for the neural net.

"Better fasten my overhead belt, anyway," Deuce ordered the aichy. "It's going to be a bumpy ride."

The aichy complied, and Deuce pushed himself backwards, a huge smile breaking across his face. Hunter Castle was coming to the Moon, and all the rumors Deuce had ever heard about the man were coming with him, pulled along by the tractor beam of his fame and his mystery. It was typical of people to believe he had a special spaceship. Also, a magical computer, a rejuvenator that kept him immortal, and a complete amusement park beneath his incredible mansion in Earthside New York.

Little could be beyond the man who headed an empire of corporations, who controlled fleets of spacecraft, who owned sixty-five percent of all the viso-beamnets and one percent of all the redeemed land on Earth.

But the best one he'd ever heard was that Hunter Castle was Elvis.

He snickered to himself and lit a cigarette. Tapped for the levy, lower because he was smoking inside his own vehicle and his car would process the air. Took a drag and watched the smoke curl slowly in front of him.

If he played his cards right, maybe Castle could be his fairy godfather. Okay, maybe that was a leap. But hey, maybe it was one he could take.

But before the deal, he had to make a few calls, see how the cards were shuffled.

He cracked his knuckle and got to work.

FIVE

"Roger and Abraham are on the verge of Registering a hit," one of Deuce's Smith contacts whispered. Deuce amplified his voice in the stillness of the aichy as it neared the Borgioli Building, a magnificently tacky conglomeration of spires and turrets trembling with bilious colors that rose at the end of a shaft called Carlito's Way.

"Thanks." Deuce made a mental tally of what he owed this particular stoolie. It was gonna take more than toilet paper. "I'll square up with you once things settle down."

"Sure thing, man."

That made all six Families—his own included—considering the assassination of Hunter Castle. He knew it was all knee-jerk. No one would dare touch a curly salt-and-pepper hair on Hunter Castle's head. It would be like whacking the president of the Conglomerated Nations: Castle was the very public head of a vast corporate entity, and like Yuet Chan said, the Families would risk being shut down entirely if the truth of any "accident" were ever discovered.

But, man, everyone was acting like *lunatics*.

And for someone who lived on the Moon to call another Moonsider a lunatic, you really, really had to be out there.

"Yes, Mr. Borgioli," his aichy agreed. "A perfect night for lunatics." Had he spoken his thoughts aloud? Deuce wondered. He'd have to watch that.

His comm badge vibrated again. He hit it, closing his eyes and stretching his legs. Realized he was hungry. He had been going full tilt and was due for some caloric intake.

"Yeah."

"It's Selene." A friend of Sparkle's—her supposed roommate, in fact—and Deuce's deathbed obligation object of protection. She was a very strange girl, usually had a kind of vacant look on her face you usually attributed to someone who was either not too bright or nearsighted. She was kind of jittery. Also, he was not sure that she liked him. However, he had an obligation to protect her that he would never violate on account of petty personal reasons, or any reason.

"Yeah, hi, Sel," he said, sitting forward.

"We're at work. This new girl, Cynthia, called me from the pit. There's this icky guy asking offensive questions about us dancers. It's gotta be *him*."

His eyes shot open. Every protective impulse in his body went on full alert. "Is *she* okay? Are you okay? Where is he? What's he done? Are the house animals on it?"

"It's probably nothing, Deuce. She'd kill me if she knew I'd called you. But you told me to let you know if I ever saw anything."

"I'm on my way." He didn't even think about it.

He swooped away from the Borgioli Building, away from the meeting, away from the summons of his Family Godfather. "Hang on, baby," he murmured, and floored it, zooming down shafts and through narrow tunnels narrow as Earthside pneumatic tubes and used for the same purpose—the chuting of packages and small objects like aichy batteries. He didn't even have the credits for all the violations; he made an advance against his next paycheck and prayed that by the time the first installment was due, he'd even have a job.

Damn, for this, Big Al would have his head.

And he'd be perfectly within his rights to cut it off himself.

SIX

The Man in the Moon, according to the Euahlayi
Aborigines of Australia (as retold for modern
Moonsiders):

Eons ago, Dreaming in the Dreamtime, Baloo the Moon decided to visit Earth. In all his radiance, he descended and touched his glowing feet to the red earth.

He soon came upon two exquisite maidens splashing in a river. His shimmering reflection entranced them, and they shyly but eagerly invited him to ride in their canoe.

But when he put a foot into the little boat, it rocked and tipped with his weight. Without further ado, Baloo fell into the dark water, and his beauty was quelled.

The girls laughed and laughed at him. Why, he was not a handsome, moonlit warrior at all! He was not a king! He was a *boy*!

Baloo was mortified beyond words. To the sound of their laughter (which some have likened to the giggle of the kookaburra) he fled home, to the sky.

For a few days he stayed hidden from sight. Then gradually, he recovered from his humiliation and gave it no more thought. Slowly he grew round and bright and full of courage.

He decided to resume his adventure on Earth. But when he descended, he saw his reflection in the river, and heard an echo of the laughter of the two maidens. Ashamed, he began to shrink away.

Thus, every month Baloo grows round and proud and bright, and every month he remembers his embarrassment and shrinks into nothing but a shadow.

By their own estimation and their own Family lore, the Van Aadamses had never condescended to walk among mortals. Other Families might get wiped out in turf wars; other Families' Godfathers might expire garrotted on a walk with the wife and kids. Not the Van Aadamses. They didn't have a Godfather. That was too . . . ungraceful. They considered themselves a privately held corporation, their best interests administered by a C.E.O.

The worst thing that had ever happened to the Van Aadams Family (or at least, that they admitted), was twenty-five years previous, when the wife of a high-ranking cousin had planned to run off (as in, to Earth) with a notorious Scarlatti drug dealer. The story went that the loving couple lasted less than two days.

Lasted, as in dying in agony from Topside-induced radiation burns all over their bodies.

Deuce used to fantasize he was secretly the child of these two star-crossed lovers. That had been before he knew about sex and nine months and all like that. Joey had filled him in when he was seven.

Heavily inbred even back in New Australia, Earthside, the Van Aadamses boasted a long, proud tradition of smooth, elegant, and successful capers, as opposed to the violent actions of a gang like the Smiths, the chaotic unpredictability of the Scarlattis, or the ineptitude of the Borgiolis. They always seemed to be able to pull off the fantastic. Everything they touched produced income and enhanced their already considerably enhanced image.

Everyone owed them favors, some over centuries, and like the Chans, they had their hands in everything. Their conversations with other Families ran to, ''Well, we agree with that, but then again, we own twenty percent of this situation.'' They were prep-school snobs steeped in Old-School formality. They admired their allies, the Chans, mostly because the Chans as a Family predated them by several centuries.

They still detested the Scarlattis for poisoning their well.

Mingling with the upper classes of the Earth and the Moon, they were the aristocracy of the Casino Families. Their casino, the Down Under, was the carpet joint of all carpet joints, the plushest edifice Deuce had ever been inside in his life. Expanses of spun burgundy-and-black carpet ran under the feet of the Moon's most prestigious inhabitants. Chandeliers that weighed a ton each at the one-sixth gravity of the Moon glittered and shimmered. The gaming tables and *vingt-et-un* horseshoes gleamed of mahogany and ebony from actual reconstructed Earthside rain forests, the most radiation-free that money could buy.

Deuce was supposed to change his clothes before he went in there, even though he was relegated to the employee entrance: coat and tie and slacks with creases, the whole nine yards. He kept a sharp black Italian suit in his locker and changed when he took his dinner break, preparatory to this, his last stop.

But now, on the rarefied lowest level, farthest from Topside and all its environmental hazards, reserved for the fancy folks but on the same floor as the stage entrance, he burst through the main entrance like a bank robber in his black craterleather.

"Excuse me, sir," murmured a platinum blonde in a strapless black evening gown. "Unfortunately, we have a dress code."

"Yeah," he said. His blaster was in his hand, but at least he had the presence of mind to hide it in his pocket. Still, pleasant alarms were bonging like arriving elevators as he crossed the lobby.

Eyebrows raised as he dodged around rejuvved matrons in flashy gowns and men in tuxes. This section of the Down Under didn't have customers; it hosted patrons. The intimidated riffraff, officially allowed if they had the right clothes, kept their distance and stayed on the upper levels, where it was all comers. Here, the Down Under entertained the highest of the high rollers, the kind of people who didn't even carry their own chips because money was well, rather *untidy*, wasn't it, darling? The casino provided pretty girls in sexy dresses and handsome young men in penguin suits to cart around the loot.

He ran to the stage entrance of Sparkle's review and flashed his Liaison badge. Made himself smile. Said, "Wow, what's with the alarms?"

"Deuce?" He turned at the whisper of his name. The speaker was Brigham, one of his Mormon buddies. Brigham was a stage security guard. A casino animal, but he was not an animal at all. He was a big kitty cat. Word was that the B-man had four wives. It was probably true. He looked tired all the time.

Mamma had thought Mormons were *pervertitos* and worked with the Catholic Ladies Association to ban their filthy polygamous marriages on the Moon as they were on Earth. But that was one fight that had been lost by the Families. It was way too much fun to take a ship to Moonbase Vegas and get married in the very spacy Mormon Temple. The MLF had been instrumental in obtaining for the Mormons their right to legally boink as many ladies as they were physically able.

Mamma mia, what a religion!

"Where's my girlfr—where's Miss Selene?" he asked carefully.

"Onstage." Brigham pointed to the viso scan. Deuce caught his breath. There she was, his vision of loveliness, his queen, not Selene, of course, but Sparkle. She towered above a misty fogbank of icy "Venusian" landscape in a crown of glitter and peacock and ostrich feathers (not that he had ever seen a peacock or an ostrich), and a little jeweled collar that draped between her magnificent *poppas*. Her platinum ponytail matched her thong, which matched her skates.

Selene and the other girls gathered in the background in a sort of ta-da! group pose. Selene did not go topless, and most of the rest of her was pretty well covered. She wore a bodysuit of icy blue and matching tights. Here and there was a cutout to reveal some skin, but the whole thing was kind of dull. Sparkle said Selene dressed in the shower stalls. Everyone else let it all hang out. Deuce figured she had been instructed to wear more clothes as a condition of employment. Because the fewer square inches of clothing you wore, the more you made, so who would opt out if she could make the extra pasta? Whatever the case, it had to be that there was something not quite primo with her actual terrain, as opposed to the contours of her landscape, because the girl did have curves in all the right places.

While they posed, Sparkle executed a swan-dive thing—there was a name for it, but it escaped him—as cymbals crashed and a volcano exploded in the background. Then the other girls swarmed around her like butterflies. Next would come a roundhouse kick, executed flawlessly on ice skates.

What total, utter class.

"That guy that's been bothering them," Deuce said, remembering himself. "I got commed and—"

Brigham warningly cleared his throat, and said softly, "Give me your blaster, Deuce."

"Mr. McNamara?" A trim, manicured security guard approached Deuce pleasantly as another, less distinguished one flanked him. The trim one had an Earthsider Greater Australian accent. "May we be of service to you, sir?"

"Outta my way." Deuce spun to the right and started behind the scenery. The two men trailed him but kept pace. "That bastard's bothering the girls again, and as usual, you morons aren't doing a thing about it."

"We haven't been notified of any problems," said the distinguished animal.

"Well, I got notified."

The thing was, Sparkle had asked Deuce not to let people know about their relationship. For good reason: It was irregular for a showgirl at one casino to be with a Family Liaison from another casino. His obligation to Selene was a different matter. Selene was not a native; she'd come up about two and a half years ago. She was the niece of R.J. Earthshine, an N.A. acquaintance of Deuce's who had been whacked a few months after Selene's arrival, in a Vendetta (since settled) between a Scarlatti Member and a Scarlatti Affiliate.

Deuce had felt very badly about the death. R.J. Earthshine had been an informant of his who had gotten in the way trying to get some info for Deuce on an entirely different matter—namely, the obtaining of a safe combination to add to his collection. Wholly by chance, Earthshine had been in the wrong place at the wrong time. With the simple opening of the wrong door, they'd juiced him without bothering to ask what he was doing there.

Deuce was completely opposed to the killing of N.A.'s unless they did something worthy of the punishment. Contrary to the opinion of many other Members and Affiliates, Deuce believed the N.A.'s had every bit as much right to life, liberty, and the pursuit of a house percentage. Most Family people considered them an expendable resource whose relatives could be fairly cheaply bought off—on the order of paying a pollution levy.

Deuce had fought his way to the crime scene to be with Earthshine for his last moments on the Moon. Fought was the operant word; no one wanted to let him through. In a rage, he had broken the arm of the Affiliate—the Scarlatti Member remained unidentified to this day; only his colors had been recognized—and had to do all kinds of humiliating things to stay out of Vendetta with the guy, including pay the Family six thousand credits.

To add to the insult, the amount of the payment had been determined not by the Charter Board but by the Scarlattis, which was also irregular. But what could he do? As with Mamma's will, no one would back him up. Big Al had been mortified by his behavior, which was to his way of thinking like running over a man to save a dog.

As he lay dying, R.J. Earthshine made Deuce promise to take care of his niece, Miss Selene. Deuce privately thought, *Niece, schmiece, this Earthside babe's his girl*, but he had accepted the deathbed obligation. That she was working for the Van Aadamses could have been messy, as Deuce was the House Liaison for the Borgiolis, but he made sure he lost a bundle in the Down Under at faro to smooth things over. That was acceptable. And a lot of good had come of the situation: Watching out for Selene was how Deuce had met and fallen in love with her roommate, Sparkle. Now Sparkle lived with him, although she pretended to still live with Selene.

The security guard touched Deuce's shoulder. "I assure you, we're as eager as you to resolve this issue."

Deuce frowned at him. "Resolve it? I'm going to beat the living crap out of the SOB. Stalking them in the aichy lot, leaving notes in their cubicles. Miss Selene's scared to death. So are all the others." That wasn't exactly true— Deuce had never seen Sparkle frightened of anything—but it made for good copy.

"Mr. McNamara accidentally brought his weapon into the House," Brigham said, taking it from him gently and handing it over. "He's very sorry."

"Yeah. I am," Deuce said morosely.

The man closed his hand pleasantly but firmly around Deuce's biceps. Deuce started to shake him off, realized the futility of it, realized he'd been a jerk to stomp through their fancy-schmancy lobby and into the revue. God, how stupid *was* he? Not stupid, just motivated, that was all.

Maybe Sparkle wasn't scared, but all the other showgirls sure were. The stalker had taken on epic proportions until he was the Phantom of the Down Under, some disfigured maniac who would whack them all. Exploiting Selene's connection to Deuce, the girls had come to him in a group to appeal for help, because the Van Aadamses, for all their assurances to the contrary, had been doing diddly-squat about apprehending him. Even the Borgiolis protected their employees better than this. Deuce had been after Sparkle to get a job somewhere else, but after you'd skated topless at the Down Under, there was nowhere to go but, well, down. In a manner of speaking.

Sparkle liked to say he had a streak of old-fashioned heroism in him. She said it with derision, like when you tell someone they need to clean their nose. Maybe blazing into her place of employment with his blaster dripping juice was the kind of thing she was talking about.

"Deuce, go with the men," Brigham urged, glancing around. "Don't make a scene."

Big Al would definitely kill him for this. He sighed heavily.

They squired him out and into a service elevator, and

punched in a code. Third floor, women's lingerie, carnival wheels, blackjack tables, and deep kimchee.

The doors opened. The alarms were silent. Deuce gestured toward the main casino floor, a sassy, brassy mishmash of "G'day Mate" Aussie ruggedness and Aboriginal fever dream. Sequin boomerangs and robot kangaroos, a holo of the Outback that was really quite impressive—trees and parrots and sunsets and boinga-boinga digideroos. In the center, next to the craps pit, hot Aborigine babes—mechanicals, probably—waved free drink coupons from the top of the big flat rock called Uluru. Termite mounds spewed colored water.

They ushered him past the tableaux proclaiming how you could win a free trip to Outback Land theme park, located right in the heart of New Sydney, Earthside. Just roll, baby! Roll with them punches!

"I got a call," Deuce said grumpily. "He was asking about Miss Selene on the floor."

"Did Miss Selene summon you during show time?" the other animal demanded, but the distinguished one gave his colleague a cool-it look. No doubt they could trace the call, see if she violated the rules. The Scarlattis had probably sold the Van Aadamses better stuff than they'd offered to the other Families. Everyone was always trying to suck up to the Van Aadamses.

He knew they were heading for their security station. He knew as much about the Down Under layout as a cat burglar. It was part of his job to know. Still, he acted a bit uncertain about going left past the slot machines or right past the Dreamtime Cafe, in case they'd underestimated his knowledge of their operation. After all, he was just a Borgioli. But he doubted the Van Aadamses took anything for granted; they were on top because they were careful.

Mr. Hunter Castle would approach them first, Deuce figured. Hell, maybe they'd even invited him.

His comm badge vibrated. The distinguished animal prissily pursed his lips, as in, *Tsk, tsk, you should have turned that off, old boy.* Ignoring him, he hit it.

"Earphone," he said.

"Where are you?" Selene wailed. "He left us a bucket of vomit!"

"They're in trouble," he said to the animals, contemplating making a break for it.

"We've got the situation under control," the distinguished one assured him. "Please come with us, and we'll bring you up to date."

The other animal reacted to some kind of signal of his own and closed his eyes. "Incoming trace," he said. He must have been reading it off his inner eyelid. Deuce was envious. All he could afford was a clock readout.

The two animals gave each other looks. Deuce said, "What?" but they didn't share. "We should go right over back to the stage now," he urged. "You schmos are putting all of them in danger."

"Security's already over there, Mr. McNamara," the polite animal assured him.

His buddy, Brigham. "Why doesn't that make me feel better?" Deuce said, feeling a little disloyal.

"Hey, we take good care of them," the other animal said angrily. "We're the only Family gives them pensions and profit-sharing."

"Yeah, and a one-thousand-credit deductible on their hospital bill if their legs go," Deuce shot back. Selene had been worried about that, having her grafts done relatively late in life. The man looked surprised; yeah, that was pretty cheesy, wasn't it, *mio amico*?

"Please, gentlemen, let's not bicker."

They had reached one of those ubiquitous doors that read "EMPLOYEES ONLY." Deuce half expected the Van Aadamses to have added the word, "Please."

A surly guard with a shield on his suit jacket coded it open.

On the other side stood another goombah, an older man gone to a bit of flab. Must be a pensioner of some sort; the Van Aadamses made everybody jog and watch their fat intake. Deuce's companions nodded pleasantly at him. The flabby man spoke into his wrist and gave Deuce and his new friends a businesslike wave through. It was probably all over the casino that the Borgioli Liaison had come barging in like Devon LeDare, the dashing hero on *Phases*, everybody's favorite soap opera.

The service hall was lined with official-looking portraits of the big cheeses and rows of awards the Van Aadamses had either presented to themselves or purchased from more legitimate channels: Best Cuisine, Superior Entertainment Value, and lots and lots of good-citizen-type plaques from all the charities they bribed.

The outer office of the security station itself was a spacious, carpeted room with couches and overstuffed chairs all facing a large console manned by an unsmiling woman in a burgundy jumpsuit. She was monitoring two banks of viso monitors, and her gaze never wandered from them to Deuce. She murmured almost continuously into a wire that jutted from her jawline and hooked into a cute dimple in her chin. There was a door behind her. That was where the real hardware lay. Deuce knew that there were about twenty of her ilk—more or less—back there, hunching over their Scarlatti stuff, doing surveillance on every inch of the casino on hundreds of viso scans.

The walls—which could not only listen, but talk—were plastered with posters about the Heimlich maneuver and various other aspects of first aid, as if these guys were paramedics. The upscale Moonsiders who found themselves in here would be impressed. They probably didn't know that the Van Aadams security forces had been implicated in— but never convicted of—over three dozen "accidents" in the past three years. Their signature style of execution was a dumdum that never, ever came back out. Instead it heated up inside you and microwaved your guts. No blood, no goo. Just a nice little package of dead meat boiling away inside.

But of course, no Van Aadams would even deign to discuss such a thing, much less acknowledge that they were just as ruthless in their cold, elitist way as the Scarlattis and the Smiths.

"Please, have a seat," said the distinguished animal. "My name is Geoffrey Tanzer."

"Oh, an Affiliate," Deuce said snippily, and was immediately embarrassed by his own childish bravado. He ought to be mending fences as fast as he could.

"Yeah, so am I, Mr. *McNamara*. You want to make something of it?" The other animal leaned into Deuce and pulled back his lips in a grimace that, frankly, made him look like a chimpanzee. Deuce had the absurd notion to tell the guy he had some broccoli hanging in there and realized he was getting scared. That was the kind of dumb crap he started pulling when he was at a disadvantage. Mamma used to say it was his inherited Irish gift for blarney gone terribly wrong.

Joey used to say it was because he was a dumb Mick dirtball.

"Would you like something to drink, Mr. McNamara?" Mr. Tanzer queried politely. "A cappuccino, perhaps?"

What he would prefer was to have his blaster back so he could shoot himself in the head and shut himself up.

"A *latte*, please," Deuce said. "Nonfat milk. Extra foam." Normally he would prefer the cappuccino, but *latte*, that sounded soft, appeasing, nonthreatening.

Tanzer excused himself to the unsmiling woman and pressed two buttons on her console. She didn't so much as blink. It was only then that Deuce realized she was mechanical. The Van Aadamses were heavily into circuitry. For good reason: As a rule, robots didn't join unions.

The Van Aadamses hated unions with a passion.

Deuce said to Tanzer, "Are you human?"

Taking no offense, Tanzer nodded. "As is my associate, Mr. Feist."

Mr. Feist smirked at Deuce as if their visitor was the dumbest man on the face of the satellite. Then he crossed his arms and perched on the corner of the console. "Mr. McNamara," he said, "we don't like it when people go into vigilante mode on our property. Mr. Tanzer and I have been hired to protect the people inside this casino. When you come busting in like some superhero, we have to protect them from *you*. *Capisce*?"

Deuce bristled at the dig at his Italian Membership but for once kept his cool. He crossed his legs and sat back. What did they want him to do, apologize? Pay them off? He closed his eyes. It was almost midnight. Sparkle's show was over. So, he assumed, was his.

"That nutcase accosted Miss Selene," he said. Actually, it had been Sparkle who had been physically confronted, but what would these two know about it? "He waited for her outside the stage door and tried to grab her." It still amazed Deuce that the bastard had gotten away without a scratch, or so Sparkle said. It wasn't like his baby not to maim someone who got in her face. "He's sent those girls hundreds of notes. He sent them an armed blaster."

"Yes. We know," Tanzer cut in. There was a rap on the door. "Ah. That must be your *latte*."

He rose and went to the door, opened it, was pushed out of the way as Wayne "the Moongoloid" Van Aadams hurled his prodigious bulk into the room.

"All right, where is she?" he demanded. "Where's the little bitch who called you guys?" He stormed into the room, dived at the console, and punched the surveillance droid in the back of the head. She immediately shut down.

"Who the hell are you?" he flung at Deuce.

Deuce's lips parted. He glanced at Tanzer, who hastily closed the door and walked toward Wayne Van Aadams the way you walked toward a rabid dog. Not that he had ever seen a rabid dog. Van Aadams's face was as round as the Moon. He had no chin; his head simply fit onto his neck like a peg in a hole. His features were puttylike, elongated, like someone had botched a face job extremely badly, or he had been in a fire, neither of which was the case. His lack of hair betrayed the strange little craters on his scalp—some speculated that they were pockmarks, but who the hell got diseases anymore?—that had earned him his nickname. He was overweight and his clothes, though clearly expensive, were rumpled and messy.

This revolting moron? Deuce wanted to shout in disbelief. *This is the Phantom of the Down Under who's been terrorizing your girls?* No wonder they hadn't done squat about it. A lot of stuff made sense now.

What didn't make sense is the fact that Cynthia in the pit had not recognized the "icky guy." Selene had said she was new. But the Heirs of the Families were Moonbase celebrities. There were articles about them on the viso and the zippers. She must be real new.

Tanzer sighed. "Mr. Van Aadams," he began, "this is not a good time."

"Don't you dare talk to me like that," Van Aadams shouted. Spittle flew. "My uncle will kill you."

Deuce uncrossed his legs. Perhaps, to a defenseless showgirl, this bullying would be effective. But not on Sparkle. She would have recognized him. She must have been protecting Van Aadams. She had deflected Deuce's questions about the Phantom as easily as she deflected his snap kicks during their sparring sessions.

O mamma mia, that woman . . .

She must have figured that if word had gotten out that the heir to the Family was hassling their hired help . . .

. . . and if a certain young hothead from another Family had found out and charged over to the Down Under to beat the living tar out of him . . .

. . . we might have one or two showgirls with a lot of explaining to do. And possibly no jobs.

Whoops.

"Jeez, Tanzer," Deuce said to the man.

"As you might surmise," Tanzer said to Deuce, "we've been monitoring the situation."

"Situation? What situation?" Van Aadams asked wildly. He ran his hands through his greasy hair. Yick. "What lies have they been telling you?" He didn't mean Deuce. He wasn't even looking at Deuce.

Then, as if Van Aadams could read Deuce's thoughts, he narrowed his piggy eyes and hunched up his shoulders like he was either going to charge or dig for truffles. "And I already asked who you are, didn't I? And do I know? Do I *know*?" He made a sour face at Deuce's patch. "All I know is you're a stinking Borgioli. What's a Borgioli doing on my property?"

"Mr. Van Aadams," Tanzer ventured.

"What's *your* name? I'm having you fired." Van Aadams shook his fist at Tanzer. "No. I'm having you killed. You. Scumbag," he said to Feist. "Get me a drink. *Now*."

"Yes, Mr. Van Aadams," Feist said evenly. He traded looks with Tanzer and surreptitiously pocketed Deuce's blaster as he crossed to the door.

There was another knock. Mr. Feist opened the door, blinked at the guard who had waved Deuce and Mr. Tanzer and himself into the hall, and got the heck out of there, lucky bastard.

The chubby guard hovered on the threshold. He sported an impressive new shiner. "I'm sorry, Mr. Tanzer," he said. "I, ah, didn't expect . . ." He trailed off and shrugged.

"Didn't expect what? That I could stick up for myself?" Van Aadams kicked the console desk, kicked it again, again. "Does everyone around here think I'm a wuss?"

Deuce ticked his gaze to Tanzer, who shook his head as if to say, *This is a Family matter. Don't get involved. Don't see it. Don't hear it.* Aloud, he said, "Thank you again for turning the wallet in, Mr. Borgioli. We'll contact the woman who dropped it immediately."

So that was it? They were going to cower while this maniac terrorized them and the rest of their operation? One knock on the door behind the immobile droid and they could have a dozen guys in here. He couldn't figure it. He knew this maniac was the favorite nephew of their Godfather—oh, excuse me, the Van Aadamses were led by a "C.E.O."—Chairman William Atherton Van Aadams V. *That* guy was said to be a clone of the original William Atherton, founder of the Family. In turn, the story went, that guy was created from DNA from the remains of Cornelius Vanderbilt.

And William Atherton V was devoted to this globule of hysteria, Wayne. This intellectual midget. It was a great source of anxiety within the great house of Van Aadams that Wayne was the Designated Heir. Steps were being taken to prevent it, and anybody could see why.

Deuce could also see why there were so many rumors that Wayne was a botched clone of William Atherton. Why else could such a smart head honcho put up with someone like this? Any other Family would have iced him by now.

Tanzer stared hard at Deuce, willing him to discretion. Deuce figured he could play this two ways: intelligently or futilely. He opted for getting his butt out the door asap and nodded at Tanzer.

"I hope her luck holds," Deuce replied.

"Wait a minute. Just wait," Van Aadams bellowed. "You mean to tell me a stinking Borgioli turned in a lost wallet? A Borgioli? What kind of idiot do you think I am?" He advanced on Deuce and grabbed his collar. He smelled of old whiskey and older cigars. "You're in a conspiracy with these two dirtballs to put a hit on me, aren't you?"

Deuce flared, fought like crazy to keep his cool. He said, imitating Tanzer's accent, "Mr. Van Aadams, please do unhand me."

Van Aadams was so taken aback that he obeyed, pushing Deuce backwards in the process. Deuce caught his balance, doubled his fists, and glared at Tanzer as if to say, *A person can take only so much.*

"Borgioli scum," Van Aadams flung at him. He advanced on Tanzer. "Where's that SOB with my drink?"

When Tanzer made no reply, Van Aadams struck him in the face. Tanzer was tougher than he looked; he barely registered the attack. But he touched his cheek experimentally, and said, "Mr. Van Aadams, I assure you, there's no conspiracy here."

"You damned liar." Van Aadams made to strike him again. This time Tanzer blocked him, but made no retaliatory moves. Then Van Aadams kicked him in the shin, hard.

"You're fired!" he shrieked. "Fired!"

Tanzer limped to the door and opened it. "Mr. Borgioli, if you please," he said. Deuce hesitated. Tanzer was a decent guy, and he didn't want to leave him alone with this lunatic. "Please."

Maybe what he was asking was for Deuce to go get some help. Or maybe like Sparkle, this Van Aadams employee stood a better chance if he kept his mouth shut. Well, Deuce would be damned if he'd keep *his* mouth shut.

He gave Tanzer a sharp nod and left the room.

Van Aadams barreled after him, screaming, "Where do you think you're going?"

At that moment, Mr. Feist was walking back down the corridor with a silver tray in one hand. Centered on it was a beverage garnished with a paper umbrella. He was perhaps two feet away from the other two men when he smoothly held out the drink and said, "Mr. Van Aadams, your Venus on Ice."

"Oh." Van Aadams stopped in his tracks.

Mr. Feist approached him. As he brushed past Deuce, he slipped Deuce's blaster out of his pocket and pushed it into Deuce's hand almost before Deuce realized what was happening. Van Aadams saw none of it. His eyes were fixed on the drink. The fact that he could switch off his tantrum as quickly and abruptly as a child was more frightening than his show of fury.

"What kind of rum did you use?" he asked dangerously, taking a sip.

"Atherton Gold," Mr. Feist replied jauntily. "Your favorite, Mr. Van Aadams."

"Damn straight." Pitching it back, he pointed over his shoulder in the direction of the security station. "There's a mess in there. Clean it up."

He walked past Mr. Feist, moved shoulder to shoulder with Deuce, and knocked him, hard.

"Out of my way, you lowlife wop."

Be cool, Deuce reminded himself, and pocketed the blaster before he innocently held up his hands.

He waited until Van Aadams had moved on before he turned to Mr. Feist. The outer door hissed. They were alone.

"Jeez," Deuce said.

Mr. Feist shrugged and began hurrying toward the security station door. "Geoff?"

Deuce caught up with him. "You got another way out of here?"

Mr. Feist nodded and pointed in the opposite direction. "You saw nothing." He glanced upward. "I think he knocked our hallway cameras out. We'll be on backup in another ten seconds or so."

"I saw nothing only if all the girls get to keep their jobs. And no repercussions. Against either Miss Selene or me."

"I'll try to arrange that." He paused. "I gave you back your blaster."

Deuce paused. Cocked his head. "Yeah, so? Why wouldn't you?"

Mr. Feist gave him a look. He murmured, "Use it. We're behind you. Not just Tanzer and me. It would be privately Sanctioned. Call me later."

"*What?*"

"And don't you ever, ever do that again," Mr. Feist added in a loud, indignant voice. The cameras must have gone back on.

"Yeah, sure," Deuce allowed, and ambled toward the other exit.

Use it?

On the Heir to the Van Aadams Family?

His mind raced; his heart pumped; every cell in his body danced the Lunar Madness. Who *said* to use it, two no-account security guards? Or someone higher up?

It didn't matter. No way was he getting involved. No way.

Then he thought of the showgirls—of his vow to protect Selene—and felt tempted.

He thought of Sparkle, and his trigger finger itched.

Big Al would never Sanction it. It would start a war. It had nothing to do with business and would do nothing to further the Borgiolis' interests.

But it would be a pleasure to juice that creep.

He went outside, into the seventy-four/sixty, and summoned his aichy. Lit up. Paid the fine.

He wondered what was going on in there. If Van Aadams so much as got near the girls, Deuce would do it. He'd pull the damn trigger even if the next thing that happened was him zooming out an airlock.

His aichy arrived. He tapped on his comm badge, so Big Al could read him the riot act at his pleasure, and called Sparkle.

"Yes," she answered.

"You okay?"

"Everything's under control."

"Selene okay?"

"A little shaken. What—"

At that moment, Wayne Van Aadams launched himself at Deuce's back. He shrieked like a madman, landing on top of him. All the considerable bulk of the misbegotten creature pushed him to the pavement. Van Aadams's angry fists pummeled the back of Deuce's head as if he wanted to bash his way into the meaty portion of the artichoke, his medulla oblongata. Van Aadams was no fighter, that was for sure. Just a pummeler.

"You keep your hands off my girl!" he screamed. "You lying bag of crap!"

"Your . . . ?" Did he mean Sparkle? Deuce had the wherewithal not to ask as he shot into action and executed a double-leg pickup and spin. He hoisted himself at Van Aadams, dropping his hips as he lifted him into the air. With a grunt he swung the Moongoloid across his chest, using his right forearm against the outside of Van Aadam's thigh. He underhooked the man's right thigh with his left arm, dropped to his right knee, and spun Wayne's legs across his front. Grunting, he blocked Van Aadams's legs with his left thigh as he pulled his right arm out. He drove his shoulders to the pavement—looked painful—and shot in a half nelson with his right arm while keeping the other guy's legs trapped. Then he secured a pin by driving into his chest.

"Mr. Van Aadams, I don't know your girl," he said. "I didn't even know you had a girl." Whoops, that didn't sound so complimentary.

Amazingly, Van Aadams still wriggled free. He reach into his shirt pocket and pulled out the necklace Diana Lunette had given to Joey. He must have lifted it when he rammed Deuce in the corridor; it would be natural for such a drool of a man to go picking through another's pockets just to see what was there. Must have then watched it. Must have subsequently jumped to his own conclusions.

"Diana Lunette is my fiancée," he announced. "And you're dead."

He heaved himself again at Deuce, who took a step back and executed a mighty fine roundhouse kick, if he did say so. He connected with Van Aadams's chin; the man's head jerked back and for a moment, Deuce thought he'd broken his neck.

"Listen, Mr. Van Aadams," he said.

But then he came at Deuce once more, roaring like a bull.

A crowd gathered, making what should stay very private very public. Deuce's heart sank even though he kept fighting. The luck of the Irish was not with him tonight. If he could have saved his butt with Big Al before, it was all over now. No way you punched out a Designated Heir without serious—and the operant word here was *serious*, friends and neighbors—repercussions.

"Hit him!" someone caterwauled, and Deuce wanted to wail on whoever it was to make him shut up.

Van Aadams took his blows and staggered back for more. "Just stop, okay? You're making a big mistake," Deuce said, but the bastard was making too much noise screaming at him to hear him.

Finally, at last, about a minute too late, two casino animals headed for them. If they had juice and if they trusted their marksmanship, Deuce figured he'd be dead in ten seconds. It would almost be worth it, he thought.

Van Aadams saw them, too. He shouted, "Stay back, I'm killing him myself!" and in that single moment, Deuce seized the advantage, gave Van Aadams a sharp snap kick to the shoulder, aiya!, and sent him sprawling.

It occurred to him that the animals were taking their sweet time getting to them.

Van Aadams landed unceremoniously on his can. The tourists were agog. He blinked once, twice, snake eyes. Something that looked suspiciously like tears sluiced down his pudgy cheeks.

"You dirty Eyetalian," he said, scrabbling to get up. "You're dead. I'm hitting him. Call my uncle. This man has committed a grave dishonor against the woman I love."

"Yes, sir," the guard closest to him said, not moving.

"Now!" Van Aadams held his arms out to be hoisted back to a standing position. The two guards complied, not a hint of expression crossing their faces. Not mechanical, Deuce decided. Just disgusted in a very human way.

"Your uncle is in a conference at the moment," the other guard allowed.

"How dare you. How dare you!" Van Aadams shouted, rushing both of them. They stepped back.

It occurred to Deuce that he had never heard anyone say, "How dare you!" before in real life. It enhanced the unreal, soap opera–like air of the entire experience. He almost laughed out loud because it was all just too bizarre.

"You, what are you smiling at?" Van Aadams demanded. He was like a huge child, maybe an enraged bear or even a bull. Deuce wasn't sure. He had seen very few real animals in his Moonsider life.

"Wayne?" someone called from the casino doors. It was a rejuvved, strong-jawed older lady in a black pantsuit. Not William Atherton's wife, but a close relative, that was for certain. "Come on in, dear."

Van Aadams wiped his mouth with the back of his hand, checked it as if for blood. Or excess stomach acid. "Get his full name and Membership number," he ordered the two guards. "I'm going to my uncle."

"Yes, sir," one of the guards said.

Van Aadams pointed at Deuce. "You'll be dead by tomorrow."

Deuce murmured, so only he could hear, "Your mom wants you to go in now. It's time for your nap."

Van Aadams turned a brilliant shade of purple. Deuce wondered why he did these things, these stupid, impulsive, nanner-nanner things that could get him into so much trouble.

"Wayne," the woman called pleasantly.

Van Aadams huffed and stumbled toward her.

Deuce closed his eyes. His clock blinked at him. At the moment, he didn't give a damn what time it was, but there it was anyway, blinking away.

"May we have your name and number?" the guard asked with complete disinterest.

"Sure," Deuce said. "It's Joey—" No, it might actually happen; Wayne's uncle might actually Sanction the hit, slim chance though it was. "Gianni Vitale Borgioli. Number 666." There was no such creature, but there was a file for him nonetheless. It probably wouldn't work; the Van

Aadamses were too smart for that kind of simple decoy. But what the hell.

The guard punched it into his comm badge, closed his eyes, made a few more punches, and nodded.

"It's processed, sir. I'll show it to Mr. Van Aadams." Meaning *the* Mr. Van Aadams.

"I'll contact my Godfather," Deuce said.

The other guard cleared his throat. "I don't think that will be necessary," he said in the softest possible voice.

Deuce gave a fraction of a nod. Good. They were just cackling the dice. These two fine men were going to lie to Wayne and tell him the hit had been Registered. And no doubt give a private report to Wayne's uncle to cover themselves. That meant he still wasn't in the clear. At the very, very least, he was going to have to resign as Borgioli Liaison to the Van Aadams Casino.

At the very least of the least.

Big Al would like that only slightly less than he would like the scene Deuce had caused.

His comm badge beeped. He shut his eyes tight and answered it.

"Come on in," Big Al growled, like you do when you're talking to a fugitive from justice.

"Yessir," Deuce replied morosely.

Inside the aichy, he reached for the nice snack Sparkle had made for him, partly on pure animal instinct—blasters needed refueling, so did bodies—and partly because it might be his last meal and his beloved had made it just for him. His case meal, as a gambler might say it.

And no one could say he wasn't betting the house tonight with his shenanigans.

He reached inside. He was so startled he nearly dropped the bag.

She who would not permit red meat in any form within the walls of their apartment; she who had once threatened Deuce with abandonment for bringing home a *soupçon* of summer sausage from a Family meeting; she for whom animal fat was an immoral form of toxic waste; that same she had packed him nothing less than a personal-size pepperoni pizza.

"Oh, God, she's got a terminal illness," he whispered, and he was so upset at the prospect that he couldn't eat a single bite.

He folded the bag top over and put the bag on the passenger seat. He said to the aichy, "Borgioli Building."

"Yes, Mr. Borgioli," the aichy replied.

The aichy ascended. Deuce sighed and settled in for the short hop.

He looked at the bag and thought about what was inside it.

"Oh, what the heck," he murmured, grabbed the pizza, and with a moment's fond thought of Moona Lisa, his erstwhile partner in crime, devoured the entire thing.

His comm badge went off as he was swallowing the last bite. Wow, déjà vu. His evening had started like this.

Well, sort of.

"Yeah," he said, expecting Big Al again.

"Deuce." It was Little Wallace. "Deuce, man, I *heard*."

Deuce said carefully, "Yeah?"

"About the hit. Oh, man. Deuce, you can hide out at my place. I'll code it for your voice."

"The hit."

"Wayne Van Aadams's hit on you. Is it true? He's bringing up Earthsiders?"

What?

"That's what you heard too, eh?" Deuce muttered. Well, as they always said, bad news traveled FTL—and a contract could be signed, sealed, and delivered faster than that. Whoever *they* were. By the rules of Vendetta, his contacts were going to dry up faster than helium dust. Nobody wanted to traffic with a lame-duck politician or a dead duck Family Member.

As he talked, he pulled out his blaster to make sure it was fully charged. Tonight it and his right hand might be his only friends.

There was something taped to the back. It was a business card. Good stock. Real ink, not laser written.

Hunter Castle, C.E.O, Castle Enterprises. New York, New Milan, London Redeemed, Tokyo.

Deuce was speechless. He stared at the card for perhaps half a minute, which is much longer than it sounds.

"Deuce, you scared, man?"

"Don't worry about it," he said easily, even jauntily, though there was suddenly nothing left of his stomach besides a knot. *Hunter Castle?* What was this, a joke or a secret message or what? "I've got everything under control."

"Oh. Okay, Deuce," Little Wallace said, obviously disappointed that his time had not come to spring into action. Huh, action. This was a wee bit o' too much action for one little ostensibly Irish boyo, excuse me very much. Little Wallace ought to spend one day in the real world of casino life. Yeah, sure, it gave you a rush. Like turbo-LEMs rushing two inches past your ears at three hundred miles an hour.

Still, Little Wallace didn't know that. His own N.A. world was mostly about being second-class and being controlled. It sucked big-time to be an N.A. Deuce felt sorry, and said, "But you can do me a favor, if you would."

"Sure, Deuce."

"Call me Tony."

"Oh. Sure, Tony." There was a pause. "Anything else, Deuce?"

Deuce suppressed a sigh. "Remember, we were going to use a code for each other?" Like it mattered anymore. Like not one single person on the Moon didn't know who they both were.

"Oh. Oh, right. Sorry, *Tony.*"

"I want you to go to my apartment and—" No, that was too dangerous. Everything he could think of to ask Little Wallace to do was too dangerous. "I want you to sit tight and wait for my instructions. Don't call me until I call you. Okay?"

"Sure thing, Deu—Tony. Anything for you, buddy."

"Disconnecting."

"Over and out."

Deuce hung up and let out that sigh. For his own safety,

Little Wallace was going to have a long wait.

But his own day of reckoning was here, baby.

"Borgioli Building," the aichy announced proudly.

"Fabulous." Half-expecting to be blown up, Deuce leaned back into the aichy, slipped Hunter Castle's business card into the dashboard, and set up a security shield.

"A perfect night, Mr. Borgioli."

"Same to you, schweetheart."

The aichy fell silent. Deuce sighed and said, "Lemme out. No wait." He commed his brother.

"Jocy." Punched on visual. Deuce hated visual, hardly ever used it. But this needed to be said face-to-face.

Joey's face filled the whole screen. His lips were baby blue, indicating his drug addiction or his keen fashion sense. Yet despite his filthy lifestyle, he was still good-looking. Those eyes.

Damn it, Deuce still loved the SOB.

Joey rose from his bed like Venus from the sea and hoisted himself on one elbow. "What time is it? What you want?" Joey slurred, blinking. There was an empty bottle of Tycho Delight gin half-wrapped-up in the bedspread. If Mamma could have seen him, she'd be on her knees all day at church wondering how God could so test her.

"Joey, be careful," Deuce said, then realized Diana was not about to admit to the Moongoloid that she had been screwing around, much less tell him who with. Realized also that he had already been fingered, and Joey was not exactly equipped to handle this or any situation. So he sighed, and said, "Watch yourself, okay?"

"What are you talking about?" Joey asked angrily. "Is this another lecture about my lifestyle?"

"Joey." Deuce hesitated.

"Because I don't need your so-great advice, okay? I'm doin' fine. Out."

The screen went dark.

Deuce sagged. Well, he'd put that scene on hold for now. He had his own scene to deal with.

"Okay," he told the aichy. "Lemme out."

"Yes, Mr. Borgioli."

The hatch popped open and Deuce popped out onto the blacktop.

Hunter Castle, he thought, almost like a mantra. Hunter Castle, Hunter Castle. The most powerful private citizen on Earth, soon to be here, right here, on the Moon. Deuce's game wasn't over. There were cards to be played here after all. Dice to be tossed. Odds to figure.

''Damn straight,'' he agreed with himself, squared back his shoulders, and started walking the walk to his own execution.

SEVEN

*Our Lady of the Moon, according to the ancient Romans
(as retold for modern Moonsiders):*

She was Diana, she was Selene, she was Hecate. Three
goddesses in one. The Virgin represented the First Quarter; the Mother was the Full Moon; and the Wisewoman,
the hag, was the Dark Moon. She burned with a fire that
consumed anyone in love, and you did not want to mess
with her. When she was ticked, she got you good.

Three kick-ass forms of the goddess, three Italian Families on the Moon.

And she was so powerful and needed so much respect,
this is how the ancient Romans, throwers of Christians to
the lions, used to address her:

*You who in the three forms . . . dance and fly about
   the stars . . .
You who wield terrible black torches in your hands,
You who shake your head with hair made of
   ferocious snakes;
You who cause the bellowing of the bulls;
You whose belly is covered with reptilian scabs and
   who carry over your shoulder a woven bag of
   venomous snakes . . .*

One bad lady.
Of course, the modern Italian Family Members of Moon-

base Vegas were very devoted to the Virgin Mary, being Catholics, and they would juice anyone who dared suggest the Holy Mother of God was just the Moon goddess in another form.

Deuce crossed the Borgioli Building parking lot in short order and stomped onto the pressure escalator, right foot first for the analysis. It said, "Good evening, Mr. Arthur Borgioli," and he just sighed and rolled his eyes. Back in the good old days, Joey used to beat the living crap out of anyone who called his brother Arthur. Now Deuce had returned the favor, in a manner of speaking, getting beat-up on Joey's behalf.

That Diana must be some woman. With a terminal illness, if she actually let the Moongoloid touch her.

Deuce coded the touch pad and the escalator diverted from the offices down to Big Al's bunker. Most of the Godfathers had a heavily fortified hideaway, and that's where everybody would be. His stomach did a flip and he forced himself to look calm. It was ironic how in this day and age of remote skin readers, attitude still counted big-time. You might think of somebody, "The dude's terrified. He's clammy and his pulse is on maximum overdrive, a wuss. But at least he isn't acting like one," and that was a pretty good compliment.

The red, white, and green carpet on the ramp was dirty and he was embarrassed for his Family's sake. Even their janitors were second-rate. Everybody always loved to say how you couldn't get good help these days, but the Borgiolis couldn't even get good N.A. help, never mind asking for someone in the Affiliated Fraternal Order of Maintenance and Housekeeping, because everybody wanted to work for someone besides the Borgiolis. Even persons who couldn't get anything to eat besides dog food. (Which was an old Earthside notion. Actually, on the Moon, dog food was pretty exotic stuff, because it was imported. Poor people—most of the N.A.'s—basically ate poor-people food, cheap and starchy.)

Used to be he was snooty like that, looking down his nose at his own Family. Now the best he might hope for was life on the docks. But at least it would be a life. Of sorts.

Deeper and deeper he glided, past bare rock and bright lights and the metallic crossbeams from the old mining days, marveling at how much slower their escalators were than those of the other Families. It was the same at the Palazzo, too. Supposedly the casino patrons didn't notice— rather than retrofit, Big Al had hired some Earthside casino consulting firm to do a study—but how could they not when they loped along on the dirty old carpet, listening to the molding squeal over the handrail?

He went through the surveillance tunnel, hearing but not feeling the scan, successfully resisting the urge to grin maniacally up into the camera and make some wisecrack— any wisecrack—to cut the tension. His heart was beating so fast it was fluttering. His palms were cryin' him a river. It would probably disappoint Little Wallace if he knew that Deuce had never been shot in his life. Deuce wasn't sure how badly it hurt. He knew it did hurt, though; he'd seen plenty of shot-up guys before, during, and after. But personal experience had thus far—thankfully—eluded him.

Cards to play, he reminded himself. Numbers to run. Hunter Castle, Hunter Castle. Oh, man, had he really hoped for action back in tonight's innocent hours?

The escalator diverted him to the heavily fortified entrance of Big Al's joint. Deuce was so nervous he wanted to scream. Aiming for a posture of nonchalance for the Eye, he draped his left hand on the handrail, dum-di-dum, just filin' my nails, as it carried him toward the ostentatious columns and curlicue molding of cupids and ancient Italian coats of arms. Big Al's HQ looked like a cheesy opera set. Family Members were still big-time into opera, the way they had been on Earth. And spaghetti. Very, very big on spaghetti, since it was a lot what your brains looked like after you'd been juiced.

His blaster was on max and in his hand, in his pocket. His heart was in his throat. He scanned left, right, shifty-eyed like a cowboy, without moving his head. He saw cameras and rocks and that was about it.

His comm badge went off, the signal weak. Big Al had

not sprung for booster cells with the same enthusiasm as the other Family Godfathers.

It kept vibrating. Deuce, now at the front door, was twitchy about touching it. He was afraid it would be misconstrued as a move to pull out a weapon, but he finally broke down and smacked it anyway.

"Earphone," he told the badge, and it complied.

"I have something for you," said a voice. It was not a voice he recognized. Every cell in his body went on red alert. Something for him like a shot of juice? A sweet little photon grenade bouncing this very moment down the escalator stairs? "The hit on you is not Registered," the voice continued. "The Earthside mechanics coming for you are named Club and Spade. One's a cyborg. The other's fully mechanical. They're good, but they're not perfect. They've got some weaknesses."

"Who is this?" Deuce demanded.

"Maybe a friend. Maybe not. There'll be a chance to pay us back if you survive." The connection was broken.

Us? Deuce said to his badge, "Redial."

"I'm sorry, Mr. Borgioli," the badge replied. "That line is secure."

"Yeah, okay." That figured.

Damn.

The escalator stopped. He began to code into the door when it hissed open on its own. Back-Line Tony, one of the most intensely enhanced musclemen of the Borgioli Family, stood with his hands folded deferentially before him. He filled up the entire doorway and then some; his head was inclined because otherwise it would have hit the transom.

"Signor McNamara," he said, with a bob of his head. "*Buona sera.* Your weapons, please."

Deuce blinked. Never, ever, had he been asked to disarm before going in to see Big Al. He was definitely in trouble.

As calmly as he could, he handed over his blaster.

"Everything please, sir," Tony politely requested.

Sighing, Deuce dug out his micros and his one-watter and handed them to the animal. Tony carried the pile in both hands, like it was either gold or garbage.

Deuce stood by while Tony coded the inner door. Then he moved aside, and said, "After you, Signor McNamara."

Tony smiled. Even his teeth looked enhanced. Running now was clearly not an option. Tony wouldn't get to whack him. He wouldn't even be allowed to watch. No, *this* was his little moment, sending the condemned to his fate, and he was enjoying it. Deuce slowly walked past him and, inside, allowed Tony what for him passed for the coup de grâce: Tony softly closed the door behind Deuce. He never thought a single click could be so loud.

Big Al, rotund, bald, and chomping on a cigar, was pacing in front of an old-fashioned painting of an Italian maiden holding a lamb. If you looked hard you could see that the lamb was wearing the Borgioli Family crest of three hands, one holding dice, one holding the Queen of Hearts, and one crossing its fingers. For luck or because it was lying, no one knew. But Deuce was not looking hard. He was trying to work up enough spit in his mouth to speak.

"I swear to God, that boy will be late for his own funeral," Big Al was saying. Then he chicked his big face to the right, saw Deuce, and glowered at him. Big Al had deep-set brown eyes that always looked sad whether he was laughing or plugging some chump. They would probably look sad when he was dead. "It's about time. I was just talking about you."

There were about twenty people seated around the long, shiny table littered with ashtrays, bottles of Chianti, and empty low-grav, capped glasses. They included all the capos and lieutenants, including Deuce's buddy, his cousin Angelo. Big board meeting. As they regarded Deuce, they all looked a little consternated. The reason being, Deuce supposed, that Big Al generally decided exactly when your funeral would be taking place.

Deuce looked at the rug a moment. He hoped his head bob showed the proper humility and submission to the Family's Alpha Male. He also hoped he left a big stain on the rug for them to remember him by.

"*Buona sera*," Deuce said deferentially. "Don Alberto, I'm desolated that I'm here so late. There was an incident."

"Yeah, I heard about your incident." Big Al stopped

pacing and rammed his fist down hard on the table. "Are you out of your freakin' mind?"

Deuce swallowed.

"There's a hit out on you."

"It's not Registered," Deuce said quickly.

Big Al looked surprised. "It's not?"

"Chairman William Atherton hasn't Sanctioned it."

"Well, he hasn't aborted it, either, and it went out on the viso." Big Al spread his hands on the table. Chomp, chomp, chomp on the cigar. There was some brown stuff in the corner of his mouth. The man needed a spittoon.

He needed also needed a shower. Or maybe that was Deuce.

"What went down? What did you do?" Big Al demanded.

"Godfather, nothing. I swear it on my mother's grave. He's got a terrible temper. You know that. Everyone knows that."

"Yeah, and everybody leaves him alone. You with your mouth, you must have provoked him."

Deuce shook his head. Not even for Big Al—or his own butt—would he hang Joey out to dry. "No, Don Alberto. I did nothing."

Big Al was silent for a moment. Then he said, "Do you know who's on his way here?"

"Hunter Castle," Deuce supplied.

Big Al nodded. "So as you can imagine, we have enough to do around here without your hijinks." He leaned over. Silver Tongue Tommy, their Affiliate attorney, lit the end of the cigar. "How could you make a public scene like that, and against a Family Heir? Who do you think we are, the Smiths? The Scarlattis?"

I should live so well, Deuce thought glumly. He shook his head. He said, "I know who the hit men are. They're Earthsiders. Wayne's bringing them in because his uncle didn't Sanction it. No Moonsider will go against me." And if Big Al believed that, he was dumber than Deuce had ever imagined.

"Hah. Those guys are window dressing. There's proba-bly a dozen guys who want to get in good with the Designated Heir juicing up their blasters and studying your picture. Don't be stupid, Deuce. You're already dead.'' Big Al scratched his shiny naked head. "God, I'm suffering. Hunter Castle's on his way here and here I am, distracted by a Family squabble. God is testing me.''

Deuce's heart sank. If all his life amounted to was a Family squabble, Big Al was going to abandon him for certain.

"Godfather, I'm sorry. *Mi dispiace*,'' Deuce groveled.

"Humph,'' Big Al said, unconvinced.

"So are you saying we let Deuce get hit?'' Angelo hesitantly asked. "That don't make us look too good.'' Good old Angelo, probably the only friend Deuce had in this room.

"We already don't look too good,'' Silver Tongue Tommy said. "Why piss off the Van Aadamses? Let them hit him. They have juice to spare. No offense, Deuce. You know this is business. I'm thinking of the Family.''

"Yeah, sure.'' Nobody in here gave a damn about the Family, Big Al included. It was every Borgioli for himself. That was one of the things the other Families found so uncouth about them.

Deuce wished he could sit down. His knees were beginning to buckle. He wished he hadn't wolfed down the pizza Sparkle had packed. Double whammies of fat and nitrates, triple whammies of the willies: His stomach was beginning to rebel. It would really take the shine off his machismo if he threw up on Big Al's carpet, ratty and ugly though it was.

Or on Big Al. That would get him juiced right here, right now, no questions asked.

"So maybe we let you get hit, huh?'' Big Al said directly to Deuce. His sad eyes were cold. "Maybe that's how it goes down? The Van Aadamses are off our case, and we can spend our time more productively, figuring out what to do about Castle? You like that, boys?''

"No!'' came a wail from the doorway. Everyone turned.

Big Al's daughter, Beatrice, bolted into the room. Poor Beatrice, frowzy and frumpy even in a flashy gold-lamé jumpsuit which only served to emphasize the breadth of her hips and the stumpiness of her legs; her gold jewelry that was in a word, *tout*; with her frizzy black hair, her hard, big features, and small, narrow-set eyes. Stiletto heels that could put your eye out, when all the showgirls wore flats except on stage. In a past life, Beatrice no doubt made a fine barrel.

Poor Beatrice, and poor Deuce, because he felt like a creep for noticing all her bad qualities when she in turn adored him and found absolutely no fault with him. He wanted like anything to tell her about his liaison with Sparkle, but of course he couldn't. That made him feel like worse than a creep. He wasn't the kind of guy to mess around on someone, and Beatrice considered them practically engaged. All that stood in their way, she believed, was Deuce's rank in the Family. He was sure she was working on Big Al night and day about that.

Back-Line Tony followed closely behind her, holding out his arms in a gesture of helplessness. How *did* you prevent the boss's daughter from crashing a meeting, deck her?

"You can't touch him," she said to her father. "Daddy, please." She threw her arms first around him, and then around Deuce. "He didn't *mean* to do anything wrong. Did you, *caro mio*?" She smiled up at her Romeo hopefully.

"No," Deuce managed. "Of course I didn't." He looked at Big Al, who glared at him as if he could devour him in one bite, spit him out in tiny pieces, and grind those pieces into the flocked carpet that was as fashionably incorrect as Beatrice's outfit.

A comm line squeaked from the table. Big Al slammed a fist on it, even though you didn't have to touch it at all, and barked, "Yeah."

"It's Johnny Canoe. *Gambler's Star* is docking. Castle's on the Moon." Which was dramatically stated if not totally accurate: A ship as big as his would necessarily orbit, and he and his crew would shuttle down to the surface and through the passenger shafts. The only ships that actually landed were freighters and other vessels. They touched down outside the domes and their cargoes went in tubes that led directly beneath the surface to the docks. But Canoe was close enough.

Which was too close for comfort. Everyone went bananas, talking at once: *We need to go to the Smiths. We need more blasters. Blasters, hell! We need whatever the Smiths have. We need to join forces with the Van Aadamses. They'll have his ear. We need to buy up his stock and get in bed with him But all his stock is privately held. We need, we should, we better,* but what everyone was really saying was, *We are crater-deep in trouble.*

"What we need is to hit him," Johnny Canoe said, and it took Deuce a minute to realize Canoe was talking about Castle.

"That's the dumbest thing I ever heard." Silver Tongue Tommy shook his head. "He's too big. Too public. Earthside would use that to shut us down."

"Yeah," Angelo interjected. "Don Alberto, you know they're always trying to shut us down. They hate us because they let go of all that profit. Two-faced politicians. What we need is to make nice to him."

"Make nice?" Ninety-Days Nino scoffed. "You ever made nice to a rattlesnake?"

"I never seen a rattlesnake," Angelo retorted.

"Well, you don't make nice. You stick out your hand, it bites you hard and shoots poison into your veins and you die."

"What we need is to find out what everybody else is doing," Big Al said.

Mamma mia, there was his trump card.

Deuce brightened. He said, "What you need is a spy."

Everyone stopped talking and looked at him. After a beat, Big Al said, "Spies we got plenty of."

"Not a spy like me. Think about it." He sensed that he should sit down, take a couple liberties, make them forget they had just about condemned him to death. "Let it get around that you threw me out of the Family. I'm persona non grata. I can watch everybody. Maybe even infiltrate Castle's organization."

"You already watch everybody," Silver Tongue Tommy said.

"But if he's N.A., he can watch better. Nobody pays no

attention to N.A.'s," Angelo cut in, obviously attempting to help his old *amico*.

"And you can protect him at a distance, so you don't have to challenge the Van Aadamses," Beatrice added. For once, Deuce could have kissed her. His thinking exactly, although he hadn't had the guts—or the brass—to say it.

"That's dumb, Bea," Big Al said, but it was a reflexive comment. Deuce could see the wheels turning. He could see Big Al agreeing. Protecting Deuce while he was spying on everybody including their archnemesis was good business practice.

"I know I have to prove myself to you," Deuce said. "And to the rest of the Family." He made a little bow at the group. "I have to atone for my intense stupidity. So I'd be motivated to do a good recon job." He thought excitedly about the card in the dashboard. This couldn't have gone better if he had planned it this way. Was there a God or what?

"It's got its merits," Silver Tongue Tommy observed.

Nino added, "And this way, we don't got to waste Deuce. After all, he *is* Family. Even if he was adopted." Yeah, what a *paisan*. Deuce owed him a ton of credits from last week's poker game, and the guy was worried about collecting. Sure, Nino could put in a claim, but who knew where he stood in the lineup of Deuce's creditors?

"It's bad for our image not to let him get wasted," Johnny Canoe said on the comm line. "He did a dumb thing."

"Van Aadams started it," Beatrice interjected. Apparently she didn't know they'd come to blows over a woman. By mistake, sure, but it would have broken poor Beatrice's heart. "That's the word on the street. We look second-rate if we kill one of our own for defending himself. What was Duchino supposed to do, let the Moongoloid beat him to death?"

"Beatrice, show respect," Big Al remonstrated, but he was smiling. "After all, Wayne Van Aadams is the Heir."

"*Mio Padrino*," Deuce said, "my Godfather, I'm not so sure of that. There's a movement in that Family toward securing a replacement."

"There's always a movement," Big Al said, unimpressed.

"A big movement," Deuce improvised. "Organized. Some pretty well placed people are in on it."

"Oh, and how would you know that?" Big Al demanded.

Deuce pursed his lips. "I can't say right now."

"Anything you want to say to me, you can tell the boys," Big Al said expansively.

Deuce shook his head. "You know I pride myself on accuracy, Godfather. I've never misinformed you about anything, have I?"

Big Al thought a moment, shook his head. As Deuce knew he would. What Deuce was pretty sure Big Al didn't know was that he, Deuce, had also not always come completely clean with him about everything he'd discovered. There was no percentage in indiscriminately dumping everything in the lap of a man who wasn't smart enough to appreciate it. Withholding information was almost a loyal act, not that Deuce had all that much loyalty anyway, because sometimes you didn't want to present Big Al with a lot of data that was just going to confuse him. Him and the other Borgioli mucky-mucks weren't the sharpest tools in the shed, to put it kindly.

Which was why Deuce saw no reason to mention what Mr. Feist had said to him, or that someone else wanted Deuce to be thinking right now about Hunter Castle.

"Do it," Beatrice urged her father. "Kick him out so he can stay in with us." She took Big Al's palm and pressed it against her cheek. "*Papà, per favore.* Protect my Duchino."

Jimmy the Painter raised a hand in objection. "Big Al—"

"Shut up, Jimmy." Big Al's eyes shone as he regarded his daughter. The story went that her mother had died in childbirth, but how do you figure that in the twenty-second century? It made as much sense as diseases. "All right, *cara*, for you. We'll replace him with, who? Snake Eyes Salvatore? A moron, but no more a moron than this moron.

Arturino, one more idiotic situation, and I'll pry your head off with a fork. You got that, boy?"

Big Al would, too. And he had the forks to do it with.

Deuce nodded. "*Mille grazie*. It's more than I deserve."

"Oh, hell, what are uncles for?" He opened his arms and caught Deuce in a bear hug, wrastled, playfully slapped his face. "You're Maria's boy, may she rest in peace. My sainted sister Apogia would never speak to me again if I killed you."

Ninety-days Nino rolled his eyes. Deuce grinned at him over Big Al's shoulder, hah-hah-hah. *Don't try this B.S. at home, Nino. This is for trained professionals only.*

"Okay, how you gonna do it?" Big Al asked. "How you gonna find out what everybody's doing about Castle?"

"Dunno yet," Deuce said . "But I'll get to work on it."

Big Al nodded. "I'll give you two days to come in with something useful," he said.

Deuce swallowed hard. "How about two weeks?"

"One week."

Deuce nodded in agreement. One freakin' week? Not even a Scarlatti could get anything worth getting in a week. Jeez.

"Get outta here, then." Big Al waved a hand in dismissal. "Meantime, we gotta notify the Charter Board we've thrown him out. Then we gotta get ready for the war council."

The others nodded, some reluctantly. Deuce mentally took down the names of the ones who weren't so overjoyed that he was walking out of there alive.

"Daddy, give us an hour before you notify the Board?" Beatrice asked coyly. She slipped her hands around something more comfortable, which was Deuce's neck, and rested her head on his shoulder. Deuce went redder than the unworn spots in the carpet. Some of the guys looked away. This girlie stuff was embarrassing to their machismo.

"If that's what you want, kitten." Big Al regarded her affectionately. Then over her head, he gave Deuce a look that told him he still had his forks sharpened and his juicer charged.

Beatrice took Deuce's hand. "Come on, Duchino," she

purred. "For sixty minutes, you're mine. We'll go someplace private."

Nino grinned back. *Don't try this at home, either, sucker. Or your woman will kick you down to hell and back.*

Deuce pretended not to get it.

Even though he knew he was gonna.

EIGHT

An hour later, Deuce emerged from the Borgioli Building, still fully expecting to be blown up. What happened in that hour, he never told a living soul.

But he promised himself a memory wipe someday, when he could afford one.

At the top of the escalator, there was a news zipper trailing the tail end of a story that had the word CASTLE in it. Without thinking twice, Deuce punched in his credit code to reset the article, then remembered he'd been disenfranchised and wondered if it was still good.

It took.

HUNTER CASTLE LANDS!

Mr. Hunter Castle, of unknown age, the richest and arguably the most powerful man on Earth, has arrived on the Moon. As his enormous ship, *Gambler's Star*, orbits high above the dome, he plans to shuttle to Moonbase Vegas later this evening.

His stated reason for the visit is to catch up with old friends.

Mr. Castle is a man shrouded in mystery. His financial empire is said to be worth billions of credits. No one knows his actual worth, as his vast enterprises are privately held and therefore not open to public scrutiny.

The Casino Families are, naturally, apprehensive about his arrival. However, we at the *Moonwatcher* welcome Mr. Castle and are eager to learn of his opinions of our fair city.

The good old *Moonwatcher*. No editorializing there. Maybe Mr. Castle had just purchased it.

Deuce pondered how you could deal with a man like that—who was practically a force of nature—as he climbed into the aichy. Fairy godfather or flesh-eating king of the underworld?

"Where to, Mr. Borgioli?" the aichy asked cheerily.

He deactivated the security shield and studied Castle's business card. Financial resources, huh. Since Deuce was officially N.A., he was out of a job. No more casino calls for him tonight. No more Family credits, either. He was surprised the aichy was still talking to him.

"Not sure yet. Your comm line still work?" he asked.

"All of my components are functioning perfectly," it responded snootily. Yeah, right. Like any of its components had ever functioned one hundred percent.

"Okay. Let's roll." He started dialing numbers. If he was going to be a spy, he might as well get started spying right away.

"Yes, sir," the aichy said. He was more surprised that it was still obeying him. Maybe Big Al had forgotten about it. Normally you pressed one button on the Big Secret Computer and that froze every single credit line of the poor jerk who'd just been Dis-Membered. Maybe Big Al was being nice.

It wouldn't work to keep him on the payroll, though. People had to believe he was really and truly out. He'd have to use Sparkle's aichy. Or public transportation. He shuddered at the notion of moving among the N.A. unwashed. N.A.'s who recognized him weren't going to be very nice to him because he'd been in a Family. Family Members were going to be brutal. Suddenly he felt like some poor schmuck stuck outside a dome with a bad air tank strapped to his back. Like he was working for oxygen, too. Because what if Big Al ultimately decided that he hadn't performed, and kept him out of the Family for the rest of his life?

What if he became an actual N.A.?

He threaded the card between his fingers, did a few passes, a few card tricks. Just how many of these little suckers were there in circulation? Who else was staring at one and making plans?

Deuce spent an hour or three hunting down Castle connections. He found out from Jésus Armstrong that a trio of guys dressed in Castle Enterprises one-pieces were shooting pool in the back of Trini Golden's Cues and Brews. Deuce's aichy dutifully deposited him at the side door.

It felt like old times. Before he had officially started working for the Family, he used to do odd jobs for Trini— collecting the empties, cleaning out the ashtrays, assisting with carting the drunks out into the alley. He got to watch Trini's small bookmaking enterprise, had even done a little numbers running for the man. It had been a great job for a teenager.

Now Trini was dead and his niece, Estrella, ran the operation. Estrella had been one of Deuce's first liaisons. She was married now, with quadruplets and a husband who strutted around like a bullfighter. Not that Deuce had ever personally seen a bullfight. Or a horse race. Or an NFL football game. Lots of Moonsiders were in the same predicament.

But that didn't stop anybody from placing bets on games, races, and other sanctioned forms of animal cruelty. Which brought him to an old sore point with the Families: How come the Department of Fairness allowed Earthside greyhound and horse racing and bullfights and like that, then made it illegal to gamble on them anywhere but on the Moon?

He pushed open the old-fashioned door—no airlock; this was *not* the place to be if the dome ever blew—and paused to light a cigarette in order to give himself a moment to adjust to the dim light. His badge queried for the pollution levy; he accepted it. Amazing. His credit line was still open.

Estrella was behind the bar, swiping receipts. On the P.A., some guy was sangin' a sad ol' song about losing his gal or his aichy or his dawg or whatever. And there they were, three guys with beards and hair over their ears in bright orange one-pieces with CASTLE emblazoned across their backs in big black letters.

Estrella gave him a nod. She swiped another receipt, neatened up the stack, and leaned on the bar.

"*Hola, guapo*," she said.

"Same to you." He smiled. "*Cerveza, por favor.*" May as well push it on the credit before it was cut off, maybe forever.

She had Bad Moon on tap—local stuff, tasted kind of like raspberries. She poured it and handed it to him. He lifted the mug, said, "*Salud*," and drank.

"Heard you had some trouble," she murmured. "Heard it was pretty bad."

He traced a little smiley face in the condensation on the side of the glass, ran his finger down to the counter, sighed, and nodded. She tsk-tsked. Gave his arm a pat. He couldn't remember why they had de-liaised, and while he loved Sparkle more than anything in the universe, he felt somewhat wistful. Estrella was motherly and warm. With Sparkle, you pretty much had to stick to being a grown-up.

He ticked his eyes left without moving his head. "Those guys said anything interesting?" Pulled out a chip from the Inferno just in case his credit closed before she charged him for the beer. And to be nice.

"Put away your money, *chingadero*." She grinned at him. She dropped her voice. "He wants to build a casino."

He almost spit out his beer. "*What*? Here? On the Moon?" he whispered.

She reached over and brushed an errant strand of hair away from his forehead. "Where else, *mi amor*?"

Where else, indeed. The only place you could build a casino was on the Moon.

"How? Who's he got?" No one could Charter a seventh Casino Family without the unanimous consent of the existing six Families and the approval of the Department of Fairness. And who was going to sanction more competition?

"You expect *them* to know?" she asked dryly, indicating the happy trio of Castle employees.

"Little pitchers have big ears." He got some of his best pieces of information from guys who had no idea what they knew. The trick was in putting all the pieces together.

She shook her head. "Not these pitchers, *cabrón*."

He picked up his beer mug and wandered over to watch the game. The lower gravity was playing havoc with their strokes. Or else they were lousy players.

They noticed him after a minute or so. Caught sight of his Borgioli patch. One looked interested, one glowered, and the third one chalked the tip of his cue. Deuce didn't know what to make of all that.

"You guys just landed," Deuce began.

"Yeah. So?" said the glowering one, who had dark hair and a beard. The interested one, who was skinny, and, to tell the truth, challenged in the appearance department, cocked his head and observed.

"Let me buy you a beer. Welcome you to town." Deuce nodded at Estrella. She raised her pointer finger to indicate they were comin' up.

The guy who had been chalking his cue said, "Why?" He was a redhead. Natural, probably. Earthsiders didn't go in for all the retrofitting Moonsiders did.

Deuce made a show of blinking and appearing confused. "Why? Cuz that's the way we are around here. Neighborly."

"I heard you guys knife each other's grandmothers," the bearded one said.

"Only if it would be good for business," Deuce returned, and the three laughed.

"Hey, he's all right." The redhead laid down his stick. "We'd be happy to drink with you, Mr. Borgioli."

"Actually, it's McNamara," Deuce said. "I'm a Member, but I was adopted." Word of his disinheritance must not have gotten out yet. This wasn't like Big Al. Yoikes, had someone hit the Godfather?

Estrella brought the beers on a tray and put them on a dining table beside the pool table. Each of the three Castle men took one, gave Deuce a nod, and drank. The ugly, skinny one screwed up his face.

"Oh, *God*. What's this stuff made out of? Radiation run-off?"

"Takes some getting used to," Deuce said. "Couple, three weeks. You guys'll probably be home by then."

"Yeah, I *wish*," said the redhead. The bearded one elbowed him to shaddup.

Deuce backed off, leaning against the pool table to the left of theirs and sipping his beer. The visitors set down their mugs and resumed their game.

"So, you're local?" the bearded guy asked Deuce.

"Local as the beer." Deuce sipped. "Never been Earth-side."

"You want to play the next round?" he asked. Typical Earthside arrogance; he figured he could beat the dumb local boy.

"Naw. I'm really good. Sometimes I hustle," Deuce drawled.

"We're pretty good ourselves," the bearded one retorted. "Even at low grav."

"Well, don't say I didn't warn you," Deuce said. He pulled out a chip. "Let's play for hard stuff. No credit lines." He made as if to confess something humiliating. "I'm in Gamblers' Anonymous. My Godfather would hit me if he found out."

The guys looked impressed.

From his pocket he pulled a deck of cards. All Family Members carried at least one at all times. "I'm high, I break the balls." He flashed the Smile. "So to speak."

The bearded one waved him off. "That deck's got to be marked."

"*No, paisan.* I swear it."

"Miss," the man said to Estrella, "a pack of cards, please."

She brought one over. Her deck *was* marked.

Deuce broke some balls.

Deuce left Trini Armstrong's Cues and Brews with a pile of strange-looking coins that he immediately took to an offtrack (how much farther offtrack could you get? There was no horse racing on the Moon yet, though everyone wanted to be the first to import it) betting establishment and discovered they were Castle company coinage and no good on the Moon.

That was okay. Because what he also left with was the fact that Castle had been seen in the company of the high roller Angelo had called Deuce about, Epperson-Roux. A guy like that would be easier to find out about than a direct target.

Deuce also got the bearded guy's comm-linkup number, which Deuce copied off his badge when the guy pulled it out of his pocket to add a couple more no-good coins to the pile they had paid off Deuce with.

The comm-link number was worth its weight in gold. Any decent Family recon man could use something like that to hack into a guarded system. That plus Epperson-Roux's name plus the business card, and the dice were a-shakin'.

It was time to plant somewhere and do some thinking. He climbed into the aichy. It still liked him. Maybe Beatrice had arranged this.

He closed his eyes. It was 4 A.M. Sparkle would not be expecting him yet.

He hoped she would be pleasantly surprised. He'd slip between the sheets (she loved fabric sheets, not all people used them anymore, preferring enhanced air), cuddle up, wrap those sinewy long legs around himself, and—

"Mr. Borgioli?" the aichy interrupted.

"Yeah?" He opened one eye.

"Sir, there's something in my exhaust manifold."

"Something like what, dear?"

"A bomb, sir."

Deuce pushed on the door. "Shut down. Exit me."

"I'm sorry. I think I'm going to explode."

"Exit me!"

The aichy stopped moving and the hatch popped open. Deuce leaped out and rolled into a ball, covering his head. When nothing happened, he shot around a corner, collapsing against a Dumpster. Scrabbled to the farside of it, shut his eyes, and braced himself.

A woman in a blue dress walked by. He cried out, "Duck and cover!"

She stared at him, walked on.

"Lady!" he shouted, and grabbed her, hustled her toward the Dumpster.

"Rape, rape!" she screamed.

"Oh, for God's sake." He threw her to the ground and landed on top of her. "Stop wiggling."

"Lady, are you a Caputo?" someone called. Deuce looked up. Two Caputo Family Members in blue-and-white starfield jackets hurried toward them.

Deuce shouted, "Kiss the dirt! There's a hit going down."

Instantly the two men joined him behind the Dumpster, flattening themselves with their hands over the exposed backs of their necks.

There was a roar, then the walls shook. Smoke billowed from around the corner. The Caputos rolled like salamis, drew their weapons, and shot in the direction of the blast.

Deuce groaned miserably and let the woman up. She smacked him. "You bastard! I'm calling the police."

"Lady, he just saved your life," said one of the Caputos. He looked at her with disdain. "And you're just an N.A." The implication being, Deuce knew, that the Caputo Member would not have risked himself for an N.A. It was that kind of world.

She got up and sneered at the three of them. "You're all going to be sorry," she said. "The Revolution is coming and the Families will fall."

Deuce frowned at her. "Lady, save it for your next rally. It ain't smart talking to three Family men that way."

"I'm not afraid of you." However, she was shaking. She was very plain and very young and had perhaps unknowingly dressed in Caputo blue. "No one is afraid of you anymore."

The Caputo who had spoken to her idly aimed his blaster in her direction. "Then they're *idiotas*, like you. *Fatti sparare*." Which meant "Go shoot yourself." Which she, not being Italian, would not understand and, therefore, not do.

She humphed and said, "You haven't heard the last of

us.'' Then she raised her fist. "The Moon for Moonsiders!''

"Oh, God, she's MLF," the Caputo said to Deuce, who nodded tiredly.

"Yeah, thanks for giving us all the tobacco pollution levy," Deuce said snidely. "And you're welcome for the saving of your life. Think nothing of it."

"I wouldn't have been in danger if it weren't for people like you," she shot back, and stomped off in the direction she had come.

"*Vaya diablo*," the talkative Caputo murmured after her. "*Strega*." He nudged Deuce with his blaster. "What's going down? Did you perp the hit or was it perped on you?"

"I'm not sure it was a hit. I think it was just my aichy blowing up," Deuce told him and his *amico*. "It seemed the quickest way to make you listen. I was having some trouble with the broad."

The Caputos traded looks. "What, you forget to get a tune-up?" the first Caputo cracked, and they both laughed uproariously.

"Hey," the other one said. "You're Deuce McNamara. I know you from the House, *paisan*." Meaning their casino. He held out his hand. "You gave me a good tip on a horse once."

Deuce remembered him. His name was Marco, and he was Family, a real Caputo. In return for the data on the nag—Pineapple Princess—Marco had let it slip that Roger Smith, co-Godfather of the Smiths, suspected his mistress, Alicia Vera, of being unfaithful. Which, of course, she was—everybody knew that, except the poor putz, who worshiped her—but the fact that he was getting nervous was important information.

"Marco," Deuce said warmly. Then both the Caputo comm badges went off.

"Earphone," the two said in unison. Deuce waited, straining to eavesdrop. Both Caputos listened carefully. Both barely reacted, scarcely registering the surprise he nevertheless read in their eyes. They shifted toward him, focused, narrowed.

"Let's go," Marco said coldly to his brother Caputo.

Without a word, they rose, blasters still drawn, and moved away.

"Hey," Deuce protested, but he knew what had gone down: Official word had been sent out by the Charter Board: He was Dis-Membered. He was scum. He was dirt.

He was N.A.

Even if it wasn't forever—he hoped—it felt awful. Like in one of those old movies where the guy pretends to be nuts to expose the mad scientists who were experimenting on their patients in the insane asylum, but then the one guy who knows the hero is really an undercover reporter ups and dies.

He exhaled smoke from the blast and shrugged. Aw, hell, at least he wasn't dead.

The Caputos disappeared into the smoke without a backward glance. Alarms sounded. Deuce's comm badge queried him about his need for medical services. He told it he was fine and trudged desultorily toward the wreckage.

There was debris everywhere, flivvers and melted wires and components that had been fused by the heat. He kicked at a grommet and watched it roll across the tunnel floor.

In the middle of the rubble his aichy was a ruined hulk. It lay on its side like a dying animal. He crouched over it.

"How ya doin'?" he asked.

"Perfect night," the aichy wheezed. He touched it, swore he heard a gasp.

It's just a car, he reminded himself, but he was sad anyway. They had gone through a lot together, this ol' aichy and him. Took it for a sizable loan for an old ex-friend, who'd had some bad luck and needed to get back on his feet. It had been in really horrendous shape—Deuce had had to put more into it than it was worth, and would have been royally pissed off if anyone else had palmed such a heap off on him—but what the hey. The man had needed credit badly. Desperate men do desperate things.

"Yeah," he said, lifting Hunter Castle's amazingly unblemished business card from the wreckage, blowing the ash off it, sliding it into his pocket. "No kidding."

NINE

Brush Burner, a tale of the Moon from the Old West (as retold for modern Moonsiders):

Seems it was time to saddle up and mosey on down the Santa Fe Trail with the herd. Just as he was putting his hardtack and salt pork back in the saddlebags, Cooky glanced up at the setting Moon and said, "Lookee, boys! Some woman's burning brush on the Moon."

"Ain't no woman, Cooky," some ol' cowboy says. "It's a cowboy."

"Woman," Cooky says. "They're the ones cause all the commotion in the world."

"You're blind," says another cowboy. "It's a man, pure and simple."

The argument gets hot enough to brand steers. Colt .45s (a type of ancient materiel blaster) get drawn.

"Y'all hesh!" the trail boss orders. "You're gonna cause a stampede, and the herd'll run from here to the Moon if y'all don't pipe down."

That was that, and the cowboys never did know if it was a man or a woman burning brush on the Moon.

And in those days, matters like that was important.

And speaking of women who set fire to the property, Sparkle *was* home.

And she was waiting for him.

She was reading off a mini in the kitchen and looked up

when he coded through the front door. Her long, tall body was swathed in a slinky black kimono open to the waist and a pair of black-satin boxer shorts. Nothing else. Not a stitch. Her feet were bare, which he dug big-time. It gave her a certain look, he did not *sais quoi,* free and feral.

She touched the pad to save her place. Her fake blood red nails were off. Likewise her heavy show makeup. Her platinum hair rose up into the air and tumbled over her shoulder in one of those fountain-style ponytails she favored. She looked fresh and dewy and naturally young. Which she was; she was only twenty-four to his twenty-five. He figured she would look like this when she was 124, no rejuv necessary. Big blue eyes, a small, turned-up nose, cupid lips. Soft features belying the fact that she could crack a man in half without so much as breaking into a sweat.

His baby.

He smiled weakly. "Hi."

She cocked her head in the direction of the door. They always came in through the garage. "Where's your car?"

"It got blown up. I had to escalate home."

She nodded slowly. "Guess you had a bad night all the way around."

"You could say that." He hissed open the fridge and got himself a Bad Moon. As a rule she liked him to drink out of a glass and as a rule, he did it, but right then he was too tired and too downhearted. He swigged back the bottle and realized he should have gone for the hefty bottle of Atherton Gold they kept in the pantry. When a guy needed a drink, he didn't need a beer.

As she watched, he flopped down into one of the kitchen chairs. Took another swig. Then he angrily ripped off his patch and tossed it onto the table. There was a smattering of credit chits and a financial report on the table beside the mini. She'd been reading the *Wall Street Journal.* Most of the other showgirls stuck to *Cosmo* or *Fabricated Beast,* some weird boycake thing they were all into. Not his girl.

Mamma mia, she deserved so much, and he was in no position to give any of it to her.

"Sparkle, we have to talk," he began. "I'm PNG. Persona non grata. I'm out of the Family. For now.''

She tapped the *Journal* off, her expression unchanging.
''I know.''

''Oh?'' He waited. Had she known or had she guessed?
She said nothing. Sparkle was like that, didn't waste much
energy on words. He respected that. It was a good quality
for the girlfriend of a Family Member to possess. Only now
he wasn't a Family Member. He was N.A., like her.

''How do you know?'' he prompted.

''Well, Deuce,'' she drawled, ''it was all over the casino.''

Yeah, it would have to be. He said, ''Did you hear about
my um, contretemps with the Moongoloid?'' When she remained silent, he added, ''You should have told me who
was bothering you girls, Sparkle. You should have trusted
that I would take care of it.''

She looked at him meaningfully. He flushed. ''Better
than I did tonight. I got caught off guard. If I'd have
known, I could have been better prepared.''

It was obvious she didn't believe him. Still, she said,
''Yeah. Sure, Deuce.''

''You should have told me about him and Diana Lunette,'' he added. ''You know my brother was with her.''

Sparkle blinked, not following him. ''What I'm saying
is, about her seeing the Moongoloid.''

Sparkle took this in. Then she nodded to herself. Deuce
hoped she let him in on her little secret. Sparkle said, ''She
told me she was getting engaged to someone very rich and
important. I thought she meant Joey.''

And it was so like Sparkle not to mention it to Deuce.
He was almost angry, except that he remembered that he
himself had decided not to talk about Joey around her, because all that came of it was him feeling like a putz. A
man did not like to feel like that around his baby.

''Engaged?'' Deuce grimaced. ''To *that*?''

Sparkle shrugged. ''He's a Designated Heir.'' Almost as
if she agreed with Diana's actions: If you're a rich big shot,
it don't matter if you're a repulsive lunatic.

''Well, Van Aadams should realize she's not a nun, not

with her lifestyle.'' He flushed. Her lifestyle was very similar to Sparkle's lifestyle.

"Listen," he went on, "I'm only out of my Family for appearances. I suggested it. I can move easier this way, check out the situation.''

"The situation," she repeated.

"Hunter Castle." He frowned and looked around. "Where's the dog?''

"Lying down. She wasn't looking too well when I got home.''

Deuce flashed on the pepperoni. A wave of guilt—and, if it be known, pure unadulterated fear—washed over him. Had he killed the dog, too?

Before he could confess, Sparkle went on, "She got into that pizza I packed for you.''

"Oh, I'm sure that wasn't it," he said generously, scooting his chair over and sliding an arm around her waist. "Maybe she's going to have puppies." He waited for a reaction.

She stared at him. "How? We never let her out.''

"Yeah, well, you never know.''

"Yes, you do, Deuce," she said. "You do know. And she's not.''

Okay, so that wasn't the basis for her kindnesses of late. He switched the subject. "If you want to leave me because of the N.A. thing, I'll understand." His voice caught, but he forced himself to remain steady. "It should only be temporary. But it's not what I came in with.''

"It's not what you'll go out with, either, dunce," she said, and put her arms around him. She parted her lips and half closed her eyes, murmuring, "Jeez, you are stupid.''

Then she kissed him.

Now, before Sparkle, Deuce had been around a little. It was difficult, growing up close to Beatrice, who had just kind of assumed they would liaise once they were both old enough. As far as he knew, Beatrice's virtue was still, ah, intact, or else she had gone the way of many a Borgioli girl, gotten drunk, and donated the Family virtue to some youngblood in the back of his flashy aichy. He, however, had honed some of his negotiating skills learning about the mysteries of love from girls other than Beatrice, ostensibly without Beatrice's knowledge. Girls like Estrella.

So, he had been kissed, many times.

But he had never *really* been kissed until he had met Sparkle. Here was the best kisser on the Moon. Here was a woman who could flatten a man with ten seconds *bocca bocca,* here was the reason kissing your opponent into unconsciousness was illegal in kickboxing.

Her soft, creamy lips moved over his mouth, caressed the corners, smoothed his closed lids—it was 5:30 A.M., just in case anybody needed to know—fondled his temples, the hollows of his cheeks, his earlobes. She breathed warm kisses into his ears until he heard himself whimper.

Then, finally, he kissed her back, knowing he didn't give as good as he got, except that you had to give him points for sincerity.

"Oh, Deuce," she whispered, and his eyes flew open, because she was being lovey-dovey again. Soft and warm and cozy, as she curled around him and nuzzled the stubble on his chin. "Deuce, I was worried about you."

He almost fell off his chair. For Sparkle to say such a thing was unheard of. He cleared his throat, as alert as if the house had informed him that it, too, had something in one of its ducts.

"Baby?" he ventured. "Has something happened to you?" She smiled at him. Dreamily. He blinked rapidly. Five thirty-two. Thirty-three. "Are you going to die or something?"

"What are you talking about?" She tousled his hair. Playfully. He stared at her.

"Are you taking drugs?"

She smiled again. "Come on. It's been a bad night for both of us. Let's go to bed, then you can tell me your plan."

"Okay," he said hoarsely, allowing her to lead him into the bedroom.

Moona Lisa, from her doggie bed in the corner, raised her head and wagged her tail. She started to get up, but Sparkle said, "Stay." She hunkered back down and gave Deuce a big, brown-eyed look of adoration.

Deuce smiled at her, and said, "Hi, girl. You okay?"

The dog wagged her tail so terrifically he was afraid she might smack herself in the head with it. He went over to her and squatted, rubbing the back of her head and her bulbous little tummy. She whined and exulted, letting him go back to his other woman only after a couple hopeful pleas to stay.

Sparkle brought the bed down from the ceiling. There were black-satin sheets on it. Before tonight, they hadn't owned black-satin sheets. Sparkle had gone shopping.

Sparkle hated to shop.

She touched her kimono and it floated low-grav to the floor in a shimmering pool of ebony. The boxers followed.

She looked at him expectantly. Fumbling, with much less grace, he began to undress. She sauntered to the bed and climbed on, reclined, waiting with her head tipped back, her platinum hair waving like shiny seaweed in the subdued light. They had once spent an entire afternoon programming the illumination to their specs. Whoa, baby, those test drives . . .

"Sparkle," he said hoarsely, and joined her on the bed. She put her arms around him, and he melted against her sinewy body. Then he thought, *Wait a minute. We* both *had bad nights? Both of us?*

What had happened to her? Had someone spilled the beans about their secret romance?

"Sparkle?" he said. "What did you mean when you said—"

"Kiss me," she ordered him, pulling him on top of her.

"Hold on," he protested.

"That's just what I was going to say to you," she cooed as she grabbed the low-grav bed sashes.

It was noon when they both woke up, one in the afternoon by the time they managed to make some cratercafe and toast. Casino life was like that.

They sat in bed together, sipping and noshing. Deuce was pensive; his days of *latte*s on the house were, at best, on hiatus.

"And Feist was the one who gave you Castle's card,"

Sparkle said, continuing their conversation. Moona Lisa wiggled on her treadmill, seemingly none the worse for wear. Deuce was relieved and contrite, and vowed that if anyone ended up murdering her with nitrates, it would be Sparkle, and it would be an accident. He was the only one around there dumb enough to kill her with misplaced kindness.

Sparkle held out her hand, and Deuce gave her the business card. She scrutinized it like a police detective, turning it over, finally holding it to the light. She said, "It's authentic."

"How do you know?" he asked, but either she didn't hear him or she ignored him.

"And no one in your Family knows you have it."

He almost said, "My sort-of ex-Family," but he knew she knew what she was saying. "Yeah. No one knows. At least, that I'm aware of. I snagged a low-level comm-link number, too. Off a Castle guy. And a name of some newcomer connected to him. Epperson-Roux."

She rolled over, taking most of the sheets with her, but that was okay because she was the one who was into sheets. The satin caressed his hip, and Deuce stirred. "Honey," he said, putting his hand on her thigh.

She rolled back with a mini in her lap and sat up, scooting back against the pillows. The headboard said, "Hello, Miss Sparkle," and shaped itself to Sparkle's previously programmed specifications.

"Let's see," she said.

Deuce scooted up next to her. The headboard said, "Hello, Miss Sparkle." Sparkle chuckled under her breath.

"I don't get no respect," he growled theatrically. His poor aichy. It would never call him "Mr. Borgioli" again. Heffernan Cleanup had dragged it away. He had managed to charge the bill to his credit line, but it had finally been canceled soon after that. Escalators and tubes were free for the N.A.'s. It had been hell taking mass trans home, sitting among so many hopeless, exhausted people.

He had planned to convert his investment line into usable credit the first thing when he got home. Now that he was home, maybe it would be the second thing.

"Whiner." She showed the mini, let it scan her eyeball and her thumbprint, and said, "Open." She typed a few commands even though it could take voice. Deuce watched the boxes twirl and unfold as she navigated her way through a field of directories. She was accessing the address on Castle's business card. It was the same thing Deuce had been planning to do.

There was the trill of a phone, and then a voice, "Welcome to Castle Industries, a service conglomerate." On the screen, the company's standard comm-link hookup code appeared beneath it.

"Well, *that's* special," Deuce said, unimpressed. "What's the use of a card? You could get that number anywhere."

"I'll try using the comm-link number you got from your pool player," she said, wiping a scanner over the numerals.

"First, I want to convert my investment line," he said.

"Yeah." She looked sad. She'd worked hard on making his little fund grow.

That done, they tried the guy's linkup number. They got the same recording, with the suggestion that they leave a voice message for Mr. Marion Clemens.

"Hi, Marion," Deuce began. He squinched up his face and blinked at Sparkle. He didn't realize men could be named Marion. "This is Deuce McNamara. The local you met at Trini's. All that coinage you gave me's no good on the Moon, bro. Gimme a call. Number's on redial. Maybe we can have a rematch. Disconnect." He looked at her. "Now for Epperson-Roux."

Sparkle nodded. She said to the mini, "Give me information on Epperson-Roux, R-O-U-X. It's hyphenated."

"There is no data available," the mini said cheerily.

"How about Epperson?"

"I have data on two hundred twenty-five thousand individuals named Epperson," it was delighted to report. "Would you care to narrow your search?"

Sparkle thought a moment. "Make the subject inclusive with Moonside and casinos and Hunter Castle."

"There are no data available within those parameters."

"Narrow it to Moonside and casinos," Sparkle suggested.

"Twenty thousand individuals named Epperson have visited Moonbase Vegas for gambling purposes. Sixty-five individuals named Epperson are employed in the Moonbase Vegas gambling industry."

Sparkle said, "Expand your search to casinos and Hunter Castle."

"No data available."

"Narrow to Hunter Castle."

"No data available."

"Well, damn," Deuce said, frustrated. "What the hell's with that? I'm going to find that sucker if it's the last thing I do." He thought a moment. "Tell it to access Castle personnel records."

Sparkle did. The mini said, "Those data are controlled."

Which of course was expected. Sparkle said, "State nature of control."

"Password required."

Deuce brightened. Passwords were no big deal. In fact, they were one of his specialities, like combination locks. "Okay." He cracked his knuckle. "Let me scan in, Sparkle. I'm going to get to work."

Leaning over him, Sparkle picked up the mini and put it down on the nightstand. She said, "I'm cold."

Deuce was nonplussed. Sparkle was never cold. Half her dance routine was comprised of spinning half-naked on the ice, and the way he figured it, she had gotten used to the chilly air. She was almost kind of in trouble for it at work, too; half the excitement of the act was to watch the topless showgirls, ah, pucker up. Sparkle puckered no longer.

He gave her a kiss. "You know there's nothing I'd like to do better than do everything some more." He reached for the mini. "But I gotta strike while my iron is hot."

She glanced downward. "I'll say."

He managed a smile. "You're scaring me, baby."

The grin grew. "I don't think so, big guy."

"Oh, hell." He left the mini where it lay. "What's another minute or two?"

"Another minute, my butt," Sparkle growled, and patted his side of the bed.

Half an hour later, Deuce's hand shook from exhaustion as he picked up the mini. He did about an hour of hacking, got nowhere, dressed, and hobbled out of the house.

In his tender boyhood, Mamma told him all this weird stuff about how girls were fragile and delicate and lots of them weren't too keen on "physical matters," as she put it. Deuce wondered where these girls were. He had never met a single one of them.

He used the comm linc in Sparkle's aichy, placing calls one after another after another, taking them as often as he placed them, until he sounded to himself like a race announcer. In rapid order, he accumulated data on Castle: he was a hundred years old, no, six hundred, no, a thousand; he had no children, he had seventeen children, he had a son; he was a clone, he was a cyborg, he was a homicidal maniac.

He had put a hit out on every Godfather; he was the son of every Godfather; he had had sex with every Godfather.

He was on the Moon to: collect a debt, kill everyone, close down all the casinos, build a new casino.

"Which he cannot do," Waxing Littlemoon, a cocktail waitress who also oversaw the Frankenstein over at Smiths' Wild West Casino, stated flatly as she chomped on her gum and smoothed her very short gingham skirt and miniature apron. Mamma had not permitted him even to talk to women who chewed gum. They were cud-chewing harlots and loose, diseased women.

Deuce missed Maria della Caldera. But the simple days were gone forever. And it was decent of Waxing to talk to him. As he had expected, most of his Family connections were snubbing him. Which would make his spying mission interesting, to say the least.

The Wild West was a rock'em, sock'em cowboys-and-Indians Western town complete with real live mountain lions, horses, and horse poop. Their girls were eight feet tall, and they wore skimpy cowgirl skirts and Indian thongs. Nobody protested the stereotypes. Nobody cared anymore.

Money mattered more than some old sense of lost heritage.

The girls sported tiny holsters tied to their thighs that held pretend revolvers full of maraschino cherry juice. Folks ordered all kinds of fruity drinks to get them to hoist their nice long legs onto a chair, withdraw their little guns, and give 'em a shot in their Sex on the Moons or their Libration Libations or whatever. You got to say, "Juice me, baby." It made the tourists feel dangerous like evil Family hit men.

"Our Family is not going to agree to it and neither are the Scarlattis," Waxing continued. She nodded as someone came up to try the Frankenstein, which was four old-fashioned slot machines bolted together. The Smiths were into antiques to complement their Wild-West thing. You fed the machine enough for all four machines and pulled one handle. Deuce had never seen it pay off. "Way I see it, anyone who buckles and gives in to him will be whacked the way the Scarlattis whacked the Mitchells," she added.

"Your Families are still in Vendetta," Deuce observed languidly, meaning the Scarlattis and the Smiths. "You guys didn't, ah, roll the Die, did you? Like some kind of university prank?"

"Oh, right."

"With your secret weapon," he went on. He always fished about the secret weapon.

She always laughed.

"Alls I can say is, make sure your enviro-suit is in good working order. When we blow the dome, you'd better be prepared." She laughed some more, alternating chuckles with cracks on her gum.

"Okay, okay." He sighed. "Don't tell me, even though I'm good to you."

"Baby, toilet paper don't begin to pay for that kind of information. Not that I would give it to you," she added hastily, as a CYA move. You never knew who was listening.

"I want to meet some of his guys," Deuce said.

She waved a hand. "We've got large quantities of them giving us their paychecks. They drink a lot, too. They've got these stupid little coins, ya know?" she gabbled on.

"We told 'em no way. Credit lines or gold or whatever, but not your weird little pennies. Damn."

"Caputos are taking them," Deuce said, to needle her. However, it was true. "So are we."

"We, who? I know you're N.A., baby." Her voice was harsh.

"Then why you talking to me?"

"Cuz you'll do something. You'll pull up before you crash. I've got faith in you."

He was touched. He had never realized before that some people bought his bullshit. Maybe that meant it wasn't all bullshit.

"Look, our doors are open twenty-nine days out of twenty-nine," Waxing said. She gave her backside a delicate scratch. It was covered with lacy undergunnies that she had once informed him were itchy as all get-out. "Even for the disgraced, as long as they're young, hung, and handsome." She dimpled at him.

"Waxing," he said cautiously, "ah, uh—"

She snickered. "Relax, Deuce. I know Beatrice Borgioli is lying in her bubble bath humming the 'Wedding March.' "

He reddened. Women talked too much.

"Listen, I'll give you some free drinks and maybe steer you in the right direction, and you can find a way to make it worth my while. Deal?"

He held out his hand. "You're too good to me."

She took it, rested it against her ample chest. "You know it, baby."

Waxing let him play blackjack at the tables where the Castle boys sucked down the free stuff and made insulting remarks about Moonsiders. They also let something loose for free: they hated Epperson-Roux because he was a "prissypants."

Well, it was something.

To Deuce's relief, he got some kind of similar break at each of the other casinos, even if it took some fishing to find someone willing to deal. Usually the person who decided to stay in touch with him was a woman. Sometimes, though, some male he'd done right by retained his memory of the event.

Everybody seemed open enough to being of service, but Deuce harbored no illusions. As John Scarne, the Earthsider patron saint of gambling, had written: "There is nothing more futile than the attempt to cook up betting systems that will overcome adverse odds."

Basically, what it boiled down to was that the guy with the power—the guy who had whatever it was you wanted, be it funds, information, an introduction, whatever—couldn't offer you an even-up proposition. If you won, and he had to pay, he couldn't give you exactly, precisely, what you wanted. He had to maintain some kind of advantage or edge over you. He had to have a better chance to come out on top every single time he dealt with you. Bad guys like Wayne Van Aadams maintained that advantage through intimidation, threats, and violence.

Good guys did it by setting up their operations with that premise firmly in mind. They either levied you a direct charge or paid you off at less than the correct odds. That percentage take was the price you paid for dealing with the guy in the first place. That was the basis of all relationships.

Including Deuce's passion for Sparkle. She had the power—he was in love with her—and she could name the odds. There had to be something in it for her, guaranteed. That was okay. He expected it. He would think there was something wrong with her if she didn't work that way.

So what was her percentage now that he was Dis-Membered? Or was he asking the wrong question? Maybe he was more attractive to her now that he wasn't considered a Borgioli. But what nine-foot-tall showgirl would ever want to hang out with an N.A.?

Hard to say. But he did know she had a limit; everyone did. You couldn't expect to walk into a situation, figure out the size of the house bankroll, then bet the full amount. If you won, you bankrupted the other person. If you lost and decided to bet the full amount of the house bankroll again, you'd have another shot at shutting them down. Casinos and bookies and girlfriends and best friends would have all gone out of business long ago if there were no limits.

And as with casinos, people, at least Moonsiders, didn't operate on the hope that on occasion they'd beat the other guy. Survival depended on extracting something from every transaction. The more action you were into, the more likely you were to survive. Which was why long-term relationships were difficult at best. Breaking a heart was the same as breaking a bank.

So he went to see the people who would see him, not filled with gratitude, but curiosity about their expectations. And he fervently hoped none of them was waiting to blow him up in order to collect a reward from Wayne Van Aadams.

Somehow Deuce had thought Castle's low-level employees would be different from everybody else's low-level employees. But they weren't. They were just as ignorant, petty, ill-informed, clever and, thank goodness, greedy. A few of their own wacky coins here, a few there, and he left Dodge with a lot more in his saddlebags than he had ridden into Dodge with.

The word was, Mr. Castle was taking meetings, lots of them, more meetings than the president of the Conglomerated Nations. He was taking them with the Godfathers. He was taking them with major players and Heirs, Designated and otherwise (which probably meant Yuet and her stepbrothers). And he was hanging around with Epperson-Roux, whose files were way, way, way secured. In Sparkle's aichy, Deuce had tried to hack into the man's life history a dozen different ways, and each time he had come up dry: ACCESS DENIED. PASSWORD REQUIRED. SYSTEM SECURED.

Blink, fade to black. Each time he tried to get in, the screen would disconnect, leaving Deuce frustrated and the aichy idling along, waiting for destinations.

There was a bit of interest at the Scarlattis' Inferno: a new statue of Mephistopheles covering the Ditwac display case. Deuce wondered if the figure, with its pointy beard and devil horns, was a holo obscuring the Ditwac or if the statue was hollow and the Great Die and its case were inside.

He wondered how many people thought the five-spot meant that Castle was going to mow a Family down.

Or that the Chans would fold now that Dai-tai was really, truly on her last legs. There was a sick joke going around: *Has Dai-tai cashed in her chips? Yuet better not bet on it.*

Word was that Yuet had armed herself in a very big way against a possible hit at the funeral. Would Castle do anything about it, such as help or hinder?

His badge went off. He took the call.

"Cheetah's Gaslamp," said the voice. It was Mr. Tanzer. "Half an hour."

"Are you crazy?" Deuce said. "No freakin' way."

"Safe passage. Guaranteed. We don't want an incident," Mr. Tanzer assured him.

"Yeah, and I'm Hunter Castle's Heir," Deuce muttered under his breath. He said more loudly, "No funny stuff. I got friends."

"You have our word."

"Oh, your *word*. In that case, I'll rush right over."

He disconnected. Their word.

Which was, he had to admit, probably good. After all, they were Van Aadamses, employees of a guy who had publicly threatened to whack him.

The rock got bigger, the place got harder, the space between got smaller.

TEN

Cheetah's Gaslamp was a sleazy little joint off a big sleazy square once known as One Step Park. Now it was just the Park. It was created to commemorate the landing of Neil Armstrong. They had taken a holocast of his footprint up Topside in the dust and put the copy down here with a statue of him beside it. The original was still Topside in a bubble inside New Luna Park, the lame Moonbase theme park.

The idea of One Step had been to make a community gathering place—*We are the Moon, we are the children*—but somehow it became the place where the community gathered to take drugs. *We are the Moon, we're all on Mars.* It was a sad crazy quilt of shanty buildings made of cast-off materials lining dirty tunnels where you did not want to go, not even to take one small leak for man, brimming with "bad characters and indecent women," as Mamma used to say.

There was always talk about clearing the area out and cleaning it up, but nothing ever happened. The Moonsider Liberation Front loved to point to it as a symbol of the deteriorating family values that legalized gambling inevitably brought with it. The Families loved to point to it as a symbol that nothing halfway decent got done on the Moon without their assistance. "The Families *add* value," as Godfather Giancarlo Caputo had once asserted.

Around six o'clock, Deuce took a deep breath, made sure his blaster was fully charged, and studied the area. Next to the Gaslamp was a pawnshop protected by a shield and a man with long gray hair and a gray beard seated behind a counter reading what looked from this distance like a racing form. Of course, Deuce's first guess when anybody was reading anything was that it was a racing form.

But you couldn't see anything through the windows of the Gaslamp because it didn't have windows. It didn't even have a proper sign, just a hand-painted thing that floated from one hook that said, "CHEETAH'S" with a picture of a strange, spotted dog beside it.

Deuce sauntered through the broken airlock. The floor was sticky, and the tables were scarred. It was uncommonly dark, and the air was thick with smoke. Through the murk a couple beer signs glowed, and just inside the door, a one-armed bandit with a holo poker game ka-chinged as an unsmiling large woman with no hair whatsoever except on her arms pulled the sleek silver arm, let go, looked at Deuce, and began to cry.

"My luck's run out," she said miserably. Her lips were bright blue, and she had a tattoo of some ethnic sort embedded in her scalp. And a handful of cracked-off neural enhancers. "It's run out."

He nodded. Sooner or later, it usually did. The Families banked on that fact of life.

"It ran out yesterday," she said, picking a scab on her head that encircled the enhancers, as if someone had tried to dig them out with a spoon.

"Mmhmm." He coughed and squinted hard past her. No doubt someone had jimmied the smoke detectors. The people inside couldn't afford the pollution levy for one puff, let alone the campfire they had going.

"I'm out of luck." The woman sighed and wandered off. Maybe that was her line to draw something with luck to her, so she could sap it away. In this place, she must be one starving parasite.

Some of the bar's other patrons observed the exchange: tattooed guys, stoned guys, short girls with blue mouths whose bones stuck out every which way because they never got enough to eat, and, in a strategic corner, none other than his buddies, Mr. Tanzer and Mr. Feist.

Deuce wondered if his own luck had just run out.

The two men sat crowded in a booth so dirty you could probably get a disease just by sitting in it. Deuce's blood pressure hopped, but he fought down his concern and did the attitude thing, even though the Gaslamp was full of the kind of guys eager to do a hit for cash money, maybe even a onechip, maybe a shot of Tycho Delight or its knockoff, rip-off competitors.

With measured steps, Deuce sauntered over to their booth. "Gentlemen," he said. "*Buona sera.*"

"Good evening, Signor McNamara," Mr. Tanzer replied. He was wearing a real silk carnation in his burgundy-and-navy suit.

"Still employed, I see," Deuce responded.

"And you are not," Mr. Tanzer rejoined, looking uncomfortable. "Would you be our guest for a cocktail?"

"Just tell me what you want."

"Please, have a seat." Mr. Tanzer gestured. "And would you mind turning off your comm badge for a few moments, sir?"

That made Deuce even edgier. "Because why?"

"Because we've endangered ourselves coming here, and we need to know we have privacy."

While he considered, the two animals made a show of taking theirs off, deactivating them, and putting them on the table. Anything happened, Family security and/or medical would not be called. Not that that would be any big deal, at least to Deuce.

Deuce said, "I'll turn it off, but I'm not taking it off." He made a show of doing so.

Mr. Tanzer said, "All right, Mr. McNamara. We're on equal footing now."

Mr. Feist glared at Deuce. "The hell we are. He can turn his on anytime he wants."

"Yeah," Deuce said, "and seeing as I am currently Dis-Membered, I will get zero backup from my ex-Family."

"You mentioned friends," Mr. Feist said, well, feistily. "Or was that just something to say?"

That ticked Deuce off. "Plus I have no idea if you're wearing extra chatterboxes up your asses." He was embarrassed at his own crudeness. He cleared his throat. "Ah, if you are carrying other communications devices on your persons."

Mr. Tanzer jumped in. "I can assure you that we are not. We wish to remain strictly anonymous."

"So you call me on an unsecured line and meet me at the front door in your colors." He didn't know if he liked this cloak-and-dagger stuff. These guys were not guys he connected with. They were not guys he trusted.

Mr. Tanzer sighed. "Please, sit down."

Reluctantly, Deuce complied, facing them.

"Have you thought about what we briefly discussed?" Mr. Feist asked.

"Yeah. So how is the big guy involved?" He eyed them both, hoping they would at least give him a hint. They remained silent. He pressed, "How do you know him?"

Deuce lifted a hand at the waitress, who nodded in a tired, bored way.

"Look, fellas," he said. "I'm not sure I have time for overthrowing the kingdom just now. Your Heir has called a hit on me."

"So if you kill him first . . ." Feist said, then looked embarrassed. Family business didn't work that way.

"Do you actually think I'm here because I want to help you kill that gravoid?"

The waitress came over. He asked for craterwhiskey, remembered his credit situation, and said, "Make that Atherton Gold. And put it on their line." Mr. Tanzer nodded to the waitress and ordered two more for him and Feist. She trudged away.

"How come you gave me Hunter Castle's card?" Deuce pushed.

Mr. Tanzer paled. He held up a hand. He whispered, "Please, keep your voice down, Mr. McNamara. We're taking a great risk."

Deuce narrowed his eyes. "No kidding. I hope this is not news to you, either. Why?"

"We prefer not to say."

"Then I prefer to go. If you don't tell me what this is about right now—"

"Oh, hell," Mr. Feist said. "It's Miss Sparkle de Lune."

Mr. Tanzer sucked in his breath and pursed his lips. Deuce bored in on the chatty Mr. Feist.

"Mr. Wayne finds her . . . attractive," Mr. Feist rattled on.

Deuce blinked. He retorted, "That don't wash. Mr. Wayne's interest is otherwise engaged. As in, he's engaged to Diana Lunette, the broad he thinks I boinked behind his back."

"Engaged?" Mr. Tanzer echoed, clearly astounded. He looked at Mr. Feist. "Does Chairman William Atherton know of this?"

Mr. Feist shrugged. "Who knows? You know how he is about Mr. Wayne. It won't matter anyway." He turned his attention to Deuce. "Mr. Wayne has also attempted to, ah, force his attentions on Miss Sparkle."

"*Bastardo*," Deuce said between clenched teeth. His fists rolled into balls. Then he pulled himself back from the brink of manly jealous fury and mentally replayed the conversation up to that point. "And this has what to do with Hunter Castle's business card?"

"There are certain *other* parties that hold Miss de Lune in high esteem," Mr. Feist filled in, speaking quickly, like he wanted it all out and over with. "Besides Mr. Wayne. Certain parties that don't want her bothered."

"*Hunter Castle*?" It took everything in Deuce not to fall out of the booth.

"Or perhaps someone in his employ," Mr. Tanzer said hastily.

"Someone like who?"

Mr. Tanzer cleared his throat. Maybe because, Deuce realized, belatedly, that he should have said "whom." "We were contacted by an unknown party within the Castle organization, who asked that we protect the young lady and 'take care' of her 'bothersome paramour.' "

"Are you talking *assassinio*?" His heart skipped a beat. Did they know about him and Sparkle? *We both had bad nights*, Sparkle had said. Like, someone hassling her about a secret boyfriend? If you had the hots for a lusty, tall lady, the main man in her life would be a bothersome paramour, was that bullshit or not?

They knew. Someone knew.

And someone cared enough to kill over it.

Deuce reached his hand under the table for his blaster in his pocket but didn't bring it out. He started darting his gaze left, right, looking for an *assassinio* guy. The whole room looked to be full of *assassinio* guys. "Girls, I don't know from the love life of Miss Sparkle." He hesitated, decided he'd better give a little to be more convincing. "I have a deathbed obligation to protect one of her girlfriends, Miss Selene Earthshine. That's why I came to your House."

"Therefore, your interests are aligned with those of our contact in the Castle organization," Mr. Tanzer whispered patiently. "You now know that it's Mr. Wayne who has been bothering Miss Earthshine as well."

"But that don't mean I was going to whack him. I'm not in the position to start a war, Mr. T. Maybe beat him up in private so his honor isn't shredded, maybe request that my Godfather parlay with your Godfa—your C.E.O. But I'm not Devon LeDare."

"You have no Godfather now," Tanzer pointed out reasonably. "You have nothing to hold you back. Especially if, as you say, the hit on your own person has not been aborted after all."

"Wait a minute," Deuce said slowly. He had the distinct impression that he'd been had. It was true. He had no Godfather. And no Family to answer to if he offed a Family Heir. Hell, if an N.A. offed a Godfather, even, there were no political consequences among the Casino Families. The *cretino* got life in prison unless the Families got to him first (which they usually did), but it didn't affect the Families' interpersonal relationships.

Had he been maneuvered out of the Family on purpose? Had Hunter Castle somehow arranged it? So he could kill two birds with one stone, as it were, get rid of two of Sparkle's bothersome paramours?

Sparkle and Castle?

Deuce scowled and thought hard. No, he himself had

been the one to suggest he be kicked out of the Family. He was just being paranoid.

"Why you two?" he asked. "I mean, how did Castle pick you? How did he contact you?"

"We got the card," Mr. Feist snapped. "That's it. Just showed up in our lockers."

"You want to subcontract the hit." Deuce frowned at them. "You wanted to pass the buck. So you taped the card from your locker to my blaster to get my attention, is all. Castle is not trying to contact me personally."

"No," Mr. Feist admitted.

"But you did. You had that Cynthia girl scare Selene to get me over there. Get me mad enough to jump him."

Mr. Feist shrugged. "Maybe."

Deuce tried another tack. "Why are you so keen to have Wayne whacked? What is Castle offering you? You'll have to break your allegiance to do it."

Mr. Feist knit his brows. "We're motivated. Let's leave it at that."

"Is there something wrong with your C.E.O.? I mean, he's not that old. He's got a lot of tread left on his tires, especially if he re-ups for rejuv. Or what? Is he sick, like Dai-tai?"

"Mr. Wayne is unsupportable," Mr. Tanzer said slowly. "He must be stopped."

Deuce pounced on that last word. "From doing what? Stopped from making your lives a living hell?" He narrowed his eyes. "You guys have a personal beef against him, don't you."

Mr. Feist tensed all over. He set his jaw and looked somewhere past Deuce. Stonily. Like he was going to spill his guts. *Viola*, the weak link. Deuce ran through a list of possibilities. What was Wayne famous for?

"He's bothering your women, too," he said. "Wives, sisters—"

"Daughters," Mr. Feist supplied, at the same time Mr. Tanzer said, "That's ridiculous."

"Of course." Deuce brightened, then realized what the men were telling him. Female relatives were a big deal in his Family. Look at Mamma, merely a friend of Big Al's sister, but canonized when she died. Look at Beatrice, who lived like a princess. He touched his heart. *"Mi dispiace. I don't mean to sound glad about your dishonor."*

"Dishonor?" Mr. Feist echoed hotly. "You moron, we're talking about our little girls, not our gambling debts."

Deuce sensed he'd said something wrong but couldn't figure out what. He said, "Didn't Chairman William Atherton make it up to you?"

Mr. Feist's face turned a brilliant shade of scarlet. He raised his fist into the air; it hovered there quite dramatically. Then he slammed it down on the table. "No one can 'make it up' to us, you Family piece of garbage!"

Deuce nodded understandingly, although he still did not understand. In his world, slights—including physical injuries, insults, deaths, and disappointments—translated into acts of dishonor. Dishonor could be rectified, with apologies, cash, or retribution. Maybe it was an Italian thing. It was clearly not an Australian thing.

"So," he said, trying to work with their worldview— what was that word Sparkle used? their gestalt—"word got out about your tragic situation with your daughters on account of Wayne, and Mr. Castle—or someone who works for him—enlisted your help to get rid of a common enemy. On account of Wayne was bothering his local girlfriend, Miss Sparkle de Lune."

"It seems that way." Mr. Tanzer was pale and shaken. The Moongoloid must have really hurt his kid. Maybe even killed her. "At any rate, we assumed our contact meant Mr. Wayne. He's the only bothersome paramour we know about, at any rate."

Great, Deuce thought. *Fabulous*. Someone in Hunter Castle's organization was urging people to whack Miss Sparkle's boyfriend, and these two clowns invite him out for a nightcap. No secret was ever one hundred percent. You had to assume someone knew or would eventually know. Maybe that time had come.

If so, no wonder he didn't have a car anymore. And wouldn't it make spying on Castle even more fun?

And to think he'd been seeking Castle people out all night. He was amazed he was still alive.

"Why Miss de Lune?" Deuce asked. His nerves were revving up to overload. His trigger finger was itchy. Someone turned on the jukebox, and he jumped a mile.

Mr. Tanzer managed one of his snooty smiles. He was also nervous. That made Deuce more nervous. Deuce looked harder at the tough crowd. Lots of blue lips. Lots of anger at the raw deal life had handed them. Mr. Tanzer said, "Perhaps you should ask Miss de Lune."

"What's it to you?" Mr. Feist demanded. "She's not *your* girlfriend."

Deuce replied smoothly, "Castle is dangerous business. I don't want to get mixed up in anything to do with him. I'm surprised you guys did."

"If you need more incentive than honoring your blood oath and saving your own life," Mr. Feist said, "I'm sure Mr. Castle is prepared to reward whoever takes care of the problem."

Deuce shook his head. "Can you imagine what they'd do to anybody who offed a Designated Heir?"

"I don't care," Mr. Feist announced "Like you said, we've got a beef."

"A beef?" Deuce leaned forward. "You've got a death wish, is what you've got, *paisan*. I'm outta here." He ticked the blaster up to max, still leaving it in his pocket. He rose and turned his back on them, tensing for a blast. Then, as carelessly as he could, he headed for the door.

"Wait," Mr. Tanzer called.

Ka-zing! From nine o'clock, a beam sizzled past Deuce's head and exploded against the wall. The bar shook. Bottles on shelves behind it popped and spewed craterbooze and nicer stuff straight into the air like geysers.

Deuce whirled around and dropped to the floor as another pulse went off. Mr. Feist was sprawled ten feet beyond him with an exploded chest. His innards were pumping, shining, and smoking. At the very least, the guy had been telling the truth about being human.

Mr. Tanzer fell under the table and hurled himself in Deuce's direction, scrabbled up beside him, and said,

"Help me, and I'll help you." He touched his own lapel, looked back. "Oh, damn. My badge is still on the table."

Help him what? Die? Deuce gestured for the man to get behind him, succumbing to that pesky heroic streak once more. "Where's the *assassinio* guy?" he hissed at Mr. Tanzer. "Who is he?"

"We weren't followed," Mr. Tanzer said. "I swear it."

"Yeah, and I'm the Borgioli Godfather," Deuce flung at him. "I was so *stupid* to believe you! This 'safe passage' deal, that was just a little something you two cooked up to get me to show up, wasn't it?"

"Look out!" Mr. Tanzer cried, as another beam flashed in their direction. It missed the men but took out most of the wall behind them, which exploded in a shower of packing material. The Cheetah, apparently, was built mostly of old transport crates. The interior of the wallboards crawled with roaches that skittered toward the lights of the beer signs.

Deuce swore and pushed Mr. Tanzer down, then fired off a couple pulses into the haze and the rush of silhouettes heading for the door. Faces swarmed into the light like figures from a bad dream or a floor show headlined by some Earthside magician. Spooky, freaked out, terrifying in their urgency. Deuce kept hold of Mr. Tanzer, both to protect him and as an anchor against the panic, which he was not new to. You're in a Family, you know from panic.

"Come on," he said to Mr. Tanzer, grabbing him by the collar and dragging him along the floor, which was slick with red human blood and squashed roach carcasses. Mr. Tanzer did his best to crabwalk along—he was no slouch in the save-your-butt department—and together they fell outside.

Deuce half dragged, half threw the Van Aadams man into an abandoned construction tunnel filled with empty Bad Moon cans, organic garbage, and cigarette butts, the carcass of an aichy—oh, God, don't let it be his own poor baby!—and, curiously, large crates marked, "PAPEL DEL BAÑO." Despite his predicament, Deuce's interest piqued. Toilet paper? Sitting out in the open? What, didn't anybody around here speak Spanish?

Well, that would have to be checked into later. He reset himself on the matter at hand, which was surviving to fight another day.

The light was bad, and he could hardly see Mr. Tanzer, who crouched gasping beside him. He touched him, said, "You got any weapons?"

"Yes. I've a 457 Copernicus and a Kepler SIG-Sauer."

Wow. Deuce was impressed. He'd never even held a Kepler. And the Copernicus did 457 pulses a minute. Another time, another place, he'd ask to fire off a couple blasts with each. "You a decent aim?"

"Decent enough."

"Then shoot to kill, okay?"

"Of course." Even now, the guy sounded like he had something to prove.

The heavy pounding of footfalls preceded a bulky figure bursting through the broken airlock. Black hair straight up on end, black eye patch, black clothes, he swiveled in their direction, dropped to one knee, and fired. Brilliant red juice lased directly overhead. Deuce and Mr. Tanzer answered with their blasters. In their assailant's charger flash, Deuce saw a bright gleam that ran along the arm, where a juice blast had burned away his black-leather jacket. The arm was metal. But the head looked human, lips drawn back in a ferocious snarl, a single eye narrowed as the figure took aim. So what was shooting at them was probably the cyborg of the Earthside un-welcoming committee, name of Club or Spade.

"And you weren't followed," Deuce said in disgust, even though he knew he was beating the deadest of horses. It was that smart mouth of his . . .

"We had an operative in the bar who assured us we were fine." Like that let them off the hook. Mr. Tanzer angled left and shot off three pulse-rounds.

The figure made some unintelligible comment about their mothers and dodged back into the airlock.

"An operative? Like an accomplice?" Deuce asked, taking advantage of the respite to check his charger. He thought about comming for help, but who? No way was he dragging his baby into this.

"Oh, damn." Mr. Tanzer sighed heavily. Deuce glanced at the man. He was whiter than white. "Damn it to hell."

The fat, bald lady with the scabby, tattooed scalp staggered awkwardly through the lock. There was an arm around her neck, held by a man with a bad blond toupee and a blaster smashed in her ribs. The woman's hands were stretched Topside.

The arm around her appeared to be made of flesh; the face above hers was blank and sullen. The figure moved awkwardly in the low gravity. It had to be the android, since their chassis were organically grown, whereas cyborgs were pieced together from mechanical parts and whatever was left of some human. Cyborgs were usually created after accidents. The Earthside cyborg population had shot up after the Quantum Instability Wars. They weren't manufactured on the Moon, but they were allowed. Still, you didn't see so many.

So they were both there, Mr. Club and Mr. Spade, in the bar into which no one had followed Mr. Tanzer, Mr. Feist, and Mr. Deuce.

"That's your operative? That . . . schizo?" Deuce asked, astonished.

"You didn't suspect her, did you?" Mr. Tanzer's voice was tight and high. They both ducked a long blast. The tunnel shook as if from a moonquake. Deuce cast a nervous glance at the crates of *papel del baño*. If he had to sneak behind them for cover, he would, but it would be a painful sacrifice if they got juiced.

"Doesn't matter if I suspected her or not, *paisan*," Deuce snipped, being defensive because no way had he guessed about her. "They did. Is she human?" If not, he had no problem with whacking her if it would save their butts.

"Oh, yes," Mr. Tanzer whispered. "Very human."

Deuce cocked his head. He looked from the man beside him to the mountainous bald woman and back again.

"Oh, my God," he said. "That's your kid. Bringing her here, you risked her life."

"Look at her. She has no life. She was beautiful. Clever.

He did that to her. He put those tattoos there. She was so sweet. Now . . .''

"Give it up, and I'll let her go," the android called.

Deuce thought, *No way*, but he wasn't sure what was going to happen now. One of the reasons the N.A.'s hated the Families so much was that the Families didn't worry if civvies got in the way of their Vendettas and wars. But Deuce had always worried plenty. He had always tried very hard not to harm any innocent bystanders. If you enlisted, you were a soldier. But if you were just some poor Joe on your way home after a tough day, you deserved every chance to continue your course on the straight and narrow.

"Save her," Mr. Tanzer said to Deuce. Then the Australian jumped up, took aim, and got blasted for his effort. He was thrown against the wall behind him, and crumpled to the ground.

"Daddy!"

While the android was distracted, Deuce tried the same routine, only he managed to hit the bad guy, who let go of the girl. She raced toward her father, her arms outstretched.

Deuce blasted like crazy, the pulses pounding the front of the Gaslamp. By the time the debris stopped bobbing around, the cyborg was no longer there.

He joined the injured party. Still alive, Mr. Tanzer said, "Shit," in his perfect high-class Aussie accent. Deuce pressed his hand against the man's chest, felt the heat and the bubbling skin. Mr. Tanzer's mouth pulled back from his teeth in agony.

"Daddy." She flung herself across her father, who winced. Deuce thought about suggesting she restrain herself, but it didn't much matter. The light was already leaving Mr. Tanzer's eyes.

"The documents," Mr. Tanzer said gasping to his daughter. "My pocket."

She plunged her beefy hands into his sticky suit jacket and pulled out a minicard and a data rod.

"Get it to the right people," Mr. Tanzer said. "Take care of her, Mr. McNamara. If you take it back to them, they'll help her. Castle doesn't know. . . .''

"Doesn't know what?" Deuce asked unhappily. "Take them what? Them who?"

"We were following Wayne . . . everywhere . . . we saw, we knew . . ." He grabbed Deuce's hand. "Take care of her."

"Sure. I will," he said, sighing. *Another* deathbed obligation. "What about Mr. Feist? He got anything needs saving for the right people?"

"No. His daughter is dead. I was the one."

The woman burst into tears. "Oh, Daddy, don't go. Don't die."

A huge blast zinged over their heads. Deuce pushed the woman's body flat onto the ground and returned fire.

It was time to get the hell out of there. "We gotta go," he told the woman.

"No," she said. "I'm not leaving him."

"You gotta. He's gonna die anyway." He made a face. "*Mi scusi*, Mr. Tanzer, but you know it's true."

"Go with him," Mr. Tanzer begged his daughter, as another blast blew up the tunnel floor, showering them with chunks of rock the size of toilet paper rolls.

"No!" She threw her arms around her father.

Mr. Tanzer looked pleadingly at Deuce.

"C'mon, lady," Deuce said.

"No," she screamed. "I'm staying with him."

Mr. Tanzer kept looking at him. Deuce sighed hard, aimed his blaster, and blew more guts out of the Australian security guard.

His daughter started shrieking and launched herself at Deuce. Deuce was about to knock her out when Mr. Tanzer emitted a long, low wail. A bubble formed over the general vicinity of heart, expanded, and popped, spraying Deuce with hot blood and sizzling pieces of lung.

"Oh, my God," the woman screamed, pummeling Deuce. "You murderer! You murderer!"

He fended her off easily, bypassed a dozen chances to make her go limp. He'd never be able to carry her even at low grav. So he grabbed her hands and yanked, hard. "C'mon. Your *babbo* wanted you to live."

She spit at him.

"Listen, about that luck of yours," he began. "It already ain't so good, so don't tempt fate here, okay? Let's get the hell out of—"

And then they were almost on top of him, the cyborg and the android, right ugly-lookin' mates, and Deuce leaped to his feet.

"Grab your dad's weapon!" Deuce shouted at the woman, but she was on her hands and knees screaming.

At that moment the door to the pawnshop opened. Juice streamed from the doorway, and a voice cried, "Run!" as the assassins turned to confront the new enemy to their rear.

Deuce grabbed the woman's hand and hightailed it down the tunnel. He shouted into his comm badge for Sparkle's aichy as explosions made his ears go numb.

Tanzer's kid was clumsy, and her uncontrollable crying made her clumsier, but somehow they stayed alive until the aichy arrived. Deuce heard the *NA-na NA-na* of the Lunar Security Forces and prayed they'd get there before whoever it was at the pawnshop was dead and the bad guys had resumed their regular programming.

He half guided, half threw the woman into the aichy. To the craft, he said, "Punch it, Mabel," which of course it didn't process. That had been an old joke between him and his old aichy. "Take off."

"You are not yet seated."

"Oh, for God's sake!" He flopped into the chair.

"Fasten your seat belt and that of your companion."

Sparkle had programmed in this crap. She was a safety freak. She had never considered the possibility that someone might be shooting at her as she entered her vehicle.

"We're fastened, goddamnit!" he shouted, yanking on his seat belt. He snapped the woman's belt around her bulky stomach. Belt her was what he wanted to do. She just sat there, helplessly staring ahead. Now was not a particularly convenient time for her to go into shock. "Okay now, Your Majesty?" he yelled at the aichy. "Get us the hell out of here!"

"Thank you, Mr. Temporarily Accepted Driver. Destination?"

"Home," he said, then realized it would probably take

him to Selene's. "The home of Deuce McNamara."

"Will comply."

A low-slung, black vehicle was roaring up behind him. He ascended, saying, "All levies will be paid," wondering how, wondering if the aichy would believe him.

Ka-zing. Ka-zing! Juice to the right of them, juice to the left of them. He wondered if the aichy would get the hint and kick it.

The woman just sat there. The aichy, to Deuce's dismay, wasn't much more animated.

Deuce said, "Hang on!" to the woman, who made no response, and "Manual override!" to the aichy, which did, releasing the controls at once.

As the black aichy bulleted toward them, Deuce flew like a damn eagle.

Not that he had ever seen an eagle, just the Eagle One in the Moonbase Vegas Museum.

"Hey, hey, we're going to be okay," he said to the woman, patting her, feeling more generous toward her now that they were in the process of escaping. "Miss Tanzer?" he queried, hazarding a glance at her.

She had slumped against the passenger door. Her eyes were as blank as her father's had been.

It wasn't until that moment that he realized that all her luck—every last gasp of it—had finally run out.

ELEVEN

Evasive maneuvers through the vast underground maze of Moonbase Vegas were part of every growing Family boy and girl's catechism. With perhaps too much ease, Deuce lost the black, low-slung aichy in the dark, narrow recesses of forgotten mining shafts, or else it lost interest or got called home. He didn't care why it wasn't there, but he logged all its distinguishing marks and ran its number through the aichy's mini. Nothing came up. No registration, no record of ownership. *Quelle surprise.*

Miss Tanzer's back was dripping with blood. She had been juiced in the construction tunnel. Deuce hadn't even noticed, and he was sorry for that. He had dragged her along without realizing she was probably in a lot of pain and certainly dying. He hoped her father understood that Deuce had tried like hell to honor the deathbed obligation. Or maybe Mr. Tanzer hadn't expected it would do any good, that she would die along with him. The two of them must have been through a special kind of hell in their years together.

He wondered if there was a heaven, and if they'd both arrived there yet. What was your angelic ETA after you died? As far as he knew, both the Catholics and the Mormons still believed in heaven, and the Mormons' was on the same star that gamblers considered the luckiest— OUQT2, otherwise known as the Gambler to, well, gamblers, and Paradise to the Mormons. The Mormons used to have a different lucky star; Paradise was a relatively new

location for them. As Brigham had explained it to him, one
of their big cheeses had a revelation that God had personally relocated to this star on account of it gave Him a better
view of the Moon. It had been almost enough for Deuce to
convert.

Then Sparkle had pointed out that this revelation had
occurred about the same time that the Mormons had gotten
in thick with the Van Aadamses.

So, as he still considered himself an Irish Catholic, he
now made the sign of the cross on Miss Tanzer's cooling
forehead and whispered, ''Happy landings, kid. Make that
giant leap. Amen.''

Her sightless eyes stared straight ahead. He was not un-
used to the presence of death, but he hated it when the
innocent bought it. It was not just. Not right.

To him, it was a personal dishonor, and no one could
ever compensate him for his part in it.

He aborted the homecoming program and zoomed
around for a while, making sure he wasn't followed, wondering what he should do with her body. His fingers were
aching to check out the minicard and the data rod, but he
kept his eyes on the readouts. No sense getting sloppy. He
punched in the location of the pawnshop and discovered it
was owned by a Mr. Levi Shoemaker, an N.A. who lived
not far from his old friend, Little Wallace. Deuce wondered
if Shoemaker was a good Samaritan type or formerly on
the payroll of Tanzer and Feist. Could be that was why the
boys had insisted on the Gaslamp; that is, to take advantage
of their top-notch security forces, ranking up there with
their A-#1 surveillance team.

Finally he decided there was nothing to do but take her
in. Hell, if the hit men knew him on sight, they probably
knew his home address, his comm-link number, and his
underwear size. It didn't matter if he went home.

None of his security fields appeared to have been tampered with—but then, they didn't have anything as fancy
as Scarlatti equipment—and, holding his breath, he glided
into the garage. He cast a glance at his silent companion
as the shadows slid over her. Her profile was nice, but her

attractiveness ended there. People always said of certain girls, usually if they carried a few extra pounds, "It's such a shame. She has such a pretty face." Miss Tanzer did not. It was scarred and cratery. Maybe once she'd been a looker. Probably just wishful thinking on her father's part.

With a sigh, he shut the aichy down. Reluctantly, he searched Miss Tanzer's pockets, not liking to disturb her but liking less leaving her in peace, and possibly remaining ignorant about other aspects of his situation.

Her ID tagged her as Alitji Anna Tanzer. She had been thirty-two. She was—had been—on medication for depression. That surprised him. They could zap your brain now to fix you. Maybe she had had some other condition that prevented a permanent fix.

"Ah," Deuce muttered to himself as his hand wrapped around a jade green vial with etched panels of glass into which lotuses had been lased. He held it to the dome light of the aichy. There was a familiar faint pink opalescent sheen to the liquid inside it. The cap was sealed with a Chan chop. He opened it, sniffed, recognized the signature scent of jasmine.

They couldn't zap your brain if you were addicted to Chan drugs.

"Oh, girl," he said sorrowfully to the dead woman, and, shaking his head, put her things in his own pockets. She also had the data rod and minicard her father had made sure she took. He was dumbfounded to find that her father had allowed her into that awful part of town without so much as a miniblaster on her. And him in security. Had he wanted her dead, like Mr. Feist's poor kid? Was he tired of seeing her so disheveled and crazy? Desperate men, desperate deeds.

He left her in the car because he didn't know what else to do with her and went into the house.

Sparkle wasn't there. She was probably still at work, if she still had a job.

He tapped his comm badge and asked for Selene's line. Let them trace it. Let them just try to hassle her. He had an obligation, and all the Families honored those; there were so many of them, with so much dying going on all the time.

"Deuce?"

"You okay, moonmaid?"

"Mmm-mmm." Selene was speaking in that weird little singsong people used when they weren't alone. He wondered if they were on earphone or what.

"How about your friends?"

"Everyone's fine."

"Tell them all I called."

"Will do. Bye!"

Moona Lisa skittered out to greet him. She looked real good. For her. Pizza appeared to agree with her.

He got out the Atherton Gold and poured himself three fingers spread wide. It went down hot and smooth and very expensive. It had been a gift from the same old ex-friend who had sold him his lemon of an aichy and who had lusted after Sparkle.

Jeez, what did his woman have to do with Hunter Castle? He thought back to how she had announced that the business card was authentic. Why hadn't he demanded to know how she knew? Why was he such a doormat around her?

One more drink, and then he armed the door and put his blaster in the charger. Got out his secondary and checked it, doing a few fast draws in the bedroom mirror to see if he had screwed the pooch with too much liquor. No problemo. He was as agile as ever. If they tried to take him at home, he'd be ready.

He put the secondary on the kitchen table and made sure the dog had water. She walked in a circle, or the closest to a circle she could get, then flopped down beside him and laid her head on his instep. He murmured, "Nice baby," and laid the data rod, the vial, the minicard, and Castle's business card in a row beside the secondary. He hissed open a drawer and got out one of the minis and pushed in the data rod. He took another hit of Atherton Gold.

The rod opened up and announced, "DOSSIER, MR. WAYNE VAN AADAMS. HEIR, VAN AADAMS FAMILY."

Somebody had been very thorough. The guy was thirty-six, weighed 320 pounds at full gravity, had a drug habit. There was a detailed readout of his weekly schedule, including approximate times for meals.

Last Friday, Wayne had made a call at 4 P.M. to Diana Lunette and told her to meet him later in the Down Under's main bar. Deuce wondered what kind of woman found the Moongoloid preferable to his brother, what kind of woman allowed a hit to go out on an innocent man just to shore up her odds of hitting the jackpot—marriage to a Designated Heir.

A call to Wayne's bookie. Deuce scanned the list of bets he'd made. What a putz. Bad calls, all of them.

Another date with Diana.

Bingo. A call had been made shortly thereafter to Mr. Club and Mr. Spade of Earthside Los Angeles. Now quartered in the Moondust, a hotel owned by the Van Aadams group. If Chairman William Atherton didn't know about it, then he was getting real sloppy.

This was interesting. And very strange. Wayne had made an appointment to meet with Gino Scarlatti yesterday. He noted the address; it was in a bar called the Crater Club in the worst part of town, worse even than One Step Park. There were no notes, and no way to tell if the meeting had been kept. So, was Gino a nervous wreck these days because of something he had going with Wayne Van Aadams? Was the Moongoloid in on the Ditwac thing? Man, that'd be a hoot.

Deuce put a bookmark in the dossier and went down a couple layers. Names and dates spewed forth like a roll of toilet paper bouncing down a flight of stairs.

There was the hit assignment on him, Deuce. It was formatted exactly the same as Borgioli Family hit documents. They were fairly standardized and usually went through channels at the Charter Board without a hitch. You declared Vendetta, paid levies, you got it stamped six ways to Sunday, you got it Sanctioned by your big boss, and you were on your way to reclaiming your honor.

Only, Wayne had skipped a few steps. Deuce punched the document to holo and examined it from both sides to see if it bore William Atherton's signature and lightmark.

No. So it wasn't Sanctioned after all. Still, Wayne's money and this incomplete form had brought the Earthside mechanics up to do some dirty work. Deuce was amazed that William Atherton hadn't put a stop to it. Maybe he was too distracted by Hunter Castle.

Deuce hacked at it for about fifteen minutes. Then he opened another layer and discovered something else that was interesting: additions to the hit, made only hours ago: Geoffrey Tanzer and Fabiyan Feist.

He sat back for a moment, digesting the information. The Moongoloid must have heard about the plan to whack him and retaliated. But why was he meeting with a scumbag like Gino?

He hacked around for a while longer. He tried to cancel the hit on himself, but it wasn't his lucky day, and he had to leave it as it was. As far as Club and Spade were concerned, they were still employed.

Damn.

Maybe he could at least cancel Wayne, then. He looked for more data about the Moongoloid. Here was one: His heart was in bad shape. He'd had it replaced once, but there was some kind of malfunction, some problem with his immune system.

"Good," Deuce said, and meant it.

The fact of the immunological problem gave even more credence to the rumor that Wayne was a clone of the C.E.O. You'd think where there was one clone, there'd be two. If that were the case, you'd also think Chairman William Atherton would deep-six the defective one and use the other.

Unless Wayne was the best of the lot. Cloning still didn't work all that great.

Look at poor little Moona Lisa.

Naughty Wayne had been arrested Earthside for indecent exposure, sexual harassment, and unbecoming public behavior. Considering how prudish they were Earthside, none of that was particularly shocking. It could happen to anybody.

Letters to a sister away at school. Letters to his uncle sucking up and asking for money.

A call to Hunter Castle about their upcoming meeting.

What? Deuce nearly fell off the chair. Moona Lisa yipped. Yes, a call, and here was the number, a different number from the one he had.

Deuce ran his tongue around the rim of the shot glass, poured himself another small nip. Talk about your heart condition. He stared at the number and wondered what to do. Castle's line was secured for sure and locked like a Family vault. Maybe if you dialed it without some secret code, you blew up.

Maybe Wayne had dialed it and he was dead, which would explain the fact that he had not been at Cheetah's Gaslamp with his bad guys. Hell, for all Deuce knew, he'd been waiting in the alley and had juiced Alitji Tanzer from the relative safety of the stacked-up toilet-paper crates.

He said to the mini, "Make a call. Here's the number." Then he stopped and chewed the inside of his cheek. "Pause." If he called from here, he had no doubt Castle would be able to trace it even if he did tell the mini to secure it. Should he go offsite, then? And what, maybe run into those two goombahs?

"Well, hell," he said, as the dog shifted her weight on his instep and looked up at him adoringly. "Continue call." He squinted—Sparkle contended he needed optical enhancements; he contended she just liked to give him the business about being older than her—and read off the numbers as they got dialed.

"Hold, please, Mr. McNamara," the mini said politely.

Deep breath in. The dog shifted. Deuce rubbed her under the chin with the toe of his boot.

Breathe in.

Breathe in.

He remembered to exhale once he began to see spots.

The number rang. Twice, three times. Then a metallic voice said, "Please show your card."

"My card?" Deuce asked uncertainly.

The line disconnected.

"Hey," Deuce protested. He told the mini, "Dial again."

As before, it complied and the metallic voice asked him to show his card. He scratched his head. Then he glanced down at his hand and picked up Hunter Castle's business card.

The card vibrated like an excited little pet.

On a hunch, he held it against the screen. There was a little *bong*, like when he had incoming. He lifted the card off the screen. A long number appeared across the face of the mini. It looked like another comm-link number.

"Connecting," said the mini.

"*Viola*," he whispered.

"Welcome to Morehouse Financial." Wow. Morehouse Financial was a very hoity-toity brokerage house. You had to be a billionaire for them to have you as a client.

"Your account number, please."

He paused. He didn't have an account number there. This had to be a mistake. He grinned. Yeah, like a mistake that might enable him to do something like check Mr. Castle's account balance.

A holo face popped up and smiled expectantly at him. "Your account number, please."

He winked at her just for the fun of it. "Hey, baby," he murmured. "Howya doin'? My name's Deuce."

"Deuce is accepted," she mouthed. "Your account has been authorized for five thousand shares of Palace Industrials. Thank you."

Deuce was speechless. Palace Industrials was a Castle company. A privately held Castle company. One you could not buy stock in.

There was another *bong*. A quicktime appeared in the upper right of the mini screen. It was a facsimile of Hunter Castle, nicely digitized. The salt-and-pepper hair, the dark eyes, the funky little goatee.

The grin.

"Greetings, Mr. McNamara," it said in Hunter Castle's thick Southern accent. "I'd appreciate a meeting tomorrow. Five P.M. Moon Standard," he added, as if it was an afterthought.

The mini shut down. Deuce said quickly, "Immediate reboot, redial."

The mini didn't respond.

Had he just gotten bribed to kill Wayne Van Aadams? Five P.M. tomorrow *where*?

About two hours later (and where was Sparkle?) Deuce managed to get the mini back up. It didn't give a damn about Hunter Castle's business card anymore. Deuce's private credit line had been used to purchase the five thousand shares. Without Deuce's authorization. And no way to liquidate them unless he could sell them back to Hunter Castle. He had about four hundred credits left to his name.

The mini had no suggestions about where to meet Castle. On his alien ship from another planet?

He went through the rest of the things he had lifted from Miss Tanzer. Plugged in the minicard. There were two full sets of Papers of Affiliation for Geoffrey Tanzer and Fabiyan Feist, their heirs, and blood relations, for the Smith Family.

They had planned to jump from the Van Aadamses, the classiest Family on the Moon, to those union-loving thugs, the Smiths.

He sat for a full minute, bemused. Given that they had a beef with the Van Aadamses, maybe needed to get out of there if they succeeded in getting Wayne killed, why go to the Smiths? Why not go with Castle?

Castle doesn't know . . . if you take it back to them, they'll help her.

He searched the card, but there was nothing else on it. He sat for a while with the dog resting on his instep and twiddled his thumbs.

There was a noise outside and he jumped, realized it was Monday morning, therefore trash day, and leaned back in his chair with a sigh. He drank some more Atherton Gold. He was known as a champion liquor-holder; along with hustling pool he used to make spending money as a kid hustling tourists on his liquor capacity. One of the few people he had ever lost to on a regular basis was Sparkle. In fact, that was how they had gotten together, trading shots in Selene's living room and arm-wrestling. Selene had acted strange that night, blinking a lot; he thought she'd been jealous and maybe blinking back tears, but she had seemed really happy later, when Deuce and Sparkle had told her they were in a liaison. She promised not to tell a living soul.

Had she kept that promise?

He decided to have another whack at Marion Clemens's comm link. This time he managed to enter an unsecured area having to do with Clemens's job as a cargo steward. He hacked and slashed his way through a lot of peripheral garbage about shifts and Moontime extra pay and a break schedule. Unions. All they did was talk about how much they didn't have to do and how much they were going to get for it.

OSHA REGS.

OVERTIME ON LUNAR HOLIDAYS.

LUNAR DOCKING FACILITIES: GAMBLER'S STAR FREIGHT.

Viola.

Deuce read about that and made a call.

Then something very sad and very ghoulish occurred to him:

Miss Tanzer was still in the aichy. There was no uncomplicated way to take her to her relatives.

And it was trash day.

Desperate men.

''Forgive me,'' he whispered to the bundle wrapped in garbage bags as it bounded down the chute and was delivered directly into the truck, untouched by human hands, unseen by human eyes, unmourned by human hearts.

Except his.

About three hours later, Deuce put the vial of Chantilly Lace in his pocket and took Sparkle's aichy to the cargo docks. Little Wallace was waiting beside the empty *Phoenix* bay. He was dark and chubby and wore his hair in dreadlocks that bounced around his head. His moon-shaped face was beaming with excitement. He looked left, right, and over both shoulders as Deuce approached. Deuce had to hide his grin at how obvious Little Wallace's precautions were, but sobered when he reminded himself that he was sticking Little Wallace's neck out simply by meeting him.

"Hi, Tony," Little Wallace said softly.

"Heya." Deuce sauntered over, not a care in the world, tra la la. He held out his hand. Little Wallace looked left, right, and over both shoulders before he shook it.

"You find Castle's cargo bay?" Deuce asked without preamble.

"It's heavily guarded," Little Wallace informed him. "Moonforce and private security, too." His eyes were practically spinning. This was the most thrilling thing that had ever happened to him.

"Where is it?"

"I'll take you," Little Wallace said eagerly.

Deuce shook his head. "If they catch you, they'll can you at the very least. I don't want you to lose your job." Such as it was. Little Wallace was not only N.A., but non-union. It was incredibly stupid of the Non-Affiliateds—they preferred to be called Independents—not to band together, but all attempts to do so had ended in chaos and their grungy equivalent of turf wars. The Moonside Liberation Front laid the blame for their inability to get along at the door of the Casino Families, and they were partially correct to do so: Each Family had a special division whose sole purpose was to keep the N.A.'s all stirred up and unable to trust each other.

It had been equally incredibly shortsighted, if not stupid, of the Families not to extend Family Membership—or at least, make Affiliation easier to achieve, which it was not—to the people they'd hauled up to build Moonbase Vegas. Plumbers, electricians, physicists, air-conditioning guys— it had taken tens of thousands of hardworking men and women to build the enviro-dome and the apartments and the streets and, of course, the casinos.

At first they would come in shifts of six months, then a year, then they started bringing their families up. Then the families started needing schools and hospitals and the rest of the things that come from living somewhere for a long time. And then, before you knew it, they started calling themselves Moonsiders and refused to relocate back Earthside because they had friends and jobs and connections, their kids were in the middle of their school years, and Earth just didn't feel like home anymore.

So instead of a transitory workforce, you had disenfranchised colonists. An underclass that worked like dogs to ensure that the Casino Families would have everything they needed to fleece every Jimmy-Bob and Jeez-Louise who walked through the airlocks, built by guys who had to learn the hard way that if you stayed out too long, you got radiation sickness.

Ergo, as Sparkle would say, a pissed-off underclass.

Some of the N.A.'s did make deals with the Families, and some of them did form unions, and so doing business with the N.A.'s was a helter-skelter, confusing situation requiring negotiating teams. Ergo the Family departments set up to "facilitate" all that—which happened to be the exact same departments that made sure the waters stayed muddy.

Deuce had no direct personal experience, but he supposed things were just as screwed up Earthside.

"Little Wallace," he said, feeling guilty, "you do realize I'm an N.A. myself now." He didn't want his number one fan to harbor any illusions of vicarious grandeur.

"You'll get back in." Little Wallace smiled at him. "I have faith in you, Deu—Tony."

Deuce pressed his hand over his heart. "I am truly touched."

Little Wallace's eyes got shiny. "Hey, man, you know I owe you my life. C'mon. I'll take you to his cargo bay."

"No way. It's too risky." He held up a hand. "I insist."

"Aw."

"I'll tell you what I find," Deuce dangled. "Hey, I've got some T.P. for you, too. It's in the locker in sector seven." It was the last of his stash, unless one of his other informants hadn't taken their payola from his lockers on the Strip. He would have to find some more goodies to thank Little Wallace with. He had done him an enormous good turn here. He remembered the *papel del baño* and thought he'd see if he could salvage it. He also remembered that he should look up Levi Shoemaker, owner of the Alamo—that was, the pawnshop next to Cheetah's Gaslamp.

It was incredibly selfish of him not to have checked on the man's welfare before now.

He fished out a voicer and handed it to Little Wallace. "This will let you in. Go on, now. I'll get back to you later."

Little Wallace stared down at the voicer without moving. Not for the first time, Deuce wondered if his informant's mother or father had gotten too much radiation. Sparkle's great-grandfather had belonged to the Atomic Veterans, which had given her a jump start on her height. Lots of showgirls had AV ancestors.

Funny how things worked out sometimes.

"Someone's looking at us," Deuce said, which wasn't true. He wanted to send Little Wallace on his way. "Get outta here. Get back to work."

"Okay." He hesitated. "You'll call me later?"

"You've got my word." If he was still alive to do it. He didn't suppose you went snooping around Hunter Castle's stuff unless you were willing to accept a set of possible consequences, one of which might be another bomb in your tailpipe.

As Deuce anticipated, Castle's assigned cargo bay was enormous. Whatever lay beneath the shield must be heavy.

The rent on that puppy would have set him and Sparkle up for life. The cost of usable space on the Moon was astronomical.

Pardon the pun.

There were guards all over the place. Some wore the white suits with the black crescents of the Lunar Security Forces, the official authority in this man's enviro-dome. The private troops had on brown and khaki, and either they were seriously enhanced or shoulder pads, knee pads, and thigh pads were all back in style. Both forces were wearing infrared detectors in the dim cavern and both were armed as if they were on the front line of a particularly vicious war.

Deuce bellied along some junked transport crates with his binocs and squinted as he changed the focus. It was

10:07. In seven hours, he had a date with Hunter Castle or a facsimile thereof.

Two of the security guys meandered toward each other. They had voice-dampers on, fancy stuff. You could hear more in an anechoic chamber than someone who had a damper on. Studying them, Deuce zoomed in on their mouths. He was pretty good at lipreading, if he did say so.

"This is a waste," one said to the other. "Why are we guarding a lot of nothing?"

The other one shook his head. "I just collect my check, friend. Mr. Castle knows what he's doing."

Deuce grinned. Hmm. Was this part of a script for the benefit of snoopy types like him or were these two loose lips honestly beefing in public? Where they guarding a lot of nothing or was there something worth stealing under the shield?

He was about to move to a new locale when the ground beneath him shook. The air thundered as if someone had broken the sound barrier, which did not normally happen on the airless Moon, once, twice, three times, and all of a sudden the armed guards were bringing their weapons to bear and keeping to their posts—well trained, these guys— while the dock security and dozens of workers started running in the direction of the explosion.

One said to the other, "What the hell was *that*?" And the other whipped out a blaster and dropped to one knee.

Deuce stayed where he was, looking for an opportunity to move closer in the confusion.

The one still standing tapped his ear, and said, "Some guy just got blown to bits opening up a locker."

Deuce whispered, "No," and ran toward the smoke.

TWELVE

This was the news story that would have run if Little Wallace had been in a Family:

Mr. Wallace Busiek, AKA Little Wallace, was blown to bits while opening a locker in sector seven. There wasn't enough of him to do anything with except to verify his identity with a DNA scan.

But he was an N.A. His death was not newsworthy.

Sparkle held Deuce as he slumped against her wet, supple body. She murmured, "It's not your fault," and part of his brain registered bitterly that this, too, was not the Sparkle of old, not his taciturn beauty, his wry girl.

"They meant to get me," he said.

He found himself thinking of Selene's uncle. Another innocent N.A. who'd opened the wrong door and died for it. He remembered the guy dying in his arms, blood burbling out of his mouth as he gasped, "Gee, gee, gee," like he was amazed he was hit. Then protesting, "No," and he was dead.

As soon as the explosion in the cargo bay stopped going off in his head, Deuce called Sparkle. She was at Selene's, where the rest of the world apparently still assumed she lived. He didn't remember how he'd gotten there, except that Sparkle's blood-drenched aichy was now parked in the garage.

Blindly he had stumbled into the apartment and waited for her as she had come out of the shower. One look at his face and she hadn't even toweled off, just knelt on her long,

long legs and held him. It was Monday, the traditional showgirl's day off. Selene had taken one strangely blank look at the two of them and left them alone.

"How could I do that to him? How could I have been so stupid?"

"Deuce." Sparkle ran her fingers through his hair.

He looked up at her, handed her a towel. Took her dark blue kimono off the hook beside the shower. "Jeez, you gotta get away from me. They might kill you, too. Don't you see? All the innocent people, they—"

"Deuce."

He rocked backward on his heels and stood, holding out his hands as if to stop her from coming any closer. When all he wanted was her closeness.

"How could I have given him that voicer?" He had played that moment over and over in his mind. "My damn vehicle had just been blown up. I'd been chased all the way home. Why didn't I think of the locker?" He began to pace. His stomach was churning. His heart was about to beat itself out of his chest. "I was so smug. I've always thought I was better than him."

She dried off and put on her kimono. Then she led him into the bedroom.

She loved him into forgetting, almost.

Afterward they lay together, Deuce staring at the ceiling, Sparkle looking nowhere, quiet; this was the Sparkle he knew. They didn't touch. He wondered what she was thinking, if she was laying out a plan of attack or retreat.

If she was sorry she'd ever met him.

If she was thinking about Hunter Castle, a man who would kill for her.

If she was thinking he was also a man who would kill for her.

Deuce heard the garage door. He tensed and reached for his blaster. Then the bedroom door hissed and Selene stood before them with a plastic casino tray and three shot glasses of liquid the color of dark honey.

"I went to the store. I got you some Atherton Gold," she said in a funereal voice. She was almost as tall as Sparkle, and did her hair in a fountain of gold with copper highlights, held in place with a huge, jeweled, gold barrette. She had dyed her big eyes lavender, with earrings to match. Her clothes were off-duty showgirl except that, as always, they covered the vast majority of her territory, sweats decorated with teddy bears with glowing jewels for eyes. She had on gold sandals. She was always a little too decorated for Deuce's taste, and also not very smart.

Her apartment was like her clothing, all gold and swirls and teddy bears. There were teddy bears in every room of her house including the spare bedroom that was supposed to belong to Sparkle. As if they made her innocent. Deuce used to imagine that people would take one look at this place and know that Sparkle didn't really live here.

"*Grazie*, Selene," he said with appreciation.

She answered, "*Prego*," just like she was Italian, and gave him a sad little smile.

Sparkle got up, took the tray, nodded her thanks. Without a word and without hesitation, Sparkle handed the first shot to Deuce. He threw it back. The second. The third.

His insides still churned. His heart still bruised his ribs. His hands shook.

"Well," Selene said, and left them alone again.

Sparkle put the tray on her dressing table next to a pile of fake blood red nails. She was dressed in workout clothes; she had been on her way to the dojo when he told her about Little Wallace. Today was not a day she usually went. It occurred to him that maybe she had set up a sparring session with Diana, hoping to make her see reason.

She looked so young. In his mind he saw blood dripping down her back and shut his eyes. The image lingered, burned.

"We've been stupid, thinking we were a secret," he told her. "He knows."

She opened a drawer and handed him a full bottle of an off-brand whiskey. He opened it and chugged from the bottle.

"Sparkle," he said, "we have to talk."

"We will," she promised. "Later. After the shock has worn off." And the booze, too. That was what she meant. She was being polite.

"We're not going back to our place," he told her, tasting the fire, wiping his mouth with the back of his hand. "I won't have you and the dog blown up on account of me. We'll get her picked up and brought to you, and you'll stay here like you're supposed to be doing anyway."

She didn't argue. It occurred to him that he had had a lot to drink and not very much sleep. He was exhausted but not drunk, but he sure wished he was.

"F'once, you'll do it my way," he murmured.

"Sure, baby," she said.

He didn't know he'd fallen asleep until he turned over in the soft bed with a teddy-bear quilt around him. He jerked awake, saying, "What?" He was lying on something. He touched his pocket and realized it was the Chan vial. Sparkle would be very upset if she knew he'd brought drugs into her vicinity.

"Sparkle," he began, determined to push everything out into the open. "Castle put a hit out on the Moongoloid because of you. Maybe it's on me, too."

He waited. She said nothing. He was devastated by her silence, which felt an awful lot like a confession. She seemed not at all surprised to hear that Hunter Castle might have put a hit out on her boyfriend. "Moongirl, I need to know about Castle. I need to know why he's protecting you. I need to know how to get in touch with him."

"I don't know," she said, shrugging. "I don't have a special number for him or anything. I did call that generic line off the card again and left a message. But he hasn't returned my call."

A message about what? "Why would he go to all the trouble of hiring guys to watch over you?"

She sighed. "Deuce, I really don't know. I was as surprised about it as you."

He half closed his eyes and murmured, "Sparkle, please just tell me. How does he know who you are?"

"We met each other once," she said. She moved her shoulders. "I never slept with him, if that's what you're wondering."

His mouth dropped open. "You never . . ."

"I got introduced to him at a party about three years

ago. I gave him my opinion on a stock buy. Palace Industrials.'' She shrugged again. ''That's it. I spoke to the man for perhaps fifteen minutes.'' She looked off into space as if remembering the details. ''He sent me roses later. Real ones. To thank me.'' She smiled wryly, and said with a touch of pride, ''It was a good tip.''

And? And? He wanted to know, but he'd already pushed fairly hard. And she'd been very forthcoming. For Sparkle.

''How did you know about Palace Industrials?''

She narrowed her eyes. ''Look, either you trust me, or you don't.''

''It's not that I don't trust you, baby, it's—''

''That you don't.'' She looked angry as she stood and crossed to the closet. She opened the door and rummaged around for something. ''Look, I told you. I met him once. One time. Oh, he also gave me a diamond bracelet.''

What? ''Why didn't you tell me this before?''

Whatever she was looking for wasn't there. She crossed back to the bed and stood beside it. ''My past is my past.'' She picked up the craterwhiskey bottle and took a slug, which astonished him. Sooner red meat than booze—and cheap booze at that—for his baby's temple.

He started over. ''I bought stock in that very company today. He let me do it. We've got a meeting.''

''Mmm.'' No expression, no reaction. Then she took another swig of whiskey. ''What does he want?''

''I don't know. Maybe to juice me for daring to love you.'' It was supposed to be a joke.

No, it wasn't supposed to be. He was angry. He was worried. He was tired and sick to his soul.

The door hissed. Selene carried in an enormous gift basket done up in colorful plastic, the kind the high rollers got in their hotel suites.

''Uh,'' Selene said uncertainly. ''This came.''

Deuce said, ''Wait. It could be loaded.''

Selene shook her head. ''I passed it through our detector. It's clean.''

''You think.'' Deuce reached to take it from her.

Sparkle gestured to her dressing table. ''Here. Thanks, Selene.''

Selene set it down and handed Sparkle a strip. Sparkle keyed acceptance of the gift and jogged in a couple more numbers. A little something for the delivery union, Deuce supposed.

He peered through the wrapping. Champagne. Chocolates. Orchids.

From Castle, he guessed. He felt a surge of dark green jealousy. He felt stupid for coming to Sparkle and baring his soul. She was playing a lot of games, and apparently he didn't hold any of the cards she needed.

Selene said to them, "Guess what."

Neither Deuce nor Sparkle guessed.

"It was just on the viso in the store. Gino Scarlatti was just found tortured to death." She swallowed. Her eyes bulged. Deuce managed to notice all this by sheer force of habit. You would have thought she harbored some feeling for the former Mr. Scarlatti. Or maybe she was just scared.

"Was a hit Registered?" Deuce asked.

"They didn't say. They said he's been dead less than twenty-four hours."

So, what was it, the lady or the tiger or something behind door number three? Was Gino wasted for having a meeting with the mutant or helping with the tipping of the Great Die or for something else altogether?

He exhaled heavily. He would not wish death by torture on anyone, not even the Moongoloid himself. The Families had had years to perfect slow, agonizing torment that made you look forward to dying like a little kid looks forward to going to New Luna Park. He had seen guys like Back-Line Tony come out of those soundproofed rooms and retch.

And cry.

Selene said, "You want more hooch?" A gesture of appeasement, perhaps, for not doing as he had asked and handing him the basket. Or better yet, for not calling him to the door to check it there. She was his responsibility. If the gift basket had blown her up, it would have cast him in dishonor, either posthumously or living, even if he was N.A. for the rest of his life. He had been a Family man when he had made the promise.

"Yes, please, Sel. I'd love some more hooch." She

seemed upset. An unidentified Scarlatti had killed her uncle; maybe she was wondering if this particular Scarlatti was the one who'd whacked him. People with beefs thought like that.

"He wants soup," Sparkle interjected. "How about some minestrone?"

Selene nodded and left. Deuce said, "If this is from a certain friend of yours . . ."

Sparkle opened the wrap, found a gift card, read it, put it down. "It's from 'a friend.' And it's not for me. It's for you."

He scanned the card. Typed. *To: Mr. Deuce McNamara. From: A Friend. With Regards.* "Well, I don't suppose it's Chairman William Atherton, apologizing for the mindless cruelty of his chosen Heir." He cocked his head. "It's not from you?"

"No." She peeled away the plastic, plucked out a roll of toilet paper stuck on a stick like a marshmallow, and showed it to him. He touched it. Nice material. Then she picked up a small gold box and opened it. Fished out a set of keys. Aichy keys.

Deuce's brows shot up. She held the keys out to him. They were on a monogrammed chain that read, "DMcN."

There was silence between them as they gazed at the keys, then at each other.

"Sparkle, tell me the truth. Are you pregnant?"

She gazed at him levelly. "Why would you ask me such a thing?"

"I'll take that as a no." She was silent. "Okay, then." He scratched his nose. "We're going to de-liaise. At least until this is over."

She raised her chin as if he had punched her. "No."

"Yes." He trailed his hand along her cheek. "You're the best thing in my world, baby. I won't let you get killed because of me."

The shocked girlfriend was gone, replaced by the female kickboxing champion of Moonbase Vegas. "Give me some credit."

He managed a sad smile. "Can't. I'm broke."

"Look, I don't know that bastard Castle," she insisted. "We have no connection."

"Let me know if he calls you, please?" he said softly. "And tell me if Wayne Van Aadams tries to contact you. Please let me in on what's going on."

"I don't know what's going on!" She flared. Her shoulders tensed. Sparkle had a pretty bad temper, which she usually kept under wraps with a lot of sparring sessions and some very heavy meditation.

"Okay, sweetheart," he placated. "Okay, baby."

She held out the keys. "Let's go home."

"You are not going there," he said firmly. "I am not going there."

"We'll be okay." She made him take the keys. "It's obvious you've got some friends."

"I was Little Wallace's friend."

"Yeah. Well." She leaned sideways and riffled through the basket. "Look. Real water." She held up a fancy bottle with a jeweled neck. "Let's get crazy." She unscrewed the top, put it to her lips, and drank. Then she handed it to Deuce.

She's upset. Afraid, he realized. *She's trying to be a tough guy, but she's as scared as I am.*

Trust her?

He was trying to trust her.

He drank the water. Sweet, fragrant, devoid of recycling filtrates. What an amazing luxury.

"I'm going to hole up at Little Wallace's," he told her, trusting her that much, handing back the bottle. "I'm coded for his door. I'll call you later."

She drank more water and carefully screwed the cap back on. Her hands were unsteady.

He bent to kiss her. She kissed him back, her eyes closed. She looked young and vulnerable. He knew better.

He turned his back, opened the door, and shut it behind him on the best card ever dealt him.

In the hallway, Selene came up to him with the same tray, this time covered with a bowl of steaming soup and a Bad Moon beer. Deuce took the tray from her because it looked as if she were going to drop it, and she wrung her hands. He had never seen anyone actually wring their hands before. Nor had he ever de-liaised from someone he was madly in love with. It was a week of firsts, this.

"Thanks for helping us with that moron Van Aadams," Selene said. "I never would have guessed him as the Phantom. I mean, really. He's a Designated Heir."

"Imagine that," he said dully.

"I don't understand why William Atherton insists on leaving the Family to him. It's too weird."

"Yeah."

She seemed nervous. "That new girl Cynthia saw him on the floor, but she had no idea who he was. That's even more incredible to me. They fired her."

"What about you?"

She shrugged. "Well, they know about our obligation, so it would look bad to get rid of me. Except that now you're N.A." She pulled a sad face. "Because of this, huh. Because I called you for help."

"No, not really."

She shook her head and touched his cheek. "I know that's not true. I'm sorry I got you into so much trouble. If it makes you feel any better, all the girls are talking about the way you dropped everything and came to our rescue."

She didn't know the half of it. He managed a wink. "Hey, that's what heroes are for." And putzes.

Maybe Sparkle was right. Maybe he did have a self-esteem problem.

He got serious and touched her arm. "Selene, take care of her. I give you that obligation, if you'll accept it."

"Huh?" She stared at him with her purple eyes.

"Her car's a mess," he said. "I'll take care of it before I go. Here are the keys to a new one." He thought a moment, held them tightly. "Never mind. She drives the old one. I'll box up her stuff at home." He couldn't hire anyone else to do it; it wasn't supposed to be there in the first place.

Selene's lips parted. "You're *leaving* her?"

He swallowed hard. Tears welled in his eyes.

"You can't do this," she said. "You love her, Deuce."

"Sel, stay out of it," he replied gently. "There's a lot

more going on here than you know. I don't want you in-volved. It's for your own good. Hers, too.''

"Sparkle can take care of herself. You know she can."

"Yes, she can." He turned his back.

Selene hissed the bedroom door open. It shut behind her. Deuce stood on the other side, feeling very much on the outside of everything he knew and held dear.

He guessed he'd have to learn how to live without her.

And figure out where the heck he was supposed to ren-dezvous with Hunter Castle.

And figure out a way to stay alive until then.

He looked back at the door, half-waiting for the sound of weeping.

There was none. That was the way she was.

A diamond bracelet?

Or perhaps she had no tears for him.

PART TWO

From the Captain's Log of Gambler's Star :

Well, I've kicked over the anthill and they're scurrying like crazy. Their antics would be humorous if they didn't involve the loss of life.

The Families spend an inordinate amount of time defending their pie rather than looking for opportunities to bake new ones. They're completely convinced they can neither create, nor manage, anything more than what they already have. How very wrong they are.

That is, the old ones feel that way. My hopes lie with the younger generation, although it concerns me to see how easily they discard their loyalties and form new alliances, only to discard those when they prove inconvenient.

The boy is more than I'd hoped for. I'm not certain how much he's figured out, but I was pleased when he made the connection with me. I don't suppose it's occurred to him that I employed an old magician's trick, which my great-great-many-times-great granddaddy used to scam the ignorant backwoodsmen he visited with his magic wagon. Pick a card, any card ... from my marked deck. If it's the Queen of Spades, its duplicate is under your chair. If it's the Ace of Diamonds, I've taped a rhinestone to my assistant's frilly garter. The Five of Clubs, it's inside my hat. Such an obvious trick. But when one's audience wants you to be the master of

173

all you survey, they willingly go where you direct them. Not so much sleight of hand, as sleight of mind.

And so it was with Deuce. It was not the business card that allowed him access to Morehouse Financial, nor his name, but his voice. He could have said anything to that holo and he would have received his shares of Palace Industrials. I'm certain he would be disappointed to know that.

I'm also certain that someday, he'll realize what I did. And that I had seeded the situation with other ways of contacting him, and vice versa, if he had not gotten the Morehouse phone number.

Common but clever, he alone seems to have a set of unchanging principles by which he lives. Even Sparkle de Lune is movable, changeable. No one, not even she, is aware of her value. But I think she's beginning to realize her gift.

Deuce's strength of character sets him apart, and keeps him alone.

I feel a sad kinship with him.

I sincerely hope I will not have to destroy him.

But no one individual is more important than the Cause.

Hunter Castle

THIRTEEN

Deuce's new aichy was a stunner. Low-slung and wicked, the SX-777 shimmered like the Crab Nebula, lavender and pink and white on a slick black base. The interior was real Sandia leather, not crater, (at least, so he believed) and it boasted not one, but two, comm links, ambient interior lighting, and enough pressure-point monitors to finally get straight who the hell he was and how much he weighed.

He debated a moment before climbing inside, and ultimately decided that the giver, if hostile, would have found a cleverer way to get rid of him than giving him a brand-new car and then blowing him up inside it. Still, as the door opened, he hesitated. Maybe a possible execution by your Family, an attempt on your life, and four deaths, one of them N.A., in two days had a way of making you cautious.

He checked all the comm systems in case there was a note from his fairy godperson. No dice. No history on the registration, although it was indeed registered. The sales and freight records were sealed, which you could do on the Moon if you were a Family Member. If you weren't, the records remained open by law.

So the vehicle had been purchased by a Family Member, or on someone's behalf by a Family Member, or by someone rich enough to buy the silence of the Department of Lunar Vehicles.

That didn't leave Sparkle out. He had no idea how big her credit lines were; whenever she had recommended he buy something, she'd bought a bit of it, too. She must have a very nice portfolio by now.

Settling into the soft, cushy seat, he instructed the aichy to remember his stats and to call him Deuce McNamara. Next he voiced all the locks and security systems. Then he ordered the Moon roof open and took the little honey out for a spin, his ability to enjoy the smooth handling non-existent.

Deuce realized he was flashing his new acquisition all over Moonbase Vegas and dipped downward into the CC levels—cables and coils—where Cheetah's Gaslamp once had been.

The pawnshop was leveled, but he stopped and looked around, poking through the wreckage to see if Levi Shoemaker had made it out. There was no way to tell.

The crates of *papel del baño* had likewise disappeared without a trace.

Deuce told the aichy to take him to Shoemaker's apartment building. It was a pretty decent place, freshly painted and with some nice touches like music on the escalators. Plants in the vestibules on each level. Pawning must be a better business than Deuce would have thought.

Shoemaker lived on one of the upper levels. Used to be locations like that indicated a cheaper rent rate, as people used to believe the closer you were to the surface, the worse your chances of getting hit with radiation. It was the same kind of thing that still went on with the casinos. People were still uneasy Topside.

No one answered Shoemaker's door. Deuce started to leave his Family business card in the mail slot, thought better of it, and decided to call him once he got to Little Wallace's place.

Back in the fancy aichy, he got commed.

His stomach jolted. He told his badge to push it through the aichy's speakers and made sure he sounded calm.

"Yeah."

"Hey, idiot. Where's your picture?"

It was Joey. Deuce said, "Visual," and found himself leaning slightly forward. His brother had taken a shower. His brother was dressed. His lips were still blue, but he looked a hell of a lot better than the last time they'd spoken. "Joey."

"What's all this I hear?" Joey knit his brows and opened his arms. "They threw you out?"

"Yeah." Deuce couldn't tell him the truth. He wasn't trustworthy.

"Those bastards. I'd like to—"

"Your line secured?"

"Who gives a damn? You're Maria della Caldera's boy!"

"Adopted boy," Deuce said, thoroughly enjoying this. He was deeply moved.

"Whatever. They pull your credit? Those bastards. Hey." His face got huge. "Whose car you driving?"

"A friend's. It's a loaner." Which might or might not be true.

He whistled. "Maybe you don't need my help then." He sounded aggrieved.

"How'd you find out about my disgrace?"

"Beatrice. She was crying her eyes out. This don't look so good for your engagement." He made a face. "It's not so great for me, either."

"They'll forgive you. They loved Mamma so." Deuce grinned. Good ol' Joey, a true Family man. He could be trusted to look out for Number One. That was okay. The mere fact that he had called was enough for Deuce to forgive a lot.

He just wondered what Joey's angle was. And he was impressed with Beatrice for keeping the con going. But what if it wasn't a con? What if Big Al had pulled a double cross on him, gotten him out for real and for good?

"So you're a PNG and an N.A." Joey rolled his eyes. "You'll be lucky if they serve you in restaurants."

"I know. But what can I do?" His stomach lurched. If this was for real, he was also S.O.L.

"How you fixed for funds?"

I'd be fixed better if you hadn't been such a selfish bastard, Deuce thought, but held out a hand, said, "Oh, okay."

"Listen, I got friends need things done." He scratched his cheek. Joey usually scratched his cheek when he was nervous. Like when he was going to bluff in poker or when he was going to lie.

"Like what?"

"Oh." He paused. Clearly he hadn't thought that far ahead. "Well, one of them wants an update on the Smith's secret weapon."

Deuce laughed. "Don't we all."

"No, listen. Guy I played cards with this morning, he tells me the Scarlattis stole it."

"Get outta town."

"Truth," Joey said. "That's how's come the Ditwac is messed up. For payback. Or the beginnings of it," he added ominously.

"Not for the Scarlattis stealing the Smiths' cache of Chan drugs," Deuce said slowly, as his mind began to work.

"Drugs, schmugs. Everybody steals drugs all the time. Who'd upset the Ditwac for that? No, it was for stealing the Smith's secret weapon," Joey insisted. "The souped-up QIC."

Deuce was thunderstruck. "Like who in the Scarlattis do they think stole it?"

"Dunno." Joey scratched his cheek again. "Who was that guy got whacked?"

"Gino? You're telling me *Gino* stole it? Hey, Joey, you puttin' me on?"

"Deuce, this guy will pay you four thousand credits for new information." He actually turned red. "And I'm putting some money in your account on my own. You're my brother."

"Who was this guy you played cards with?" Joey scratched his cheek again. "Joey, *mio fratello*, look. I know you are not telling me the entire story here."

"What?" Joey asked, all wide-eyed innocence.

"Who was it told you that Gino Scarlatti stole the Smith's big toy?"

"Okay. It was a dame," he added. "That's all I'm saying."

"Don't you trust me?"

"Hey, since the Scarlattis invented all that weird crap,

I'm not doing full disclosure on no comm linkups. *Capisce*?"

"*Si*," Deuce said. A dame. "Hey, Joey, is it Dian—"

"I gotta go," Joey said, glancing over his shoulder. In the background a shadow moved.

Deuce's heart leaped into his skull. "Joey, behind you . . ."

"Yeah, doll, just talkin' to my bookie." Joey said to the shadow. He raised and lowered his eyebrows. "Can you place those bets for me, Carson?"

"Sure. *Ciao*," Deuce said, and disconnected.

Gino Scarlatti steals the weapon from the Smiths.

He makes an appointment with Wayne Van Aadams.

Now he's dead.

Tanzer and Feist talk to Deuce about offing Wayne.

Wayne adds them to his hit list.

Tanzer and Feist are dead.

Tanzer dies with a dossier and Smith papers in his pockets. He makes sure his daughter gets the Smith papers and apparently wants Deuce to take her and the papers back to them to protect her with Smith Affiliation.

"Oh, God," Deuce whispered. None of Tanzer's deal was important to the story. Club and Spade, while important to Deuce personally, were also extra baggage. The boiled-down, take-home message of importance to the Moon at large was this: Gino Scarlatti had stolen the secret weapon from the Smiths and given it to the Moongoloid.

Wayne Van Aadams had the weapon.

Wayne Van Aadams.

No, that had to be wrong. It was too horrible to be true.

For about an hour, he stayed in the aichy and made exploratory calls, none of which went anywhere. He lurked around as he drove, hiding behind corners, going down the side streets. Like you could lurk very well in a car like that. Finally, satisfied that he was still alone, he slunk over to Little Wallace's cinder-block apartment colony, Moon over Miami.

In somebody's dreams who did not live there, pal.

The Miami was total N.A.: one big square of iridium-colored Moon dirt adobe. No frills, not even lined parking spaces. No playgrounds for the kids, just an empty lot littered with broken glass and Bad Moon cans.

The place reeked of things that were too old, and hardworking people who did not have that many credits that they wasted them on bathing all that often. Deuce remembered all the many times Little Wallace had shyly invited him over. Deuce had never gone. They'd met now and then in bars, and Deuce had bought him beers on occasion, but Deuce had never gone to his home. Now he was ashamed of himself, of his snobbery. Concerned about his great reputation, he hadn't wanted to be seen in an N.A.'s neighborhood if he didn't have to be. As far as he'd been concerned, the more business they could conduct offsite, the better.

Now Wallace was dead, and he would never know that Deuce had never seen a place more inviting than the decaying and anonymous hovel before him.

"Watch your car, mister?" asked a girl in ragged clothes with a bandage over one eye. She didn't look like she could do much if someone messed with the aichy, which stood out like a pile of estate jewelry amidst the dross in the parking lot. Still, he nodded and swiped her account strip, realizing the exchange of financial information gave someone a fresh trail to him.

Hell with it.

He went through the main entrance and escalated to the twelfth floor, Little Wallace's floor. He coded Little Wallace's door, pausing on the threshold when the door hissed. Almost as a reflex, he found himself wishing for a font of holy water so he could cross himself before he went in. For all he knew, the whole place would blow as soon as the floor recognized his foot pressure.

Nothing happened as he walked in and a dingy overhead light dimmed on. The light said, "Hello," in a friendly, noncommittal way, illuminating a dull, ugly square of a place dominated by a floorside sofa bed, an ancient viso, and a coffee table with a heating element on the top and a deepfreeze beneath. An alcove for storage and another for prayers, and that was it.

What a wretched existence. No wonder he had loved living Deuce's life.

Deuce sat on the sofa bed. The room was eerily silent. No dog to gabble happily that he was home. No furnishings calling him Miss Sparkle.

He didn't think he could bear staying here. But he figured if he could just manage to stay alive until five, he'd have a much better picture of the lay of the land.

He opened the freeze and found an off-brand frozen dinner of craterchicken, mashed potatoes, and peas. He cooked it and devoured it. Then he picked up the viso control and flicked it on. *Phases* was on. Somewhere in a reclaimed Earthside rain forest, Devon LeDare was crashing through a doorway, surprising guys with guns that shot actual bullets, as opposed to the blasters they had here on the Moon. They were drug dealers who had kidnapped LeDare's wife. Deuce was disappointed. He hadn't seen an episode in almost a month and nothing new was happening.

He fished around the sofa for a mini, found none. You couldn't live without a mini in this day and age, could you?

There was something on top of the viso. Nodding to himself that he'd located it, he got up and crossed to the box.

It wasn't a mini, but a small stack of printed pamphlets. Intrigued by the feel of paper, Deuce picked them up.

THE MOON FOR MOONSIDERS. TELL THE FAMILIES TO GET THE HELL OFF OUR ROCK!

N.A. = FREEDOM!

"Little Wallace?" Deuce asked quietly, perplexed. He riffled through the stack. They were propaganda pamphlets for the MLF. Had Little Wallace been a member?

Deuce opened one of the leaflets. A very unflattering pic of Big Al was overlaid in a holo over a shot of a man lying in a crater. The dead man had been dug up. The caption read. "WHEN YOU GO TOPSIDE, NO ONE CAN HEAR YOU SCREAM."

"Yeah, so?" Deuce asked, irritated. Nothing made any noise Topside. There was no freakin' air on the surface. You could blow up the entire Moon and you wouldn't hear anything. Was that the fault of the Families?

And anyway, Deuce recognized the dead man. It was

Bernie "Best Bet" Borgioli. Bernie had skimmed funds off the top of the Borgioli house percentage for years. Big Al had known about it and let him live. Hell, even let him do it, although it was terrible for their image as well as the morale of the more honest Borgioli affiliates (if such could be found.)

Deuce had no idea why Bernie had been so favored, but he had been. Bernie had met his demise not at the hands of Big Al, but at the behest of Chicky Smith, who had caught him, ah, in a delicate position with Chicky's midget girl friend, Angelina Rille. Angelina, who had never bothered with leg extensions (then again, not all women did, although all showgirls did), measured in at only five-foot-three. She was probably the shortest woman on the Moon except for lady tourists, and everyone thought she was a freak. Apparently at least two men on the Moon thought otherwise.

But the implication of the pamphlet was that Big Al had killed Bernie.

Hey, you got whacked on orders of Big Al, nobody ever found you again, much less dug you up in a freakin' crater. That was one thing Big Al was definitely good at. This pamphlet was not only inaccurate, it was insulting.

But the next one was worse. It showed—

The door hissed. Deuce dropped the pamphlets, pulled out his blaster, and crouched behind the sofa bed.

None other than Angelina herself stood in the doorway. She glanced up at the light and yanked out a blaster, throwing herself back outside.

"Come out," she ordered.

She wasn't ugly or even freakish, just strangely little. Deuce wondered if she was also a good shot, which would be even stranger. Family girlfriends stayed oddly vulnerable. He supposed it was because when you were in Vendetta, you never messed with peripheral Family. That was one thing that had made the Scarlattis' genocide of the Mitchells so heinous.

Another was that they had never officially declared Vendetta against them.

Deuce didn't move. If this little lady was here to rub him out, she'd have to make some effort.

After about half a minute, she said, "I know somebody's in here. Come out or I'll just start shooting."

In someone's home in the middle of the day? He didn't think so. The cops would be there before her weapon had time to recharge.

He waited some more. There was silence. He bet she was calling in that she'd found him.

Deuce got up from behind the couch—his knees cricked; man he was tired—and glided to the still-open door. With the agility of a well-practiced kickboxer, he aiya'ed! through the threshold, spotted her murmuring to herself, batted her hand from her comm badge, tapped it off, and said, "Come in here."

"Who . . . ?"

"Don't give me that," he said, but she still looked blank. "How much am I worth?"

"I'm sorry?" She moved her shoulders. "What are you doing in Wally's apartment?"

"It won't do any good to play dumb, doll," he said threateningly.

She brightened. "You're Deuce," she said. "Wally's friend."

He decided to admit it. Hell, if she was here to hit him, she already knew who he was. "Yeah. Deuce. Yes." He held out his hand for her to come inside. She demurred, standing her ground. "*Mi scusi*, but it's cold in here," he added, indicating that they should get away from the doorway.

"You've got people after you," she said angrily. "Which is why Wally got killed." Her eyes flashed. She was actually pretty good-looking in her odd, elfin way. Perfectly proportioned. Just . . . little.

Short. That was all. Short.

He held out a hand and smiled the smile that worked on all but a few. She took a deep breath and sailed past him into Little Wallace's room.

"Who'd you call?" he asked. He watched her, wondering if she should tell him the truth.

She looked down at the floor and spotted the pamphlets. Her mouth twisted unhappily at the picture of Big Al and Best Bet. "I thought you didn't know who I was."

"In relation to Little Wallace. Wally," he added smoothly.

Her eyes filled with tears. "He loved it that you called him that. He loved your whole stupid Family thing." Tears spilled down her cheeks. "Your whole stupid Family thing that got him killed." *And Best Bet Bernie, too*, he thought, *only that had been* her *whole stupid Family thing*. And if he had the latest information (who knew anymore?) she was still with Chicky Smith, which was unbelievably stupid. But that he kept to himself.

"*Mi dispiace*," he said automatically, realizing it was just about the worst thing he could have said, because only the Families spoke Italian anymore. Not even N.A. Italians—if there were such people—spoke Italian. "Signorina, uh, that is, Miss Angelina—"

"Oh!" she sobbed, and fell into his arms. She threw herself around him and wept hard, bitter tears. "I loved that big lug. I loved him."

He thought she might mean Best Bet, but he said carefully, "Little Wallace?"

She regained her composure, pulling herself out of his embrace and wiping her face. "He was a brother to me."

"In the movement," he said, guessing. She flushed to her roots. "In the MLF."

"He shouldn't have told you," she blurted, then covered her mouth when she realized what she'd done.

"Yeah, well." He didn't know what to say. He felt like he'd been had. He was almost angry at Little Wallace, but not really. Being in the MLF was probably the biggest excitement N.A.'s could find. But Angelina? She was liaised inside a Family.

She ran a hand through her hair and looked at him with real terror in her eyes. As well she should: If the Smiths found out she was in the MLF, they'd probably do the crater thing on her, too.

The MLF was as big a thorn in the side of the Families as the Department of Fairness back on Earth. The MLF were like unbearable little mosquitoes, just kept biting at you and biting at you and buzzing their little buzzy B.S. to the Fairness flacks in a perpetual attempt to get rid of the Families. It was foolish of them: Lose the casinos, you lost the lifeblood of the entire Moon. The MLF thought otherwise, thought they could figure out some way to support the population in a "decent" way (their word, give me a freakin' break).

Every once in a while, a MLF leader disappeared.

"Miss Angelina," he said, touching his heart, "I have no beef with you. But you have to tell me who you called."

She shook her head. "I got a machine. I had only started to leave a message."

"Tell me the truth. I won't hurt you."

"You'll sell me out the minute there's profit in it. That's they way you all are."

"Would Little Wallace have agreed with that notion?" he asked softly.

They regarded each other. Fresh tears slid down her face; her eyes must have recharged. She said, "He believed you to be a man of honor."

"For all of me being a Borgioli, that's true," he said, then remembered Best Bet Bernie, his brother Borgioli, and tried to frame an apology.

She must have read his expression, for her mouth twisted in an ugly smile, and she said, "I've made some big mistakes, Mr. McNamara. The size of which you can only begin to imagine."

"Hanging with the MLF being the biggest," he shot back at her. "Hey, Miss Angelina, what do you want with these people?" He tapped the pamphlet with his fingertips. "You have a Family liaison. This isn't for you."

"What are you doing here?" she demanded, changing the subject.

"I'm asking you the same thing," he said.

She threw back her head. "I'm collecting Wally's things for his mother."

"Oh." Deuce was sad, and very sorry, as he thought of Little Wallace's mamma, even though he had never met her and had no idea what she looked like. Red eyes from crying, a tight, thin face from not eating. It was always the mothers who suffered the most.

She looked at him. He decided to be straight with her, mostly because she probably knew what the deal was with him if she'd talked to Wally lately.

"I'm N.A. Got kicked out of my Family for some of those honkin' big mistakes you were just mentioning."

"At least you didn't end up in a crater," she said bitterly. "Yet."

"Don Alberto ain't like that," he said, but that wasn't exactly so.

She sat down on the sofa bed and picked up a cushion, hugged it to her chest. He couldn't help but stare at her legs. They were so short. Chicky Smith was one kinky *paisan*.

"What're you looking at?" she flung at him. He made a, "Who, me?" gesture and picked up the pamphlets he'd dropped on the floor.

"It really was a machine," she said. "Not everybody likes to stay in constant contact all the time. I only got as far as leaving my name."

"Truth?"

"Truth." She looked at him askance. "Why are you so nervous?"

"I'm N.A., and there are two Unsanctioned hit men after me," he told her. "It might be safer for you if you left."

"Oh, I was followed here," she said. "Chicky's men follow me everywhere."

"They know you're in the MLF?" he asked, taken aback.

Through her tears, she gave him a sly half grin. "Give me some credit. They think Wally was a distant relative, is all."

He grinned back, but in the back of his head he wondered if perhaps that was why Little Wallace had been killed, instead of because of him. But no, it had been his locker that had blown Little Wallace up.

"A distant relative. How come they believe that?"

"I set it up that way," she retorted. "Give me some—"

"Okay. We'll work on that credit thing." What a

strange, short, interesting woman. He couldn't help but like her. "Now, what are we going to do about each other?" She didn't react. He wasn't sure she was following him. "I got something on you, and you got something on me."

"Is there a reward out on you?" she asked.

"You mean, wanted dead or dead? Sure."

"Well, there's also a reward on naming members of the MLF," she countered. She reached in her pocket. He tensed. She pulled out an account strip.

He raised his brows. "You're going to bribe me? Won't Mr. Smith dislike that?"

"I'll deal with that later," she said. "You know how it is." When he didn't respond—because he didn't know where she was going with that—she asked, "You know, with women and Family guys. We can tell a lot of little fibs. Don't you have a girlfriend?"

Too many people had been inquiring about his love life lately. He tried to look calm. "No." And that was the truth, wasn't it?

"Oh." She hesitated. "A guy like you, I would have thought you did."

It was a compliment. Or else he took it as such.

She rose and put the strip back in her pocket. "You can't begin to imagine what your life as an N.A. is going to be like," she said pityingly. "Especially since you're Dis-Membered. Dis-Affiliated would be a little better."

"Yeah, I figured that," he said sorrowfully. "I've already had to escalate my way around a couple times." It really sucks."

She laughed harshly. "Oh, man, you're really going to be in for it." She took a breath. "There's an MLF meeting on the twenty-ninth. Maybe you should go."

"Don't tell me about it, Miss Angelina," he warned her.

"Why not? You're N.A. now."

"I might try to Re-Member. Or go to a new Family."

She laughed again. "Who're you kidding? You're out for the rest of your life. Look, the MLF can offer you a lot of good things. We're looking for guys like you, guys who can get things done."

Was she really so naive, or was she really so clever? He shook his head.

She persisted. "We're tired of being pushed around. It's time to get serious."

"Miss Angelina, I don't want to know too much about your private business. Really." He flashed her the Smile. "I like you." The twenty-ninth. He should get the location, too.

But the problem was, he did like her. He didn't want to know about her revolution. Didn't want to have anything to report on it, dumb though that might be. They'd never get anywhere worth going anyway. And more importantly, he had to concentrate on the matter at hand. Namely, seeing if Wayne Van Aadams really had the Doomsday Machine.

She flashed him her own version of the Smile. "Okay, you win. Help me pack my friend's stuff, and I'll forget I ever saw you."

Angelina left at four with three sad little boxes piled in her arms like baby animals. The sofa bed and the combo table had come with the big box that was the apartment. Three boxes. Not much to show for a man's life. Deuce hoped Little Wallace's cause had given him some measure of meaning.

Besides being morose, Deuce was exhausted. All he wanted to do was hiss out the sofa bed and go to sleep. He had barely enough time to shower. Places like this charged you in advance for a ration of water and utilities, and it was always a scramble to make your ration last. It was a holdover from the early days, and good enough for N.Λ.'s.

At 4:45, he de-escalated out of the building, found the urchin who had volunteered herself to guard his car—she was merrily playing low-grav hopscotch with some other urchins; anyone could have planted any number of bombs in the exhaust of his new speedster—and gave her permission to go off duty.

Then he got into the aichy, said, "Take me to your leader," and leaned back. The aichy knew who its leader was, or must have been preprogrammed for this interesting little journey, because it said, "Yes, Mr. Deuce McNamara.

We will dock with *Gambler's Star* in approximately ten minutes.''

Deuce closed his eyes and took a deep breath. *Mamma mia*, what a good guess. Or else he was just too dumb to live that it had taken him this long to figure that this aichy was not so much a gift as a ticket to ride. Maybe it was the revelation about Wayne and the Smith weapon that had helped him correctly spin the tumblers. Helped him hit the reset button in his brain, as it were.

It was 4:48. ''Arrange my arrival time for twelve minutes,'' he told the machine. ''Five o'clock exactly.''

''Yes, Mr. McNamara. Five o'clock exactly.''

''Warn me of any dangers you notice.''

''No dangers perceived at present, sir.''

It took off.

He took another deep breath. No dangers at present.

He hoped that was a good guess, too.

FOURTEEN

L ooking back, Deuce would be amazed at three things: that
as nervous as he was, he could actually doze off en route
to his first meeting with Hunter Castle; and that as tempting
a target as he was, no one killed him before he got there.

Doze off he did, in the twelve minutes he had left of his
life B.C.—Before Castle—jerking awake when the aichy
announced, "Excuse me, Mr. McNamara. We are being
guided into a docking area by *Gambler's Star* traffic control."

That was the third amazing thing. He had expected to be
moved over past a lower level of Bugsy Siegel, down Si-
natra, and into Shaft THX 1138, where he would board a
shuttle that would take him through a surface airlock and
up to the orbiting ship. But what happened was, he somehow went directly through the airlock in his aichy. Apparently he was surrounded by some kind of enviro-shield.

It wasn't until that moment that he realized he'd lost his
enviro-suit in the explosion that had taken the life of his
aichy. Talk about terrifying.

He looked up and tried to whistle. Anyone who had ever
watched a viso had seen *Gambler's Star* speed grandly
across the screen during the station identification of the majority of the channels, those being the ones Castle owned.

But when you saw her in person, you almost wet your
freakin' pants.

She was enormous, larger than any cruiser or transport
Deuce had ever seen. You could fit several hundred aichies

just like his inside her, maybe several thousand. From this angle he couldn't see her in her entirety.

You could call her ostentatious, only she wasn't. You could call her a miracle of modern engineering, which she was.

Completely black, her running lights were like small, snakelike eyes blinking on dorsal fins. Rows of illuminated windows ringed the starboard side, which he was facing, and shadows moved across them. How many hundreds were in her crew?

He started taking mental notes. The slight bulge at the stern must be where her reactor was. He couldn't see as far as the bow. She was as sleek as a matte black stingray (not that he had ever actually seen a stingray); he thought of flatphotos he had seen of antique flying craft like the Stealth bomber of the twentieth century and the *Kitty Hawk* aircraft carrier from the same era, and gas movies of later vessels like the *Harsh Mistress*, the battle cruiser upon which nine thousand had lived during the Quantum Instability Wars.

As he craned his neck, he was startled when it seemed that the section nearest him disappeared, flickered, then reappeared at a slightly different angle. Must be the docking illumination. But no wonder people thought it was from another planet.

His aichy canted at an angle at the same time that a docking hangar slid open gracefully and slowly. From somewhere in the bubble memory of his mental associations, Deuce found himself humming "The Blue Danube," an ancient Earth waltz.

The aichy neared the hangar. Deuce swallowed hard. "It's a perfect night for a rumble."

"Yes, Mr. McNamara. I hope you're packing a weapon," the aichy replied, and Deuce managed a grin. This car was a sassy little thing. Well programmed, too. Whoever had done it had to have a sense of humor.

He relaxed a tad. Hell, Castle was just a man, he could point at you and you wouldn't disintegrate into dust. It wasn't like an invasion or anything. Perhaps it didn't have to mean the end of life as everyone knew it.

It wasn't like the aliens were landing.

Except that Deuce was twenty-five, and Castle had never been here in Deuce's entire life. On a verified visit, anyway, he reminded himself. More people had claimed to see Castle than Elvis, but no one had ever paid any attention. They figured he'd come the way he had come, with fanfare and hooplah and scaring the wits out of everybody.

The hangar door did something weird, unfolded or expanded, so that the aichy passed through an aperture much larger than it had at first seemed to be. The speaker in the aichy pulled in sound: pfft, pfft, he heard the exchange of vacuum for air, as brilliant lights burned across his field of vision. He squinted. He waited for the sound of the airlock shutting, heard nothing.

Then the lights dimmed to a manageable level, and he unbuckled his seat belt.

"Please exit," the aichy told him politely. "Have a pleasant stay."

The wing door popped open. Feeling for his blaster, Deuce climbed out.

The docking area was painted with Castle's colors. Black was predominant, with just a hint of orange here and there, in racing stripes and flickering stars in the corners that shifted in hue and intensity. Holos, maybe.

If it had been up to Deuce, he'd have used colors like dark purple, blue, and black, done a medieval theme. Castles. Maybe superimposed a dragon, a sword, something like that. Castle didn't have an actual logo, just his name in hurried-looking letters.

Two tall men—that is, tall for men—in white suits and wraparound sunglasses appeared on an overhang maybe twenty feet above Deuce. Hail, the bothersome paramour. Moving in unison, they started down a flight of stairs. They were handling the lower gravity beautifully. They got down to Deuce's level and approached. Both had black-and-orange handkerchiefs in their breast pockets. He wished he had called Sparkle, at least to say good-bye, just in case.

"Mr. McNamara, hello," said one of the men. Coming in at about seven and a half feet, they were twins, or clones, with long, chiseled faces, gray-and-blond goatees, and loose blond hair that brushed their shoulders. As one, they removed their sunglasses and put them in their breast pockets behind the hankies. They had steel gray eyes, a bit blood-shot and tired-looking. If they were mechanicals, they were damn good ones. It took a lot of tinkering to imitate human frailties such as exhaustion.

"Gentlemen," he said, succeeding at a businesslike, not-totally-terrorized tone of voice. "My card." He gave them Castle's business card, just in case proof of purchase was required. His own card was now obsolete, and he had no idea if these guys would understand the situation if they ran it through and it came up bogus.

"Thank you, sir," Man in White A said, taking and pocketing it as if it was the most normal thing to do.

Man in White B moved to one side and made a sweeping gesture. "If you please, sir."

They went through a door, and Deuce started digesting everything he saw as fast as he could. The passageway they walked through was sleek and curved, well lit, and the bulkheads—probably he would call them walls, since so far this ship looked nothing like a ship—were holos of a pasture. On his right, two beautiful white horses galloped in the background. As Deuce and the Men in White combo walked along, the holo parallax shifted in perfect synchro-nization with his speed. The horses whinnied. He smelled grass and the merest bit of horse manure. It was by far the best holo he had ever seen.

Even more amazing, however, was that the horses gal-loped across the passageway and cantered alongside Man in White B, now on the opposite wall. They continued frol-icking back and forth the entire length of the passageway, which seemed to go on and on and on.

"How old is this vessel?" he asked Man in White A, because he was overwhelmed and needed to say something. Better a question than a dumb remark designed to display his keen wit and total absence of astonishment.

"It's been in Mr. Castle's family for generations," the man replied. "Of course it's continually updated."

"Oh, of course," Deuce retorted with a hint of sarcasm, and shut his eyes in self-recrimination. It was 5:07, if any-one wanted to know.

''Mr. Castle is waiting for you in the conference room,'' Man in White B said helpfully. Deuce wondered if these two guys ever beat people up. If, when they did, they asked you if you preferred a black-and-orange hankie or a more ordinary white one for your bloody, broken nose.

''Guess he's pretty busy taking over the Moon, huh,'' Deuce drawled. He wanted to kick himself.

''Mr. Castle is always busy,'' Man in White A said.

They departed the pasture when they turned a corner. This was a marine-themed area, with pounding surf and sandy beaches. Deuce swore he smelled the salt air. Gulls squawked. You couldn't have birds on the Moon because they needed heavier gravity to swallow.

They came to a pair of doors holoed with swirls of ocean waves and Castle's immense yacht, the *Huntress*, cutting through the water. Deuce had also never seen an ocean. The seas of the Moon were dry as the rest of the Moon, of course. But right then Deuce was sweating so much he could probably fill the Sea of Crises.

The doors hissed open, and Deuce took a long, slow breath as the men disengaged and left him.

The conference room was as big as the hangar he'd been docked in. The ceiling rose from a sharp angle beginning at the top of a panoramic window revealing black, starry space and soaring to what he supposed you would call a skylight. How you got windows like that on a spaceship, Deuce had no idea. They made him horribly nervous.

Enormous statues of knights in shining armor—the proper Castle motif at last!—flanked a conference table that seemed as long as the horse-pasture corridor. The entire joint glittered with trophies. There were lots of shiny old-fashioned hardbody ones, the kind with angels and guys in togas and eagles with their wings spread. What a lot of weight to cart up here. There were holos, encapsulating the winning moment: Castle flying across the finish line in a footrace; Castle jogging to the tennis net to shake the hand of his vanquished foe; a yacht emblazoned with *Gambler's Star II* on its hull sailing past a buoy with all hands in natty orange-and-black sailing outfits cheering. Criminy, how many yachts did the guy own?

There were pictures on the walls, statics and gas, of Castle shaking hands or otherwise mugging it up with all kinds of celebrities, from movie stars including Devon LeDare, to the famous pop group, DaVinci and the Variations (their current number one hit: "The Old Moon in the Young Moon's Arms"), to the current president of the Conglomerated Nations. Brag, brag, brag.

And centered in Deuce's field of vision, seated at the end of the conference table, sat the big man himself, Mr. Hunter Castle. Deuce was almost shocked. Not big. Not tall, not imposing, but yet the air surrounding him crackled with authority and command as he spoke into a bank of comm links, raising one hand toward Deuce in a request for a minute or two to tie things up.

He wore a black suit, a better choice than white for his salt-and-pepper hair, his nearly black eyes, the devilish goatee. And far better than orange, which would have billed him either as a tourist or a Borgioli pimped up for a hot date.

Thanks to Sparkle, Deuce knew a bit from fashion, and he knew this suit was hand-made for this man and this man alone. It was nice material. Expensive. Maybe even real wool.

"I don't care, Charlie," Castle was saying. "Buy it." He disconnected manually and looked up at Deuce. He smiled and rose. Okay, he was a bit taller than Deuce had guessed. Still, not a frightening man.

"Good evening, Mr. McNamara," Hunter Castle said. His voice was deeper than on the viso.

"*Buona sera*," Deuce replied. His voice was higher than in real life.

"I hope you had an uneventful journey."

"As uneventful as they come," Deuce replied. "It's a nice vehicle."

"Thanks. I make them. Would you care for a drink, *signor*? I believe your favorite choice is Atherton Gold. Mr. Wong." At a wave of Castle's hand, a uniformed man came gliding into the room from a side door with a silver tray, a bottle, and two shot glasses. The man was a mechanical.

"Speaking of shots," Deuce said boldly, though of

course no one had uttered the word, ''Mr. Castle, you got a hit out on me?''

Castle blinked. Then he chuckled and gestured for Deuce to sit down. Deuce stayed standing. Castle shrugged and poured the Atherton Gold. What was he going to do, slide it down the table like a beer mug down Trini Golden's bar?

''I see you're the kind of man who dispenses with unnecessary pleasantries.'' He took one of the shot glasses. The robot started down the table toward Deuce with the tray.

Deuce said carefully, ''I've had a long day, Mr. Castle. You probably sat in your fancy stuffed chair studying market reports, but I've been a lot more physically active.''

The robot approached him and extended the tray. Castle said, ''Have a drink. You look like you could use one.''

Deuce scratched the back of his neck. ''How do you expect me to look, with what you've put me through?''

''I?'' Castle looked aggrieved.

''Yeah.'' Deuce slugged back his shot. It hit the spot.

''I was going to propose a toast,'' Castle said. ''To my casino.''

''Oh, yeah,'' Deuce said. ''I heard about that.'' He looked at Mr. Wong, who dipped the tray toward him. Deuce poured himself another shot. Castle still did not drink.

''We'll be joined shortly,'' Castle said.

As if on cue, the doors hissed, and another man walked into the room. He was of medium build, with sandy brown hair and do-nothing, see-nothing eyes. He wore a boring gray suit. He would make a perfect *assassino* because he was completely forgettable.

Deuce swallowed hard.

''This is Mr. Epperson-Roux,'' Castle announced. Epperson-Roux inclined his head.

No kidding? Deuce leaned forward. The mystery man himself.

''*Buona sera*,'' he said.

''*Buona sera, signor*,'' Epperson-Roux replied. Deuce was intrigued not only that he replied in a Family way but by the man's impeccable accent. Was he a Family man?

He wore no colors. More significantly, there wasn't a speck of black or orange on him.

"I hope the aichy was to your satisfaction?" Castle asked, and that was the end of the spotlight on Mr. Epperson-Roux.

"*Sì, grazie*," Deuce said uneasily, wondering if he was supposed to wax on about the car or grovel or what. He said simply, "Thanks for the lift." He fished the keys out of his pocket and held them out to Castle as if he understood that the fabulous speedster had been nothing more than a loaner.

Then, exhibiting a bravado he suddenly felt nowhere in his body, Deuce pulled out a chair and sat.

Mr. Wong went to a wet bar to the left and got another shot glass. He poured Epperson-Roux a drink.

"We were just toasting the future," Castle told the newcomer. He and Epperson-Roux both drank. Deuce hesitated.

"Mr. Castle, I mean no disrespect, but you can't just waltz onto our turf and start playing with our toys." At least Deuce didn't think he could. Probably, if anyone could, it would be him, though.

Epperson-Roux gave Castle a look that Deuce couldn't decipher. Nevertheless he logged it for later and waited for Castle to respond.

"We?" Castle echoed.

Deuce fought his nervousness down. *He's just a man*, he told himself. *Just flesh and blood. No big deal*. "The Families."

"Oh, I'd heard you were N.A.," Castle said, possibly not realizing this was a grave insult. Or possibly not giving a damn.

Deuce said nothing. Castle appraised him. "Which is why I invited you here. I need someone neutral to go over things with."

"Someone neutral?" Deuce glanced at him sidelong. "You try to whack me, you let me buy stock, you give me, I mean, lend me, a car, and you think I'm neutral?"

Castle laughed. "I knew I'd like you. I propose a toast. A different toast," he added, as Deuce started to protest. "To the beautiful Miss Sparkle."

Deuce's mouth dropped open as Sparkle entered the room and sat down beside him. She was wearing a slinky silver jumpsuit he'd never seen before. Her platinum hair was pulled back and dangled down her back like a silver waterfall with a strobe light on it. She had on fairly heavy makeup, and her nails were still on.

She was gorgeous.

Mr. Wong waited for instructions. She said politely, "Water, please," and he moved away to fulfill her request.

"Sparkle?" Deuce murmured. She gazed at him with her heavily lined eyes and she looked like someone else, like someone he'd never boinked before. "Baby, what's going on? Why are you here?"

"It seems we have a mutual friend," Castle supplied.

"Yeah?" Deuce asked belligerently. "Who?"

Castle smiled at him. "You."

Sparkle didn't smile. She didn't do anything. Then he saw she had on a diamond bracelet. He had never seen that bracelet before. He had never heard about it until today. Her and her real red roses.

Flaring, Deuce pushed back his chair. "I'm going now."

"Where?" Castle asked. "To do what?"

He was blowing it. Who wouldn't, after the day he'd had? Big Al would kill him if he walked out of this room. Or someone else would.

"What do you want with us?" Deuce put his hand on Sparkle's shoulder. "I don't like games." He looked around. "But you do, don't you, Mr. Castle?" He pulled his deck out of his pocket. "Tell you what. You're low, you tell me what's going on. High, I stay with no questions asked."

Castle shook his head. "That's probably a marked deck."

Deuce drew himself up, but it was Sparkle who said, "Mr. Castle, Deuce is a straight shooter." Sparkle's highest compliment. He calmed down a little.

A little.

Castle shrugged. "You should know, *mademoiselle*. All right."

Deuce laid the deck on the table and shuffled the deck.

He had Sparkle cut. He shuffled again, walked the seventeen miles down to the end of the table, and fanned the deck out on the table. For a moment he was distracted by the very large array of comm links, screens, and scanners on Castle's console. He didn't believe he'd seen that much communications hardware in his life, even when he and Joey had gone to Moonport Traffcom with the Boy Scouts.

Castle picked a card and turned it over. It was a seven.

Deuce closed his eyes and wished on the gambler's star. The real one.

He had an eight.

Castle chuckled. "All right." He moved his shoulders. "It's no mystery, Mr. McNamara. As I said before, I'm here to build a casino."

Deuce frowned at him. "That's not a good answer."

"It wasn't a good question."

Deuce gathered up the deck with one flick of his wrist. "The only way you can do that is if all six Families agree to let you in. And who's going to make that happen?"

Castle just smiled.

Deuce persisted. "I know you're loaded. But with all due respect, you can't just buy your way onto the Moon. The Families built this place with their bare hands."

"I thought your people did the real work," Castle jibed. "The Non-Affiliateds, I mean."

Deuce opened his mouth to protest, then realized he had a possible new angle here. He raised his chin. "We prefer the more politically correct term of Independents."

"Of course. My apologies. And to you as well, ma'am," he added, inclining his head toward Sparkle. For a minute Deuce thought the man was going to air-kiss her hand. Hunter Castle was every inch the slick Southern gent, oozing magnolia blossoms while he held all the aces.

Deuce flashed, "You can't just come in and play the table maximum."

"No?" Castle continued to smile at Sparkle.

"No." Deuce fought down his growing anger. "Look, even though I won the wager, I still don't know what you've got planned, and I sure don't as hell know why you sent for me."

Castle ticked his gaze toward Deuce and held up a finger. "Not sent for you. Invited you."

"Yeah, well. For a guy like you, it's the same thing, isn't it? This is not a table I can walk away from."

Castle chuckled again. Deuce didn't like all this chuckling.

He looked at Sparkle, who, while appearing perfectly at ease, wasn't relaxed, either. But, damn it, she looked like she belonged here. Like it was okay if Hunter Castle air-kissed her hand.

On the other hand, Epperson-Roux was clearly nervous. That was interesting.

"I sense I need to prove myself to you," Castle observed.

Why? He'd already proven himself to the entire satellite. The Families were going berserk.

Deuce glanced around at the trophies, the photographs, and thought of the twin Men in White, created or hired on in Castle's own image. The guy was ultracompetitive. He wanted everybody to buy his B.S. In short, it was bugging him that Deuce was not acting all polite and solicitous.

So Deuce decided to bug him some more, see what happened. "Yeah, you do need to prove yourself to me," he challenged. "Because so far I'm not all that impressed."

"I'm sorry I'm such a disappointment to y'all," Castle replied, not looking sorry at all.

Deuce waited. He didn't know what else to do.

They sat in silence. Sparkle sipped her drink. Deuce tried to swallow. Finally, Castle cocked his head. "I've been planning to hand a lot of money out to show my goodwill. My respect, as it were."

Deuce flung out, "It'll cost more than a few measly shares of Palace Industrials." He realized it sounded like he could be bought after all—which he probably could; maybe it depended on who was selling what—and tried again. "What I mean is—"

Suddenly Sparkle sat up a little straighter. She said in a strange, dreamy voice, "A wrestling match."

Castle looked at her eagerly. Deuce frowned and said, *"Cara, mi scusi?"*

Her eyes closed, opened. She stared as nothing, gaze vacant, the way she did when she was figuring amortization rates or counting cards. Then she nodded. "Your man against his man."

"His?" Castle leaned forward.

"Deuce's." Then she shook her head and cleared her throat. Her lids fluttered. Softly she murmured, "God, I'm thirsty."

"Mr. Wong, fetch the lady a drink," Castle said. "A real one. That's it, then. We'll hold a wrestling match."

Deuce watched in amazement as Sparkle threw back a shot of Atherton Gold. She was turning into a regular booze hound.

"*What*?" Deuce said in total bewilderment.

"You and I are going to hold a wrestling match," Castle said again, as if Deuce merely hadn't heard him. He looked at his associate, Epperson-Roux. "What do you think, Emerson?" Emerson, huh? Deuce took note of the usage of the first name and started his own little subdirectory on the meeting: SEEMINGLY MEANINGLESS DETAILS.

Epperson-Roux said, "I can't really offer you an opinion, Mr. Castle." Item Number 2 of SMD file: *Mr. Castle.*

"Sparkle, what the hell are you talking about?" Deuce demanded. Whatever he had expected from this meeting, it was not to be arranging wrestling matches. Castle grinned at Sparkle and Deuce as if they were the cute couple they were supposed to be. Deuce suppressed the urge to whirl around to see if a blaster was aimed at his back.

"I'm not sure," she said softly. She looked tired.

"What are the stakes?" Castle asked, watching her closely.

"If Deuce wins, you triple his stock holdings," Sparkle said. "His Palace Industrials." Deuce was even more flabbergasted.

"And if I win?" Castle asked. He stroked his goatee. "Dinner with you, Miss Sparkle?"

"No," Deuce said flatly, at the same time that Sparkle said, "You're on, Castle."

"All right, then." Castle looked pleased. Deuce was not so much, but at least she hadn't called him, "Hunter."

"Wait. Stop. I don't get any of this," Deuce said.

"We'll drum up a little interest," Castle went on. "We'll sell tickets and donate the money to the schools. The Independent schools. Not the private Family schools."

Mr. Epperson-Roux nodded. "Excellent idea, Mr. Castle. That will go a long way for you."

"At whose casino?" Castle asked. He shook his head. "Bad idea. Everyone will think that means something. Neutral territory, then."

Deuce said in surprise, "Schirra Hall?" It was the N.A. convention center and pretty much of a dump.

Epperson-Roux said, "It will please the Independents."

"Agreed," Castle said happily. "How about next Saturday?"

"It's probably booked," Deuce said, cast adrift. No, make that drowning. "Some concert or something."

Castle waved his hand over the table. Deuce realized he had a built-in mini. "Let's see. That's the twenty-ninth." He looked up. "You're right. It's a, hmm, political rally. Probably MLF." He shrugged. "I'm sure they could accommodate us for a sizable donation to their schools, don't you think, *signor*?"

"Beats me." Deuce didn't get this at all.

"I'm sure they could," Epperson-Roux said warmly. He reminded Deuce of a schoolteacher, kind of prim and nicey-nice.

"Great. I'll get my people on it." Castle hesitated. "Unless you want your people involved, Mr. McNamara?"

Deuce was just about to tell him to give him a break; they both knew he didn't have any people. Then it occurred to him that he just might have. With this kind of wager in his pocket, he could grab a lot more action than you got with a few rolls of toilet paper.

"With all respect, Mr. Castle," he said, "Miss de Lune and I have another appointment. We'll have to get back to you on all the details." He and Miss de Lune had some big-time talking to do.

Sparkle uncrossed her fabulous legs and stood in unison with Deuce.

"Very well." Castle hissed a square on the table, and a

business card appeared. "This is Jameson Jackson's number. He's my executive assistant. He's at your full disposal. Call him anytime."

Sparkle slipped the card into the bodice of her jumpsuit. Deuce frowned. He would have been happy to hold it for her.

"It's been delightful," Castle said, including them both. "I look forward to more of these little meetings. Oh, and to expedite that . . ." He handed Deuce back the keys. "Please, I insist."

As nonchalantly as he could, Deuce took them, and said, *"Mille grazie, signor."*

"Prego," Castle answered.

They all shook hands, including the mysterious Emerson-Roux, and then Deuce and Sparkle were escorted back to the hangar by his old friends, Clones A and B. It was only then that Deuce noticed the sleek black stretch aichy bouncing on the air at the far end of the vast hangar.

"You come in that?" he whispered to Sparkle, who nodded.

"I'd better come with you now, though," she said.

"Yeah, you'd better." He was reeling.

"By the way, I kenneled Moona Lisa," Sparkle said.

"You went to the apartment?" He was furious. "Sparkle—"

"It was fine. There was no action," she said, shrugging.

That was puzzling. He would have at least expected a bomb.

They reached the beautiful aichy. Deuce told it to open the doors, made sure Sparkle was in okay, then climbed in his side. He revved the engine as a matter of habit—his old car, you had to make certain it was going—and it sounded like he was a kid trying to show off, *vroom, vroom.* The combo pack watched them leave, their hands folded. Deuce fought back a nervous desire to wave at them. They wouldn't think it was cute or funny.

He had to stop caring what people thought.

He was silent as the *Gambler's Star* guidance beam lowered him away, then disconnected. He took the wheel, holding it tensely.

Sparkle asked the aichy, "Can you give us a secured cone of silence?"

"Yes, Miss Sparkle," the aichy said brightly. Hey, what was this, community property?

"Guaranteed?" she pressed.

"Yes, ma'am. Mr. Castle has programmed me for absolute passenger privacy."

"If you believe that . . . ." Deuce began.

"I do believe it," she replied.

His lips parted. He stared at her as red flushed up her cheeks. "What the hell is going on, baby?" he asked, looking at her. "What were you doing there? What's all this *schiamazzo* about a wrestling match?"

She took a couple of seconds to answer. Then she sighed, and said, "He sent the stretch for me. He said you'd be there, and I should be, too, since I was your partner."

His partner. Interesting choice of words. He kept looking at her. "How did he know you're my partner?"

"I doubt there's much he doesn't know," she replied, echoing his own sentiments.

"What did you two talk about before I got there?"

She just looked at him. "Deuce, our pasts are past," she said. "You and I agreed to that when we got together."

Deuce ran a hand through his hair. "Hell, Sparkle, I never dreamed your past included Hunter Castle."

She looked at him levelly. "And my present? What does my present include?"

A diamond bracelet? he wanted to say, but he grasped that she was speaking of time, not loot.

"I hope that you're still my baby," he said, embracing her.

She kissed him long and hard and only the way she could. They'd been de-liaised less than half a day. Not even, really. They hadn't done any of the normal things couples did to unencumber themselves vis à vis finances, possessions, all that stuff. The thought of actually going through with it was more than he could bear now that they were in each other's arms.

She broke contact long enough to whisper, "Autopilot. Go half speed to your destination."

"Yes, Miss Sparkle de Lune," the aichy said cheerfully. "Violations levies?"

"Charge them to Mr. Castle."

"I am fully authorized to comply," the aichy informed them. "In addition, I have been requested to inform you of any suspicious activity in my scanning vicinity."

Deuce made himself pay attention to the matter at hand. "Honey, please. Tell me what's going on. What's with this wrestling deal?"

She touched her forehead. "It just came to me to suggest it. I suddenly had the idea. I could see it plainly and clearly, as if it were already happening." She made a little movement with her shoulders. "It was like that with the stock tip I gave him. For Palace Industrials. I was looking at the *Journal* that morning, and I noticed the name. When I met him at the party that night, I saw the certificates in his portfolio, as if he already owned them. I felt compelled to tell him to buy it. I didn't know why then, and I don't know why now."

He scratched his face, realized that was Joey's habit, not his, and put his hand in his lap. "Are you telling me you have what, female intuitions?"

She looked at him so hard it made him nervous. As if she were asking him to tell her what was going on. "No one I know has intuitions like these," she said finally. "At least, that they've told me. Sometimes I feel things, and they turn out to be true."

"Such as?"

She slid him a coy glance. "Such as you'd never have the balls to de-liaise with me."

He narrowed his eyes and lifted his chin. "Bet me."

"Because I'd bust 'em," she said.

"*Amore mio*," he whispered. He melted against her, losing himself in the softness of her body, the heady fragrance of her perfume, Lycanthrope, the cool metallic slickness of her hair. The tang of whiskey and water on her tongue.

"Just try it," he said adoringly. "You'll be sorry, Miss de Lune. You'll be crying."

"You'll be limping, Mr. Deuce McNamara."

"I bet you."

She breathed warm breath into his ear. "What do you bet me?"

"Another kiss."

"Either way, I win," she said.

He decided to go for it. "Then, marriage."

She stared at him for a full minute or two (which is actually a very long time if you're holding your breath, waiting to be executed, or waiting for a woman to agree to your proposal). He could not tell if she was going to kiss him or deck him.

Then she smiled like some young girl he had never seen before in his life. "Jeez, Deuce," she said. "Talk about brinkmanship."

He licked his lips, but he wasn't about to back down. It had been said. He wasn't going to unsay it. It would hang between them for the rest of their relationship, which he predicted would be shorter if they didn't settle it. Who set the fire on the Moon? Deuce or Sparkle?

"Okay, talk about it," he challenged. "Say what you're thinking. Do you see that in your magic cards?"

She took a quick breath. "He wants to introduce himself to the Families. Putting on the match is like throwing an open house."

He was taken aback by her evasion. Disappointed. But the truth was, as far as the match went, he was actually beginning to like the idea. Talk about your big-money game. When would he ever have a chance to double-down like this again? It beat being snubbed by Caputos.

"Except we don't want him to open a house."

She leaned against the passenger door and put her shoes in his lap. She was so beautiful. "He's here, Deuce. We have to deal with him."

"By holding a wrestling match," he said.

She smiled, shrugged. "Why not?"

"Sure, why not?" he echoed. "Why not hold a wrestling match? And why not marry me too?"

She cocked her head, stared at him for another good long while. It was like some kind of tantric question-and-answer period—talk about your brink—when she finally moved one shoulder, and said, "Well, okay, what the hell."

And that was about the one hundred and third thing he was amazed at that day.

FIFTEEN

Deuce and Sparkle were busily installing their upgrade in the romance department when Deuce's comm badge went off. He groaned; Sparkle said, "Take it," and she was right: With this much action going on, he had to stay connected.

Even if he far preferred the action in the aichy.

"Deuce, it's Selene," she whispered. "I'm in trouble."

"Sel?" He half sat up. Sparkle unwrapped herself from around him and looked at him. He switched the call to the aichy's surroundsound system.

"Talk to me," he urged Selene.

"Some guys have kidnapped me." Her voice trailed off. "Oh, God, they're coming back. Deuce, Deuce, come quickly."

"Where are you? Can you get on visual?" The screen stayed blank. To the aichy, he said, "Begin trace. Selene, keep talking. Speak to me. What's going on?"

"No!" she screamed.

The line went dead.

"These are the transmission coordinates," the aichy announced without being asked, and flashed them on a screen in the center of the console.

"That's in the middle of Van Aadams territory," Deuce said. "It's a private club that looks out into the Big Shaft. The Last Call."

"Let's go." Sparkle said to the aichy, "Head for those transmission coordinates. And fasten our seat belts."

"Yes, Miss Sparkle de Lune," it said happily.

"Wait, I'll go manual," Deuce said, disengaging the autopilot. He hung a left and flashed into a tunnel with a sign over the entrance that read, DANGER. CONDEMNED. DO NOT ENTER. He knew it wasn't condemned. He had put the sign there himself.

His comm badge went off again. He tapped it. "Yeah, baby, hang on. I'm—"

"Artie, we're screwed up," Joey said. He came on visual. He was naked, in bed, and he looked the worst Deuce had ever seen him. White-faced, his eye sockets purple, his eyes sunken like he was dead. "We took some bad stuff."

Oh, God. "Joey, did you call the Godfather? He'll send over Dr. Machiatto."

"*O mamma mia!*" Joey shrieked. He slammed his fist into the pillow and burst into tears. Then he started throwing up. Then his back arched and he began to shriek in agony, rolling from side to side and clutching his stomach. "Artie, help me. Diana, she's dying."

"Diana?" Deuce echoed. "Diana's there?"

"Yeah. We were partying. Got back t'gether. She brought some stuff." His eyes rolled back. Then he blinked hard and wiped the back of his hand across his eyes. Deuce saw blood.

"Show me what you took," Deuce said.

"She brought it with." Joey held up a small green bottle. Clearly embossed on the label was the Van Aadams coat of arms, a sun whirling like the wheel of fortune. Deuce closed his eyes. Wayne Van Aadams must have decided to whack her for not being the pure angel he had dreamed of. Now she was sharing her fate with his brother.

"I should've told you something," Deuce began, meaning Van Aadams's insane jealousy and the hit that had sprung from it, but now was not the time. "I'm calling *il Padrino*. You need medical attention. You've probably been poisoned."

"No," Joey begged. "Don't tell Big Al. I'm so humiliated. I'd rather die than let him see me like this."

"*Giuseppe, per favore—*"

"*No, mio fratello.*"

Deuce looked at Sparkle and made some calculations about obligations, the thickness of blood, the depth of his love for her, and accompanying desire to protect her. "You go get him."

She shook her head. "You need my help to get Selene."

"No. Get my brother. His coordinates are—"

"I know where he lives," she said, clearly displeased. Deuce had never taken Sparkle to see Joey. No one in the Family including his own brother knew about their love.

Deuce punched in for a cab. He said to the aichy, "Stop for passenger transfer."

"You take care of him," he said to Sparkle. "Comm a doctor on your way over to meet you there. I'll take care of Selene."

Deuce drove the aichy two levels up from the Last Call and loitered in the parking structure of Velvet Drive—"velvet" being slang for "winnings," which is what tourists were supposed to spend on these three levels, where the fanciest, flashiest, and most-marked-up merchandise on the satellite could be purchased.

He moved under the assumption that Selene was once again the bait to get him to come in without thinking, blaster blazing, like at the casino. Which was why it was important to go in slow, even if the thought of Selene with that monster made him shudder.

This time, he held at least one good card: Years ago, he and Snake Eyes—his current replacement as Casino Liaison—had broken into the Last Call to reclaim a shipment of cigarettes the Van Aadamses had "diverted." They'd made it look like they'd come in the front door, when actually, they'd used an abandoned air-enhancement duct in one of the walls, which Deuce had pinpointed in an old set of blueprints. The blueprints he'd sneaked out of a safe in the Down Under during a routine Liaison visit. One of his operatives, a girl named Sheila, had distracted Sammy the Abo, the then–Down Under Liaison, long enough for Deuce to spin the tumblers and pop out the data rod. The safe had not been well armed; who gave a damn about old building plans? He scanned them into his mini, put them back, and no one was ever the wiser.

But now he was almost sorry he knew about the duct as he slithered through it on his belly. It was filthy and filled with rotting debris. There was no illumination except for Deuce's flashlight, and it did a great job of showing him the desiccated rat corpses he was crawling over.

Then, dead ahead, the light revealed an overhanging panel that had come loose from the top of the duct and was blocking Deuce's way. He considered yanking it free, but it was firmly attached at the one end to the ceiling. A better solution was pushing it back into place and making sure it was secure. He winced at the noise he made, muffled though it was, and crawled on.

Then the locater on his flashlight revealed that he was about eight feet directly above the transmission coordinates of Selene's cry for help.

He stopped crawling and pressed his ear to the duct floor, pushing a dead animal out of his way. For a moment there was silence, and then he heard voices.

"He should be here by now." It was Selene. And she wasn't shrieking, not one bit. She was as cool as a cucumber, which Deuce had seen, in salads at the casino buffets.

"Unless he doesn't give a damn about you."

Deuce froze. He had only heard that voice utter eight words, but he knew who—correction, what—it was: Wayne Van Aadams's android hit man, Mr. Club or Mr. Spade.

"It doesn't matter if he gives a damn about me. He has an obligation. Which he'll honor better than you've honored yours."

"Hey, we thought we got him." Another voice, very garbled. That had to be the cyborg.

"You should have verified the hit before you told Mr. Wayne that you got him," she countered.

"How were we supposed to know this was more than a routine hit?" the garbled voice demanded. "Some love triangle—"

"That's Signor Wayne's take on it," she said. "And as far as he knows, that's all this is. But McNamara's going to get in the way sooner or later. It's better for me if he's dead, like my stupid ex-husband. You don't need to know why. I'm paying you enough that you should just do it without any questions.''

Get in the way? Stupid ex-husband. Signor Wayne? Deuce narrowed his eyes and stared absently into the beady gaze of the rat beside his head. It blinked back at him. He swallowed. It was a live one. It sniffed at him. He clenched his teeth and tried to shoo it away. It stood its ground, sniffing, its little red eyes blinking in the flashlight beam.

He inched away from it and the panel beneath him began to give way. Catching his breath, he grabbed it and held it, but he couldn't put it back perfectly into place. As a result, he had a view into the room. Bad blond toupee, black hair, and Selene, who looked left, right, and said, ''What was that?''

''Maybe he's here,'' the android replied.

''Take a look around,'' Selene ordered them.

They picked up weapons, Mr. Club and Mr. Spade, and left the room.

Selene sighed heavily, raised her arms, lifted up her sweatshirt, and scratched her back.

Her back with a prominent Scarlatti brand, deep and ugly and unmakeoverable, crawling up her spine. Which explained her choice of overly covering dancewear.

You did not submit to a Scarlatti brand unless you were a Scarlatti.

Selene stretched backward, gazing straight up at Deuce's peephole with her big-eyed stare.

With her unusual eyes.

Her eyes that had shown up two and a half years ago in the company of a man who was not her uncle and never had been, this said ''uncle'' whacked by two Scarlattis, one of whom had not been identified.

But maybe the dying man had tried to identify the Scarlatti Member: ''Gee, gee, gee no,'' he had moaned. Deuce was almost moaning now: Why hadn't it ever occurred to him before?

Viola. Gino Scarlatti.

Next, the Scarlattis had demanded that Deuce pay six

thousand credits to stay out of Vendetta, and Mrs. Gino had disappeared.

Word on the street was that six thousand smackers was what ocular implants plus a body makeover cost on Earth, and people had teased Deuce that he had paid for a new look for her. But nobody ever expected to see her back on the Moon.

Could Selene be Mrs. Gino Scarlatti in a new body with new eyeballs? The Scarlattis might have brought her back to be an undercover spy. Maybe while on recon—or maybe because she had come back specifically to kill Gino—she had found out that her ex had stolen the Smiths' secret weapon. Maybe he had copped to it in order to save himself. Maybe he'd promised to cut her in on the action. And maybe she had decided to handle that action on her own instead of reporting back to her bosses. Then she had sold out to Wayne Van Aadams and one of them had killed Gino.

And now she wanted to kill Deuce because he hung around too much, might find out, and might at the very least reveal her to the Scarlattis, who would kill her in a worse way than she had killed Gino. And the only damn reason Deuce hung around too much was on account of the deathbed obligation R.J. Earthshine had extracted from him. R.J. Earthshine, who had loved Selene and wanted her to be protected.

Poor sap.

"See anybody?" she called out.

"Just me," said the Moongoloid. He waddled in alone, just a monstrous ball of weirdness bouncing along in crocodile loafers Deuce craned his head and caught a glimpse of Wayne's face. His eyes were bright red and his nose was running. He didn't bother to wipe it.

"My fiancée is dead," he said, sniffling. "I've got her body in my aichy."

"Oh, I'm so sorry," Selene said, trying to sound sympathetic. But her voice was high and hopeful. "And that awful man who led her astray?"

The Moongoloid pursed his lips. His jowls bounced in the low grav. "No. She was waiting for him at his brother

Joey's apartment. I guess she decided to share her stash a little early." He sighed heavily. "I told her to stop taking drugs. I told her something would happen to her someday if she didn't."

"So McNamara's still alive," Selene said, clearly disappointed. A lesser man's feelings would have been hurt.

"Diana died because she promised to be true to me. And she broke that promise." Van Aadams gestured at Selene. "You haven't kept your promise, either, Mrs. Scarlatti."

"I'll get it for you," she said, backing slightly away. Better that she run, Deuce thought, his old protective habits rising to the forefront of his impulses.

"When they found Gino's body, they searched his place and inspected his credit line. There was no payment and no device," Van Aadams said. "Which may mean that he didn't hand it off. Either it's still where he hid it, or someone stole it."

Deuce kept spinning the tumblers. He sagged with relief. Wayne Van Aadams did not have the weapon after all.

The rat blinked at him, approached, nibbled on his jacket. He raised a hand. It squeaked and darted away.

Selene said, "What was that?"

"Don't try to distract me," Van Aadams said. He advanced on her and raised his hand. "If you don't find it soon, I'll give you what I gave Diana."

The Moongoloid hit her, hard. Deuce winced as she cried out and crumpled to the ground. Slowly he began to slither backwards. Then he stopped as more footsteps entered the room, and watched as the cyborg and the android came back into the room. They stared down at Selene, but neither of them said a word.

"Club, you cover the back door," the Moongoloid said. The toupee nodded. "Spade, take the front. She said he'd come for her. I'll be in the bar. Let me know when it's over."

"What about her?" Club asked.

"Lock her in here. I'll deal with her later."

The three left the room. Deuce waited for the click of the door, then slowly inched back the panel and dropped like a cat to the floor.

She was out cold. There was a huge goose egg on her forehead. Not that Deuce had ever seen a goose.

One of her eyes had been knocked loose. It protruded strangely from the socket. He wondered if she could see him while she was unconscious. The thought gave him the willies.

"Okay, Mrs. Gino, let's go." He looked around. There was a table pushed against a wall and a couple of chairs beside it. Wasn't there some experiment with a chimp and a banana that had these ingredients?

He pushed the table beneath the ceiling breach, put the table on top of the table, hoisted Selene fireman-style over his shoulder. Her long legs dangled like those of a very large black-widow spider. Which he had never seen. He groaned. There had to be an easier way to stay alive.

How he got her up into the chute he would turn into another legend, but after some huffing and puffing, he managed it. He took off her sweatshirt and tied her wrist to his ankle so he could drag her along behind him.

The overhanging panel posed a problem. As he passed beneath it, it came loose again, and smacked Mrs. Gino in the head. He had a sinking feeling she might be dead.

He had the same feeling about Joey. He wanted like anything to comm Sparkle and see what was happening, but he knew he had to maintain silent running. Or crawling, as it were. And crawling fast, because given Wayne's attention span, the Moongoloid would be checking in on her anytime now.

How he got her undetected into the waiting aichy was more stuff of legends, but she woke up just as he peeled out and took off. She saw him, gasped, and then smiled the fakest smile this side of a pit boss who has to hand some high roller a record-breaking stack of chips.

"Deuce, you saved me," she simpered.

"Can it, sweetheart. I know everything. Signora Scarlatti." She apparently was not aware that one of her eyes was hanging loose, because when she widened them, it hung out even farther. Deuce said, "Your makeup's running."

She felt her face, found her eye, and muttered an Italian swear word under her breath.

Deuce said, "Where did Gino stash what he stole from the Smiths?"

She licked her lips. "Why should I tell you?"

He pulled out his blaster. "Because otherwise I'll juice you, *signora*."

"You have an obligation to protect me."

"I'll break it. On account of my brother, I'll do it," he said, making a show of putting his finger on the discharger.

She goggled at him. "*You*?" That made up a little for her disappointment that he had not met his Maker. She regained her composure. If sweating bullets counts for composure. A lesser woman might have wet her pants by now. "This has nothing to do with your brother."

"The way I see it," Deuce said, slamming into another "abandoned" tunnel, "the Moongoloid whacked Diana because he thought she was seeing me. You were in a perfect position to disabuse him of that notion. But you let him believe it—hell, you probably suggested it in the first place—because you wanted me dead. You knew he was gonna kill her, and I'll lay odds you knew how. And you didn't care who went down with her."

He commed Sparkle, who said, "We've got a doctor, but it's not good, Deuce. Is Selene okay?"

"Oh, yeah. Just ducky."

"Deuce?" Sparkle sounded confused.

"She's with me. I'll tell you all about it when I get there."

Deuce glared at Selene. She spit on the floor. "I'm also the dame who asked your brother to give you four thousand credits for information on the weapon. *Cretino*. If I knew where it was, I would have taken it myself and given it to Wayne."

"So you tortured Gino to death because he didn't spill?"

"I didn't kill him." She looked angry as hell. "In fact, if I knew who did, I'd kill *them*. He's no good to me dead, is he?"

That made sense. Now he was sorry he'd kidnapped her. He wasn't sure what to do with her.

"Baby? We're on our way," he said to Sparkle.

"Let me give you coordinates," Sparkle replied. "Van Aadams sent some goons for Diana's body, so we've moved Joey to a safer location."

"Oh?"

"Yes. I have a condo Topside."

Deuce's lips parted. This was news to him.

But then, so much of his life was.

SIXTEEN

"They'll be looking for you, you know," Selene snipped as Deuce painstakingly sneaked through various tunnels and shafts on his way to the surface. "Wayne will be furious."

"That's the least of your problems, Sel," he gritted as he kept to the darker sections of the base. "What's your real first name, anyway? I don't think I ever knew it."

"Viviana."

"Viviana Scarlatti. How exotic." He was being mouthy because he was scared. His stomach was doing flips. He always knew deep down that he loved Joey, but the realization that he might lose him was almost paralyzing him. "You know, something's been bothering me. I can't believe you would actually think I'd turn over information about the Smith weapon to an unknown party for four thousand credits." And he couldn't believe his brother hadn't told him the unknown party was Selene.

She shrugged. "Maybe I didn't think you would. Maybe I just wanted to see what you would do."

That made sense. "And I can't believe you're involved in this. Criminy, Sel, I mean Viv, giving something like that to Wayne Van Aadams. Are you out of your freakin' mind?"

"Maybe he wasn't my real customer."

He chewed on that a minute. "But to give it to anybody on the Moon. If it is really as bad as they say it is—"

"Maybe it wasn't anybody on . . ." She clamped her mouth shut and looked out the window.

Maybe it wasn't anybody on the Moon? Someone on Earth, then? Holy moley. He said offhandedly, "Oh, yeah, I heard about some deal with the DFs going down." Meaning the Disenfranchised Families, the eight who had gone back to Earth only to have all the Earthside gambling action pulled out from under them by the League of Decency.

She muttered, "I'm not saying anything else."

Or what about Hunter Castle? Had he told Gino Scarlatti how to steal the weapon? All this *schioccezza* had coincided with his arrival.

"Talking to me may be the only way you can stay alive," he pushed. "If you're into something big, you can bet they'll find you and shut you down. Permanently."

She shrugged. "You'll have to torture me to make me talk."

"Like you did to Gino."

"I told you before, I didn't do it." She glared at him.

"Uh, then, of course I believe you." He tapped the archy console. "Maybe I'll just pull over and let you walk home." She paled, said nothing.

He decided to give up for now. He was more scared than before. He wasn't sure he wanted to know what she was involved in. Ignorance can be lifesaving.

Yeah, but if someone had the means—and the motive—to blow him and every other Moonsider to kingdom come, didn't he have a patriotic duty to stop them?

He drove in silence. Finally they got Topside. They flew over New Luna Park, the amusement park. Despite the fact that it was nearly midnight on a Monday, there were a few tourists shuttling around the rides—the carousel, the Ferris wheel, and the bumper cars that looked like antique lunar landers—a few more coming out of some show, and still more in the carny section where the games were. The tourists were fascinated by the low-grav effects on things like throwing balls at bottles, that kind of thing. Too bad all the games were fixed.

There was a line for the Heinlein Catapult, the fastest

ride in the park. It was like a big curved set of rails that ramjetted you straight up, up, up, released your vehicle, and you sort of rocketed free for a few seconds, then floated down. Deuce thought it was pretty terrifying, but the Earthsiders loved it.

Finally he touched down and hesitated about getting out. He'd lived below the surface his entire life. Then he caught Selene smirking at him, and he told the aichy to open the doors.

His blaster pointed at her, he had her climb out first, and followed her out her side. The aichy sat on a nice octagonal landing pad. Beyond them, a pebbled walkway led to a gazebo illuminated by klieg lights and decorated with what had to be fake flowers. A pleasant trickle of water gurgled as if from a fountain. With his hand around Selene's arm, they went around the gazebo and down a walkway festooned with more artificial flowers. The fountain was from the naked-nymph period, probably a copy of something famous in Earthside Italy. Chubby cupids with water jugs were pouring the water into a pool while stone fish raised their little heads domeward and spewed water into the air.

Speaking of air, it was not bad up here. He inhaled deeply, trying to calm himself down as he bounded along, his mind filled with images of Joey in various states of dead.

They came upon a cluster of two-story buildings, very nice and streamlined, possibly real wood (but that would have been ridiculously expensive). As instructed, he dashed to the second door in the first building and spread his hand across it, opened his eyes wide for the scan. Sparkle told him she had programmed in some security.

"Hello, Mr. Deuce McNamara and Miss Unidentified Visitor," the door said, and opened.

Deuce was unprepared for what he saw: a holo of a flower garden—roses, long purple things, what he thought might be daisies—complete with floral air enhancements and birdsong. Couches ran along the length of two walls. On the other, a huge screen ticked with stock prices in one quadrant, while in the others, viso channels and text news flickered silently.

On a table beside one of the couches was a basket of fruit.

And Hunter Castle sat on the couch, munching an apple.

"Mr. McNamara," he said, smiling and rising. "And this lovely lady is?"

"Someone you don't need to meet," Deuce said tersely. "Where's my brother?"

Castle looked taken aback by Deuce's bad manners. Deuce didn't care.

"With my physician." Castle jerked his head in the direction of a door. "You were wise to get him immediate attention."

With Selene in tow, Deuce brushed past him and hurried to the door, hissed it open. It was a bedroom, but not heavy on the sleeping function. The enormous bed, settled on the floor, was an ebony ocean of sleek black sheets and waves of pillows. In the middle of it, Joey lay pasty and sweaty.

A man in a white coat stood next to Sparkle, and they both hovered over the still form.

Deuce gestured for Sparkle to come over. He murmured, "Watch her. She's the widow of Gino Scarlatti, and she just tried to kill me," and handed over both his blaster and Selene.

Sparkle looked astounded but nodded. No questions. What a fiancée. She said, "Selene, let's go in the other bedroom, shall we?"

Joey moaned. Deuce hurried to his side and took his cold, clammy hand. "*Mio fratello.*"

He said, "Artie." Moaned again. "*O mamma mia*, my guts are all chewed up."

Deuce was shocked. The doctor gave a quick nod of assent, and Deuce took Joey's hands in his.

"You're going to be all right. We're growing you some new organs right now," the doctor said to Joey.

Joey sighed. "Clones, *fratello*. You know they're never as good."

"Well, in your case, I'm sure the liver will be in better condition," Deuce said, trying to make him smile. Joey only groaned again.

"Hey, Artie, we had good times, didn't we? Remember

when we used to steal the Rollers and zoom all over the place? Mamma was sure we'd kill ourselves.'' Joey coughed. ''You were a terrible driver. Such a klutz.''

Deuce's throat tightened. ''The worst.''

''Remember when we met Crazyhorse McCarthy? He let us sit in the *Moonshot*?''

The *Moonshot* was the legendary Roller that McCarthy had ridden to glory decades before in a famous early Moonside race. ''*Sì*, I remember.''

''What happened to those days? We were such bad boys. But we were brothers.'' His cold hand closed tightly around Deuce's. ''Arturo, I love you. I feel so bad about the money. Mamma wanted you to have it. That's why I drink and take drugs. Because I know I'm evil. I should die and leave you everything. If I live, I'll share. I swear it. I just wanted to be a big man, *capisce*?''

''*Fatti sparare*,'' Deuce murmured.

The doctor cleared his throat and gestured for Deuce to come away from the bed. It was not a room made for dying, or for sleeping, or for reminiscing. The walls were black and silver, the ceiling covered with mirrors. On the floor was a man's black silk bathrobe trimmed with orange.

If Deuce could have seen red when he closed his eyes, he would have. As it was, he saw that it was just after midnight.

''I'm Dr. Harriot.'' The doctor fwapped off a glove and offered his hand. ''Mr. McNamara, your brother is very sick.''

Deuce's heart leaped to his throat. ''How . . . how sick?''

The doctor glanced in Joey's direction. ''If Miss de Lune hadn't called me when she did, he would be dead by now. We may have caught it in time. It was a poison. Something Earthside banned decades ago. It came in this bottle, made to look like Chan drugs.''

Deuce thought of the vial of supposed Chantilly Lace he had in his pocket. His skin crawled. He pulled it out and handed it to the doctor. ''Is this the same thing?''

The doctor held the vial to the light. Then he pulled the stopper. He took the vial over to some testing equipment set up on top of the dresser and did stuff to it, dropped some in, stirred it around, added stuff. Deuce watched closely. He heard a muffled smack and a thud in the direction Sparkle had taken Selene.

The doctor said, "This is pure Chantilly Lace. Pretty container. Unusual."

"Okay." Deuce took it back and stuck it in his pocket before Sparkle could see it. She would not like drugs in her place. And what was with this place? Was there any end to her secrets? "Tell me more about Joey's situation."

"I took various cultures, and we're growing him a new pair of kidneys, a stomach, some bowel, pancreas . . ." The doctor trailed off. Apparently the list was very long. "You were right about his liver. It's in terrible shape. He would probably have died from that alone within the year, unless he had gotten it checked."

"*O, mamma mia.*"

"It's Chan drugs, not alcohol," the doctor added, gesturing to Deuce's pocket "He's severely addicted. I'm not doing anything about that right now, but he will have to be taken off them. They've already caused terrible damage."

Deuce nodded. "*Mille grazie.* Strip my card, and I'll pay for everything."

The doctor waved a hand. "Mr. Castle has already authorized payment."

"I insist."

Dr. Harriot demurred. "Please, that's not my area of concern. Take it up with Mr. Castle. Now I must get back to my patient."

Sparkle joined them, closing a door behind her. A hair or two had come loose from her ponytail. She looked at Deuce significantly. "Selene decided to take a little nap in the guest bedroom."

"I'll have to ask you to step out so he can get his rest, too," Dr. Harriot told both of them.

Deuce nodded, and they walked toward the guest bedroom door. As soon they were out of earshot, Sparkle murmured, "I knocked her out. What's going on?"

"She's Gino Scarlatti's ex-wife. She's working with the Moongoloid to kill me." He hesitated. "There's a lot going on, baby, but I think you'd be safer if you didn't know about it." He opened the door and peeked in. Covered with a blanket up to her neck, Mrs. Gino looked fast asleep.

Beside the bed, a silky black-and-orange men's bathrobe pooled on the floor after someone had taken it off. Deuce noted it, said nothing. Closed the door.

Deuce whispered, "We gotta get her out of here."

"Yes," Sparkle agreed.

The doctor said, "Sssh," and they crept out.

Castle stood when they came into the living room. Formal thing, wasn't he. He said, "How's he doing?"

"Better," Sparkle answered.

Deuce put out his hand even though he would rather it be a fist. "Thank you for taking care of my brother," he said. Maybe the man did it for Sparkle, but he had still saved Joey's life.

Castle looked intrigued. "It's my understanding Joey Borgioli cheated you out of an inheritance."

"That's our business," Deuce said firmly. Now was not the time, and Castle was not the man to discuss this with.

Castle rocked back on his heels. "Ah admire loyalty, even when it's misplaced. Y'all do realize, of course, that he's blown his entire fortune on drugs." Deuce was taken aback. "Drugs are a filthy business." Castle finished his apple and genteelly wiped his mouth with a napkin. "They'll be banned from my casino. All mah employees will submit to drug tests."

Deuce blinked at him. This man was nuts, and he himself was nuts, too. Because if Joey pulled through this, Deuce didn't give a damn about the money.

Sparkle approached, said, "Mr. Castle, I . . . we really do appreciate your help, but now Deuce and I need to catch up on a few things."

Castle inclined his head, folding the napkin several times and laying it next to a plate that contained the remnants of his apple. "In that case, I'll be leaving."

"I'll see you to the door," Sparkle said, like it was her door to see him to.

"And I'll see you at dinner." Castle winked at her.

Deuce seethed.

As soon as he was gone, he whirled on Sparkle. "What

was he doing here? And what are you and Joey doing here? Why didn't you take my brother to my Family?''

She remained silent. He was too on edge to keep his mouth shut, even though he knew he should. ''And what's his bathrobe doing here? Orange and black, those are his colors.''

Sparkle stared at him for maybe half a minute. Then she went back into the bedroom, was gone for about half a minute, and returned with the bathrobe. She threw it at him.

He caught it. Turned it over. In huge block letters was a name: *Alex Van Damnation*, the friend who had sold him the aichy.

And tried to steal Sparkle from him.

''There's a quicktime waiting for you.'' She spoke through her teeth as she picked up a mini and handed it to him. He stared at it and thumbed it. ''Hello, Mr. Deuce McNamara. You have an incoming,'' it said to him.

''Yeah, yeah,'' he said impatiently. ''Open it.''

A miniviso centered itself on the screen and began to run.

His eyes widened. It was Alex Van Damnation, AKA ''Moonman,'' of the Conglomerated Nations Wrestling Foundation.

''*Alors*, Deuce,'' Moonman said. He was from France. ''It's been a long time, eh, *mon copain*?'' His hair hung in curly ringlets around his round, flat face. Everything that could be broken had been, and his features were compressed. His dark blue eyes still gleamed when he smiled, though, and he still wore his signature handlebar mustache.

''Sparkle, what's this?'' Deuce said unhappily, moving to turn it off. But the Moonman continued.

''Ah tried to make a deposit to your investment account for the money ah 'ave owe you. It was *fermé*. Clos-ed. Ah know it's been a while. Ah just want to tell you ah am sorry, man.''

''Yeah, right,'' Deuce murmured.

''I'm coming to ze Moon for ze big wrestling match, Deuce,'' the quicktime went on. ''I heard about ze prize money from Sparkell. I want to make a comeback on the Moon.''

Deuce narrowed his eyes at Sparkle. "What'd you do?" She looked at him blankly, like Selene might do. "Did you ask him to do all this because I'm in a jam?"

"You have a self-esteem problem," she said crisply. Apparently he'd hurt her feelings.

"Thank you, Dr. Freud," he retorted, then lowered his head to his chest with a long, unhappy breath.

Now he was trying to hurt hers. He said to the mini, "Quicktime on."

"Recording," the mini reported.

"Moonman, I've got a situation here. I'm P.N.G. Maybe next time."

"He's already bought a ticket," Sparkle said. "He's due in Thursday night."

He rubbed his forehead. "You set this up?"

"He's your friend."

And she was his girl. And what did that mean anymore? "Does he figure that, too?"

She gestured to the room. "Yeah. And yeah, I own this place, and yeah, Castle came here to save your brother's life. And no, I did not sleep with him in the guest bedroom." She crossed the room and headed for the front door.

"Baby?" he called softly. But the front door was already hissing shut behind her.

He told the mini. "Cancel last response. Retape."

"Taping, Mr. Deuce McNamara."

"Moonman, glad you're on your way." He made himself smile. "I sure could use your help. End."

"Send?" the mini asked helpfully.

"Yeah, before I change my mind."

He went into the master bedroom. Joey's eyes were closed. He looked deader than a doornail. Not that Deuce had ever seen a doornail.

The doctor said, "There's nothing you can do here. I suggest you get some air." Deuce hesitated. Was there a con going on? Should he leave his brother alone with this man?

"Go on," the doctor urged. "Go for a drive. Get some coffee."

Coffee. Deuce's eyes widened. *Coffee.* He remembered

Gino bragging on his new espresso machine, his nervousness joke about nobody touching it, not even Andreas.

"Sure, okay," he said quickly. "That's a great idea. I'll just comm the Borgioli Family to let them know Joey's with you," he added as a very subtle threat. If anything happened to Joey, there'd be hell to pay, and Harriot would be writing the check.

He hurried into the guest bedroom. Selene was coming around. She glared up at him, and slurred, "I'm gonna scream."

He saw his blaster on the dresser near the door, picked it up, and pressed it against her cheek. "I don't think so. Come on. We're walking out of here, and you ain't saying nothing to nobody." She started to speak. "Because if you do, I'll call the Smiths."

Her mouth shut.

There was another door from the guest bedroom to the living room. They walked through and left the condo without incident.

She got into the car without any trouble.

Then she leaped toward the console and punched on a comm line, so Deuce punched her out again. He almost felt sorry for her. It was like the old days, when she'd been a punching bag for Gino. Him and his hyped-out lifestyle and his espresso machine.

He descended below the surface and began tiptoeing around again. Mrs. Gino was still unconscious. He drove carefully, sure there was a search party out for her.

Sure enough, when he dipped into an offshoot of Bugsy Siegel Way, two aichies got on his tail and started blasting.

"What have we got?" he asked the speedster as he began evasive maneuvers. "Colors?"

"By colors and configuration, one Smith car and one rented vehicle," the aichy reported. "One moment, please. Rental registration is blocked."

Deuce frowned at the screen. "A Smith car? Can you reconfirm?"

"Yes, Mr. Deuce McNamara. A Smith speedster, model—"

"Never mind." He'd have to figure that out later. "Any cyborgs? Androids?"

"One of each in the rented vehicle," the aichy supplied.

Club and Spade. That he expected. But the presence of the Smith aichy was a puzzle. "You armed?"

"Oh, yes, Mr. Deuce McNamara. It's a perfect night for a rumble. I have two pulse cannon and three attack lasers."

"All right." He whirled around. "Attack mode. Designate the rental Target A. The Smith vehicle is Target B."

"Confirmed." Pulses of energy blasted past the aichy. Its stabilizers began working overtime.

"And we're Target C," Deuce muttered under his breath.

"Evasive maneuvers," he ordered.

They were converging on him, one to the left, one to the right, following in as he dodged into a utility tunnel. A freight transport hurtled toward them, then slammed on its forward thrusters and ducked into an artery. Deuce saw the driver waving his fist at them as he flashed past.

He floored it—in a manner of speaking—and screamed toward the worst part of town. The two vehicles followed, working together. They were careful of oncoming traffic. So was he.

"Cables and coils," he instructed the aichy, and he rocketed downward.

Through the debris and the dirt and the poor and the sick, they blasted at him. He blasted back.

The Smith vehicle began to fall behind.

"Target B has received a hit," the speedster confirmed. "But we did not hit it."

"No?" He hazarded a glance around. The Smith vehicle nose-dived into a ramshackle building. There was no explosion.

His comm badge went off. "We'll be in contact," said a voice he vaguely recognized.

"Who are you?" Deuce shouted.

"They have disconnected," the aichy informed him. "The line was secured. Target A approaching at three o'clock. They are firing."

Club and Spade. The burst reached the passenger side of

the aichy. Deuce closed his eyes and waited for impact. Felt the rocking, gentler than he had anticipated. They must have been too far away to waste him.

He looked over. They hadn't been too far away to waste Mrs. Gino. There was a huge hole where her right side had been, and she was very clearly dead. Her eyeballs ricocheted all over the interior of the vehicle.

NA-na NA-na. The police were coming.

Club and Spade tried one more burst, then pulled up and away, leaving Deuce with the prospect of dealing with the cops. He wasn't sure how he would explain the presence of one dead Scarlatti broad in his front seat, so he got the hell out of there.

He gave the Missus a half-decent burial inside a rusty Dumpster.

Then he headed out to get himself just what the doctor ordered: a cup of coffee.

From Gino Scarlatti's fancy-schmancy new espresso machine.

SEVENTEEN

Deuce needed to be incognito. He didn't know if that meant using the damaged but still beautiful aichy was in or out, but he damned the photon torpedoes and went full speed ahead. If his hunch was correct, he had to move fast.

He landed at an offsite parking lot for workers and told the aichy to configure a strip that would forward the parking fee and potential vandalism damage (after all, this baby was sure to engender class envy) to Hunter Castle. It was not a problem, the aichy told him.

He got out amidst the stares and glares, darted away, and ducked into a surplus store. He bought himself a black duster and a wide-brimmed hat. Staring at himself in the mirror, he did not recognize any atom as belonging to Deuce McNamara. Satisfied, he hopped a workers' tube that would land him at the Inferno.

Mass transportation was free, and you didn't have to have any kind of card to use it. He didn't know how *that* had happened—if the Families had run these things, there'd be a charge, you could be sure of that—but now that he was cash poor, he didn't mind the lack of asset exploitation.

The tube zoomed along through the rock, came to a station, jerked to a halt. A couple of tired-looking people got off the tube and a couple more got on. Everyone was in shabby clothes and everyone looked like they couldn't care less about the grand and glorious fact that they were alive. The air was dusty, and Deuce found himself laboring slightly to breathe. Maybe over time they got brain-damaged from not enough good air.

WILL WORK FOR OXYGEN.

The man's sign wasn't so funny in retrospect.

He wondered if the guy had gone to the Palazzo to get the dishwashing job. Deuce hoped he had.

A male N.A., maybe thirty, maybe fifty, gestured to Deuce. "I know your face," he said. "You're the guy who's arranging that wrestling tournament."

Uh-oh. He said, "No, I'm not," glancing left and right over his shoulders.

The guy smiled and raised a fist. "Right on," he said. "Give us N.A.'s something to be proud of." Deuce was stunned. "The Moon for the Moonsiders!"

"Waidaminute," Deuce protested, sweating more than ever. How many milliseconds ago had he made that arrangement with Hunter Castle?

"The Families suck," someone yelled.

Someone else cheered.

"They suck the big one!" Deuce's new friend went on, enjoying himself.

A woman in a drab brown dress put her finger to her lips. "Careful," she whispered to the crowd.

"Yeah," Deuce added, rising.

"I'll be there, man," Deuce's buddy promised. "Hundreds of us will. We understand the symbolism, man. Archangel and Gamma Lord. That's how it all started. Now we're going to take it back."

Deuce shook his head vigorously. He had not gotten the symbolism, not before. "Sorry, you got the wrong guy."

"The Inferno," the tube announced. Deuce hoisted himself up and made his way to the exit.

He stepped into the seventy-four/sixty and took a deep breath. The air was definitely better out here.

Sometimes tourists freaked out when they came to Moonbase Vegas. Claustrophobia was a common problem. They felt like they were suffocating. They became obsessed with the dome. How thick? How sturdy? Right now, Deuce felt twice as hemmed in; if only the tourists knew how much more there was to worry about.

On the escalator to the next level, he accidentally bumped into a Caputo. "Hey, watch it, dirtbag," the Caputo said, turning around and drawing on him. Deuce glared back at him and reached for his own blaster. Remembered he did not want to draw attention to himself.

"Who you looking at, N.A.?" another Caputo demanded, crowding him.

This wasn't going to lead anywhere good. Deuce left his blaster in his pocket, and said, "Sorry."

"That's better," the first Caputo said. "Next time, watch where you're going."

"You freakin'—yes, sorry," Deuce said. He memorized the face. He was going to get that face someday and hang it on his wall.

He looked at the glittering Strip with new eyes: saw the tourists falling all over themselves; saw the Family members strutting around like they owned the place, which they did; saw the N.A.'s, trudging like they were at full grav.

He burned to be in Family colors, even Borgioli red, green, and white. This undercover thing had humbled him, that was for sure. He would never have dreamed he'd miss the perks of being a Borgioli wiseguy.

He stepped onto the escalator and trekked along. The neons flashed, the holos danced. Fire blasted from the volcano in front of the Inferno. Clowns from the Caputos' Cirque de la Lune capered and pranced, trying to lure the crowd from the Inferno to the Lucky Star. A few rabbits bounded after them. Scores of tourists crowded the boulevards, pointing at the sights and weaving from a combination of exhaustion, low gravity, and free drinks.

Deuce couldn't help but stop and admire the scene for a few heartbeats. After all, this was his town. And it was a mighty cool one.

At Donna MaDonna's he thought he saw Angelina Rille, the petite queen of the MLF, but he couldn't be sure. He moved on. He had a Doomsday Machine to lift. If it was still there.

"Hey, Deucie, where've you been, honey?" asked a hooker at the door to the Inferno. This was Bambi, with her own name tag on, and she had on a sheer red bodysuit, silver high heels, and nothing much else.

"I'm, um, trying to be unnoticed," he said in a low voice, winking at her conspiratorially.

Her face fell. "Good idea," she said. "They're going insane in there. My best friend Kimba is missing." Her lower lip quivered. "And as soon as I've saved up the fare, I'm getting the hell out of here."

Now is not the time, he yelled at himself, but his stupid streak of heroism kicked into overdrive and made him say, "They been threatening you, baby?"

She nodded and burst into tears.

Instantly a Scarlatti doorman dressed as a devil glided over to them. "This man bothering you?"

"No." She shook her head vigorously. Deuce watched the animal take note of her name tag. He didn't like the expression on the doorman's face. He pulled his hat lower. "He's a really good friend," she went on.

"N.A.," the doorman sneered, but so was Bambi.

Deuce fished in his pocket and produced the brand-new strip the aichy had created. "How much you need?" From afar, the doorman watched, bored, reassured. Assuming, no doubt, Deuce was purchasing her devilish services.

"No, no," she said, eyes widening. "It's all right."

He took her hand and said, "Get out your card." She did, probably from force of habit, and he swiped his against hers for fare back to Earth. So he'd pay Castle back one millennium at a time. Or when his local boy beat the wrestler Castle no doubt would import from Earth.

"I can't take this, Deuce," she said gratefully. "Not unless I sleep with you a hundred and twenty-two times."

He smiled faintly. "Give me a rain check. We'll catch up someday Earthside."

"But you hardly know me."

He leaned forward and brushed her cheek with his lips. "Not that I wouldn't want to," he said in her ear, and went inside the casino.

She followed him in. "Deuce . . ." Grabbed his hand.

"I, ah, need to find a friend," he said, shaking her off

with the first lie that came into his head. "A guy friend of mine."

"Oh. Maybe he's in the Passion Pits." She took his hand. "I'll take you there."

Oh, *fabulous*. "I can find my way."

"No." She looked up at him with huge eyes. "The doorman saw me take your money. If I don't go to the Pits with you, he'll report it as suspicious activity."

That would not be good.

She popped something small and hard into his palm. "Put that on," she whispered. "It's some of the new Scarlatti hardware they didn't sell to anyone else. If you've got a weapon, it'll shield it from the detectors."

He was impressed. Wished he'd known about it earlier so he could have brought a weapon. His blaster was hidden in the bushes—transplants in transplanted earth—near the parking lot. "Thanks."

They walked past holo doors of crimson flame and theatrical smoke that enhanced, rather than dirtied, the air. Music with synthetic violins jittered up and down his spine and set his teeth on edge. A tourist couple stumbled through the fire, laughed, and stumbled back the other way. Jeez, didn't they have holos Earthside?

Bambi didn't notice. She was staring straight ahead.

"Oh, my God, it's Andreas," she whispered. "I did something to, um, really piss him off."

Deuce really didn't want to see him, either. "Uh-huh," he said uncertainly.

"Come here." Bambi darted through the flames and pushed on the black wall. A door opened inward, and she and Deuce practically fell into a hall.

"Are we near the Pits?" He was confused. He concentrated, trying to remember where Gino's office was from here. He closed his eyes.

It was even later than he thought.

"Whew, that was close." She smoothed her hair and clothes.

He oriented himself and began walking with her. Left, right, two doors, six feet, a right . . .

Bingo. They were standing directly outside Gino's office.

Now what could he do with her to get her out of the way?

"C'mere." He smiled at her. "Suddenly I feel . . . friendly."

"Oh." She dimpled. "I'm told I have that effect."

Ten feet, twelve . . .

"Let's go to the Pits," she said.

"Too public." He put his arm around her waist and led her toward the door. "What about in here?"

She went white. "That's Gino's office. It's locked."

"Oh," he said innocently. "I heard that he, uh, bought it. That it is his office no longer, but a storage closet."

She licked her lips nervously. "No one's supposed to go in or out. Andreas said the Family would go into Vendetta over his death and for me not to pay any attention because Gino was a thief, anyway."

His ears pricked. She was talking too fast. She was very scared.

"Vendetta against who?" He should have said "whom." He didn't think she would notice.

She paled. "Kimba saw it, not me." She thrust her strip at him. "Take your money back, Deuce."

"Saw what, honey?" He put his hand on her shoulder. She folded herself against him, leaned forward, and buried her face in his chest. She began to cry. "You mean, saw who killed Gino?"

"Andreas said it would cause a war if it gets out," she whispered. Her words were muffled. "He said he'd kill Kimba and me if we said anything. And I haven't seen her in days."

He was surprised Andreas hadn't already killed Bambi as well. "Let me help you," Deuce urged. "Tell me who did it, Bambi. I'll protect you."

She shook her head and dug her hands into his pockets, whimpering.

"I'll get you off the Moon," he promised. "I will." She sagged against him. She'll get you off him. He held her. "Hey, it's me, Deuce. You don't need to be afraid of me, too."

She led him down a maze of corridors and into the back entrance of the Pits, where the girls took their dates. There was a door marked "Bambi" and on the other side was a room the floor of which was an immense bed with red-silk sheets and black pillows. Above the bed was a shelf and on that shelf, a holo of Tina Fracci, the actress who played Devon LeDare's wife on *Phases,* in her altogether; a cut-crystal pitcher of water and a couple of matching glasses, some massage lotions, and an assortment of marital aids. Also, a very shiny, brand-new copper espresso machine.

Deuce stared at it. "Is that Gino's?" he asked, trying to hide his astonishment.

"Hey, I earned it," she retorted. She lay on the bed and held out her arms. "Let's don't talk about Family business," she said huskily.

She was trying to distract him. As surreptitiously as he could, he commed himself on audio. His badge beeped. "Earphone," he said, then pressed his finger against his left ear and frowned.

"*Mi scusi,* you're breaking up," he said to his "caller." Then, to Bambi, "Ah, my comm system's acting up. I'm going to have to take this on audio. Would you mind giving me a few minutes?"

She looked put out. Then perhaps she remembered that he had comped her a free trip to Earth. She touched his hair. "Sure, baby," she said silkily. "I'll be down the hall in Crescent's room. She's packing. Call me when you're finished." She left the room.

Deuce immediately locked the door, and with the crafts-manship of a skilled locksmith, completely dismantled the espresso machine. He examined each and every piece of it. Damn. If Gino had once hidden something in it, it sure wasn't there now.

He didn't go to collect Bambi, but she rapped on the door and hurried inside.

"I have to go," he told her. She looked alarmed, and he took advantage of that. "Things are happening. That call I got . . ." He let his voice trail off meaningfully. "You have to tell me, Bambi. I can only help you if you come clean. Who whacked Gino?"

She jerked away from him and reached for the door. He caught her arm and held her gently.

"Signorina," he pleaded.

"Van Aadamses," she whispered finally, not looking at him. "Two of their security guards killed him. Andreas is furious with us because Kimba and I tried to shake down Gino's sister for some um, money Gino owed us, and she gave us the espresso machine instead and Andreas said now it will get out about his death."

He stopped listening. Two Van Aadams security guards. Mr. Tanzer and Mr. Feist had killed Gino. They had tortured Gino in order to . . . in order to . . . make him tell them where he had hidden the weapon.

And then they themselves had taken it.

Mamma mia.

He wrapped his arms around her. She put her hands in his pockets as if to keep them warm and huddled against him.

"Now I'm dead," she murmured.

"No. You did the right thing, telling me. Now I can protect you."

She dug around some more, like she wasn't going to give up on the Pits portion of their evening. "Ooh, is this Chantilly Lace?" she asked brightly as she dug the vial out of his pocket. Like she had forgotten about everything else, such as that her life was in danger. Lace addiction was like that. Before he could react, she uncorked it.

"No," he said, trying to grab it from her. It fell to the floor. The vial broke open.

Bambi said, "God, Deuce, I'm sorry," and dropped to a squat to retrieve it. "Hey, what's this?" she asked.

It was a long black cylinder approximately the size of one of those little stampers they gave you to fill out keno cards with. It had fit inside the curved side of the larger vial.

Deuce stared at it. Tanzer and Feist had killed Gino because Gino had the Smiths' secret weapon, and they were going to make sure the Moongoloid didn't get it. They were going to give it back to the Smiths in return for Affiliation in the Smith Family.

On his person and that of his daughter when they had died, the Tanzers had had three items, and he had begged

Deuce to take "it" back to them. Which implied that Deuce had that which should be taken back.

Deuce snatched the vial and the black cylinder back from Bambi.

"Go out the back way," he whispered. "Comm Angelo Borgioli. Tell him you came from me. Tell him the words, 'to the Old Country.' Give him the credits I stripped you. He'll take care of the rest." She blinked at him and shook her head. "I swear it. Don't pack. Run." He knew Angelo would come through for him. He was the Family transport man, and he was Deuce's friend. He wouldn't ask questions now. Later, yes. But Deuce would have to deal with later when the time came. And speaking of which, his time was almost up.

He had the weapon.

He had had it all along.

And obviously, the Smiths knew it, or they wouldn't have shot at him.

He ducked outside, his hat low over his forehead. The Scarlatti devil security guard barely glanced his way.

He made it to the tube.

He made it to the aichy.

And then his comm badge went off. Swallowing hard, he tapped it.

"Yeah."

"*Cretino. Idiota.* Come here now," Big Al ordered.

"*Mi dispiace*, Don Alberto," Deuce said, exhaling. "I'm in the middle of something and I can't—"

"What? What did you say? You *can't*? You freakin' double-crossing scumbag, you get here in ten minutes on your own or you'll be here in five in a hearse."

Which didn't make a lot of sense, but Deuce said tiredly, "*Sì, Padrino.* On my way."

He disconnected and found God.

Real quick.

EIGHTEEN

Big Al was in a lather. He saw Deuce alone, not a good sign. He showed him a viso commercial about THE MOONMATCH OF THE CENTURY featuring none other than the most famous wrestler on Earth, Hang 'Em High Harry, who dressed like an old-fashioned outlaw complete with chaps and gun belt. There was an insert of Deuce kickboxing, which he supposed implied that he was going to wrestle Hang 'Em High Harry himself, which he had never agreed to. And never would.

"What the hell are you doing?" Big Al screamed at him. "You're supposed to be spying on everybody!"

"I am. I am, Godfather," Deuce assured him. "I've been to Castle's ship. I—"

"You two are listed as impresarios. What the hell is an impresario? I for one am not very impressed."

"It was supposed to be a little bet," Deuce said in a penitent voice. "Something to like, you know, bond with him."

"I'll bond you with him. With a laser. In a crater. You." He jabbed his index finger at Deuce. "You are currently a PNG and an N.A. You're not some high-ranking Family man can make deals with anybody. Who the hell do you think you are?"

"This is actually good for us," Deuce insisted, sweating. He had the Smiths' weapon in his pocket, and his Godfather was so incredibly stupid that he didn't dare so much as hint

239

at the larger picture he was currently starring in. "It gives us leverage."

"*You* it gives leverage."

"And you're my Godfather," Deuce pointed out.

Big Al had nothing to say to that. Perhaps it was dawning on him the opportunity they had before them. Just in case, Deuce added, "I'm learning all about his operation."

"Oh, really?" Big Al's sad eyes bored into him. "Then perhaps can you clue me in to the fact that Emerson Epperson-Roux is the deputy director of the Department of Fairness. And he's living on that SOB's freakin' ship?"

Deuce blinked. That he had not known.

"Of course I knew that," Deuce said. "I had a drink with him earlier this evening."

" 'Earlier this evening.' What the hell's wrong with you? You sound like a Van Aadams, 'earlier this evening.' During what part of this evening were you going to tell me about it?"

"I'm desolated," Deuce said. "You see, Don Alberto, Joey, he's not so good. He's very ill."

"What?" Big Al's mouth opened, closed. "Maria's Joey?"

"My Joey," Deuce retorted.

Big Al picked up a phone. "Where is he? The clinic?"

"No, Godfather. He's in a safe house. Some dame tried to poison him."

"*Puttana.*" He spit on the carpet. "Who is she? Has a hit been Registered on her?"

"We don't know who she is." Him and his big mouth.

"Give me her description. We'll find her."

The door opened, and Beatrice sailed in in an evening gown of white fluffy stuff and ribbons in her prodigious hair. It was 3:00 A.M. At the sight of her, Big Al softened. He wagged his finger at Deuce. "This is not over."

"*Sì, Padrino.*"

Beatrice threw her arms around Deuce and covered his face with kisses. "*Mio Duchino,*" she cried, "it's been two whole days. I've been so worried about you. Working undercover!"

"Yeah, well." He slumped beneath the weight of his

guilt at her happiness over him. "I'm . . . tired, Signorina Beatrice."

"You're so formal." She giggled at him, and then at her father. Her ribbons flowed around her bare shoulders. "*Papà*, he's bringing so much honor to the Family. No one else has a deal going with Hunter Castle. Not publicly, not like Deuce."

Big Al cocked his head. He looked as if someone had shot him. *Now* he got it. Now that Beatrice had translated for him.

"That's true," Big Al said. He was silent a moment. "Maybe it's time to bring you in, Arturino. Put your colors back on your sleeve." He smiled at Beatrice. "We can announce your engagement to Beatrice at the same time."

Beatrice squealed with joy. Deuce stood stunned. Then he coughed into his fist, and said, "Godfather, such an honor. I can hardly speak."

"Then it's settled."

Deuce raised his hand. "Except Castle is dealing with me *because* I'm N.A.," he said. "He told me he liked it that I was neutral."

"Neutral, schmeutral," Big Al said expansively. "Surely he must know we would never kick such a clever boy out of our Family, eh?" He tousled Deuce's hair. "Eh?"

"Godfather," Deuce said carefully, "I can still do a lot of good out in the field. It's not time to call me in yet." Wasn't this something, talking Big Al out of what he, Deuce, wanted? If he was back in the Family, they would protect him against the Smiths and whoever else might be after him by then. Theoretically, at least. He wasn't sure if anybody could protect him. And they hadn't exactly pulled out any fine weaponry before. "Let me get through the wrestling match."

Big Al shrugged. "I'll talk to the rest of the Family. We'll work out a plan." He beamed at Beatrice. "Now, you young people enjoy yourselves." At Deuce, he wagged a finger. "Be sure you show respect to my little girl."

"Of course, Don Alberto," Deuce said with a bob of his head.

As soon as Big Al left the room, Beatrice leaped onto

him, throwing her legs around his waist. "*Amore mio*," she crooned. "You're mine at last." She nuzzled him. "My father was going to agree soon anyway. I think people *know*."

"Know."

"About us, silly." She kissed him.

"Ah." He made a recovery and eased her off his body and onto her own two feet. This situation was almost more dangerous than the other one. If Big Al found out about Sparkle now, Deuce was as good as dead. "I have to go, Bea. I have business."

Her eyes shone. In their Family, having business was very manly. It usually meant you were either going to make some money or kill someone.

"All right." She stepped back and admired him. "I like your black clothes. They make you look like a spy. Very dangerous."

He wished he loved her. She was a sweet girl. "You take care," he said sincerely. Perhaps if he found someone for her . . .

"*Addio*," she whispered, blowing him a kiss.

"*Addio*." He saluted her and quickly turned away.

He ramped up and took a long look at the aichy, which he had dared to drive over because he had not dared to be late for his meeting with Big Al.

He sighed. He told it, "I want you to take yourself on a long trip around the base. If you're attacked, fight back to the best of your ability. Take as many of the suckers as you can. If you win and are not followed, return to the Topside coordinates."

He swore the aichy hesitated. Then it asked, "If I am followed?"

"Attack until you're blown up or you run out of fuel. If you run out of fuel, crash but don't harm any innocent bystanders. Be especially careful of N.A.'s. Try to make it so they won't be able to tell if I was inside without running a DNA scan." That would buy him a little—a very little—time.

"If I am outgunned?"

"Same as above."

It did hesitate, damn it. It did. "I will comply, Mr. Deuce McNamara."

It took off. He watched it go.

"*Addio*," he whispered, and trudged, exhausted, into the shadows.

NINETEEN

In the dead of night, Deuce found a flophouse, paid for his bed with a few Borgioli onechips he dug out of his pockets, and fell asleep with a neon sign flashing GIRLS GIRLS GIRLS on his eyelids. He dreamed of eyeless women and men with no innards. He dreamed of wedding dresses in tall and squat sizes. He dreamed of Earth, a shining planet populated by horses and seagulls.

After a couple hours, he got up. With people looking for him, he had to be careful. He had a plan, but he wanted to think it through before he put it into action.

DAI-TAI CHAN, CHAN FAMILY GODMOTHER, DEAD AT 89.

That was what the zipper said, and more. She had looked far older than eighty-nine, and that was a young age to die these days. She must have been addicted to her own drugs.

He read on, discovered that the cremation was scheduled for later today, it now being Tuesday, at one o'clock in the afternoon. There would be bloodshed; Yuet would be armed against the inevitable assassination attempt orchestrated by Cheung and her other stepbrother, Sying. Perhaps their plan was to be co-Godfathers like the Smiths.

And then he read something that made him ill:

Bambi Moonchild, a hostess at the Inferno, was found dead at approximately three this morning. The medical examiner has determined that the cause of death was accidental.

That was all. But it was more than enough for him. The

deaths of girls like Bambi were not usually mentioned in the *Moonwatcher*. It was a planted story, designed to warn someone or inform someone or scare someone. Or all three.

He crossed himself, and whispered, "Be with God, *bambina.*" It was time to play his hand before someone else called it.

He took no mass trans, but walked to the Strip and stood hidden, watching the glitter and the giddiness, knowing the violence that bubbled beneath it and rose occasionally to the surface. Containing that spillover was what the Charter Board and the Department of Fairness were all about. The Families and all they represented could go to hell as far as outsiders were concerned—as long as they continued to provide revenue. Casino profits were taxed, and taxed heavily.

Who cared if the players changed, as long as the money came in?

He ate in a dirty coffee shop filled with dispirited N.A.'s talking about the upcoming wrestling match. He felt like a putz that he hadn't connected this match with the big one back in Earthside Las Vegas. But that had been ancient history. He'd always liked to think he was studying up on the future.

His badge vibrated, and he jumped a mile. Tapped it and whispered, "Yeah."

"Why are you whispering?" Big Al yelled.

"Godfather, I'm, ah, casing a joint." He was glad for perhaps the two millionth time that Big Al had been too cheap to spring for the personal locators that nearly everyone wore these days.

"What for?"

He dithered a moment. He couldn't tell Big Al he was trying to figure out how best to unload the Doomsday Machine. "Information. Castle's inside."

"Oh, *really*," Big Al said frostily. "That's pretty interesting. Considering he's in the next room drinking a Bloody Mary and listening to Bea play the piano."

Deuce closed his eyes. It was 10 A.M.

"Listen, we're entering into a treaty with the Chans," Big Al went on.

"Us and Castle?" Deuce asked, surprised.

"Us," Big Al said ambiguously. "Against Yuet. With Cheung and Sying. God forbid that they should have *regular* names."

"Oh." Deuce was sorry.

Since Joey's predicament, Deuce found himself heavily in favor of halting drug production. Yuet was the only potential heir who felt the same way. He had often imagined himself being of service to her in some way. Now he was going to help her enemies end her life.

He heard Big Al say, "No, Bea, not right now. Go ask Mr. Castle if he'd like some more champagne."

Champagne? "Are we in a treaty with Castle, Don Alberto?" Deuce asked.

"We being the Borgiolis?" Big Al asked pointedly. "Go see Cheung. He's in the bunker. Report back." He disconnected.

Deuce felt half in the swim and half out. Big Al was still bossing him around, which Deuce found reassuring. On the other hand, he was playing his cards awfully close to his vest. Deuce had no beef with that. So was he. However, this was a delay he did not welcome. Every second he had this cylinder-thing on him was another second he could end up like Miss Bambi Moonchild.

The Chans had a bunker inside the casino, but he would have assumed Yuet would have commandeered it. That Cheung was already in it did not bode well for the beautiful heiress.

Through long years of experience, he expertly melted into the crowds and ducked behind buildings as he made his way toward the Pearl of Heaven.

Then, at the side entrance, he saw Sparkle with Quon, the good old Liaison to the Borgiolis. He was stunned. Their heads were together like they were reading something together or telling each other a secret.

He commed Sparkle and whispered, "Baby, I'm behind you. Is it safe?"

"Yes," she said, half-looking over her shoulder. He separated himself from a curved wall and hunched down, walking toward them with his hands in his pockets, his blaster on kill. Sparkle had good judgment, but Quon might not.

"*Buon giorno*," Deuce said. "I assume we're here for the same reason." Quon looked nervous. "To pay our respects to the Family on the death of Madame Dai-Tai."

"Whom do you represent?" Quon asked. "Whom." Maybe he was classier than Deuce had thought.

"I'm expected," he answered cryptically. Sparkle gave him a little frown, which he pretended to ignore. If something went wrong, he didn't want anyone to think they were in it together.

But what was she doing here?

Quon looked left, right, took a deep, deep breath, and murmured, "All right. Come on."

He coded them through the door, put out a hand, and coded another door to his immediate right. Deuce mentally nodded to himself. He knew where they were. Two corridors and five rooms over was the counting room. The next door held a safe he knew the combination to. They kept spare pharmaceuticals in there for air enhancement. Last he'd checked, anyway. For all he knew, the formula for Chantilly Lace was in there now. He thought of the cylinder in his pocket and swallowed hard. Would it blow up if you got jostled too much? Was there a timer on it that would go off if the right guy didn't punch in the secret code?

Quon brought them to a corner and looked around it. He motioned them to stay back. Deuce whispered to Sparkle, "Why are you here?"

"I'm not sure," she whispered back. "I had another feeling . . ."

Suddenly they were surrounded by men in suits holding blasters and submachine pulsers aimed directly at their heads.

Deuce and Sparkle threw themselves into defensive stances as Quon shouted, "Stop! They're on our side."

"Good," said a female voice. The black-garbed guys parted, kowtowing low to Yuet Chan, who was dressed in a beautiful brocade robe of jade and salmon that dragged on the floor. Her hair was loose. She didn't look like there was a war on.

Quon stared at her. "But I thought . . . I thought . . ." He stared at Deuce. "You were sent by Big A—"

Sparkle grabbed Deuce's blaster from his pocket and shot the man. Staring in disbelief at his own steaming organs as they tumbled from his body, Quon moaned and fell to the floor.

Yuet inclined her head in Sparkle's direction. Then she said to Deuce, "Miss Sparkle has led me to understand that you represent powerful antidrug forces who wish to ally themselves with us."

Uh-oh.

"His brother is almost dead from Chantilly Lace," Sparkle allowed.

"You are Independent," Yuet observed. "Do you come with many followers?"

"We've never had a leader before," Sparkle replied.

Deuce said smoothly, "But there's no reason we can't have one now," and looked back at Sparkle.

Yuet's eyes glittered. She looked eager. "Are you authorized to make a treaty?"

"I'll have to get back to you on that," Deuce replied. "To tell you the truth, we were basically here on your average freedom-fighting mission. We didn't realize you'd already won."

"Just tying up loose ends." Yuet glared at her *assassinio* guys. "Don't just stand there. Clean up this mess."

They hopped to and dragged Quon and his accessories away. Yuet said to Deuce and Sparkle, "May I offer you tea?"

"How very gracious," Deuce answered, kowtowing. "We really don't deserve such an honor." He couldn't wait to get Sparkle alone and find out what was going on.

Yuet took them to the bunker, which was more like a miniature Chinese palace with pink-and-green stuffed furniture, wooden tables with bronze characters on them, and enough communications equipment to rival Hunter Castle's conference room. The woman who brought them tea was Roxy, who Deuce winked at, and she had to hide an answering grin. Good for her; in the time he'd been off duty, she'd backed the right horse and gotten herself a promotion to key lackey.

They drank their tea in silence. Yuet said to Sparkle, "As always, I'm indebted to you," and they both kind of regarded Deuce the way you do a baby, like everyone owns it and is proud of it, and then Sparkle said, "Madam, we're sorry to cause such insult, but we do have to go."

"Yes," Yuet said. She reached forward and kissed Sparkle on the cheek. Then on the lips.

Deuce wondered if he was next, but he was not. She only smiled and nodded at him, and that was that.

Outside, Deuce whirled on Sparkle. "What the hell was that?"

"We're old friends," she said calmly, walking on. Her face was glowing.

"I was sent in by my Godfather to back Cheung."

"I know."

"Then why—"

She took his blaster out of her pocket and handed it to him. "If you'd gone in there gunning for her, you'd be dead, too. She'd already won. Quon didn't know it."

"Sparkle, what's going on with you?"

She stopped, looked at him, shook her head. "Deuce, I had this . . . feeling. I *knew* what was going to happen. I knew I had to take care of you."

"So you saved me again with your psychic awareness." He couldn't help his sarcasm, hated his mouthy self for it.

"I guess."

"And what is it with the wrestling-match notion? Everyone is comparing it with that one they had back on Earth. That Archangel thing. It's too big, Sparkle. It's making people nuts. And remember the outcome of that fight."

She kept walking. They were beyond the Pearl of Heaven and reaching the vast display windows of Donna Ma-Donna's. Momentarily he was distracted by a set of mechanical mannequins dancing to "Shine On, Silvery Moon" as they modeled UNDERWEAR THROUGH THE CENTURIES: chastity belts, black bustiers, gravitassels, and less.

Again, he thought he saw Angelina Rille, this time rounding a corner.

"Where's Selene?" Sparkle asked.

"Dead," he said, turning his attention back to her. "My fault."

"Good." Her voice was terse. She sure hadn't had any ESP about that little piece of work being Mrs. Freakin' Ex–Gino Scarlatti. Maybe she felt guilty about it.

"Look," he began, "I'm going to go talk to the Smiths."

"*What*?"

"Yeah. I figure it's the only chance I have of—"

A man rushed in front of them and lobbed an object at the window of Donna MaDonna's. Deuce got a flash of metal; the man was his old friend, his cyborg hit man. "The Moon for Moonsiders!" he shouted, like he was fooling anybody that he was MLF.

Deuce grabbed Sparkle. "Kiss the dirt!" he yelled, and threw himself on top of her as they fell toward the ground.

The window of Donna MaDonna's exploded. Glass geysered, whooshed inward, then showered the ground. Retro foil bustiers, black brassieres and red-lace panties twisted in the blast. The mannequins squeaked and squealed, piling one on top of the other like dead bodies.

There was blood on Deuce's fingers as he peered through them.

"Oh, my God, my God," someone wailed in the distance. "We're going to die."

Juice pulsed at them. Bursting from the rubble, the android joined his better half and they fired off weapons that took out parts of the sidewalk. Swearing, Deuce shielded Sparkle with his body and dodged the beams as best he could. His blaster was nowhere to be found. He hunched over her and began to pull her out of the line of fire, slicing open his legs and hips with each movement as he crawled over the wreckage.

In the opposite direction, barreling down the street, someone in a car with Smith colors on the side jumped the curb and headed for them.

Then a large, dirty aichy screeched up at ninety degrees. A door opened. A hand extended.

"Get in, get in!" shouted the owner of the hand. "Get her out of there."

Blindly, Deuce grabbed it. The hand pulled as he dragged Sparkle in with him, and they were crammed into a tiny space without any seats.

The door hissed shut.

The aichy screeched out of there, followed by blaster fire. Someone said, "Oh, great, now we've got Scarlattis at six o'clock!"

There was so much blood in his eyes that Deuce was blinded. He cried, "Help her, help her!" Then he passed out.

TWENTY

Deuce had a wonderful dream:

He and Sparkle were riding the horses in Hunter Castle's holo walls through breaking foam along a seashore where seabirds cawed and dipped. She was wearing a gauzy wraparound thing that streamed in the wind like her shimmering platinum hair. He was dressed like Devon LeDare, in a black-leather jacket and matching trousers. No, wait. In a black one-suit trimmed with orange. No wait, naked. He was naked.

No one was after them. No one wanted anything from them. They could ride horses naked all day and all night if they wanted. They would never get sore. The horses would never get tired.

Then someone was mumbling, and Deuce knew he was awake. Mainly, because he was not riding naked on a horse, but seated in a chair, and because he ached all over.

He was also unable to see. They'd put a hood over his head. So he ticked through a list of people whose voices he did not want to hear:

Club and Spade.

The Smiths.

The Moongoloid.

Anybody named Scarlatti, and a cast of other thousands who by now knew about Gino and the weapon and Tanzer and Feist and all the rest of the big mess.

Maybe even anybody named Borgioli, but especially Big

Al, who was probably Registering a hit on him because of what had happened with Yuet.

Mamma mia, who was left?

Cautious footsteps approached him from behind. Someone pulled his hood off and Deuce sprang to his feet. Nice young feller, blond like him. Deuce thanked him with a roundhouse kick that sent him sprawling to the floor with a grunt.

"Stop, please, Mr. McNamara," said a man with gray hair and a gray beard seated behind a gray folding table. He looked vaguely familiar.

"What's going on?" Wobbling, Deuce assumed a fighter's stance. The blond man on the floor groaned, held up his hands in a don't-hit-me gesture, and got to his feet. He backed away from Deuce the way a cardinal backs away from the Pope.

Or an N.A. from a Godfather.

Deuce's head throbbed. "Where the hell am I?"

"You're safe," the gray man told him. "Thanks, Gary."

The other man scurried out of the dim, small room. The windows were covered over. Comprehension dawned as Deuce looked at the posters on the cracked and peeling walls. THE MOON FOR MOONSIDERS! FREEDOM NOW! SEND THE FAMILIES INTO ORBIT!

"You're with the MLF," he said to the vaguely familiar man. "Who the hell are you?"

The man inclined his head. "Don't you remember me, Mr. McNamara?"

Deuce studied him. The hair, the beard. He imagined him in various settings: Casinos, family meetings, darkened alleys, blaster fights . . .

"I'll be damned. You're Levi Shoemaker. The pawnshop owner."

"The very same." Shoemaker leaned forward on his gray-metal desk.

"Where's my . . . colleague?"

"Miss de Lune is resting comfortably. You have my word on that."

While Deuce was processing that, the perky and petite

Angelina Rille glided into the room and stood behind Shoemaker. She put her hands on his shoulders.

"He's your real squeeze," Deuce blurted.

She laughed silently. "I'm his daughter."

Deuce was astonished. "You're the daughter of a pawnshop owner?"

"Of a revolutionary," she said proudly, kissing the top of Shoemaker's head. "And the man who saved your life."

That was true. "Why?"

Shoemaker laughed. "I slept with her mother."

Deuce rolled his eyes. Fabulous. He was sitting here with a goose egg on the back of his head and cuts all over his butt and this guy was a comedian.

"Why did I save you? Which time?" Shoemaker asked, looking amused. "When I commed you and told you about the Earthside hit men? When I disabled the Smith pursuit aichy? I could say it was for humanitarian reasons."

"And I could say that was a load of crap."

Shoemaker's eyes danced. A smile wisped across his face. "Honey, get the man a chair. Mr. McNamara, we've been following you for a long time. You seem to be something of a humanitarian yourself."

Deuce glared uneasily at him. "Following me?" Angelina nodded. So he *had* seen her loitering around Donna MaDonna's. "Well, you'd better let me go. I got a tracking device on. All these attempts on my life lately, I got security."

Shoemaker folded his hands. "We searched you, Mr. McNamara. What you have is an unusually strong code of ethics about many things, but especially N.A.'s. You give money to the poor. You tell them where to find jobs. You try your best to keep us out of your battles."

"Yeah, well, big deal," Deuce said. "Whacking you guys is bad for business."

"As are turf wars," Shoemaker said. Deuce waited to see where he went with that. "By the way, Yuet Chan was declared the new Godmother today. There was no violence. There will be no turf war at the Pearl of Heaven. I thought you'd want to know."

"Old news," Deuce tossed back. *Today*? he thought. As

calmly as he could, he added, "What day is it?"

"You've been out for a while. It's Thursday. The nineteenth. About noon."

Deuce shrugged. As surreptitiously as he could, he checked for his blaster. He didn't have it. Nor did he have the cylinder.

"What did you do with the item?" Shoemaker asked.

It must have fallen out of his pocket during the confusion. "Oh, no," Deuce said. "No way I'm handing the Doomsday Machine over to a bunch of fanatics."

"Deuce," Angelina reproved, as she put a chair beside him, "we are not fanatics."

Deuce felt dizzy and nauseous but his wounds didn't bother him. They must have let a doctor at him. "Okay, here's the truth. I lost it during the melee. It's gone."

Father and daughter looked at each other sadly. Shoemaker said, "Mr. McNamara, do you realize what that was? Not a weapon of destruction, but an economic weapon. It was a new way to store energy. A revolutionary sort of fuel, as it were."

Deuce guffawed. "And you know from revolutionary, eh? Look, Mr. Shoemaker, I mean no disrespect, but that sounds far-fetched. The Smiths don't make batteries. You've been snowed." He thought for a moment. "So I guess the reason you saved me is out the window."

Shoemaker watched him closely. "That's one of the reasons we saved you."

Uh-oh.

"Well, I don't have it. Period. The end. It was nice of you to save us, but I'll just be getting my associate and we'll be leaving, thank you very much."

"Mr. McNamara, listen to me." Shoemaker grew very serious. He resembled the pictures of God the Mormons had shown him in their efforts to convert him. "I want things to be good for my daughter. I want my grandchildren—should Angelina present me with any—to have a grand future."

"Then send 'em Earthside," Deuce responded, which, to him, was a completely reasonable solution. "They'll only be N.A.'s here. Down there, they're regular people."

Shoemaker sighed. Angelina held out her hands. " 'Regular people'? Don't you think that's unfair, being labeled at birth as something less than others? Don't you find that a little strange?''

''Well, they can always try to Affiliate,'' he added, feeling defensive. ''That's almost as good.''

''The Family system is a caste system. Like old Earthside India,'' Angelina explained with a hint of impatience. ''We were founded on the principles of democracy.''

''Not Moonbase Vegas, sister,'' Deuce retorted, and then was sorry because that was indeed truly low and disrespectful. Sister? Mamma would have given him a smack. ''*Mi scusi*, but—''

She dropped her hands to her side and turned to her father. ''That fuel could have freed the N.A.'s from dependence on the Families. And . . . oh, Daddy, there's no reasoning with him.''

''I think you're wrong.'' Shoemaker winked at Deuce. Deuce did not like any men winking at him for any reason. ''I just don't think we've gotten through to him.''

She said, ''There's not enough time to get through.''

He hated this act, pretending like the guy being interrogated wasn't in the room, especially since the interrogatee usually had live wires clipped to his nipples not long afterwards.

He folded his arms across his chest and shifted his weight to one hip.

''How come Chicky Smith hasn't killed you?''

Shoemaker gave her another loving pat. ''My girl is very brave.''

''Very dumb.''

''When you believe in something, we call it courage, not stupidity,'' she said. Her eyes flashed.

She was short but pretty.

And stupid.

''And you two believe in . . . ?'' He glanced left, right to make sure no one else could hear him. ''Taking over the Moon so you can be in charge. You, the Families, what's the difference?''

''The difference is, we want to lead our people to freedom from economic slavery," Shoemaker said.

"Yeah, well, that's what our Godfathers want. For their people." He paused meaningfully. "That is, if I was still a Borgioli."

"Angelina tells me you have hopes of Re-Membering."

"Yeah, well."

"By giving them the cylinder?"

"Maybe." He was a little surprised they didn't know the truth about his supposedly only being a temporary N.A. He half expected that they had spies in the Borgioli Family. They seemed like those kind of people.

His kind.

He grinned at them, which threw them both off. "Now that you know I don't have the what, energy source?, I'm no use to you," Deuce said. "Let me go, and no one gets hurt."

"Oh, Deuce," Angelina said gently. "I know you wouldn't hurt a fly."

"I mean no disrespect, Miss Angelina," Deuce replied, "but I have hurt flies and worse. And I probably will again."

"That remains to be seen." Shoemaker put his hands on the desk. "Please, come and say hello to someone who has wanted to meet you for quite some time."

Deuce was instantly on alert. "Like who? Where?"

"It's just a short walk," Shoemaker assured him.

Deuce felt compelled to warn them. He knew the MLF could be a little rowdy, but these two seemed pretty naive. "I'm a Registered kickboxer. My hands and feet are deadly weapons."

"Yes, yes, of course," Shoemaker said. He took Angelina's hand. Deuce couldn't help but stare at her. The fact that she had liaised with not one but two Family members intrigued him. She must have attributes not immediately detectable to the eye. And she must be cold-blooded, if she could do the love thing with two pretty savvy Family men solely for political reasons.

Or maybe she was passionate about her beliefs. Yeah, he liked passionate better.

Speaking of which: "Where's Sparkle?" he asked again.

"I promise you, she's all right. You saved her life."

"Proof would be good."

"In a few minutes, I'll take you to her."

They walked outside. Two guys in camouflage with badges on their sleeves that read MLF Unit One snapped to attention, presenting arms. They had juice superpumpers, which were illegal. The Borgiolis only owned a couple hundred of them.

"At ease," Shoemaker told them, and the soldiers moved to parade rest. Deuce was a little more impressed by his host. He seemed not so much a little old junk dealer as the seasoned head of an elite private army.

"You're what, a general?" Deuce jibed.

"Commander in chief," Angelina filled in proudly.

Deuce whistled. "The big cheese? How many are in your outfit?"

"You don't need to know that." Shoemaker was pleasant, but there was an edge to his voice. He sounded very commanderish. Angelina was clearly digging it.

Past Quonset huts that bore an amazing resemblance to the first lunar colony, they made a left and marched alongside a row of storage units. Definitely from one of the later Apollo missions, maybe 21 or 22. It occurred to him they might have the real falcon feather and the four-leaf clover. He'd ask them sometime when they weren't so preoccupied.

Behind the storage units was a small A-frame building with a military-looking sign over the door, dark blue letters on a field of gray. CHAPEL.

"You're fully equipped," Deuce said.

Shoemaker opened the door. "After you."

"Oh, no. I ain't going nowhere first."

"I'll go first," Angelina said. She went right in, which still didn't prove anything because you would know just from her height who she was. No password or secret handshake required.

Deuce hesitated, adjusting to the light, looking for the holy water.

"Go on in," Shoemaker urged.

Must be Protestant. There was no font. Mormons also

did not have fonts. Wouldn't that be something, a revolutionary movement run by Mormons.

Cautiously, he went in.

It was a very plain church with maybe ten pews on either side and a narrow center aisle. There was a raised altar at the far end, carpeted in red, with a large cross hanging from wood paneling. No figure of Christ on it. No statues of the Virgin. No votive candles. No stained-glass windows. A sign that read, PLEASE KEEP YOUR VOICE LOW. NO WAGERING.

Deuce relaxed a smidge. Maybe these guys wanted to believe they were intrinsically different from the Families, but they weren't so much if you had to keep them from betting in church. What was life but one big crapshoot, anyway?

A gray-haired woman was sitting in one of the front pews. Angelina slid in beside her, spoke to her, and gestured for Deuce to come forward. He didn't move. Broads carried juicers same as guys.

The woman half turned her face, and her profile gave Deuce pause. It was a profile he knew, but couldn't place.

"It's all right." Shoemaker came up behind him. "I guarantee your safety."

"Like you did at Cheetah's Gaslamp?"

Shoemaker tsk-tsked. "Geoffrey Tanzer and Fabiyan Feist were two of our best."

"Best what, torturers?"

Shoemaker looked unhappy. "They went a little too far."

"A *little*?" Deuce raised his brows. "You people are worse than us. What were they going to do to me if I didn't do what they wanted, cut off my"—he glanced at Angelina—"fingers?"

Angelina said defensively, "Meeting you there was their call, not Daddy's."

"And Tanzer gave his unarmed daughter your precious cylinder?"

Angelina persisted. "Because she was unassuming."

"And no juice?" Deuce pressed.

Shoemaker stepped in. "Geoff believed her craziness

was her best weapon. It would have looked suspicious if a woman like her had been packing arms.'' The man shook his head sadly. ''They didn't know you were still targeted for a hit. They had been assured it had been called off.''

''Assured by who?''

Shoemaker sighed. ''Assured by someone in our organization who made a mistake.''

''Yeah, well, maybe it was those two that made it. Did you know they were going to file Papers of Affiliation with the Smiths?''

For an instant Shoemaker looked shocked. Then he said, ''Of course.'' A beat. ''It was a miscommunication.'' Another beat. ''Did you bury her somewhere? Give her respect, as you would say?''

''Yeah,'' he said. ''I took very good care of her. You can tell her family I'll be in touch with the particulars.''

''Thank you. And again, my apologies. As my daughter said, Tanzer and Feist set that meeting up with you before clearing it with me.''

''To do what? Kill the Moongoloid? Take over?''

Shoemaker hesitated. ''They wanted to enlist you in our movement that day.''

''Fabulous.'' Maybe this was a bunch of crap. Maybe Shoemaker had planned to juice all three of them, grab the vial, and kill Spade and Club, too. Or maybe, like Selene, he'd also been in cahoots with the two hit men. Funny how Shoemaker alone had survived the melee, and how he was still alive.

On the other hand, Deuce was also still alive.

Deuce walked down the aisle and stopped beside the two women in the pew. The stranger looked up at him.

She had to be Little Wallace's mamma.

''Mamma Busiek,'' Deuce said shakily. ''My respects. I'm so sorry for your loss.'' A speech often heard in Family circles. He and Joey used to joke that they should get little pins to signify how many funerals they had attended, with special gold ones for perfect attendance. You got one of those pinned on your suit when it was you lying in a casket.

Mamma Busiek touched his hand. Her face was blotched from crying. ''My boy owed you his life,'' she said.

"It was nothing. He accidentally took a Family package once," Deuce said. "I helped him give it back." In the beginning of their relationship, he had kind of milked Little Wallace's innocent error to get him to tell him things. Inflated his own part in it.

"Many Family Members would not have bothered," she insisted.

That was true. "Others would have," he retorted.

She smiled triumphantly at Angelina as if to say, *You see? He's a nice young man.* "He admired you greatly," she said. "He knew you weren't like the other Family parasites. He believed you could be turned to the light." She raised her right hand as if she were taking an oath. "He believed you would lead your Family out of the wilderness and onto the path of righteousness."

"*Signora,*" Deuce began. "I'm a Catholic, not a, um, whatever it is you are."

"I'm a member of the Synodic Synod. A woman who has seen the truth." She talked in that strange singsong preachers used. It gave him the willies. "We need a prophet to drive away the Pharisees. We need a Messia—"

"Now, let's don't get carried away," Deuce said nervously. He tried to help her to a standing position, but she was staying put. "Please."

"And the Lord cried, 'Let my people go!' " she shouted. "Hallelujah!"

"I think that was Moses." Deuce swallowed. "Please, Mamma Busiek. I came to give you my respect. Not, ah, anything else."

"But you know you're the one, don't you?" She lowered her voice. "We are many, Deuce McNamara. We are legion. You'll need a lot of followers to part the Red Sea."

"Up here we have the Sea of Tranquillity," he reminded her.

"You'll need a fortune." Her eyes glittered. He had no idea what she was talking about. "And it can begin with a widow's mite."

He blinked. Now she'd lost him. Shoemaker came up beside him and laid a hand on her shoulder and faintly smiled at Deuce in a fatherly sort of way. "A mite is a small coin," he explained. "In the Bible, the widow didn't have much money, but she gave all she had to the cause. To her, it was a fortune."

The cause? "*Mi scusi*," Deuce said to the woman. "I don't know from the Bible. Like I said, I'm Catholic."

"But you're a Moonsider, boy," she said, her eyes shining. "Don't you see? You're one of us."

"Yes, he is," Shoemaker agreed.

Ka-blam.

He got it.

The MLF was a cult of religious fanatics.

"Oh, no," he said, shaking his head. "Excuse me, but I've got a busy day, and it don't include this kind of stuff." He brushed past Shoemaker and stomped down the aisle.

"And a little child shall lead us!" the woman called after him.

He was met outside by Angelina, who apparently had gone out a side door and darted around to the front.

"Why didn't you guys tell me you were nuts?" he said accusatorily.

Her cheeks were red. From hurrying, possibly, or from mortification that their secret was out, probably. "We aren't."

"Coulda fooled me." He jerked his head in the direction of the church. "Jeez, I feel sorrier than ever for Little Wallace, hanging around with a bunch of lunatics. Except that his *mamma* really loved him."

Shoemaker arrived next. He scratched his forehead. "Well, that didn't go as I'd planned." Deuce looked at him. "She's been rather emotional since her son died."

"Emotional? Does she carry snakes around, too?" Deuce asked, stuffing his hands into his pockets. "I want my colleague."

"The MLF is not a religious organization," Shoemaker said. "It just so happens that Mrs. Busiek has found comfort in her religion because of her loss."

"Her loss is your loss," Deuce said, "if you'd hoped her pitch would make me want to sign up."

Shoemaker and his daughter traded glances. Apparently that was exactly what they had hoped.

"You don't realize the unique position you're in," Shoemaker went on. "We need a symbol."

"You mean a patsy." Deuce eyed the guys with superblasters. "I want my colleague *now*."

"They're going to sacrifice you." Shoemaker held out his hands. "They're going to let you get killed."

Deuce shrugged. "Thanks for the news bulletin." He wished he knew exactly what the man was talking about.

"It'll look like an accident. There are things going on you don't know about, young man. Backroom deals. Double crosses. The Families are trying to outmaneuver each other in what they perceive as a fight for survival before Castle even begins to threaten it."

Deuce nodded. "I can understand that. I perceive my own situation as a fight for survival."

He walked up to Angelina, cupped her head, bent down, and kissed her. "Please, she's not just my colleague. She's my fiancée," he murmured. "Let me see her."

She wrapped her hands around his wrists. "All right."

He kissed her again. "You should find a nice boy." Gave her father a look. "One who isn't wacko and one who doesn't torture people worse than Family Members do."

"Deuce . . ." She inhaled, held it, exhaled. "Have a nice life."

"I will."

"It's going to be short," Shoemaker said.

"That a threat? Because we can take it outside, now," Deuce said. Then he realized they were legally outside. "Or Topside," he added. "Anytime you want."

Shoemaker sighed. "I have no quarrel with you."

Deuce raised his chin. "Maybe not at the moment." He saluted Angelina.

"You can't just walk out of here. It's not safe for either of us." Shoemaker raised a hand at a soldier, who doubletimed it over to him. "Get Mr. McNamara a car and a driver." He looked at Deuce. "People think you still have the cylinder."

"Your concern for me is touching."

Shoemaker put his hand on Deuce's shoulder. "Think

twice, McNamara. Your world has turned upside down in the last few hours. The balance of power has shifted. The rules, such as they are, have changed.''

Deuce raised his chin. ''That's no big deal. They've changed before.''

''Not like this. Hunter Castle has never been here before.''

''Officially he's never been here before.'' Deuce turned to go.

A black stretch aichy zoomed up silently beside him. The driver's window rolled down and an incredibly sexy redhead in a chauffeur's uniform smiled coyly at him. He was surprised. This was not the type of MLF chauffeur—chauffeuse?—he would have expected.

''Thanks,'' he said to Shoemaker. ''I'll send her back in one piece.'' To his surprise, there were tears in Angelina's eyes. ''Don't, like, pray for me or nothing.''

She smiled. Maybe the tears were just an allergy. ''I wouldn't dream of it.''

''Okay, now I want my lady,'' he told her. ''Then we'll get the hell out of your hair.''

''And go where?'' she prodded.

''Don't worry about us. I've got a plan.''

''I'm sure you do. I just wish it included us,'' Angelina said with a tinge of wistfulness in her voice.

TWENTY-ONE

As soon as Deuce and Sparkle cleared the MLF compound, Deuce called Joey. He was tired and he sounded okay.

The MLF stretch limo had a viso, and he and Sparkle—who was, indeed, also very much all right—caught up on the prodigious amount of news that anchorman Ram Chander had to share with them. First there was Madame Dai-Tai's spectacular cremation inside some kind of little temple which they also burned up, for which the Chans had to spend tons on pollution levies. It was reported that Yuet's stepbrothers, Cheung and Sying, had left for pressing business on Earth before the funeral and "were not expected to return to the Moon for some time." Yeah, no kidding. He wondered how many different shuttles they were sent home on, six?

Then there was Donna MaDonna's blowing up in slow motion. Ram Chander told everybody how the MLF had been blamed but denied responsibility.

"Earth officials have been contacted for comment, but the representative for the Department of Fairness, Mr. Emerson Epperson-Roux, has stated that if this latest act of violence can be traced to any of the six Casino Families, their Charter will be revoked. This could prove disastrous for the local economy, which relies almost solely on tourism, for—"

Deuce surfed the channels.

". . . and I want to share my Lucky Plan with you before I die," a man in a very nice blue suit was saying. It was the Lucky Luciano Get Lucky Quick man with his inter-minable infomercial. It was on at all hours of the day. "I can double-down anytime I want. I can break the bank with only fifty credits in my pocket. I can—"

Deuce changed.

"—latest experimental Roller is rolling off the assembly line in New America!"

Deuce watched for a moment. The Roller was a squat, boxy vehicle comprised of a cabin of reinforced stainless steel atop huge balloon wheels. They were based on a com-bination of the old lunar landers and the Vectran air bags that had been deployed during the Pathfinder missions to Mars in the twentieth century. Someone had once told Deuce they looked like "tanks" or "Humvees." He'd never gotten around to bringing up graphics of such antique vehicles, but now he thought about him and Joey zooming around on them and getting into trouble, and felt a strange surge of protectiveness toward not just his brother, but all the innocent people on the Moon.

"—deplorable violence," Hunter Castle was saying on Channel 17. "Ah am certain that the authorities will deal out justice to the perpetrators of this heinous act. Donna MaDonna's is an historical landmark of Moonbase Vegas, and—"

" 'An' historical landmark?" Deuce sniped. "Where does he get off talking like that? And how would he know what's a landmark and what isn't?" He made himself shut up; he sounded like a jealous, petty, small-minded *scemo*.

And jealous.

Sparkle said nothing. Then she patted his hand on her knee, and said, "You're pretty nervous, aren't you?"

He nearly had a heart attack. Wow. *Empathy* from Spar-kle. Or was she simply being psychic?

"Not so much." He shrugged his shoulders and caught her expression of disbelief. "I call meetings with Rog and Abe Smith all the time time."

"Me too." She went back to watching the viso.

Maybe it was a joke, and maybe she meant it.

"Look," she said, pointing to the images.

"Interest is heating up for the Match for the Moon,"

Ram Chander said excitedly. "Local Independent Deuce McNamara is taking on Hunter Castle in a wrestling match sure to pull in a lot of money for local Independent schools. Even though the two men have not divulged the identities of their contestants, the wagering has already begun. As of this broadcast, Castle is favored to win by a margin of fifty to one. The match, which will be held—"

"Turn it off," Deuce said. Fifty to one. He hoped he lived long enough to get whupped by fifty to one. His stomach was in a knot. "This is nuts. All it was supposed to be was a little bet."

"For some people, there are no little bets," Sparkle remarked.

"You got a feeling, good or bad?"

She shook her head. "Neither." Then she said, "The MLF. You don't think they're an offshoot of the League of Decency, do you?"

"Whoa. You think?" Deuce blinked. "You know, now that you mention it, Signora Busiek was your standard religious hardliner."

"It's something to think about," Sparkle said.

"Oh, and I was running out of things to think about," Deuce replied archly. He winced. His mouth was getting ahead of his blood pressure. He said to the chauffeuse, "Can you get me a comm line that looks like I would think it's secured, but it's not?"

She grinned at him in the mirror. "A disinformation web? Sure." She pressed a button. "Any calls you make will be picked up all over the base."

"Okay, here goes." He dialed Angelo, his Borgioli cousin. "*Paisan*," he said. "It's Deuce. You'll never believe this. That thing Gino Scarlatti stole? Guess who has it."

The aichy zoomed on toward the Wild West.

Casa de Smiths:

Down in the bunker, there was no yeeha! rootin' tootin' town of yesteryore. There were metal walls covered with banks of communications and surveillance equipment. There were guys who had never smiled in their lives totin' blasters, and more unsmiling accountants, lawyers, runners, and nervous-looking Affiliates than Deuce had ever seen. It was a regular factory of anxiety down there.

At the end of a table almost as big and long as Hunter Castle's, the two dark Smith co-Godfathers, Roger and Abraham, sat like cigar-store Indians, grumph, humph, no how, no way.

And all of this was for Deuce.

Who had shown up empty-handed.

"Which is the point, ain't it?" he drawled at the two stone-faced men.

No one moved for the longest time. Then Abraham said out of the corner of his mouth, "Clear the room. The dames, too."

Faster than a race announcer could shout "And they're off!" everyone, even that sexpot, Alicia Vera, scurried out like there was a rabbit to chase. Sparkle looked like she was going to make a big deal out of being asked to leave, but she unfolded herself from her chair and sauntered out very slowly, letting her hips roll from side to side.

"Who is that?" Abraham asked Roger, who was making sweetsy with Alicia Vera as she posed by the door in a vampy curve and admired him.

Sparkle languidly turned her head and smiled at him. Abraham smiled back. "A pleasure, Miss . . . ?"

"De Lune. Sparkle de Lune." Like a duchess, she left the room slightly behind Alicia Vera.

Abraham turned to Deuce. "Your woman?"

"My associate." He wished he could just cop to it. Beatrice thought they were engaged and Sparkle . . . well, he supposed she was unemployed by now, not having shown up for work since last Sunday. Maybe she had arranged for leave. He'd have to ask. Not that she'd tell him.

"Your associate in blackmailing us?" Roger said, leaning forward in a manner meant to be threatening. Which it was.

Deuce swaggered a bit even though it was the last thing on the Moon he was up to. He sat down and crossed his legs at the knee. Yow. His painkillers were wearing off. He kept steady.

The Smiths looked like they might swoop down and devour him, he was so cavalier in their presence.

Okay. Grounded and ready to run, he said, "You must know that I have nothing but the deepest respect for you and your House. You are everything a Family should be, powerful and ruthless, and—"

"What do you want?" Abraham interjected.

Stay on target, stay on target, Deuce ordered himself. He opened his hands as if he were holding a little chick inside them. Not that he had ever seen—

"Let's kill him," Roger said. "I'm too busy for whatever this . . . *N.A.* kid has to say to us."

Deuce pulled a sincere expression. "Don Roger, Don Abraham, a miracle has befallen me. A miracle and a curse. I have learned the secret of your secret weapon." Now was the part where he had to pull the biggest bluff of his life.

"You have." They looked completely unimpressed.

He uncrossed his legs and leaned forward. "Which is to say, there isn't any."

They stared at him. He was afraid he'd miscalculated. Very afraid. Afraid enough to have a heart attack at his young age and in his excellent physical condition, except for lately because he was under so much stress.

Mamma mia, he even blathered in his head when he was nervous.

"What makes you think this idiocy?" Abraham asked, rising. He was at least a million feet tall. Deuce craned his neck to look up at him. He made himself not burst into tears or a hysterical, terrorized fit of laughter.

"Let's just say I put a few facts together. As in, Gino Scarlatti thinks he's stolen the Doomsday Machine, but how come he thinks that? You would never in a million years let a *cretino* gravoid like him get near such a thing. And your guys in their fancy aichies are shooting at me and never quite hit me. But they're *Smiths*. And I ask why don't they aim better?" He caught his breath. "Because then there won't be anything to collect from the wreckage."

"Or anything to copy or steal," Abraham pointed out.

"And the MLF thinks it's some kind of energy source or battery or whatever, and—"

Roger's dark face went red with fury. "Who the hell do you think you are, barging in here and—?"

He was right. Deuce nearly keeled over. He was right! He had correctly called their bluff. *They had nothing.*

"Godfather, I mean no disrespect," Deuce said, laying his hand over his heart, mostly to keep it inside his chest. "I am not trying to jerk your chain. I'm trying to save my own life. I have let it be known that I have come to see you. I let the entire satellite believe that I am returning to you what is rightfully yours, even though maybe someone grabbed that cylinder during the explosion at Donna MaDonna's and is trying to get the goody out of it like they're cracking open a walnut."

He held out his hands again. He was gesturing with them like an Italian, like a Family man, which was what he supposed he truly was and always would be. "And maybe they got it open and found out there was nothing inside that was worth all their troubles. And then they figured the cylinder they found is a decoy that *I* planted during the explosion because I'm out to rule the Moon or something with the real one, which they assume I still have. And which I have now brought to you." He took another breath. "And no one, including anybody in your own Family, ever has to know that all I did was sit here and sweat."

"Well, you're right. That cylinder was a decoy," Abraham cut in, also looking unhappy. "We have dozens of them. We have the real weapon hidden safely away."

"I know," Deuce said patiently. "I will go to my grave knowing that." He held out his hands. "You see, gentlemen, if I did not come to you and return what was yours, my own Godfather would have wanted me to deliver it to him. Truth," he said at their surprise. "The MLF even kidnapped me to give it to them. They tortured me, but still I held out. No one would believe me that I lost it or that its very existence was a big lie—I mean, a, um, prevarication that you have used for generations to intimidate everybody. I would never have had any peace unless I came to you and pretended to give it back."

"You have no Godfather. You're not in a Family," Roger said. The wheels were turning. Deuce wanted to dance an Irish jig, except his behind and his legs were on fire.

"I tell you now that I was Dis-Membered over a trivial matter and then retained to spy on everybody during the invasion of Hunter Castle," Deuce said. He figured if Beatrice and Big Al were sippin' cider with Castle, Castle might know about the spying thing. There wasn't much percentage in keeping secret what surely was not secret. "I also tell you that I believe you took advantage of his arrival to add some confusion of your own, for your own reasons. In coming here, I'm laying my life at your feet."

"In exchange for?" Now Roger Smith was almost grinning. Deuce wanted to let out a war whoop the likes of which had never been heard in Comanche Nights!

"In exchange for you acting as if I did give you the weapon, for then protecting me."

Roger said generously, "Do you want to Affiliate with us?"

Deuce knew that would be coming. He bowed his head sorrowfully. "Again, I mean no disrespect. *Daverro daverro*, which in the language means 'really and truly.' You know it's a cross to be a Borgioli." He rolled his eyes. "But my adopted mother, Maria della Caldera, may she rest in peace"—he crossed himself—"thought she was bringing the blessings of the Virgin Maria to me by getting me into that degenerate Family. You know that in any Family, it's considered better to be a Member than an Affiliate. Although we also know it would be better to be an Affiliate of your House than a Member of mine, it's on my mind to lead my Family someday. Then maybe I can turn all the Borgiolis into decent people by begging you to, ah, take us in."

Their eyes popped like Moon Pies. "Merge with the Borgiolis?"

"If someday it was possible," Deuce said. "Who knows what the future will bring? If I had the opportunity to rise to the top, I would do the best thing for my Family that would class it up." But he would not Sanction a hit on Big Al. No way.

"Maybe killing you would be better." Roger looked at Abraham.

Deuce said, "I thought of that, too." Boy, had he. "But think of your reputations. I bring you the weapon, and you whack me?"

"There is that," Roger admitted.

"I am the man who returned your weapon to you, and now your friend. When I want, I'll be Re-Membered like that." He snapped his fingers. "I'll rise like cream. Who couldn't, in the Borgiolis? And then, when the time is right . . ." He smiled. Maybe that part was a bit of a fib, but by then, the tides would have changed again, wouldn't they?

"You let Gino Scarlatti steal that Chan vial because he'd stolen your other cache of Chan drugs," he went on, resuming his bluff. "You wanted to see how he was doing it. Somehow, Gino and Wayne Van Aadams got it into their heads that what Gino actually had was your weapon."

Abraham smiled. "Somehow."

"We were two dishonors behind by then," Roger said. Abraham flashed him a warning glance, and Roger looked uncomfortable. And in that moment, Deuce knew an important piece of information: the Smiths had not repositioned the Ditwac. Otherwise, they would have counted it as the restoration of one, if not both, of those two dishonors.

Then who had repositioned it?

"We need you to prove your loyalty to us," Abraham said. "I want you to sign Papers for Honorary Affiliation. That's essentially a treaty between you personally and our House for the rest of your life."

Deuce pretended to consider, but of course he would sign. There were benefits to be had, plus he really had no choice. What was he going to say, no? "I have associates to consult," he said slowly.

Abraham snorted. "The Borgiolis."

Deuce smiled faintly. "Associates, not embarrassments." He allowed his glance to flicker upward. As in, toward the enviro-dome. And Castle's massive ship that hovered there.

"Sign, or you won't leave this room," Roger growled.

Deuce inclined his head. His bluff was finally being called, and he was out of steam. "Godfathers, it would be an honor."

Roger hit a comm link on the side of his chair. "Ten-Stop, come in here."

Deuce knew that Ten-Stop Theo was the Family Registrar. He would ensure that the Papers were properly drawn up. Deuce blinked a few times to moisten his eye for the scan. There were perhaps two drops of moisture left in his entire body. Except that he was positive that any second he was going to wet his pants.

"Welcome to our Family," Roger said. He pressed the link again. "Bring us champagne. And get Deuce McNamara's *associate* in here." He winked at Deuce. "Nice setup, kid," he murmured.

"Don Roger, thank you so much," Deuce said feelingly. The room spun, but he kept his bearings.

Barely.

The Smiths gave Deuce three bodyguards for protection, but the biggest protection they gave him was letting it be known that he had returned their secret weapon intact and that they were satisfied that he had not penetrated those secrets. Otherwise, he would be dead.

In their absence, Selene's apartment had been ransacked and his and Sparkle's had been torched. People looking for the weapon, people looking for him. Deuce wondered if Club and Spade had given up now, or if he was still a target.

After grieving together over the loss of their material possessions, Sparkle collected Moona Lisa and decided to go to the Topside condo, check on Joey, and pull herself together. Deuce sent two of their Smith bodyguards with her. He took the other one and told him to wait outside the Borgioli House while he paid his respects to Big Al.

He walked into the entrance of the casino amid the mandolin music and the holos of gondoliers, the leaning tower of Pisa, and some really busty peasant girls squishing grapes for wine with their bare feet.

The huge statue of David was playing to the crowd. "Hey, I feel a draft in here! Anybody else naked and cold? But seriously, folks, welcome to the Palazzo di Fortuna, the Palace of Fortune. Speaking of fortune, anybody wanna see my family jewels?"

Deuce sighed and hurried through across the floor to the sweet melody of people calling out, "Hey, Deuce, hey, howyadoin', Deuce!" and found his Godfather in the casino's poshest eating establishment, Diana's Grove. The feature of the joint was that all the waitress dressed in tiny togas that pretty much left nothing to the imagination. Which Sparkle had told him was ironic because in the original myth, some hunter spied on Diana, goddess of the Moon and of the hunt, her being in a state of undress, and got torn to pieces for peeking at her.

Seated with some of the Family goons, Big Al was eating a huge plate of spaghetti and meatballs. He ate with his fork stuffed into his hand like he was tearing someone's head off instead of satisfying his discriminating palate.

"*Buon giorno, mio Padrino,*" Deuce said, bowing.

Big Al grunted and kept eating. He didn't offer Deuce anything, and he didn't suggest he sit down. So Deuce waited. After a time, his stomach growled loudly.

Big Al growled in return and slammed down his fork. "You," he said. "I told you what to do about Yuet. You failed me. Why haven't you checked in? What the hell have you been doing?"

Deuce didn't know where to start. He said, "I've been tying up loose ends, Godfather." That Big Al didn't know about the cylinder and the Smiths astounded him.

"Loose ends. Your *mamma* used to talk to my sister about you for hours," Big Al went on. "She worried herself to death over you. They said in school you didn't live up to your full potential."

Deuce inwardly sighed. He thought he'd pretty much put all that behind him.

"My girl loves you," Big Al went on. "I've approved your engagement. Prove yourself worthy of her."

It occurred to Deuce that proving himself unworthy might disentangle him from Beatrice's eagerness to live up to her own full potential, but there was that fork.

He said, "I'm desolated that I'm still a disappointment to you, Don Alberto."

"You're also living on borrowed time, son." His sad eyes got small and mean. "Which Beatrice is gonna collect on pretty damn soon, if you get my drift."

His drift being a little caper that included something white, something borrowed, and one blue bridegroom.

Deuce felt so cheap.

"*Mi dispiace*," he said, avoiding the issue as best he could. "I'll make you proud of me real soon."

Big Al's eyes got sad again. He laid down his fork. "You, how can I stay angry with you when she loves you so? I need grandchildren, Arturino. Once you marry Beatrice, I'll designate you my heir."

Yikes. Wouldn't that make the Smiths happy? Deuce swallowed hard.

Big Al smiled at him. Actually smiled. "Get out of here," he said. "Go spy on people. I have a headache. That you gave me."

"Maybe you should marry her," Sparkle said without much emotion. Or concern, or jealousy. But on the other hand, no enthusiasm.

They were standing with their three bodyguards in the crush waiting for the passengers from the *Arthur Clarke* to arrive. Sparkle had dressed real nice for the occasion, in a field of stars on blue velvet with a big blue bow in her fountain of platinum.

Despite the security guards, Deuce was scanning for Club and Spade. And maybe some *assassinio* guy of Castle's, who knew? Deuce wasn't sure how rough he played. But he did know Castle played to win.

"I can just imagine what would happen to my neck when she found out I had a mistress," Deuce ventured.

Sparkle raised an eyebrow. Deuce felt a rush of panic. That *was* what she'd had in mind, wasn't it?

"I'm so sorry for all the sneaking around," he said feelingly. "Now that you've been fired—"

"It's still not a good idea." She shrugged. "I don't think about it much, really."

God, she was cool. Some might say cold.

"Oh, look, it's the N.A. who's organizing that wrestling match!" a woman said in a loud voice. "Mother, it's him!"

Heads turned in Deuce's direction. He glanced at Sparkle, who shrugged and shook her head as if to say, "Beats me."

A murmur went through the crowd. A young man with bronze hair held out a mini.

"Mr. McNamara, could I have a signature? We love what you're doing for the little guy, going up against that *invader*."

"The Families are too afraid of Hunter Castle," added the woman who had first recognized Deuce. "They're going to sit by and let him take over the entire satellite!"

The Smith guards made a fan around Deuce. "No signatures," one of them grunted.

Deuce said, "It's okay."

"It ain't safe, Mr. McNamara," said the grunter.

"I'm happy to sign a few minis." Minis were pushed quickly past his protectors. He looked at Sparkle. She, too, was amazed.

"Earth shuttle *Arthur Clarke* has docked," the P.A. announced. "Passengers will be arriving through airlock Number 1028C in approximately ten minutes."

The crowd grew. People called out Deuce's name. Then, "M-L-F, M-L-F."

We need a symbol.

Uh-oh.

A visocam arrived on the scene. Then Ram Chander was standing in front of him, asking, "When did you first dream up this wrestling match to unite the Independents, Mr. McNamara? Was it when the MLF offered to back you?"

Deuce was mystified. "Ah . . ."

"He's here," Sparkle murmured. "Say, 'No comment.' "

"Sorry." Deuce flashed the Smile. "No comment."

"But Mr. McNamara . . ."

The Smith grunter moved subtly toward the reporter.

"Are the Smiths backing you as well?" Chander asked
Deuce cheerily as he backed up.

"No comment," Deuce said again, looking to Sparkle.
But her attention was riveted—*sì, daverro daverro*, riveted—on the door as the arrival light blinked on.

Soon he would be here. Alex van Damnation. The Moonman. And formerly a very close friend of Deuce's.

They had had a big fight over Sparkle. As in, Alex doing
the wrestling thing and Deuce, kickboxing. It had happened
very late in a bar after a lot of Atherton Gold, but it had
happened, and they had both meant it. The fact that Alex
had left the Moon and gone to wrestle Earthside seemed to
indicate that Deuce had won. Except that after that, Sparkle
started traveling more often to Earth. Citing business interests which, unlike most showgirls, Sparkle actually and
honestly had.

Yeah, like stock deals.

We're engaged now, he told himself. But he had to admit
he would be a lot happier when they could announce it
publicly.

With the crowd and the visocam aimed at them, they
moseyed toward the door, where an airport employee, with
what could only be described as a blue-wool bagel on her
head, posed by the lock as if it was part of the Daily Show-
case on everyone's favorite game show, *Moonspinners*. She
worked for the shuttle line and her name was Reba; on
occasion she told Deuce if there were important Earthside
people on board.

The light flashed twice, and the door opened with a low
kathummmmmm. Then passengers were streaming through
the door, all excited and eager, pointing at the one-armed
bandits and the glitz, hardly able to believe they were actually here! And other people were hugging newcomers and
showing them babies and all that. While all the while, Ram
Chander kept asking, "Are you waiting for your wrestler,
Mr. McNamara? Is this the man who'll be wrestling, or are
you still going to enter the ring yourself?"

"He hasn't changed," Sparkle observed. There was a
softness in her voice usually reserved for the dog, and of
late for Deuce.

Moonman came into Deuce's view. He was what you might call a strapping lad, with bulging shoulders and pecs and biceps and no neck, none whatsoever, inside a leotard-style top and a pair of black trousers. He was having trouble with the low grav, laughing as he bounced along with the crowd.

Deuce swallowed and briefly wished he had the kind of fiancée who would squeeze his hand and whisper, "I love you and only you, darling." But that wouldn't be his fiancée then, now, would it?

Moonman saw him. Alex's smile faded. His Adam's apple moved. Deuce realized he was nervous, too. Alex held on to his carry-on bag, crammed to bursting. Everyone went for the one free carry-on. Cargo space was very expensive on the shuttles.

The crowd deposited Moonman three feet away from Deuce and Sparkle. Sparkle moved away from Deuce and approached the other man. She kissed him lightly on the lips, and said, "Welcome home."

Moonman regarded her seriously. Something passed between them, something private and layered. And then his gaze ticked toward Deuce. He walked toward him with his hand extended.

"Deuce," he said.

"Are you McNamara's wrestler?" Ram Chander insisted.

Moonman blinked. "*Pardonnez-moi?*"

"Yes, yes, he is," Sparkle said. She sounded excited.

Deuce hesitated. Then he held out his hand. "Your goddamn cheesy car blew up on me," he said.

"You never could drive worth a damn," Moonman retorted.

Then their arms were around each other, and they greeted each other as old good friends should, with a laugh and a slap on the back.

"I didn't have an accident," Deuce said.

"Well, you bought it, *mon ami*."

"Well, you robbed me, dirtball."

They laughed again and Moonman punched Deuce's

shoulder, then wobbled backward. "Ahm going to have to readjust to the gravitee, I see."

"Will you be ready for the big fight on the twenty-ninth?" Chander went on.

"Did you take your free-fall meds?" Sparkle asked with real concern in her voice. You could hurt yourself seriously if you didn't prepare yourself ahead of time for a Moonside stay. The meds made it possible for people to shuttle back and forth between the two gravities, just as earlier pharmaceutical protocols had eased the transitions among Earthside time zones. In fact, they had been the precursors to the freefalls.

"*Oui, oui,* of course," Moonman assured her.

Sparkle took his hand. She waved her hand at Ram Chander. "We'll have a press conference tomorrow at one o'clock. Thank you. Good night."

That only drew more people. A reporter from the *Moonwatcher* arrived. Despite the efforts of the Smith guys, they were jostled and pushed. One of them reached in his pocket.

"No blasters," Deuce whispered, and the man sighed in frustration.

"We got to get you out of here," he muttered. "Now."

"Right," Deuce said. He raised his hands. "Press conference at one o'clock."

"Where?" someone called.

Deuce hesitated. Sparkle said, "In front of Schirra Hall."

"Yeah," Deuce said.

"We're going *now*," the Smith guy said.

Alex van Damnation scratched his head. "*Alors*, a lot 'as 'appened since ah was here last."

"*Pas de merde*," Deuce responded. "More than you can guess."

More than he could, too.

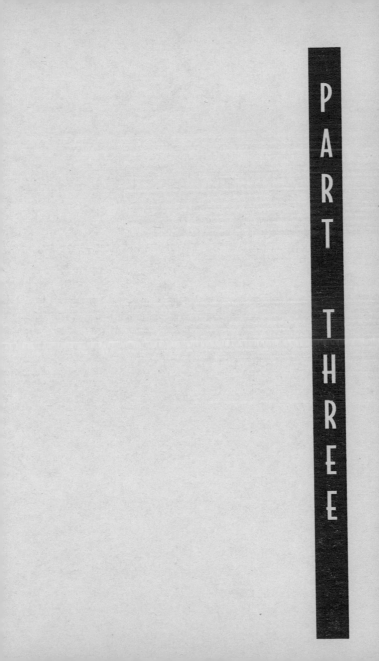

PART THREE

From the Captain's Log of Gambler's Star:

Interesting developments, as I gaze upon my lucky star, the Gambler, from the impressive skylight of my most impressive ship. Daily I discover new capabilities of the items that I salvaged from the wreck.

I am indeed a lucky man, although some would argue that there is no such thing as luck. I think it was that ol' Southern boy, Thomas Jefferson, who said, "I believe in luck. And it seems the harder I work, the more luck I have."

It seems that Deuce has become a rallying force among the Independents, who see this match as an "us"—meaning the Independents—"versus Castle" situation. I find this rather tragic; they are completely overlooking the Families, whom they regard as such a monolithic enemy that they're disregarding them entirely in this enterprise. There are so many opportunities here that they could exploit! At the very least, they could take the watchwords of the MLF—"the Moon for the Moonsiders" and unite with the Families against me.

I believe that in the long run, it's to my disadvantage that they've not done so. So many interests, so many deals to make. I've had meetings with each Family and with the MLF, but of course there is no Independent leader with whom to parlay... yet. They all want something different. None of them trusts the other. It would be easier if I had a better road map. I had assumed I would be treated as if I were attempting a hostile takeover, but that doesn't begin to describe the complexities of the situation here, with Vendettas and dishonors and obligations and more unique situations than I can keep track of. It was arrogant of me to assume that what works on Earth would necessarily work here.

However, the boy is beginning to grasp the situation, and there, perhaps, lies my hope. He really is a shrewd young man. Though I have no cause to be, I'm proud of him.

On the plus side, this place is such a pressure cooker that the wrestling match has become a way for these people to let off steam. I have Sparkle to thank for that. She's coming along nicely. I see now that games and wagering are second nature to them. It's the best way to make them sit up and pay attention.

I'll have to keep that in mind.

                                        Hunter Castle

If Deuce hadn't been there, he wouldn't have believed it. Schirra Hall was usually a drab, scummy joint with cracked seats and sticky concrete floors ripe with the smell of rancid popcorn and stale beer. On the one or two occasions he had actually been inside its doors, Deuce had contrasted it to the Family halls with their padded seats and beeyoutiful chandeliers and exorbitantly priced, watered-down drinks, two of which you were required to buy for the privilege of spending a month's salary or two to see some headliner.

But now, thanks to Hunter Castle, it was a wonderland. Its walls were freshly spackled and painted, and exquisite holo murals of various athletes popped from its sleek, undistressed walls. Sparkle told him the holos were originals by none other than Gigot de la Mere, which impressed her more than it impressed Deuce because he did not know many names of famous Earthside artists.

The flooring had also been redone, and all the seats reupholstered. The N.A.'s, in their drab Sunday best, were going bonkers admiring the upgrades. A few people were obviously hesitant to sit in them. Deuce regarded the happiness and pleasure on their faces and felt an annoying little tug on his heart. A few cans of paint, a couple nice chairs, one of those twirly light-balls hanging from the ceiling— geez, it wasn't so much that Castle had done, and yet these people were practically fainting.

Castle was not stupid, that was for sure. Or cheap.

Then a woman suddenly whirled around, spotting Deuce as he stood behind a pillar with his Smith bodyguards having a smoke, and clasped her hands under her chin.

"Thank you, Mr. McNamara," she called. She beamed at him. "Thank you so much."

Deuce lifted a finger and smiled back, though of course he had done nothing to warrant her gratitude.

Moonman had asked to be alone as he prepared for the fight. He was in the practice area, still working on his grabs and holds for use in the light gravity. Alex was doing pretty well. Unfortunately, his opponent, also warming up, was doing better. The guy had a specially equipped gym back on Earth, and he practiced at one-sixth gravity on a regular basis, just in case.

For now, Deuce stayed behind the pillar, taking everything in. Castle had yet to make his appearance. He was probably up in the sky box with the sports reporters and the big bookmakers.

A voice boomed out, "Laaaaaadies and gentlemen! May I have your attention, please! The match you have all been waiting for will begin shortly! But first, let's welcome the exquisite girls and boys of the Cirque de la Lune!"

Each Family had been invited to include an act from their revues in the pre-match warmup. Most N.A.'s had never seen these fabulous shows—they were for the tourists— and they went even crazier as trapeze artists floated down from the twirly ball and started their act. Then some contortionist-type girls trotted into the ring and turned themselves into glittering pretzels and things like that.

Deuce left and went to check on Moonman. He was sparring with Master Akira, Sparkle's kickboxing instructor and the owner of the dojo where she and Deuce worked out. Sparkle had met Diana Lunette there. Waxing Littlemoon told him that Wayne Van Aadams wanted to have a big funeral for Diana, but his Family put the kibosh on it. His engagement has not been Sanctioned, so, therefore, it had never been official. Apparently, Chairman William Atherton was furious with Wayne for embarrassing the Family by announcing his liaison with this mere showgirl all over the base, then whacking her. Bets were on that the Chairman might even disinherit him over it. Turned out that the rejuvved matron who had called Wayne in from his contretemps with Deuce was some great-aunt of his brought up from Earthside for the sole purpose of making him presentable so he could get engaged to a decent girl, and then he had gone and loused it up. No one had seen him in public since the death of his one grand love.

Deuce was crossing his fingers that Club and Spade had been called off, but of that he was still not sure.

"Hey, Alex," Deuce said, bowing to Master Akira. "How ya feeling?"

"*Incroyable.*" Alex soared into the air and feinted a bodyslam at Master Akira. Moon wrestling was not like Earth wrestling. It had a lot more elements to it. Kickboxing was part of it. Karate, too. It was really classy.

Deuce smiled. "You go out there and kill 'im, big guy."

"Zat ah will do," Alex promised. Then he got serious with Master Akira, and Deuce left again so as not to distract him.

He wandered back to his hiding place and watched some more of the show. It had been going on for over an hour. Lasers flashing, colors swirling and dancing. The enormous glowing twirly ball descended from the ceiling, opened slowly, and showgirls dressed in silver did hula dances with their arms and tossed sparkling confetti crescents at the cheering crowds. Music pulsed. For this moment, Schirra Hall was somewhere else, a sparkling fantasy world, no matter if you had a box seat or you were SRO.

Sparkle worked the *Venus on Ice* segment in rollerblades in the ring, and Deuce puffed with pride as some man murmured, "What a dame."

The media had begun comparing this match with the one that blew up Earthside Las Vegas, and that scared off a few of the Family Members. Most of them showed, however, maybe figuring if part of the Moon went, probably all of it would. Castle told Deuce he had the latest detecting equipment installed in the auditorium. The Lunar Security Forces had okayed the match, stating for public consumption that their concerns about security had been satisfied.

Finally, it was time for the "really big shew." As Deuce

went to collect Moonman, he ran into Castle and his entourage. Castle hailed him. He was smoking a cigar like Big Al might smoke. Deuce wished he had one, too.

"Signor McNamara." He smiled and puffed.

"Mr. Castle." He did not smile.

That was it. They parted to get their wrestlers.

Sprayed gold from head to toe, Moonman was dressed in purple and gold, colors that belonged to no one on the Moon, with a big M on his chest. The MLF claimed this as a direct reference to them. The N.A.'s did likewise.

"Come on, baby," Deuce said, giving him a punch on the arm. "Let's nail that bastard."

"*Allons-nous*," Alex agreed.

It was a circus going into the ring, with girls galore and a phalanx of guys on their Hoverharleys, running lights flashing. The crowd was on its feet, shrieking for their local boy. Moonman had wrapped golden bracelets around his wrists and biceps, and gold cord around his forehead, and furled a cape with gold crescents all over it. Deuce wasn't sure how the N.A. men felt about Moonman, but the women were in orbit. They loved him. They thought he looked heroic and sexy. Which why why Deuce was selling holo posters of him for two credits a whack—very cheap, cheap enough for every N.A. on the satellite to be able to afford one.

Sparkle, in a very slinky black evening gown, sat in her VIP seat in the first row from the ring. There was an empty seat in the cordoned-off area for Deuce, but he doubted he would use it. He was staying ringside, and so were his three Smith bodyguards.

Seated beside her father, Beatrice waved from the mezzanine in an area reserved for the Borgioli Family. Deuce smiled at her, for an instant awash in guilt.

Then he turned his attention to the grand entrance of Hunter Castle's boy, Hang 'Em High Harry, who was 75–0. He dressed all in black cowboy clothes—namely, a black wrestling leotard and spiked leather chaps, a bandanna, and a cowboy hat—and carried a lasso that some broads dressed as Indians set on fire. Hang 'Em High wowed the crowd with diabolical props—guns, knives, bows that shot flaming arrows, and a blowtorch that looked like an old Winchester rifle. Pyrotechnics, the opiate of the masses.

The Smith bodyguards were digging it. In their cordoned-off area, so were the Smith Family attendees.

The referee stepped forward. He would call the match, but the Charter Board was also watching via remotes stationed all over the Hall, and if there was any evidence of cheating, it would take immediate action, maybe even shut down the match.

"Laaaaadies and gentlemen, please take your seats. Mr. Castle, Mr. McNamara, into the ring with your champions, please."

Deuce's heart pumped in his ears. He could barely hear a word as the guy droned on about good sportsmanship and a fair fight and blah de blah blah blah while Moonman and Hang 'Em High sneered at each other. Deuce wanted to shout, *I am standing here with Hunter Freakin' Castle. Me. Maria della Caldera's adopted boy.*

". . . best man win," the referee finished. Deuce and Castle shook hands. Then Moonman and Hang 'Em High shook hands and bared their teeth at each other like it was a biting contest.

Deuce went to Moonman's corner and sat on a little stool, while Moonman did his opening moves. He glanced over at Sparkle. She looked intense, maybe even nervous. His Smith guys were allowed to sit around him, even though it obscured the view.

The lights swirled. The music pulsed. Over the P.A., a voice boomed, "Who will win the Battle for the Moon? Will it be the cowboy of death, Hang 'Em High Harry? Never defeated, he knows and craves the taste of blood. Brought here in the spaceship of an invader, will he rule the Moon with his blowtorch and his flaming arrows?"

As if to illustrate, Hang 'Em High strutted around the ring and shot flames so high into the air he almost singed the twirly ball.

"Or will it be our brave champion, Alex Van Damnation, the Moonman himself, who—"

"Deuce!" someone shouted.

"Deuce! Dooce! Dooce!"

Louder and louder. In rhythm to the chant, people slammed the floor with their feet. Clapped their hands. Shouted Deuce's name.

Deuce's mouth fell open. He stared at the faces in the enormous arena.

"Deuce!"

He stood up and waved. His Smith guys scanned the crowds like Moona Lisa looking for pieces of pepperoni.

"Deuce!"

People were shrieking. Some broads were crying. Waving handkerchiefs. Waving hands. Waving MLF flyers.

"Deuce!"

Dizzy, he sat back down. The audience kept it up. A spotlight fell on him, and the referee brought him a microphone. He stared down at it, having no notion what to say. He cleared his throat and glanced at Sparkle. Her head was raised proudly.

He said, "Moonman, make us proud we're Moonsiders!"

"The Moon for Moonsiders!" someone yelled.

"Moon! Moon!"

"Deuce! Deuce!"

"MLF. MLF. MLF."

People were pounding on the floor with the feet and hitting their chair arms with their fists.

"Boss," one of his Smith guys told Deuce, "it gets any wilder, we're going to hustle you out of here."

He grinned. "Some fuss, huh?"

One of his guys cracked a smile. "Yes, Don Deuce," he replied.

Deuce blinked. Don Deuce. Wow. Then he licked his lips and shook his head. "I'm an N.A., remember? Just one of the people."

"Look," one of the other Smith guards said, pointing.

In the short span of time it had taken them to talk, Hang 'Em High had leaped onto Moonman's back like a big spider and was slamming both his fists into his face. Then he peeled himself off and executed a volley of kicks and punches. Moonman staggered like a drunk. Then he collapsed against the ropes.

Master Akira helped him back to a standing position as the ref watched. Moonman raised a hand, and Master Akira signaled that he was all right.

Then Hang 'Em High threw his lasso around him, drew him in, and headbanged him, hard. Moonman doubled up and sprayed blood all over the arena floor. Hang 'Em High headbanged him again, then held out his hand while one of his ringside assistants handed him what looked to be a revolver. He slammed it down on Moonman's head.

Moonman fell to his knees.

The crowd began booing. Deuce scowled at the referee, who gave Hang 'Em High a little chat and a moment to remember his good sportsmanship.

Then he started headbanging Moonman again. Teeth flew out; maybe even pieces of bone. Deuce could hear his groans. Each breath he took sounded like someone was ripping out his lungs.

Deuce ran to Moonman, and said, "Do I drop the little white towel?"

"*Non*," Moonman said, gasping. His head was bleeding profusely. "I kill heem, Deuce." He blinked his swollen lids. "Where is he?"

Deuce said, "I'm throwing it."

"*Non*. It's my choice. My honor."

Then Hang 'Em High flew at them both. Deuce went flying into the ropes, dazed.

Hang 'Em High lifted Moonman into the air, jet-packed to one of the towers, and tossed Moonman off it. He pulled out a chain saw and revved it up. He leaped off the tower and aimed himself for Moonman, who was on his knees. His face was gushing blood. His arm was at an odd angle.

No one ever knew if Hang 'Em High would really have used the saw. Deuce, straining to pull himself together, gazed out at the crowd. He saw only one face—Sparkle's— and she was staring hard at him and mouthing, "Do it, do it." Deuce gestured to Master Akira, who handed him the white towel.

Moonman wailed, "*Non*!"

Deuce threw it to the ground.

The match was over.

The booing crowd thundered with disappointment. They started wrenching their pretty new chairs free of their bolts. They hurled their drink cups and programs toward the ring.

Dodging projectiles, Deuce gestured for the microphone. The terrified-looking referee darted forward, handed it to him, and took cover in the trapdoor in the center of the ring.

"Stop!" Deuce boomed. His voice reverberated off the freshly painted walls and brand-new flooring. "What are you doing? Act like Moonsiders, not animals! This isn't a fight to the death. It's a wrestling match. And we threw in the towel. They won."

"Deuce," someone shouted. Another voice joined that one. And another. And another. It was a wave of sound that made the entire hall vibrate.

It was the only detonation that went off that night, but it was an explosion nonetheless.

The crowds stormed the ring. The Smith bodyguards drew their weapons . . . and Hunter Castle flung himself in front of Deuce.

Then something hit Deuce, and he was out for the count.

When he came to, he was lying on his back on a massage table in a room filled with people. Something stank and burned beneath his nose, and when he got a good whiff, he was fully awake.

Beatrice's tear-splotched face hovered over his, joined by Big Al's.

"*Mio amore*," Beatrice whispered. "Are you all right?"

He nodded and licked his lips. "Moonman," he said. "How's Alex?"

"He's going to be okay," Beatrice said.

"I want to see him." He tried to sit up. The room tilted, and there were two Beatrices. Gently she pushed him down.

"Later, Deuce. See, *Papà*, how thoughtful."

Big Al grunted.

Deuce blinked hard, and asked, "Who are all these people?"

Big Al said, "Ssh, keep your voice down. Family mucky-mucks have come to pay you respect."

"Pay . . ."

"Out, out," said a voice. "He needs some rest."

"I love you," Beatrice whispered, squeezing his hand. "You, and only you."

"Come on, Bea, give him some room. Your perfume's enough to make him pass out again," Big Al said gruffly. To Deuce, he said, "I'm thinking we should announce your true Family status immediately. That you are, and always have been, a Borgioli."

Deuce licked his lips. "Let me be presentable first, I ask you," he said. "Don't do it with me lying here like a baby." He needed some time to think through all the angles of his obviously altered situation.

"But—" Big Al began, then was jostled away by Beatrice, who said, "*Papà*, you heard the *doctore*."

Then Andreas Scarlatti leaned over him. Deuce braced himself for a blast of juice and wondered where the hell his Smith bodyguards were.

Andreas murmured, "We want to pay our respects. We also want to thank you for whacking that *strega*, Mrs. Gino Scarlatti. We understand that she stole from our brothers, the Smiths, something of value that you, thank God, returned to them."

Interesting interpretation. And it wasn't exactly true that he had actually whacked Mrs. Gino, either. But he understood that Andreas was reaching out to him, so he said, "It has caused me a grave personal dishonor. For I suffered under a deathbed obligation to take care of her."

"Perhaps we can discuss compensation for this sullying of your name and reputation," Andreas replied. "It is my understanding that at one time you stated to poor, dead Gino your desire to Affiliate with us."

"*Sì*, that would be a great honor," Deuce allowed in a hushed voice. Perhaps he could become an Honorary Affiliate of all the Houses. Collect 'em like scalps. But for now, he looked left and right.

"Of course this is a private matter between you and us, more properly discussed another time," Andreas said. "Is there something we can do for you in the meantime, Don Deuce?"

He swallowed and said, "*Mille grazie*, Signor Andreas. You honor me too much."

Andreas whispered, "We have much to discuss."

Then Ten-Stop Theo, Registrar of the Smith Family, pressed his hand and murmured, "Please, sir, we need to meet tonight. Our Family and yours. You," he amended.

"Sorrowfully, our doctor reports that my brother is still very ill," Deuce said, figuring it was common knowledge by now about Joey. "I must remain by his side tonight." He was astounded by his own audacity. "*Daverro, daverro*," he added, "any other reason, of course I would be there."

Ten-Stop looked frustrated but not surprised. He said, "We've heard of your brother's trouble. We'd be glad to help in any way we can." He added under his breath, "*Any* way."

Deuce blinked. By whacking the Moongoloid? Is that what he meant? They would do that for him, a stinkin' Borgioli N.A. no-account?

He felt dizzy again and must have lost consciousness. Then a man dressed in scrubs was growling at someone, "I don't care who you are, madam. You can speak to him another time. This man is under my care and everyone must leave *now*."

The man introduced himself to Deuce as Dr. Golden, another of Hunter Castle's medical staff aboard *Gambler's Star*. As he described Deuce's condition to him, Deuce tried to take names and make out faces as the crowd reluctantly left, but someone stood in his way. Deuce looked up.

Hunter Castle smiled down on him. "Mr. McNamara, I'm real sorry," he said. "I don't know what got into Harry. Back home, we'd say he'd eaten some locoweed."

Deuce said, "You might check his urine for Chantilly Lace."

"Ah." Castle closed his eyes. "The evils of drug abuse. Again, my deepest apologies to you and Mr. Van Damnation. I would send Harry in to apologize, but he is ah, indisposed at the moment." Deuce wondered if Harry was permanently indisposed. Then Castle added, "Clearly, this debacle has played out in your favor."

"Yeah, clearly," Deuce said smugly. He wondered where Sparkle was. Master Akira glided to Deuce's side. Hunter Castle took a step back as Deuce licked his lips and said, "*Sensei*, my master, please, take me to Moonman."

Master Akira helped Deuce slide off the table. Dr. Golden rushed over, looking very perturbed. "Mr. McNamara, please lie back down."

"Later," Deuce said. With Master Akira's help, he staggered from the dressing room and into an adjoining room, much dimmer than his. A nurse stood to one side, fiddling with a small machine spewing readouts. A figure was lying prone on a gurney. Sparkle leaned over it, holding the figure's hand in both of hers.

Deuce, Master Akira, and Castle neared the bed.

Moonman ticked his adoring gaze from Sparkle to Deuce. His face fell. "Deuce, I'm sorree," Moonman moaned as Deuce drew near.

"Alex, the guy's a freakin' killer, not a wrestler," Deuce replied.

"Rematch," Moonman said gasping.

Sparkle looked at Deuce. He said, "Not a chance, dude." She sighed with obvious relief. "You hurt a lot?"

"*Non*, they gave me lots of drugs." Moonman smiled at the nurse. She smiled back. "Tomorrow I'll be better than new."

The nurse nodded at Deuce, who relaxed and sat in a chair beside the gurney.

"Listen, Deuce." Castle turned a second chair around and sat down. He clasped his hands on the back of the chair. "Emerson Epperson-Roux is calling a meeting tomorrow afternoon. With the Charter Board." Deuce waited for some shoe somewhere. "He wants you to be there."

It was another sweet moment. For the first time in his life, he was a force to be reckoned with, not Maria della Caldera's adopted boy. Very, very sweet. He said, as innocently as he could, "I ain't a Member."

Castle chuckled. His dark eyes gleamed. "Emerson has requested and received a waiver. It's at two o'clock at the Charter Board HQ." He clapped his hands and turned his attention to Sparkle. "I guess it's dinner with me, Miss

Sparkle. That was the bet, as I recall. Shall I collect now?''

Sparkle looked down at Moonman. At the nurse, who said, ''He needs his rest.''

She shrugged. ''Might as well.'' She turned—finally—to Deuce. ''I'll make this quick.''

Castle looked taken aback. Then he laughed and offered her his arm. Deuce watched them go. Sparkle did not look back.

''*Alors!*'' Moonman groused to the nurse as she pressed a pressure hypo against his hip. ''Take a care. My bottom is very bruised.'' He said, ''Deuce, that man. He will try to sleep with Sparkell.''

Deuce muttered, ''You win some, you lose some, *mon ami.*'' Sighed. Tried to think about something else. But what could you think about, when you were in love and your fiancée was with a man who had once given her real red roses?

''She told you it would be a quickie,'' Alex added helpfully.

What a comfort.

With Deuce's three Smith bodyguards in tow, he and Moonman left through a side tunnel for the Topside condo.

He was not prepared for what he saw: hundreds of people everywhere they drove, waving signs that read things like, ''Deuce Our Hero'' and waving at his car. He discovered that the aichy had an exterior microphone and put it on. Very faintly he heard:

''*Deuce, Deuce, Deuce.*''

''Holy shit,'' he breathed. Moonman stared at him. The Smith guys said nothing, but he knew they were taking notes.

He took calls:

From Levi Shoemaker, who reminded him that the MLF stood for the liberation of the satellite from oppression.

Miss Angelina, who reminded him of the same thing, also that she still thought about their parting kiss.

From Yuet Chan, who informed him that she had rushed to his side after the match, but the doctor had forced her to leave before she had a chance to thank him and his freedom forces again for helping her secure her Godmotherhood. Since he basically had done nothing but show up after the fact, it was pretty clear that she was sucking up big-time.

From Brigham, on behalf of his people, who hoped that he would accept a lovely embossed copy of *The Book of Mormon* to read "for inspiration and enlightenment on his spiritual journey from the Moon to the Celestial Kingdom that awaits the faithful on Gambler's Star."

The only major political group he did not hear from was the Van Aadamses.

"I'm going to need you guys tomorrow when I go to the Charter Board meeting," he told the Smith guys. They nodded without expression. They were still taking notes for their real bosses.

Joey was not so good, but he was better. Dr. Harriot was now surrounded by bustling nurses, emphasis on *bust*ling, ha-ha, and Joey was propped up and sipping some kind of gooey liquid through a straw.

The doctor said, "We've almost finished organ production. Then we'll have to begin trading the old organs for the new ones."

"New lamps for old," Deuce said, remembering an old fairy tale Mamma used to tell them. "If I rub his liver, can I make a wish?"

The doctor politely ignored what in his eyes was probably bad taste. He said, "Normally, I would prefer to perform a delicate operation like this in Earthside facilities. But Mr. Castle has the most up-to-date surgical theater I've ever seen."

Castle had taken his girl on a date, and now he wanted to take his brother to his fancy-schmancy ship. Deuce was feeling a bit left out of this whirligig of fun. He asked, "Mr. Castle indicate that this is all right with him?"

"He told me to tell you that he insisted. He left you a quicktime."

Deuce watched it. It was Castle, drawling, "Mr. McNamara, I would appreciate this opportunity to show you my goodwill toward the leader of the Independents and his esteemed brother." Deuce and he knew he wasn't the leader yet. But it was fabulous to imagine the great man hedging his bets in that direction.

Deuce looked at Joey before he responded. "It's up to you, *mio fratello*."

Joey lit up as one of the sexy nurses took his pulse. "Best to do it where's it's safest."

It occurred to Deuce that he still wasn't sure if Castle had ever tried to whack Bothersome Paramour #2. He had a moment where he imagined Castle holding Joey like an ace, waiting for the moment to play a full house. But there really was no alternative. After all, the Borgioli Family physician was a Borgioli.

He responded in the affirmative to Castle's quicktime and joined a very dinged-up Moonman in the front room, where he was ordering pizza for them and the Smith guys and charging it to Castle. It would cost a fortune to deliver it Topside, which was the point. The Smith guys were digging it. Moona Lisa was wriggling as if she understood every word, including "extra 'amburger, extra sausage, and extra pepperoni."

As Moonman concluded the order, he said to Deuce, "Ah wish I 'ad as good a relationship with my brothair as you 'ave."

Even the Smith boys betrayed their astonishment at this pronouncement. The fact of Deuce's protest over his *mamma's* will and the rejection of his claim was very old news.

"*Grazie*." Deuce's eyes watered. He ducked his head and gave Moon a pat. "It's good to have a brother."

"You are a lucky man, Deucement."

The dog licked his face adoringly. He smiled, cracked his knuckle, and said, "You know, Moonman, tonight I feel like the luckiest man alive."

And then some.

TWENTY-THREE

Charter Board Headquarters.

Deuce gazed up at the ornate building, with the crests of all the Families, three on three massive columns, three on the other, divided by the blind statue of Justice (executed by the same artist as did the Borgioli's David statue, only with much more respect for the subject). She wore Roman robes and held up a scale. On each side of the scale rested a die. Both of them showed sixes.

Deuce had half expected them to show fives, like the Ditwac. The Scarlattis had still not solved their mystery, and the Mephistopheles figure was still there. But that was not on Deuce's mind as he climbed the steps surrounded by his four bodyguards—for Alex, who could barely walk, counted himself among them—and stared up. He felt thirteen again, which in Family life was the age of responsibility. On his alleged birthday, after a brief ceremony (the slashing of palms, the oath of *omertà*,) Maria della Caldera and Big Al, standing in for Deuce's father, had brought the boy to give his respect to the Charter Board.

Most Family Members went through those doors maybe twice in their lifetimes, once as a kid, once as a parent.

This was a very big deal.

Especially since, at the moment, he wasn't a Family Member at all.

He wished Sparkle was here. But no one was here who hadn't been invited. The area had been swept clean of chanters, demonstrators, curious onlookers, tourists, and

299

Family Members and Affiliates. Only the heads of Families, Deuce, and Castle were allowed in.

No bodyguards, either.

So Deuce said good-bye to them at the front door and swaggered as best he could into the Charter Boardroom.

Wayne Van Aadams saw Deuce first. His face went purple; he leaped to his feet and was restrained by his uncle, Chairman William Atherton.

"Bastard! Bastard! Why aren't you dead?" he screamed. He shook his hand at Deuce. His voice screeched into the sopranosphere.

Deuce kept his cool. He said, "*Mi scusi,* but I thought this was only for leaders." He inclined his head toward Chairman William Atherton. "Meaning no disrespect to your Family, sir." The Chairman regarded him calmly, but the man's cheeks were pink. Wayne was embarrassing him.

"You bastard!" Wayne screamed. Everyone ignored him as you would a recalcitrant child, a drunk tourist, or any N.A.

"We gave the Van Aadamses a waiver for their Designated Heir," Big Al said. He added with a conspiratorial smile, "Seeing as he's the only one who's got one Registered right now."

Uh-oh. Thin ice there. Deuce smiled back. "I see."

"And why is he allowed here?" Wayne demanded, pointing. "He's an N.A., a nobody! He has his nerve questioning my right to be here when he has no right at all!"

"His presence was requested by me," Epperson-Roux said firmly. "We at the DOF feel that, due to recent events, the status quo may have been permanently altered up here, and we need to assess the situation."

"What the hell are you talking about?" Wayne shouted. Finally, Chairman William Atherton touched his arm and murmured something in his ear. Wayne clamped his mouth shut.

Everyone else looked nervous: Don Roger and Don Abraham; Donna Yuet; Don Giancarlo Caputo, who really shouldn't have bothered, since he was so old and doddering no one would pay him any mind; and Don Tito Scarlatti and the rest of the Scarlatti Select of Six, which included Andreas and four other guys, Santo, Rafaello, Vito, and Matteo.

Epperson-Roux said to the Board, "Let's begin, shall we?"

"As you wish," said a disembodied voice.

Deuce and the others stood and bowed to the scans. The Board had eyes; the Board could see if you did not pay appropriate respect. It would remember; it remembered everything: every hit, Sanctioned or not, Registered or not; every Vendetta, every dishonor.

Everything.

It calculated everything. Judged everything, decided everything.

It had been installed by the Department of Fairness almost seventy years ago, and in that time, the violence level had dipped low enough to allow Moonbase Vegas to stay open despite the earlier major *schiamazzo* by the public to close it down. Earthside had been pleased; with this setup, it could police the Families in a remote and impartial way. And collect "taxes."

The Families had been pleased because after the installation, Earthside pretty much left them alone.

But now, there was this new guy. This guy who had shown up with Hunter Castle, who wanted a Charter to build a casino.

"Let's begin," Epperson-Roux said, clearing his throat as he glanced unhappily at Wayne Van Aadams, who appeared ready to launch himself at Deuce any second. "Mr. Hunter Castle has put before the Board his desire to build a casino."

"Never," Don Giancarlo Caputo rasped. "*Giammai! Vaya diablo!*" He spit on the ground.

"Earthside is impressed with his credentials," Epperson-Roux continued. "And his stated intention to—"

"Impressed with his money!" Don Giancarlo said. He pounded the table. "Where's my nurse? I need my heart medicine. *Mamma mia*, what a shame that we are sitting here! What a dishonor."

A couple of lights on the Board blinked. Shame and dishonor logged and recorded.

"—to ban drugs from his establishment," Epperson-Roux continued loudly. "This has made the Department sit up and take notice, I can tell you." He beamed at Castle.

"What a minute. I, too, am averse to drug use," Donna Yuet insisted, frowning. "I have been granted no special favors for this courageous stand."

"Foolish stand," Don Giancarlo said. "Everyone who comes to the Moon wants to take drugs!"

"*Sì*," Big Al concurred. "This is stupid talk. We won't agree to let that man have a casino, and that's that."

"How do the Independents feel?" Epperson-Roux asked Deuce.

Everyone looked at him. Deuce had a curious sense of déjà vu. In a very real way, he was facing a roomful of hostile Family Members, fighting for his life. As nice as they'd made with their visits and their phone calls after the match, they weren't happy with his new position as the darling of the Independents. He had no illusions about that.

"I, ah," he began. He took a breath and steadied himself. "The match put a lot of money in our school fund."

"We'll equal it," Big Al said, then hesitated. "How much was it?"

"Six hundred thousand credits," Castle cut in.

Big Al frowned. "We'll make a donation," he amended.

"So will we," Chairman William Atherton added.

Deuce began to see how this could be played to the benefit of those who did not have so many benefits. He shrugged. "There's so much to be done . . ."

"We, too, will make a donation," Donna Yuet said sharply.

Epperson-Roux favored Castle with a small, fleeting smile. Deuce realized the DOF flack was going to do whatever it took to give Castle his Charter. He was even more confused about why he was here. He had no power to agree or disagree with anything. He wondered who had really requested his presence, Epperson-Roux or Castle. And if Castle, why?

Castle looked straight at him and said, "How's Mr. Van Damnation?"

"Fine. He wants a rema—" he began. Then it dawned

on him. He was here to provide an alternative solution. He said, "A rematch. But since he's too bashed up, I'm proposing a different kind of wager."

Everyone stared at him as if he were insane. Except for Castle, who almost looked proud of him. Deuce said, "A race across the Moon."

"What? *Scemo!*" Big Al cried. "Are you nuts?"

Castle crossed his ankle over his knee. "An interesting notion, Mr. McNamara."

"You and me, no seconds, no hired guns," Deuce said, as the idea blossomed in his mind. "If I win, you have to leave the Moon."

Castle smiled. "And if I win? What, *you* leave?" As if he could care less.

"Nothing of him and him," Don Giancarlo said, wagging his hand at the two men. "It's enough with that *stupido* wrestling match. Look what happened, now this boy is a big shot like a *don!*"

"Agreed," William Atherton said. "We can't base this decision on a sporting event."

"It's a good idea," Big Al said through clenched teeth. He looked significantly at each Family Member. "All Castle has to do is lose, and he's history."

Epperson-Roux turned to the Board. "Interim comment, please?"

The disembodied voice answered, "This proposition will be considered. Adjournment for one hour."

"This is unbelievable," Wayne Van Aadams said. "Uncle Will, what the hell are you doing?"

A mechanical dressed in a tuxedo appeared and made a little bow. "Please, gentlemen and lady, this way. We are serving refreshments in the salon."

"Salon. I'll salon him," Big Al muttered. As he passed Deuce, he grabbed his arm. "You do this, you better do it as a Borgioli," he said. "I knew I shoulda stopped you from holding that idiotic wrestling match. You announce here and now you're a Borgioli, or I'll . . ."

"Big Al," Deuce said softly, "think about it. If I tell them I'm a Borgioli now, they won't let me race against him. If I stay out of Family politics, they might go for it.

Then, when it's over, I'll put my colors on.''

"Gentlemen?" The mechanical whirred toward them. "Is there a problem?"

"There'd better not be," Big Al said. His sad eyes were sadder than usual. "Don't break an old man's heart, Arturino. Your mother would want you to be a good boy."

"Don Alberto, I only want what is best," Deuce said carefully.

The hour ticked by slowly as they stood in the Dutch Schulz Memorial Dining Room, drank Chianti and champagne, and ate canapés. The room was decorated with holos and oil paintings of famous men of action—Capone, Luciano, Schulz, and earlier Godfathers of the Six Families. Everyone and no one talked to him and to each other. The Charter Board had ears and eyes everywhere in the building. It had probably heard what Big Al had said to Deuce.

Finally the hour was up, and they reconvened in the conference room. The Board got to the point as soon as everyone sat down.

"There will be a race of seventeen hundred kilometers from Tycho to Copernicus, the crater above Moonbase Vegas. Each Family will provide a racer. If Hunter Castle wins, he is allowed his Charter. However, if he is killed at any time before completion of his Casino, his heirs receive fifty percent of all six Families' profits in perpetuity."

"*What*?" Donna Yuet cried.

"That's so's we don't whack him," Big Al explained, disgruntled. Clearly, that had been his plan.

"Then a MLF or an N.A. can kill him just to shake us down," Andreas said. He bobbed his head in Deuce's direction. "Meaning no disrespect, but they'd like nothing better than that we lose some of our handle."

"McNamara's not in a Family," Wayne Van Aadams jumped in. "He can't race."

"The Board concurs with Mr. Emerson Epperson-Roux's assessment that the balance of power on the Moon has shifted. If Arthur Borgioli, AKA Deuce McNamara, can provide evidence that he speaks for the majority of Independents, he will be allowed to compete. There are to be no hits on any Member or Affiliate of any House, nor on

Hunter Castle, nor on Arthur Borgioli, if he is declared a competitor, until the race is completed. All hits in motion will be canceled. A Family perpetuating a hit from this moment forward will be forced to give fifty percent of its profits in perpetuity to the survivor's Family, or in the event of no Family affiliation, to an inheritor of the deceased's choosing.''

"Notice that it did not say, 'heir,' " Don Giancarlo muttered. "This is against tradition. This is not our way."

"Don Giancarlo is right. We will not agree to this," Chairman William Atherton said, rising. "This is not the way to—"

"This is the decision of the Board," the Board announced.

They looked at each other. "A moment, *per favore*," Andreas said, holding up a finger as he tapped his comm badge. All the others did likewise. They were canceling hits. Deuce estimated that perhaps fifty men would live to game another day.

The Board continued. "If Mr. Castle loses, he will be banned for life from seeking a Casino Charter. If any Family representative wins, he will receive whatever reward his Family deems sufficient. If Mr. Arthur Borgioli wins, he will receive one tenth of one percent of Mr. Castle's profits for thirty consecutive years, which estimates conclude may range from twenty to fifty million credits; an equal amount will be given to a variety of Independent charities, which shall be chosen before the race. A method of assessing the proper amount will be agreed upon in advance and payments placed yearly in escrow accounts for Arthur Borgioli and for the charities, to be administered by this Board. Any Family or group who finds these stakes untenable may so state now and withdraw from competition."

It paused. There was some coughing from Don Giancarlo but nothing else. "There being no objections, this meeting is adjourned. Arthur Borgioli, please remain behind to discuss your situation."

The Family heads looked as if they'd been shot. In ones and twos they began to drift out of the room with steam streaming from their ears. Grinning, Hunter Castle shook hands with everyone, pointed at Deuce and winked, and took his leave.

Wayne Van Aadams bumped Deuce, and whispered, "I don't give a damn about what the Board says or does. I'll take you out anyway. I don't care if my Family goes bankrupt. Killing you is worth it. Watch your back, wop."

"*Fatti sparare*," Deuce said in return. "Look, I gave the Smiths back what was theirs but I ain't told them you were the one who wanted it. Watch your butt, or I will."

He thought Wayne Van Aadams might die of a heart attack then and there.

The Board determined that everyone not a Member of, or Affiliated with, a Family would receive a secret vote for or against designating Deuce as their race contestant. This was different from naming him their leader, which may be why not so many N.A.'s got secret visits in the night from various Family people as might have been expected. A few, yes, and the voting turnout was a little light. But Deuce won a majority.

He was in.

To keep everyone from going insane and having the opportunity to rig the course or Deuce in their favor, the race would be held in three days.

And so, to work.

"It's amazing, this peace," Deuce said to Moonman as they looked over a variety of oxygen tanks at Artemis Tifatina's supply house. "No one's died in almost twenty-four hours."

"Pair'aps your Families should take a lesson from this," Alex observed. "As the Independents are learning, there is more to be gained in working together than fighting."

"Yeah, like with your French Revolution," Deuce drawled. "You can chop heads off a lot faster if one guy shoves the victim under the blade and the other guy releases it. What do you think of this tank?"

Deuce got an incoming, and took it.

"This announcement is being simultaneously broadcast to all contestants. The race is being postponed by a day," the Charter Board voice informed him. "Mr. Castle cites transportation delays."

"Well, so what?" Deuce demanded. "We're all hurrying—"

"As Mr. Castle is not from around here, we are granting his request for a twenty-four-hour extension." It disconnected.

"Actually, this is good and bad," Deuce said. "He can get better stuff, and we can get stuff, period."

"I think you should take the money of the MLF," Alex persisted. "It is a lot. And the things you need are expensive. He must have very elaborate plans."

"If I take money from them, then they own me." Deuce had laid down a policy of accepting only small amounts of money to finance the race. This served to endear him to the N.A.'s but wasn't doing much to help him win.

He knew various players were funneling money to him through N.A. donations. Probably the MLF, too. He took the blind donations but stayed away from anything that looked like an out-and-out bribe.

"We need more money," Alex insisted. "Look at 'ow much this helmet costs."

For the first part of the race, the contestants would be dropped off at the base of the crater, Tycho. They would climb up and into it, and commandeer one of the huge wheeled vehicles called Rollers. Rollers were normally used in heavy mining and construction projects to haul immense loads over long distances. The tractor portion was very rugged and housed a powerful fusion reactor. The top speed of a Roller hauling a load was about fifty kilometers an hour, but unloaded they could run as fast as a hundred kilometers.

The racers would take the Rollers from inside Tycho to Pitatus, the crater at the southern rim of Mare Nubium. It was a distance of 450 kilometers. So, depending on how crazy (or how good) the driver was, this portion of the race could take as few as five hours . . . but most bookies doubled that amount when creating their lines.

Deuce hoped he could make it at all. As a kid, he and Joey used to mess around on Rollers. Deuce was a terrible driver. Mamma used to wonder aloud why he had not killed himself on one.

If they could not afford a customized Roller, they could use one of several provided by the Brotherhood of Wheeled Machinery, Moon Chapter Alpha. Of course everybody set to customizing very slick machines.

There would be a sprint to reload oxygen, which came in tanks the size of a violin, and then they would race cigar-shaped dust boats across Mare Nubium as far as they could take them. Then they would set out on foot. They would have to negotiate the terraces, rays, and craterlets of the interior of the crater of Copernicus, and then over the three central mountains to the finish line on the other side.

Just a friendly little hop.

Of course, no one wanted to use the cheap equipment provided by the Race Committee. Deuce had tried to sell his shares of Palace Industrials back to Castle, but the Earthsider had refused.

"You'll need 'em in your old age," he smugly told Deuce. As they were privately held by Castle, there was nowhere else to sell them. So Deuce, while potentially wealthy, was cash poor.

And so, it was time for Sparkle to come clean: yes, she had once had a fortune, but she had donated most of it to showgirls who couldn't afford the one-thousand-credit deductible for their hip operations, and to the Atomic Veterans. The rest, she would give to Deuce.

"No way," he said.

"Take it," she murmured. They were standing in the gazebo by the condo with boozy cocktails in their hands. She had on a gauzy thing that made him nuts. But her mind clearly was not on pleasure. It was on worry. "You need it. You need all of it." She shivered. "I have such a feeling, Deuce. A bad feeling. Like I'll never see you again after this race."

"Hush, now," he said uneasily. "You know I'll never forget the little people." But she was serious. She was not happy.

"I can't shake this, Deuce."

He took her in his arms. She yielded against him. "So

much of the time I can't figure you." Kissed her at her jaw-line. Her lips. "It's getting harder instead of easier. It . . . you've become so different." Kissed her again. Sparkle kisses. Those wonderful, wonderful Sparkle kisses.

"I know." She grimaced. "I feel like I'm . . . diffusing somehow." Those wondering Sparkle words. "Weaken-ing."

"Loosening," he suggested, loosening her gauzy thing. Thinking about the word, diffusing.

"Loosening, then," she agreed. "But I may tighten up again."

"Ain't nobody's business if you do, sweetheart." And he was overwhelmed by the oddest thought: It didn't matter what the percentage was. It didn't matter if he ever got something out of loving her. He loved her. That was all there was.

They sank in low grav toward the floor of the gazebo.

All there was.

In the distance, people chanted, "Dooce, Dooce, Dooce!"

Maria della Caldera used to love to tell Deuce stories about the old days in Earthside New York. (He had never figured out why people said things like "Earthside New York." There was not a Moonside New York, and it sure didn't look like there was ever gonna be one.)

Anyway, in Earthside New York, when someone in the Family met with tragedy, the other Family Members came to the rescue. She remembered stories of her grandmother sitting in the bakery her grandfather ran, weeping and ac-cepting envelopes of money from Family and friends, who whispered, "For the babies, Nonna."

"Such love," she used to say, but what Deuce heard was, "Such bribery."

He had thought of love as a kind of bribery: You don't hurt me, I don't hurt you.

Now, he didn't know what to think. Except that if he died, the worst part would be his inability to take care of his baby. His last thoughts would be of worrying about Sparkle and not of worrying about himself.

It was a very strange concept.
But he kind of liked it.

And speaking of envelopes, many were pressed into his hand. Oh, sure, a lot of them were from people who wanted something from him. Now, or later.

And some, from people like the bum who had worn the WILL WORK FOR OXYGEN sign around his neck. In clean, cheap clothes, he crossed a busy street to press three onechips into Deuce's palm. He said, "I have a good job now. I'm getting married. God bless you. Win the race for guys like me."

For no reason at all, Deuce had burst into tears as he had taken them.

No reason at all.

From the Captain's Log of Gambler's Star:

I'm in an interesting situation here. I've got to win, but when I do, I'll lose a lot of ground. Nevertheless, I'll have gotten their attention.

Still, it's time to call in the cavalry.

All's fair . . .

This is not a game. This is not about casinos and corporations and fragile egos. This concerns the future of our planet. Yes, and of the dear little Moon, too. Of the human species.

My watchwords: Plausible deniability.

For my own survival as well.

Hunter Castle

TWENTY-FOUR

With less than twenty-four hours to go before the race, the Charter Board officially made book that Deuce was the underdog. It calculated his status by taking into account the amount of money Castle and the Families were spending on their race preparations as well as the odds that had been laid against him.

It looked pretty grim. And it hadn't even speculated about his driving skills.

It was also clear the Board had selected the course from Tycho to Copernicus—a stretch of about a thousand miles—because the craters were spectacularly photogenic. In other words, the race would look good on viso, except for the bits where they went out of range of the orbiting satellites. But that would just add to the excitement.

Guess who owned broadcasting rights?

"Look at it this way, Artie. The more money he makes, the more you get when you beat him," Joey said brightly as he fielded tens of dozens of calls to N.A. volunteers out in the field. Joey was in charge of "feeding the cult," as Sparkle called it: the cult of Deuce as champion of the little people. Joey was good at it, too. Over Deuce's protests, he had whipped those poor Synodic Synod people into a frenzy. Word was that their church was a rockin' and a rollin' as they prayed for their deliverance at the hands of this new Messiah.

Joey was a new man—take that literally; if they'd used metallic parts, he'd be a cyborg by now—the most obvious thing being that women were throwing themselves at him and he was turning them down.

"They might try to get to you through me," he explained to Deuce. "We ain't had so much luck in that department, know what I mean?"

He was also becoming very good at collecting information—maybe not so good as Deuce—but now that Deuce was so high-profile, it was harder for him to get it. At first that surprised Deuce, but then he figured it was that old consciousness of entitlement thing—*I'm little, you're little, it's no big deal to tell you this.* In Joey's case, it was, *You're not the biggest kahuna, but maybe you'll tell him I told you this, and I'll get something out of it?*

And Joey was the one who located Crazyhorse McCarthy, the wizened old hermit who held the still-unbroken record for Roller racing on the Moon. He remembered the two Borgioli brothers who had tried to imitate his exploits, and offered his legendary vehicle, *Moonshot*, for the Independent cause.

Deuce was astonished. He said to Joey, "You know, maybe I might do okay."

Sparkle gazed at him from across the room and looked very worried, very unhappy. She got up and left the room. Joey, Deuce, and Moonman, who were calibrating Deuce's oxygen supply, watched her glide across the room, a vision in black silk.

Joey said, "I'm getting another glass of iced tea." When he was out of earshot, Deuce murmured to Moonman, "Let me ask you a question, and you give me an answer. Have you ever slept with her?"

"Not this trip," Moonman answered intensely, as if this were absolute proof of his enduring friendship. "Ah swear it."

Deuce waited a beat. Then he said, "If anything ever happens to me, I want you to take care of her. Real good care of her. And the dog."

"*Zut*, you fool, nothing will 'appen," Moonman said. "But ah would."

Joey rejoined them with his tea. "I'm not sure what's going to happen tomorrow," Deuce said to his brother. "I made my will. If Castle ever buys his damn stock back, you and Sparkle split the loot, okay?''

Joey looked at the floor. "I'm so ashamed," he whispered. "I treated you like crap."

"What are brothers for?" Deuce asked, but the awkward part was, he agreed with Joey. He couldn't tell him it was okay because it wasn't. "Listen, Joey, I told Moonman this and I'm telling you this. If anything happens to me, take care of Sparkle. The first thought you should have is of her. Do you promise? Take this like a deathbed obligation." Which if his *mamma* had extracted from Joey, he would probably have a good strong credit line to work with.

"This I promise you," Joey said, laying his hand over his heart. "I'll think of her first. And Moona Lisa," he added. There was a moment of silence between them. Then Joey said, "Speaking of crap, that's what you look like. You need to get some shut-eye. Castle's probably up there getting a massage and a potassium drip." Which would help keep him from exhaustion during the race.

Deuce nodded, finished his beer, got up, and went into the bedroom. Sparkle was sitting on the bed and staring into space. She turned when she saw him and patted the mattress.

"Whatcha doing, baby?" he asked, sitting beside her and taking her in his arms. "Communicating with the spirits?"

She kissed him and pushed him down into the slinky sheets.

An hour later, she awoke, screaming from a nightmare she refused to describe, and neither she nor Deuce slept for the rest of the night.

But when you're pumped, it doesn't matter if you're exhausted. As Deuce and the others were driven to the race site, Ram Chander and the other media guys were chattering away, trying to talk to the contestants through their helmets. Everybody all over the Moon was watching, and Castle was making a fortune beaming it back to Earth. Each

House had sent somebody, even the Borgiolis, and everybody looked very intimidating in their colored enviro-suits. Deuce wore black and dark purple.

"Are you ready, gentlemen?" asked Epperson-Roux, who smiled at them on the visos in their escort vehicles. He sat at a table of other dignitaries—the chief of Lunar Security Forces the mayor (whose wife was addicted to Chan drugs and got them for free); various union officials who resided in the pockets of one or more Houses; various local gaming regulators who did the same; and Miss Moon Race, some babe showgirl with eyes the color of the Earthside sky. Not that Deuce had ever seen—

Oh, and Donna MaDonna. A fund had been set up to rebuild her store, it being *an* historical monument and all.

Then, just as the race to the Rollers was about to begin, Deuce's driver from the Lunar Brotherhood of Transport Workers turned and handed him a data rod.

"I was told to give you this just before the race," he said. "I ain't read it, Mr. McNamara."

Deuce plugged it into the alchy's backseat mini. It said:

YOU SCUMBAG!

I HAVE RECENTLY LEARNED THAT YOU HAVE BEEN IN A SECRET LIAISON WITH A CERTAIN STREGA PUTTANA NAMED SPARKLE DE LUNE.

I HAVE REMOVED THIS HARLOT TO A PLACE OF MY CHOOSING.

I WANT YOU TO AGREE TO THREE THINGS, OR I TAKE HER HELMET OFF RIGHT NOW:

YOU WILL NOT THROW THE RACE TO ANYBODY.

YOU WILL ANNOUNCE THAT YOU ARE RE-MEMBERING INTO THE BORGIOLI FAMILY AS SOON AS THE RACE IS OVER.

YOU WILL MARRY BEATRICE, WHO HAS NO IDEA OF THIS DISHONOR, AND IF YOU EVER TELL HER, I WILL TAKE YOUR EYES OUT OF YOUR HEAD WITH AN ICE CREAM SCOOP AND DO WORSE TO THE SO-CALLED MANLY PARTS OF YOUR ANATOMY.

I HAVE TAKEN YOUR UNAUTHORIZED N.A. GIRLFRIEND

AND PUT HER SOMEPLACE SAFE. SHE HAS ENOUGH OX-
YGEN FOR TWENTY HOURS. AFTER THAT, PFFFFT.
    DON'T TELL NOBODY OR SHE DIES NOW.

Shaking, Deuce said, "Thanks, buddy."

The driver tapped his aichy's comm link. "I was told to
verify that you had received it," he said happily. "It's
what, a good-luck message? You know we're counting on
you, Mr. McNamara." He tapped his badge. "Message relayed and received."

"On your mark," the race master boomed into the comm
speaker in Deuce's helmet.

Deuce sat paralyzed for a moment. Then he leaped out
of the aichy and hunkered down.

"Get set."

He took a deep breath.

"Go!"

He ran like he had never run before.

In his suit up the side of Tycho, he huffed, straining even
in the low grav and in his excellent condition. Through his
helmet speaker, he vaguely heard Ram Chander shouting
out their positions and names like he was calling the nags;
it sounded like Castle, for all of being the oldest, was ahead
of him.

Gray rock, gray dust; Deuce slid down and fell to one
side. How long it took him, he couldn't say. The depth of
the crater was actually small in comparison to its diameter.
But when he finally looked over the top of the rim and saw
the row of illuminated vehicles, he almost shouted his out-
rage.

Castle's extra day had been spent transporting the experimental Roller from New America that Deuce had seen
on the MLF stretch aichy's viso. It was shiny beneath the
klieg lights, enormous and glowing in the black crater.

Unfair. Money could not stand in the way of Sparkle's
life. He should comm the Committee; he should speak up.

But he knew the ways of Families; they would probably
kill her, cover it up, deny everything. The message on the
data rod? A forgery. There would be a used ticket proving
she had left for Earthside. There would be all the evidence

they needed. It would not be considered a hit; she was only N.A.

So there would be no particular consequences as far as the Charter Board was concerned. And, therefore, no need to investigate it.

". . . the most beautiful vehicle in the row," Ram Chander enthused. "But wait, what's this? Can that be *Moonshot*? The vehicle of the legendary Crazyhorse McCarthy?"

Deuce was down the rim and halfway to *Moonshot* when Castle's enormous Roller, with *Gambler's Choice* emblazoned on the rear, took off, bouncing wildly, with its headlights flaring. The others got into their vehicles. Panic was making Deuce clumsy. Finally he reached *Moonshot* and tapped his brother, who was acting as his pit boss, on the shoulder. He pressed his gloved finger against his helmet shield. He couldn't speak; his transmissions were being picked up on viso and Big Al would hear him.

Joey cocked his head. Deuce pointed to his forehead. Joey frowned. Deuce mouthed, "Sparkle. Trouble. Big Al." He hoped Joey could see his face well enough, prayed that the visos could not. "Sparkle. Trouble. Kidnap." He prayed to God that Joey understood, but he couldn't spare any more time. It took everything in him not to yell out the words, hoping Joey or Moonman—who was waiting at the finish line—would be able to act before Big Al could.

But he couldn't take that risk. Deuce got into *Moonshot* and started across the crater floor.

He was lucky that he'd been slow. The others were all gunning for Castle, and it was making them nuts. They were ramming each other, bouncing into the air, onto their sides, on their hoods, bouncing back onto their gigantic balloon tires. It looked funny, but it was very dangerous. Deuce watched the Caputo vehicle go down and stay down. *Gambler's Choice* was buffeted by the Chan Roller, which then ricocheted and hit the Borgioli vehicle. It swerved and dogged *Gambler's Choice* again. Snake Eyes Salvatore, Deuce's replacement as Liaison, was the driver.

Deuce took up the rear, trying to stay in close but letting the others do the damage. Then one of them whirled around in a one-eighty and slammed straight into him.

For a moment he saw stars. He saw Sparkle gasping for breath.

He floored it.

The Roller that had hit him tumbled all the way back down to the floor of the crater.

Snake Eyes.

Deuce pushed harder. The old machine shook. He closed his eyes and gritted, "C'mon, baby."

"Mr. McNamara," Ram Chander chirruped in his helmet. "How are you doing?"

"You tell me," Deuce gritted, and kept on.

"Mr. McNamara? We can't hear you. Is your helmet on?"

Then he reached the rim and took the descent too sharply. He careened down the side like a skier on a ski slope. Not that Deuce had ever seen either one.

Gambler's Choice was dead ahead. Deuce crashed into him and they both flopped onto their sides. Deuce was thrown around inside like a doll; he closed his eyes and took the ride.

At the bottom, his vehicle righted itself again, but he was desperately behind.

He was going to lose.

"Two of the Houses have already dropped out!" Chander announced. The Borgiolis and the Chans are no longer in the race. What excitement! What a thrilling day to be a Moonsider!"

"Baby," Deuce whispered.

TWENTY-FIVE

The sun was beginning to rise, casting strange shadows on the rough landscape. So many craters, rises, rilles, rays. Deuce thought his teeth were going to fall out from all the bouncing.

He prayed to God Joey had understood what he was trying to tell him.

Hour after hour he jolted along, at times slamming against another Roller, falling into a crater, struggling back out. He stopped once to orient himself because he was so dizzy.

But he kept going.

He saw a flash; suddenly he shot downward at a heart-stopping pace. *Gambler's Choice* was ahead of him. He guessed that Castle had shot at the rim above him to create a landfall. The man played rough.

The man played to win.

Then, as Deuce watched, some kind of beam hit the rear of *Gambler's Choice* and the rear end of Castle's Roller was gone. Vaporized. No longer with us.

"Now . . . owe . . . us," crackled in Deuce's helmet. It was the garbled voice of Andreas Scarlatti. They must have calculated that they were temporarily out of viso range and disabled Castle.

The Families were going to start calling in the favors, Deuce realized.

He imagined Castle not surviving a blast like that. Could not imagine the Scarlattis agreeing to fork over fifty percent of their hard-extorted handle. Imagined a turf war. Imagined Earthside getting involved.

Realized the importance of saving Castle's life, and headed toward him.

After about twenty minutes, he reached the ruined vehicle. There was no one in the wreckage.

But there were deep footprints, deeper even than the dusty lunar surface should have allowed. Castle must be using hoppers, Deuce thought, a form of cheating, according to the rules.

But they were out of viso range, and who would ever know?

Deuce swore. He wished he'd thought of doing it himself.

He roared on. Then his Roller abruptly stopped. It coughed a couple more times, and then died.

Someone had tampered with his fuel supply.

"Baby, baby, I'm coming," he whispered, got out, and started running.

Without hoppers, without sleep, without a map, without hope.

Not.

It was an expenditure of energy he could not afford, but Deuce climbed a crater rim anyway. He had to get his bearings.

With a whoop, he saw the oxygen-refueling site, a large igloo-shaped container marked by a Moonbase Vegas flag not flapping in the breeze: a fat full Moon and six stars on a rainbow field that incorporated all the Family colors. Lovely thing. No marker for the Independents. Or Castle.

They'd have to get a new flag.

He saw no other Rollers, no dust, no Castle, no nothing.

He got to the oxygen-refueling site and grabbed the tank coded for him. The others would not come loose from their locked positions without the matching laser retinal scan of their respective owners.

He hustled to the row of dust boats. There were only five left. Castle was ahead of him. He staggered into the nearest one and skimmed off across the Mare Nubium, the Black

Sea, a flat plain of thick gray powder. Just looking at it made him thirsty, it was so dry.

His oxygen was not the best. It trickled in weakly and stank just enough to give him a headache. He wondered if the tank had been fully charged when he got it, and if anyone had tampered with it while it had been locked into position at the refueling stop.

He wondered if he was going to suffocate. He wished it on himself if it would stop it from happening to Sparkle.

How far behind was he? He tapped his helmet, said, "Test, can you hear me?"

No one answered.

Then, as Deuce rounded a ridge, Castle was righting his boat and climbing back into it. From the looks of the disturbance in the dust, he had had a bad spill.

"Good. Die, you bastard," Deuce said through clenched teeth, and bore down on him.

But again Castle was quicker than he. The man jumped into his duster and charged away, angling the craft just so that it geysered a hanging wake of dust that slowed Deuce up and nearly made him lose control. Deuce shouted and held on.

They began a pattern of Castle dodging and throwing up a flume, then of Deuce eating it as he shot through it. One hour, two, three, it went on. Deuce was shaking from exhaustion. He was getting light-headed again, and this time he suspected his brain was oxygen-deprived.

Deuce thought about Sparkle and how much he loved her. He thought of Castle and the billions he had, and why did the bastard give a damn about building a casino on the Moon? Because it was there? Because it was boring on Earth, as all the Moonsiders knew?

He saw Sparkle's little-girl smile in her sleep. Her fabulous beauty. He thought about how smart she was.

He got angry, then angrier such that he lost track of where they were going; he saw only that this rich, spoiled Earthsider, who had no notion of what he was doing, was going to be the reason his baby died.

So when Deuce saw that Castle had stopped again, and not only that, but there was a shuttle from *Gambler's Star* descending toward him, no doubt preparing to airlift the duster farther on the course—when he saw all that, he floored the duster and aimed straight for Castle.

And Castle waved his hands for Deuce to halt.

"No way, *bastardo*," Deuce gritted.

Castle reached into his suit pocket.

Deuce refined his aim with the pointed bow of the duster.

He showed Deuce his blaster.

Deuce braced himself for impact.

Castle shot his own duster.

Deuce swerved.

He banked and dug into the dust, throwing up a wall of it, skidding wildly until he ran into a craterlet rim and slammed to a stop.

On rubber legs, he got out. "What the hell are you doing!" he shouted.

The Castle shuttle landed a distance away. Castle tapped the side of his helmet and gestured toward him. Deuce realized his helmet comm system was out. He wondered who he had to thank for that.

Castle gestured toward him.

Deuce shook his head again.

Castle shot his duster again.

Deuce smiled grimly; what, did he figure it had worked the first time so he might as well do it again? Right before he jumped into the shuttle and zoomed away, probably with another duster in the hold? Make it look like he had piloted himself to the side of Copernicus, then walk to the finish line?

Then the man made a show of putting the blaster down and walking toward Deuce, gesturing for Deuce to hurry toward him. The shuttle pilot joined his boss.

Deuce reached in his pocket for his own blaster. Weapons had been strictly forbidden, but who was paying attention to that noise?

They neared each other. Castle made gestures. Deuce made sure the safety was off.

Castle motioned to the shuttle pilot, who handed him a mini. Castle wrote on it and threw it toward Deuce.

Deuce caught it with his left hand, keeping his right wrapped around the blaster.

"Joey contacted us. Sparkle being held Apollo 14. We'll go together."

Could this be a horrible trick to win the race? Deuce shook his head. He couldn't trust this.

He couldn't not trust this.

Castle held his hand out. Shook it hard at Deuce and pointed to Deuce's blaster. Deuce pulled away and leaped into the air for a sidekick just as Castle grabbed his own blaster back up and shot Deuce's dust boat into fragments.

Castle gestured to the shuttle, the only vehicle left.

He was telling the truth.

He had to be.

Deuce flew like the wind.

And *that* he had seen.

There was atmosphere aboard the shuttle. Deuce pulled off his helmet at the same time as Castle.

"She's being held in the Apollo 14 Memorial," Castle said without preamble. "She's guarded, but not by many." He nodded to the pilot. "Send for reinforcements."

Deuce swayed, kept a grip on himself. "Castle, she's only got fifteen minutes left. Big Al must have miscalculated, or we took a lot longer than we're supposed to."

"Get the lead out," he said to the pilot, and smiled stiffly at Deuce. "That's an old Earthside term. It means to hurry."

Deuce nodded unhappily.

The Apollo 14 Memorial was supposed to be another big tourist attraction, but nobody cared about that stuff anymore. The slightly more popular Moonbase Vegas Museum was easier to get to and contained just about everything worth gawking at while you caught your breath and tried to forget how much you'd just lost at the tables.

The crater, Fra Mauro, lay to the south of it, and it was behind this crater that they descended and crept toward the decrepit hut that housed the memorial. There were shadows and light across the silent landscape, blackness and white.

Castle had replenished Deuce's oxygen supply after admitting that perhaps someone had monkeyed with the tanks . . . but not with an eye to killin' anybody. He had also given him a new helmet, but they agreed not to speak to each other because the line might be unsecured.

Castle was in good shape, for all of being a thousand million years old and the son of every Godfather and the clone of Moses. He darted ahead with his blaster drawn. Deuce wanted to tell him to slow down, damn it. He had no idea if Castle could hold his own in a fight.

He closed his eyes.

If his time was synchronous with Big Al's, Sparkle had three minutes of oxygen left. He and Castle each carried a violin-sized oxygen tank for his baby.

Stay on target, stay on target . . .

Castle crouched behind a tiny craterlet and waited for Deuce. Deuce crab-wagged over.

Castle pointed to the man guarding the entrance. He wore a white suit, no distinguishing colors. Deuce nodded.

They separated, Castle moving to the left, Deuce to the right, trying to hide themselves as best they could.

Then Castle stumbled . . . or did he do it on purpose? The guard looked left, aimed, and Deuce juiced him. He fell.

Castle ran for the entrance. Deuce followed. The airlock was open, and they hurtled themselves inside.

In the shadows, a figure started gesticulating. Castle, startled, shot off a pulse.

Deuce whirled in a circle. There were freakin' astronauts everywhere. LEM's and pieces of matte gray equipment. It was the museum.

Castle had just shot a damn mechanical.

Deuce raised his hand to stop him from doing it again. Castle nodded.

They crept on.

They went through a cockeyed door painted with swirls like a galaxy and found themselves looking down on a lower level. Half a dozen figures were sitting in suits playing cards. A third figure, lithe, about nine feet tall, was sitting inside a display room of Mission Control reading a magazine through its helmet. The figure sat back in its chair and lifted the magazine. Deuce couldn't help the sigh that escaped him.

They had given his poor genius baby *Fabricated Beast* to read.

Two more figures came into view. One of them stood by the figure with the magazine and aimed a blaster at her, then shot into the ceiling. Debris clouded the view for a moment.

Suddenly, the figure dropped the magazine and clutched its throat.

Either the bastard had shot her, or she was out of air.

Deuce shouted and flung himself over the balcony, landing smack-dab on one of the guards.

Castle, with the reflexes of someone used to heavy gravity, made his way down the stairs, shooting as he went.

Deuce went into action: side kick to the guard's face, another, another, until he collapsed. Another assailant came after Deuce, weapon drawn. Deuce leaped into the air as juice pulsed, missing him . . . but hitting the tank Castle had brought and losing the oxygen.

Deuce used his tank as a weapon, slamming it against the guy. He supposed that to Castle, all this looked bizarrely slo-mo, but to him, it was happening too fast.

Another guy was on him.

Two guys were on Castle.

There were more guards in this room than had at first met the eye.

Deuce was on the floor now. One of the figures aimed a weapon. Deuce could see his face. He looked like he was laughing.

Then the man's mouth formed an "O," and he fell forward toward Deuce. Deuce craned his head. Castle was still being attacked, but another figure stood with a blaster extended toward the fallen man.

"*Ah got 'eem*, Deuce," said a familiar voice inside Deuce's helmet.

Moonman. Thank God. Deuce threw him the oxygen tank. "Take it to her."

Moonman ran awkwardly to the inert figure, but just before he reached her, another guard slammed into him. The tank went flying.

Deuce was being pummeled. He pressed himself into the floor and pushed up with all his might, catching the guy's foot. With his blaster, he pierced the guy's suit, hoped the suit's redundant safeties would not engage. If Big Al had provided it, they probably wouldn't.

The guy went down, his face growing red, then white as fear passed through it, leaving death in its wake.

Deuce flew across the room to the figure on the floor. Ripped off the old tank, slammed in the new.

Please. Please. Please.

She raised her hand. Patted his helmet.

Leaped to her feet.

Then more guys dashed into the room via the overhang. Sparkle, Moonman, and Deuce went into action. It wasn't like those choreographed ultimate fighting shows. There was nothing heroic or artistic about it. It was an ugly, nasty swarm of kickboxing, wrestling, and weaponry, as they bombarded the enemy and forced them back, gathering up Castle on the way—he wasn't doing too well—and moving out into the main room of the memorial.

They got outside. There were more guys. Deuce was pumpin'; Deuce was humpin'. Blasting and slamming and headbanging, whatever worked, whatever . . .

Something was descending. Reflexively he shot at it with everything he had left.

Castle, with whatever strength he had left, suddenly flung himself at Deuce. As he was dragged down, he wondered just whose side Castle was on. Then he saw the craft land.

It was another shuttle, one of Castle's.

They were saved.

TWENTY-SIX

Aboard the shuttle, winging toward the finish line, Castle told Deuce that no one else had finished the race. There had been a severe collision between the Scarlatti and the Caputo dust boats, and they had been airlifted out. The Van Aadams contestant—a woman—had broken her leg climbing Copernicus. If not for that, she would have won.

"So it's a draw," Deuce said. He didn't care. Sparkle was in his arms. Moonman—whom Joey had also contacted when he had appealed to Castle's people, having successfully read Deuce's lips—was bragging to one of the Men in White how he had infiltrated the enemy camp and bided his time, hoping the others should show. It was clear Moonman and Joey had made a better impression on them than Deuce. They were the ones Joey had contacted, and they were the ones who had initiated the rescue attempt by sending the first shuttle down to Castle's duster.

"A draw means I win," Castle drawled. It did not. There was all kinds of complicated stuff about what they would do if there was no winner, and it was going to take a trip to the Charter Board to decipher it.

"I'm going to hit Uncle Al," Deuce said, spitting into his palm. "I'll tear his freakin' head off and—"

Joey said, "Deuce, the kidnapping was a setup. Those guards were not Borgiolis, and that letter was a forgery. They were in disguise, sent there by the Moongoloid. To get you."

Deuce tensed. "Club and Spade?"

"Ah don't think so," Moonman said. "I did not see them there. Maybe William Atherton held them back. Or maybe Monsieur Wayne did, in case you survived."

Deuce balled his fists. "This isn't ever gonna end unless I end it."

"No," Sparkle said. "It's enough for now. We'll get him later."

Joey said, "The Chairman has forbidden him to leave their compound. So we know where he is."

Deuce raised his chin. "Then I'm going after him. Alone."

"What are you going to do, just walk up to him?" Sparkle sounded very frightened. Deuce reminded himself she had thought she would never see him again after the race, but she had. Not all her premonitions were correct.

"He can if he wants." Castle handed Deuce a small, round object. "This is like a Scarlatti weapons shield, only it ought to work on shielding you, too, when you violate their territory."

Deuce stared at it. "Where'd you get this?"

Castle moved his shoulders. "Friends, let's say."

"You're not going without us," Joey insisted.

Deuce shook his head. "This is a personal Vendetta, pure and simple. If I drag you into it, it'll just go on and on. I'm going in by myself."

He took Castle's shield and left.

There was a lock to the Van Aadams compound—which was a really nice rain-forest ecosystem, no expense spared—which posed no challenge to Deuce. He kept waiting to be blasted into smithereens, but the little button Castle had given him seemed to be doing the trick.

Deuce was going to have to find out more about this thing. And what friends? The Scarlattis? Well, they'd said they were his friends, too.

There were guards hither and thither, none of whom detected Deuce.

And then . . . *viola.*

The pool. And the monstrosity that was Wayne Van Aadams was swimming in it, alone. Slightly above him was an unlighted cabana.

Deuce was not so stupid as to assume there weren't on-lookers, but the cloaking device made him a little cocky. He hid behind a eucalyptus tree and shot off a pulse that zinged into the water.

At once two figures jumped into his path.

Club and Spade. The black hair, the bad toupee. They came at him like the nearly indestructible creatures they were, while Wayne screamed, "You're dead, McNamara! Dead." His ineffectual splashing, which he probably thought of as treading water, made his threats seem comical.

Deuce thought to himself, *That bastard Castle set me up. Got me to save my woman and then—*

He flew at the cyborg and the android with everything he was worth, calculating every kick to come, every punch he would throw. Shot off as much juice as he had, just to soften them up.

But they were on him in seconds. He might as well have been fighting two walls. As they bore him down and held him still to give their blows better targets, Deuce reached in his pocket for something to throw, for a recharge, for anything—

—wrapped his fingers around the little button and without thinking, threw it at them.

It exploded.

And Club and Spade did, too.

Their body parts sailed up, up into the air and cascaded down like a gory, thick waterfall.

Wayne Van Aadams was shrieking.

A light went on in the cabana.

The good-looking rejuvved Earthside woman stepped out of it. She was carrying a martini glass and smoking a cig-arette. She looked directly at Deuce, and said, "Oh, good, you're here. We were apprised of your arrival, and, frankly, we were beginning to wonder if you'd gotten lost, Mr. Mc-Namara."

Wayne stared at her. "Aunt Constance? What are you saying?"

She gazed at the Moongoloid without a trace of pity. "You are hopeless. You're an embarrassment to the Family. Please, Mr. McNamara, be our guest." She indicated her nephew, who started screaming and scrambling out of the pool.

"Thank you, Signora Van Aadams," Deuce said with respect. He took out his blaster. Mrs. Van Aadams went back into the cabana. Out of the corner of his eye, he saw her silhouette smoke her cigarette and drink her martini.

Three seconds later, Wayne Van Aadams scrambled no longer.

TWENTY-SEVEN

It was too good to be true that Deuce was not in fatal trouble with the Van Aadams, so he hid out in their rain forest for a good long time, waiting for guards to start looking for him. But the Van Aadams compound remained quiet. Eventually he found another route to the Strip and sidled into the crowd.

"It's him!" someone screamed.

Like a blaster had gone off, everyone burst into cheers and shouting. People tugged at him, yanked at him; he was carried along in a sea of wild faces as he pushed back, so squeezed he couldn't breathe.

"Dooce! Dooce! Dooce!"

"MLF!"

"Independents!"

N.A.'s swarmed around him like he was a rock star. He lost track of time, of where he was. It was worse than running out of air.

Then the MLF declared themselves his bodyguards, to be replaced by the Lunar Security Forces shortly thereafter. They were armed and warned everybody to stay back.

"Dooce! Dooce! Dooce!" Thousands were calling his name.

Thousands.

He was hustled into a little restaurant called the Right Stuff. People banged on the door, on the windows. Outside, the Strip was in a frenzy. There were riot police. Deuce's comm badge wouldn't stop going off. He couldn't hear anything it said.

In quick order, he was joined by Levi Shoemaker and Miss Angelina, his daughter. They were glowing.

"We heard you were dead," Shoemaker said. "You were an instant martyr."

"Sorry to disappoint you," Deuce drawled.

Angelina looked very happy to see him. Again he felt a pang. In another life, on another rock, maybe the two of them could have had something. Provided she came with a ladder.

"You're a force to be reckoned with," she said. "Now, more than ever, the people need a leader. A negotiator. You know what's going on down at the Charter Board, don't you?" Deuce shook his head. "They're carving us up again. Dividing the spoils without our say. We've appealed to Earthside, but—"

"Oh, *fabulous*," Deuce cut in, with the reflexive thinking of a Family Member.

"But they haven't responded. They refuse to recognize us," Shoemaker said bitterly.

"You mean the MLF," Deuce said.

"Yes, but we speak for the Independents," Angelina insisted.

Deuce gazed at her levelly. "No, you don't."

There was a beat. "We've looked out for you. Protected you," Shoemaker said.

"*Grazie*. But you don't own me."

Shoemaker sat back in his chair. "If you don't help us, we won't be held responsible for the actions of our desperate people."

"Oh, yes, you will," Deuce said. "The Families will hold you accountable." Shoemaker paled. "A lot of people could get badly hurt. A lot of N.A.'s."

"Then you'd better help us. You'd better get yourself in the middle," Angelina said.

Deuce considered. That might be true. He said, "Can you get me to the Charter Board building?"

Shoemaker clapped him on the back. "I knew you'd come around."

"Hey, I'm not carrying the flag or nothing," Deuce said. "Don't get too excited."

But they were.

An aichy was produced to take Deuce to the Charter Board building, but on the way he finally answered one of the incomings and discovered everyone had gone Topside.

He told the aichy the change of plans and joined the party. They were massed outside the condo complex in the garden. Sparkle looked both beautiful and worried as she stood in the gazebo.

"Deuce!" She ran to his side and kissed him in front of everybody, including Beatrice, who, surprisingly, did not look very upset about it.

"I guess your woman's intuition is not so good," Deuce said to her. Her answer was a small smile. Apparently she had not yet given up the worry thing.

Moonman was there, too. And Joey. Also looking worried. They weren't the only ones.

Everyone was staring up through the dome at a very bright ellipse of stars.

Which were lights.

Which, according to Castle, were government ships called by Epperson-Roux intent on keeping the Families from waging a war to the death.

Which Epperson-Roux could not confirm, he being not there.

He being missing.

"Everything's gotten so messy," Castle drawled. "What with that inconclusive ending to the race and all the Independents being riled up. Emerson told me that they're talking about pulling everyone's Charters and sending in troops to keep the peace. And bureaucrats to run your casinos."

"Do you know what else?" Big Al demanded. "That man was in the League of Decency. At the least, he should be fired from his post and thrown off the Moon."

"I think he has been," Castle said. "Anybody seen him?"

There was silence, a very hostile silence.

Castle held up a die. They drew back. It looked very much like the Ditwac.

"There are six spots on this thing," he said.

"That's right. Six." Don Giancarlo spit on the ground. "Not five and not seven. My Family ain't gonna let no *scemo* government boys steal our House from us." There were grumblings of agreement.

"Now that I have your attention," Castle said, smiling. He pulled out another die from his pocket. Shook it. Stopped. "Oh, a few things." He smiled and held out his hand. "I would like to announce my engagement to Miss Beatrice Borgioli."

Completely ignoring Deuce, Beatrice dimpled and ran to Castle's side. With a feather, you could have knocked Deuce over.

Roger and Abraham Smith frowned at him; he was no longer in a position to offer them the Borgioli Family. Deuce shrugged at them. Win some, lose some.

He had other things to offer, did he not?

"It has also come to my attention that Mr. Wayne Van Aadams, the Designated Heir of the Van Aadams Family, has been hit. My sympathies, Mr. Van Aadams." He inclined his head in William Atherton's direction. The man looked back at him stone-faced. Deuce braced himself for being fingered.

Castle went on. "And I regret to announce that the Charter Board has reported evidence that the Chan Family perpetrated the hit."

Yuet Chan said, "*What*?"

He held out a mini. "Here's the hit document. With Madame Chan's light signature itself. Verified by the Charter Board."

"That's a forgery!" she shouted. "That's absurd. Castle, you double-crossing bastard!"

He looked sorrowful. "Your House has hit a Designated Heir. That's a very serious offense, and on top of it all hits were forbidden, were they not?" He tsk-tsked. "Ah do believe your Charter may be revoked."

Yuet Chan raised her fists. "Forbidden only until the end of the race," she said, then her face flushed as if she realized that made her sound guilty. "This is preposterous. Incredible. That man supported my claim. I have no reason to wish him dead. We're an old and noble Family. We abide by the rules."

"Of course we'll prosecute to the fullest extent of the law," Chairman William Atherton said.

Deuce watched in awe. The Moongoloid's uncle had wanted Wayne hit, too. Castle had given him what he wanted. He was giving each Family what they wanted, and getting rid of his main rival for drug-free living. Or maybe he just wanted Yuet Chan's casino since he wasn't going to be allowed to build his own.

The man was a master. He was building his power base before their very eyes. Maybe Sparkle was right to stay worried.

"I would think that with the Chans so busy with legal matters, perhaps the Caputos would run their gaming operation for them?" Castle asked.

"No way! No!" Yuet shouted. "I'll call a hit on every single man, woman, and child on the Moon before I allow that. I—" She stared at the assembly and clamped her mouth shut.

Don Giancarlo smiled hugely. "We were the first ones here. Some say we should have been the only ones."

The Caputo dream restored.

And for the Scarlattis?

Castle shook the second die, blew into his fist, and threw it on the ground at his feet. Deuce waited for the six.

It was a one.

Uh-oh. Everyone stared at the man.

"You Families own Moonbase Vegas," Castle said. "And the government owns the rest of the user-friendly land. I can also see that Topside is not an attractive option. So I have put in a bid for the Darkside."

Joey said, "You're going to build an entire city from scratch?"

Moonman added, "On ze darkside? It cannot be done."

"You're nuts," Big Al said worriedly, perhaps doubting his illustrious son-in-law-to-be.

"I'll need help," Castle allowed. "I'll need new technology, which I can pay for. Whatever it takes, Andreas.''

''We'll deliver,'' Andreas said. ''Whoever of the Scarlattis joins me.'' It was obvious he knew a lot of them were going to.

''And I'll need security. I'll need weapons no one's ever heard of before.''

Saying nothing, the Smith Godfathers nodded in unison.

So, there were the backroom deals for all to see. Yuet Chan looked like she was about to throw up.

''Now, for the Independents,'' Castle said, looking at Deuce.

''He's a Borgioli,'' Big Al interjected. ''We put him undercover to spy on you all, but he's—''

Deuce cut in, ''I'm nobody, Mr. Castle.'' He looked straight at Big Al. ''I'm no longer a Borgioli, Uncle Al. It pains me to admit it, but I no longer think in that way.''

Big Al's mouth dropped open. ''If it's on account of Beatrice—''

Deuce laid his hand over his heart. ''*Daverro, daverro,* I wish for her only the biggest happiness.''

''Duchino,'' she whispered, looking wistful.

Deuce turned his attention to Beatrice's fiancé. ''And I don't speak for nobody, Mr. Castle.''

Castle smiled. ''Which is why I'd like you to be my second-in-command. Walk with me.''

Deuce looked over his shoulder at Sparkle. She was dead white. He gave her a reassuring look and joined Castle as he left the group.

''Mr. Castle,'' Deuce began as they walked apart from the others.

''Hunter.'' He pulled a cigar out of his pocket and handed it to Deuce. Pulled out another. Lit Deuce's, lit his own. Commed for the levies.

Deuce puffed. ''How did you shift the Ditwac?''

Castle only smiled.

Deuce tried another tack. ''Why'd you shift me?''

Castle stopped. He pointed overhead. ''Those aren't government ships, Deuce. They're transports carrying the materials to start building my Moonbase. Including a hell of a lot of toilet paper.''

Deuce looked up at the lights, gaped at the power of a man who could even dream this big. The potential for action.

The hope.

''How did you know you would win?'' Deuce asked.

Castle laughed. ''I always win.''

From the Captain's Log of Gambler's Star:

It's a new year. I'll leave soon. I'll leave him to do it for me while I work on the more pressing issue. The real issue. Perhaps he'll guess what I'm about when I give him access to the technology I salvaged from the crashed ship.

Partial access, of course.

Maybe he'll understand that the lesson of the city he builds is this: right idea, wrong distance.

Wrong reason.

Perhaps he'll guess when Sparkle's power grows and develops, as I predict it will.

They'll have beautiful children.

And I will give them a beautiful future.

Hunter Castle
Aboard Ship, 2143

NANCY HOLDER is the best-selling author of thirty-one novels and two hundred sf, fantasy, and horror short stories. She has received four Bram Stoker Awards from the Horror Writers Association, seven of her romances have appeared on the Waldenbooks Romance Bestseller List, and she has won several romance industry awards. Her work has been translated into over two dozen languages. She has spoken at WorldCons, World Fantasy Cons, World Horror Cons, and others. She lives in San Diego with her husband, Wayne, their daughter, Belle, and their three dogs, Mr. Ron, Maggie, and Dot.

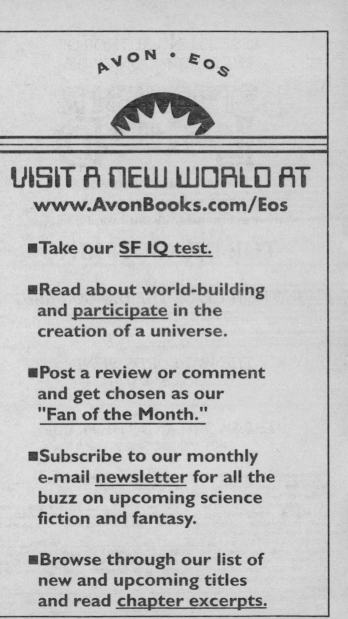